THE SHAME  ARL CABOT

Telima lashed my wrists together tightly, with the strong hands of a working girl. She indicated that I should lie on my left side, facing her. Then, with another coil of marsh vine, she tied my ankles together.

As I lay there, she unlaced her tunic, opening it. Again she looked at me. To my amazement, insolently, with a liquid motion, she slipped the tunic off over her head.

She sat on the mat and regarded me. "I see," she said, "that you must again be punished."

She struck me with savagery, four times.

I had been a warrior of Ko-ro-ba.

Now I was only a girl's slave.

THE CHRONICLES OF COUNTER-EARTH
By John Norman

now available from Ballantine Books:

TARNSMAN OF GOR

OUTLAW OF GOR

PRIESTS-KINGS OF GOR

NOMADS OF GOR

ASSASSIN OF GOR

RAIDERS OF GOR

CAPTIVE OF GOR

RAIDERS
OF GOR

John Norman

A Del Rey Book

BALLANTINE BOOKS • NEW YORK

A Del Rey Book
Published by Ballantine Books

Copyright © 1971 by John Norman

All rights reserved. Published in the United States by Ballantine Books, a division of Random House, Inc., New York, and simultaneously in Canada by Random House of Canada, Limited, Toronto, Canada.

ISBN 0-345-29538-2

Manufactured in the United States of America

First U.S. Printing: December 1971
Thirteenth U.S. Printing: September 1981

Cover art by Boris Vallejo

Contents

The Blood Mark

I could smell the sea, gleaming Thassa, in the myths said to be without a farther shore.

I reached down from the rush craft and took a palm of water into my hand and touched my tongue to it. Thassa could not be far beyond.

I took the triangular-bladed tem-wood paddle and moved the small craft, light and narrow, large enough scarcely for one man, ahead. It was formed of pliant, tubular, lengthy Vosk rushes, bound with marsh vine.

To my right, some two or three feet under the water, I saw the sudden, rolling yellowish flash of the slatted belly of a water tharlarion, turning as it made its swift strike, probably a Vosk carp or marsh turtle. Immediately following I saw the water seem to glitter for a moment, a rain of yellowish streaks beneath the surface, in the wake of the water tharlarion, doubtless its swarm of scavengers, tiny water tharlarion, about six inches long, little more than teeth and tail.

A brightly plumaged bird sprang from the rushes to my loft, screaming and beating its sudden way into the blue sky. In a moment it had darted again downward to be lost in the rushes, the waving spore stalks, the seed pods of various growths of the Gorean tidal marshes. Only one creature in the marshes dares to outline itself against the sky, the predatory Ul, the winged tharlarion.

It was difficult to see more than a few feet ahead; sometimes I could see no further than the lifted prow of my small craft, as it nosed its way among the rushes and the frequent rence plants.

It was the fourth day of the sixth passage hand, shortly before the Autumnal Equinox, which in the common Gorean calendar begins the month of Se'Kara. In the calendar of Ko-ro-ba, which, like most Gorean cities, marks years by its Administrator Lists, it would be the eleventh year of the administration of my father, Matthew Cabot. In the calendar of Ar, for those it might interest, it was

1

the first year of the restoration of Marlenus, Ubar of
Ubars, but, more usefully for the purposes of consolidat-
ing the normal chaos of Gorean chronology, it was the
year 10,119 Contasta Ar, that is, from the founding of Ar.

My weapons shared the boat, with a gourd of water and
a tin of bread and dried bosk meat. I had the Gorean short
sword in its scabbard, my shield and helmet, and, wrapped
in leather, a Gorean long bow of supple Ka-la-na wood,
from the yellow wine trees of Gor, tipped with notched
bosk horn at each end, loose strung with hemp whipped
with silk, and a roll of sheaf and flight arrows. The bow is
not commonly favored by Gorean warriors, but all must
respect it. It is the height of a tall man; its back, away
from the bowman, is flat; its belly, facing the bowman, is
half-rounded; it is something like an inch and a half wide
and an inch and a quarter thick at the center; it has considerable force and requires considerable strength to draw;
many men, incidentally, even some warriors, cannot draw
the bow; nine of its arrows can be fired aloft before the
first falls again to the earth; at point-blank range it can
be fired completely through a four-inch beam; at two hundred yards it can pin a man to a wall; at four hundred
yards it can kill the huge, shambling bosk; its rate of fire
is nineteen arrows in a Gorean Ehn, about eighty Earth
seconds; and a skilled bowman, but not an extraordinary
one, is expected to be able to place these nineteen arrows
in one Ehn into a target, the size of a man, each a hit, at
a range of some two hundred and fifty yards. Yet, as a
weapon, it has serious disadvantages, and on Gor the
crossbow, inferior in accuracy, range and rate of fire, with
its heavy cable and its leaves of steel, tends to be generally favored. The long bow cannot well be used except
in a standing, or at least kneeling, position, thus making
more of a target of the archer; the long bow is difficult to
use from the saddle; it is impractical in close quarters,
as in defensive warfare or in fighting from room to room;
and it cannot be kept set, loaded like a firearm, as can the
crossbow; the crossbow is the assassin's weapon, *par excellence;* further, it might be mentioned that, although it
takes longer to set the crossbow, a weaker man, with, say,
his belt claw or his winding gear, can certainly manage to
do so; accordingly, for every man capable of drawing a
warrior's long bow there will be an indefinite number who
can use the crossbow; lastly, at shorter distances, the

crossbow requires much less skill for accuracy than the long bow.

I smiled to myself.

It is not difficult to see why, popularly, the crossbow should be regarded as a generally more efficient weapon than the long bow, in spite of being inferior to it, in the hands of an expert, in range, accuracy and rate of fire. Well used, the long bow is a far more devastating weapon than its rival, the crossbow; but few men had the strength and eye to use it well; I prided myself on my skill with the weapon.

I paddled along, gently, kneeling on the rushes of my small, narrow craft.

It is the weapon of a peasant, I heard echoing in my mind, and again smiled. The Older Tarl, my former master-at-arms, had so spoken to me years before in Ko-ro-ba, my city, the Towers of the Morning. I looked down at the long, heavy, leather-wrapped bow of supple Ka-la-na wood in the bottom of the rush craft.

I laughed.

It was true that the long bow is a weapon of peasants, who make and use them, sometimes with great efficiency. That fact, in itself, that the long bow is a peasant weapon, would make many Goreans, particularly those not familiar with the bow, look down upon it. Gorean warriors, generally drawn from the cities, are warriors by blood, by caste; moreover, they are High Caste; the peasants, isolated in their narrow fields and villages, are Low Caste; indeed, the Peasant is regarded, by those of the cities, as being little more than an ignoble brute, ignorant and superstitious, venal and vicious, a grubber in the dirt, a plodding animal, an ill-tempered beast, something at best cunning and treacherous; and yet I knew that in each dirt-floored cone of straw that served as the dwelling place of a peasant and his family, there was, by the fire hole, a Home Stone; the peasants themselves, though regarded as the lowest caste on all Gor by most Goreans, call themselves proudly the ox on which the Home Stone rests, and I think their saying is true.

Peasants, incidentally, are seldom, except in emergencies, utilized in the armed forces of a city; this is a further reason why their weapon, the long bow, is less known in the cities, and among warriors, than it deserves to be.

The Gorean, to my mind, is often, though not always,

bound by historical accidents and cultural traditions, which
are then often rationalized into a semblance of plausibility.
For example, I had even heard arguments to the effect
that peasants used the long bow only because they lacked
the manufacturing capability to produce crossbows, as
though they could not have traded their goods or sold
animals to obtain crossbows, if they wished. Further, the
heavy, bronze-headed spear and the short, double-edged
steel sword are traditionally regarded as the worthy, and
prime, weapons of the Gorean fighting man, he at least
who is a *true* fighting man; and, similarly traditionally,
archers, who slay from a distance, not coming to grips
with their enemy, with their almost invisible, swiftly moving shafts of wood, those mere splinters, are regarded as
being rather contemptible, almost on the periphery of
warriorhood; villains in Gorean epics, incidentally, when
not of small and despised castes, are likely to be archers;
I had heard warriors say that they would rather be poi-
soned by a woman than slain by an arrow.

I myself, perhaps because I had been raised not on Gor,
but on Earth, did not, fortunately in my opinion, suffer
from these inhibiting prepossessions; I could use the long
bow with, so to speak, no tincture of shame, no confusion
of conscience, without the least injury to my self-esteem; I
knew the long bow to be a magnificent weapon; accordingly, I made it my own.

I heard a bird some forty or fifty yards to my right; it
sounded like a marsh gant, a small, horned, web-footed
aquatic fowl, broad-billed and broad-winged. Marsh girls,
the daughters of rence growers, sometimes hunt them with
throwing sticks.

In some cities, Port Kar, for example, the long bow is
almost unknown. Similarly it is not widely known even in
Glorious Ar, the largest city of known Gor. It is reasonably well known in Thentis, in the Mountains of Thentis,
famed for her tarn flocks, and in Ko-ro-ba, my city, the
Towers of the Morning. Cities vary. But generally the
bow is little known. Small straight bows, of course, not
the powerful long bow, are, on the other hand, reasonably
common on Gor, and these are often used for hunting
light game, such as the brush-maned, three-toed Qualae,
the yellow-pelted, single-horned Tabuk, and runaway
slaves.

I heard another bird, another marsh gant it seemed, some fifty yards away, but this time to my left.

It was late in the afternoon, the fourteenth Gorean Ahn I would have guessed. Some swarms of insects hung in the sedge here and there but I had not been much bothered; it was late in the year, and most of the Gorean insects likely to make life miserable for men bred in, and frequented, areas in which bodies of unmoving, fresh water were plentiful. I did see a large, harmless zarlit fly, purple, about two feet long with four translucent wings, spanning about a yard, humming over the surface of the water, then alighting and, on its padlike feet, daintily picking its way across the surface. I flicked a salt leach from the side of my light rush craft with the corner of the tem-wood paddle.

On river barges, for hundreds of pasangs, I had made my way down the Vosk, but where the mighty Vosk began to break apart and spread into its hundreds of shallow, constantly shifting channels, becoming lost in the vast tidal marshes of its delta, moving toward gleaming Thassa, the Sea, I had abandoned the barges, purchasing from rence growers on the eastern periphery of the delta supplies and the small rush craft which I now propelled through the rushes and sedge, the wild rence plants.

I noticed that one of these rence plants had, tied about it, below the tuft of stamens and narrow petals, a white cloth, rep-cloth.

I paddled over to look at the cloth. I looked about myself, and was for some time quiet, not moving. Then I moved past the plant, parting the rence and passing through.

I heard again the cry of the marsh gant, from somewhere behind me.

No one had been found who would guide me into the delta of the Vosk. The bargemen of the Vosk will not take their wide, broad-bottomed craft into the delta. The channels of the Vosk, to be sure, shift from season to season, and the delta is often little more than a trackless marsh, literally hundreds of square pasangs of estuarial wilderness. In many places it is too shallow to float even the great flat-bottomed barges and, more importantly, a path for them would have to be cut and chopped, foot by foot, through the thickets of rush and sedge, and the tangles of marsh vine. The most important reason for not finding a guide, of course, even among the eastern rence growers, is that the delta is claimed by Port Kar, which lies within it, some hundred pasangs from its northwestern edge, bordering on the shallow Tamber Gulf, beyond which is gleaming Thassa, the Sea.

Port Kar, crowded, squalid, malignant, is sometimes referred to as the Tarn of the Sea. Her name is a synonym in Gorean for cruelty and piracy. The fleets of tarn ships of Port Kar are the scourge of Thassa, beautiful, lateen-rigged galleys that ply the trade of plunder and enslavement from the Ta-Thassa Mountains of the southern hemisphere of Gor to the ice lakes of the North; and westward even beyond the terraced island of Cos and the rocky Tyros, with its labyrinths of vart caves.

I knew one in Port Kar, by name Samos, a slaver, said to be an agent of Priest-Kings.

I was in the delta of the Vosk, and making my way to the city of Port Kar, which alone of Gorean cities commonly welcomes strangers, though few but exiles, murderers, outlaws, thieves and cutthroats would care to find their way to her canaled darknesses.

I recalled Samos, slumped in his marble chair at the Curulean in Ar, seemingly indolent, but indolent as might be the satisfied beast of prey. About his left shoulder, in the manner of his city, he had worn the knotted ropes of Port Kar; his garment had been simple, dark and closely woven; the hood had been thrown back, revealing his broad, wide head, the close-cropped white hair; the face had been red from windburn and salt; it had been wrinkled and lined, cracked like leather; in his ears there had been two small golden rings; in him I had sensed power, experience, intelligence, cruelty; I had felt in him the presence of the carnivore, at that moment not inclined to hunt or kill. I did not look forward to meeting him. Yet it was said, by those I trusted, that he had served Priest-Kings well.

I was not particularly surprised at finding a bit of rep-cloth tied on the rence plant, for the delta is inhabited. Man has not surrendered it entirely to the tharlarion, the Ul and the salt leach. There are scattered, almost invisible, furtive communities of rence growers who eke out their livelihood in the delta, nominally under the suzerainty of Port Kar. The cloth I found had probably been a trail mark for some rence growers.

A kind of paper is made from rence. The plant itself has a long, thick root, about four inches thick, which lies horizontally under the surface of the water; small roots sink downward into the mud from this main root, and several "stems," as many as a dozen, rise from it, often of a length of fifteen to sixteen feet from the root; it has an excrescent, usually single floral spike.

The plant has many uses besides serving as a raw product in the manufacture of rence paper. The root, which is woody and heavy, is used for certain wooden tools and utensils, which can be carved from it; also, when dried, it makes a good fuel; from the stem the rence growers can make reed boats, sails, mats, cords and a kind of fibrous cloth; further, its pith is edible, and for the rench growers is, with fish, a staple in their diet; the pith is edible both raw and cooked; some men, lost in the delta, not knowing the pith edible, have died of starvation in the midst of what was, had they known it, an almost endless abundance of food. The pith is also used, upon occasion, as a caulking for boat seams, but tow and pitch, covered with tar or grease, are generally used.

Rence paper is made by slicing the stem into thin, narrow strips; those near the center of the plant are particularly favored; one layer of strips is placed longitudinally, and then a shorter layer is placed latitudinally across the first layer; these two surfaces are then soaked under water, which releases a gluelike substance from the fibers, melding the two surfaces into a single, rectangular sheet; these formed sheets are then hammered and dried in the sun; roughness is removed by polishing, usually with a smooth shell or a bit of kailiauk horn; the side of a tharlarion tooth may also be used in this work. The paper is then attached, sheet to sheet, to form rolls, usually about twenty sheets to a roll. The best paper is on the outside of the roll, always, not to practice deceit in the quality of the roll but rather to have the most durable paper on the outside, which will take the most weathering, handling and general wear. Rence paper comes in various grades, about eight in all. The rence growers market their product either at the eastern or western end of the delta. Sometimes rence merchants, on narrow marsh craft rowed by slaves, enter some pasangs into the delta to negotiate the transactions, usually from the western edge, that bordering the Tamber Gulf. Rence paper is, incidentally, not the only

type of writing material used on Gor. A milled linen
paper is much used, large quantities of which are produced
in Ar, and vellum and parchment, prepared in many cities,
are also popular.

I now noted another bit of white rep-cloth tied on a
rence stem, larger than the first. I assumed it was another
trail mark. I continued on. The calls of marsh gants, a
kind of piping whistle, seemed more frequent now, and
somewhat closer. I looked behind me, and to the sides.
Yet, not surprisingly, because of the rence, the rushes
and sedge, I could not see the birds.

I had been in the delta now for some sixteen days,
drifting and paddling toward Thassa. I again tasted the
water, and the salt of it was even stronger than it had
been. And the great, vast clean smell of Thassa was clear.

I rejoiced, moving ahead. There was not much water
left in the gourd now, and it was the last of several I had
brought with me. The dried bosk meat in the tin, and the
bread with it, yellow Sa-Tarna bread, now stale, was almost gone.

Then I stopped short, for tied to a rence plant before
me now was a sheaf of red cloth.

I then knew that the two pieces of cloth I had encountered earlier had not been simple trail marks but boundary
signs, warnings. I had come into an area of the delta
where I was not welcome, into a territory that must be
claimed by some small community, doubtless of rence
growers.

The rence growers, in spite of the value of their product, and the value of articles taken in exchange for it, and
the protection of the marshes, and the rence and fish
which give them ample sustenance, do not have an easy
life. Not only must they fear the marsh sharks and the
carnivorous eels which frequent the lower delta, not to
mention the various species of aggressive water tharlarion
and the winged, monstrous, hissing, predatory Ul, but they
must fear, perhaps most of all, men, and of these, most
of all, the men of Port Kar.

As I have mentioned, Port Kar claims the suzerainty of
the delta. Accordingly, frequently, bands of armed men,
maintaining allegiance to one or the other of the warring,
rival Ubars of Port Kar, enter the delta to, as they say,
collect taxes. The tributes exacted, when the small communities can be found, are customarily harsh, often what-

ever of value can be found; typically what is demanded is great stocks of rence paper for trade, sons for oarsmen in cargo galleys, daughters for Pleasure Slaves in the taverns of the city.

I looked on the red cloth tied to the rence plant. The cloth was the color of blood; I was in little doubt as to its meaning. I was not to proceed farther.

I moved the small, light craft through the rushes, past the sign. I must make my way to Port Kar.

The cries of marsh gants followed me.

The Cries of Marsh Gants

I saw the girl ahead, through a break in the rushes, some fifty yards beyond.

Almost at the same time she looked up, startled.

She was standing on a small skiff of rence, not larger than my own rush craft, about seven feet long and two feet wide, fastened together, as mine was, with marsh vine; it, like mine, had a slightly curved stern and prow.

In her hand was a curved throwing stick, used for hunting birds. It is not a boomerang, which would be largely useless among the sedges and rushes, but it would, of course, float, and might be recovered and used indefinitely. Some girls are quite skilled with this light weapon. It stuns the bird, which is then gathered from the water and tied, alive, in the craft. The birds are later, on the rence islands, killed and cooked.

I moved the rush craft toward her, but not swiftly. Then, letting it drift, I put the tem-wood paddle across the craft, resting my hands on it, and watched her.

The cries of marsh gants were about us now. I saw that her hunting had been successful. There were four of the birds tied in the stern of the craft.

She looked upon me, but did not seem particularly frightened.

Her gaze was clear; she had a dark blondish hair and blue eyes; her legs were a bit short, and her ankles somewhat thick; her shoulders were a bit wide perhaps, but lovely. She wore a brief, sleeveless garment of yellowish-brown rence cloth; it was worn well away from both shoulders to permit her freedom of movement; the brief skirt had been hitched up about her thighs that it might in no way bind her in her hunting. Her hair was tied behind her head with a strip of purple cloth, dyed rep-cloth. I knew then she came of a community that had contact to some degree, direct or indirect, with civilized Goreans. Rep is a whitish fibrous matter found in the seed pods of a small, reddish, woody bush, commercially grown in several areas, but particularly below Ar and above the equator; the cheap rep-cloth is woven in mills, commonly, in various cities; it takes dyes well and, being cheap and strong, is popular, particularly among the lower castes. The girl was doubtless the daughter of a rence grower, hunting for gants. I supposed the rence island, on which such communities lived, might be nearby. I also supposed it might be her community which had placed the warning markers.

She stood well in the light, slightly shifting skiff of rence, moving almost imperceptibly, unconsciously, to maintain an easy balance. I myself found it difficult to stand in a rush craft.

She did not lift the throwing stick against me, nor did she attempt to flee, but simply stood looking at me, watching me. She had no paddle, but, thrust in the mud near her, was a long pole which she would use to propel her light craft.

"Do not be frightened," I said to her.

She did not respond to me.

"I will not hurt you," I said.

"Did you not see the warning marks," asked she, "the white marks, and the blood mark?"

"I mean you," I said, "and your people, no harm." I smiled. "I want only as much of your marsh as the width of my craft," I said, "and that only for as long as it takes to pass." This was a paraphrase of a saying common on Gor, given by passing strangers to those through whose territories they would travel: Only the span of the wings of my tarn, only the girth of my tharlarion, only the width of my body, and no more, and that but for the time it takes to pass.

In Gorean, incidentally, the word for stranger and enemy are the same.

"Are you of Port Kar?" she asked.

"No," I said.

"What is your city?" she inquired.

I wore no insignia on my garments, nor on my helmet or shield. The red of the warrior which I wore was now faded from the sun and stained with the salt of the marsh.

"You are an outlaw," she pronounced.

I did not reply.

"Where are you bound?" she asked.

"Port Kar," I said.

"Take him!" she cried.

Instantly there was a great cry from all sides, and, breaking through the rushes and sedge, dozens of rence craft, bound with marsh vine, thrust into view, each poled by one man, with another in the prow, a two- or three-pronged marsh spear uplifted.

It was pointless to unsheath my sword, or to take up a weapon. From the safety of the yards of marsh water separating me from my enemies I could have been immediately slain, lost in a thicket of the two- or three-pronged marsh spears.

The girl put her hands on her hips, threw back her head and laughed with pleasure.

My weapons were taken. My clothing was removed. I was thrown forward on my face in the rush craft. I felt my wrists pulled behind my back, and crossed; they were instantly lashed together with marsh vine; then my ankles were crossed, and they, too, were lashed securely together with vine.

The girl stepped lightly onto my craft and stood with one foot on either side of my body. She was handed the pole with which she had propelled her own craft, which craft was tied to another of the rence craft of the men who had come from the rushes and sedge. With the pole she began to propel my rush craft through the sedge, the several other craft accompanying us, on one or the other side, or following.

At one point the girl stopped the craft, and the others did, too. She, and one or two of the others, then put back their heads and uttered a kind of piping whistle, the call of the marsh gant. This was answered from various points about us, most of which were several yards away. Soon other rence craft, with their curved prows and sterns, had joined us.

The rence growers, I had learned, communicate by means of such signals, disguised as the cries of marsh gants.

Ho-Hak

The rence islands, on which the communities of rence growers dwell, are rather small, seldom more than two hundred by two hundred and fifty feet. They are formed entirely from the interwoven stems of the rence plants and float in the marsh. They are generally about eight to nine feet thick and have an exposed surface above the water of about three feet; as the rence stems break and rot away beneath the island, more layers are woven and placed on the surface. Thus, over a period of months, a given layer of rence, after being the top layer, will gradually be submerged and forced lower and lower until it, at last, is the deepest layer and, with its adjacent layers, begins to deteriorate.

To prevent an unwanted movement of the island there are generally several tethers, of marsh vine, to strong rence roots in the vicinity. It is dangerous to enter the water to make a tether fast because of the predators that frequent the swamp, but several men do so at a time, one man making fast the tether and the others, with him beneath the surface, protecting him with marsh spears, or pounding on metal pieces or wooden rods to drive away, or at least to disconcert and confuse, too inquisitive, undesired visitors, such as the water tharlarion or the long-bodied, nine-gilled marsh shark.

When one wishes to move the island the tethers are simply chopped away, and the community divides itself into those who will handle the long poles and those who will move ahead in rence craft, cutting and clearing the way. Most of those who handle the poles gather on the edges of the island, but within the island there are four deep rectangular wells through which the long poles may gain additional leverage. These deep center wells, actually holes cut in the island, permit its movement, though slowly when used alone, without exposing any of its inhabitants at its edges, where they might fall easier prey to the missile weapons of foes. In times of emergency the

13

inhabitants of the island gather behind wickerlike breastworks, woven of rence, in the area of the center wells; in
such an emergency the low-ceilinged rence huts on the
island will have been knocked down to prevent an enemy
from using them for cover, and all food and water supplies, usually brought from the eastern delta where the
water is fresh, will be stored within; the circular wickerlike breastworks then form, in the center of the island, a
more or less defensible stronghold, particularly against
the marsh spears of other growers, and such. Ironically, it
is not of much use against an organized attack of well-
armed warriors, such as those of Port Kar, and those
against whom it might be fairly adequate, other rence
growers, seldom attack communities like their own. I had
heard there had not been general hostilities among rence
growers for more than fifty years; their communities are
normally isolated from one another, and they have enough
to worry about contending with "tax collectors" from
Port Kar, without bothering to give much attention to
making life miserable for one another. Incidentally, when
the island is to be moved under siege conditions, divers
leave the island by means of the wells and, in groups of
two and three, attempt to cut a path in the direction of
escape; such divers, of course, often fall prey to underwater predators and to the spears of enemies, who thrust
down at them from the surface. Sometimes an entire island is abandoned, the community setting it afire and
taking to the marsh in their marsh skiffs. At a given point,
when it is felt safe, several of these skiffs will be tied together, forming a platform on which rence may be woven,
and a new island will be begun.

"So," said Ho-Hak, regarding me, "you are on your
way to Port Kar?"

He sat upon a giant shell of the Vosk sorp, as on a sort
of throne, which, for these people, I gather it was.

I knelt before him, naked and bound. Two ropes of
marsh vine, besides my other bonds, had been knotted
about my neck, each in the hands of a man on either side
of me. My ankles had been unbound only long enough to
push me stumbling from the rush craft, among the shouting women and men and children, to the throne of Ho-
Hak. Then I had been forced to my knees, and my ankles
had again been lashed together.

"Yes," I said. "It was my intention to go to Port Kar."

"We are not fond of the men of Port Kar," Ho-Hak said.

There was a rusted, heavy iron collar riveted about the neck of Ho-Hak, with a bit of chain dangling from it. I gathered that the rence growers did not have the tools to remove it. Ho-Hak might have worn it for years. He was doubtless a slave, probably escaped from the galleys of Port Kar, who had fled to the marshes and been befriended by rence growers. Now, years later, he had come to a position of authority among them.

"I am not of Port Kar," I said.

"What is your city?" asked he.

I did not speak.

"Why do you go to Port Kar?" asked Ho-Hak.

Again I did not speak. My identity, that I was Tarl Cabot, and my mission, that I served the Priest-Kings of Gor, was not for others to know. Coming from the Sardar, I knew only that I was to travel to Port Kar and there make contact with Samos, first slaver of Port Kar, scourge of Thassa, said to be trusted of Priest-Kings.

"You are an outlaw," said Ho-Hak, as had the girl before him.

I shrugged.

It was true that my shield, and my clothes, now taken from me, bore no insignia.

Ho-Hak looked at the garb of the warrior, the helmet and shield, the sword with its scabbard, and the leather-wrapped bow of supple Ka-la-na wood, with its roll of sheaf and flight arrows. These things lay between us.

Ho-Hak's right ear twitched. His ears were unusual, very large, and with extremely long lower lobes, drawn lower still by small, heavy pendants set in them. He had been a slave, doubtless, and, doubtless, judging by the collar, and the large hands and broad back, had served on the galleys, but he had been an unusual slave, a bred exotic, doubtless originally intended by the slave maters for a destiny higher than that of the galley bench.

There are various types of "exotics" bred by Gorean slavers, all of whom are to be distinguished from more normal varieties of bred slaves, such as Passion Slaves and Draft Slaves. Exotics may be bred for almost any purpose, and some of these purposes, unfortunately, seem to be little more than to produce quaint or unusual specimens. Ho-Hak may well have been one so bred.

"You are an exotic," I said to him.

Ho-Hak's ears leaned forward toward me, but he did not seem angry. He had brown hair, and brown eyes; the hair, long, was tied behind his head with a string of rence cloth. He wore a sleeveless tunic of rence cloth, like most of the rence growers.

"Yes," said Ho-Hak. "I was bred for a collector."

"I see," I said.

"I broke his neck and escaped," said Ho-Hak. "Later I was recaptured and sent to the galleys."

"And you again escaped," I said.

"In doing so," said Ho-Hak, looking at his large hands, heavy and powerful, "I killed six men."

"And then you came to the marshes," said I.

"Yes," he said, "I then came to the marshes."

He regarded me, the ears leaning slightly toward me, "And I brought to the marshes with me," said he, "the memory of a dozen years on the galleys, and a hatred for all things of Port Kar."

There were various rence growers gathered about, the men with their marsh spears. Almost at my side stood the blondish girl I had first seen, she who had been primarily effectual in my capture, herself acting as the bait, the lure to which I had been drawn. She stood proudly beside me, straight, her shoulders back, her chin high, as does a free woman beside a miserable slave, naked and kneeling. I was conscious of her thigh at my cheek. Over her shoulder were slung the four birds she had caught in the marshes; their necks were now broken and they were tied together, two in front and two over her back. There were other women about as well, and here and there, peering between the adults, I could see children.

"He is either of Port Kar," she said, shifting the gants on her shoulder, "or he was intending to be of Port Kar, for for what other reason would one go to Port Kar."

For a long time Ho-Hak said nothing. He had a broad head, with a heavy, calm face.

I heard the squealing of a domestic tarsk running nearby, its feet scuttling in the woven rence of the island, as on a mat. A child was crying out, chasing it.

I heard some domestic marsh gants making their piping call. They wandered freely on the island, leaving it to feed, then returning to it later. Wild marsh gants, captured, even as young as gantlings, cannot be domesticated; on the other hand, eggs, at the hatching point, gathered from floating gant nests, are sometimes brought to the island; the hatchlings, interestingly, if not permitted to see an adult gant for the first week of their life, then adopt the rence island as their home, and show no fear of human beings; they will come and go in the wild as they please, feeding and flying, but will always, and frequently, return to the rence island, their hatching place; if the rence island, however, should be destroyed, they revert entirely to the wild; in the domesticated state, it might be mentioned, they will often come to whistles, and will invariably permit themselves to be picked up and handled.

There were several reasonably important looking individuals gathered about, and, as it turned out, these were headmen from various other rence islands in the vicinity. A given rence island usually holds about fifty or sixty persons. The men from several of these islands had cooperated in my pursuit and capture. Normally, as I may have mentioned, these communities are isolated from one another, but it was now near the Autumnal Equinox, and the month of Se'Kara was shortly to begin. For rence growers, the first of Se'Kara, the date of the Autumnal Equinox, is a time of festival. By that time most of the year's rence will have been cut, and great stocks of rence paper, gathered in rolls like cord wood and covered with woven rence mats, will have been prepared.

Between Se'Kara and the winter solstice, which occurs on the first of Se'Var, the rence will be sold or bartered, sometimes by taking it to the edge of the delta, sometimes by being contacted by rence merchants, who enter the delta in narrow barges, rowed by slaves, in order to have first pick of the product.

The first of Se'Var is also a date of festival, it might be mentioned, but this time the festival is limited to individual, isolated rence islands. With the year's rence sold, the communities do not care to lie too closely to one another; the primary reason is that, in doing so, they would present too inviting a target for the "tax collectors" of Port Kar. Indeed, I surmised, there was risk enough, and great risk, coming together even in Se'Kara. The unsold stores of rence paper on the islands at this time would, in themselves, be a treasure, though, to be sure, a bulky one.

But I felt there was something strange going on, for there must have been five or six headmen on the island with Ho-Hak at this time. It is seldom, even in Se'Kara, that so many rence islands would gather for festival. Usually it would be two or three. At such times there is drinking of rence beer, steeped, boiled and fermented from crushed seeds and the whitish pith of the plant; singing; games; contests and courtship, for the young people of the rence islands too seldom meet those of the other communities. Why should there be so many rence islands in the same vicinity, even though it was near the first of Se'Kara? Surely the capture of one traveler in the delta did not warrant this attention, and, of course, the islands must have been gathered together even before I had entered the area.

"He is a spy," said one of the other men present, who stood beside Ho-Hak. This man was tall, and strong looking. He carried a marsh spear. On his forehead there was tied a headband formed of the pearls of the Vosk sorp.

I wondered what in particular there might be to spy about on the rence islands.

Ho-Hak still did not speak, but sat on the shell of the Vosk sorp, looking down at the weapons, mine, before him.

I squirmed a bit in the marsh vine that constrained me.

"Do not move, Slave," snapped the girl, who stood beside me.

Immediately the two loops of marsh vine knotted about my neck tightened, each taut, pulling against the other.

The girl's hands were in my hair and she yanked my head back.

"He is of Port Kar," she said, her hands in my hair, "or intended to be of Port Kar!" She glared at Ho-Hak, as though demanding that he speak.

But Ho-Hak did not speak, nor did he seem particularly to notice the girl.

Angrily she removed her hands from my hair, thrusting my head to one side.

Ho-Hak seemed intent on regarding the leather-wrapped bow of supple Ka-la-na wood.

The women of rence growers, when in their own marshes, do not veil themselves, as is common among Gorean women, particularly of the cities. Moreover, they are quite capable of cutting rence, preparing it, hunting for their own food and, on the whole, of existing, if they wish it, by themselves. There are few tasks of the rence communities which they cannot perform as well as men. Their intelligence, and the work of their hands, is needed by the small communities. Accordingly they suffer little inhibition in the matters of speaking out and expressing themselves.

Ho-Hak reached down and unwrapped the leather from the yellow bow of supple Ka-la-na. The roll of sheaf and flight arrows spilled out to the woven mat that was the surface of the rence island.

There were gasps from two or three of the men present. I gathered they had seen small straight bows, but that this was the first long bow they had seen.

Ho-Hak stood up. The bow was taller than several of the men present.

He handed the bow to the blondish girl, she with blue eyes, who had been instrumental in my capture.

"String it," said he to her.

Angrily she threw the marsh gants from her shoulder and took the bow.

She seized the bow in her left hand and braced the bottom of it against the instep of her left foot, taking the hemp cord whipped with silk, the string, in her right hand. She struggled.

At last, angrily, she thrust the bow back into the hands of Ho-Hak.

Ho-Hak looked down at me, the large ears inclining toward me slightly. "This is the peasant bow, is it not?" he asked. "Called the great bow, the long bow?"

"It is," I said.

"Long ago," said he, "in a village once, on the lower slopes of the Thentis range, about a campfire, I heard sing of this bow."

I said nothing.

He handed the bow to the fellow with the headband of pearls of the Vosk sorp bound about his forehead. "String it," said Ho-Hak.

The fellow handed his marsh spear to a companion and turned to the bow. He took it confidently. Then the look of confidence vanished. Then his face reddened, and then the veins stood out on his forehead, and then he cried out in disgust, and then he threw the bow back to Ho-Hak.

Ho-Hak looked at it and then set it against the instep

of his left foot, taking the bow in his left hand and the string in his right.

There was a cry of awe from about the circle as he strung the bow.

I admired him. He had strength, and much strength, for he had strung the bow smoothly, strength it might be from the galleys, but strength, and superb strength.

"Well done," said I to him.

Then Ho-Hak took, from among the arrows on the mat, the leather bracer and fastened it about his left forearm, that the arm not be lacerated by the string, and took the small tab as well, putting the first and second fingers of his right hand through, that in drawing the string the flesh might not be cut to the bone. Then he took, from the unwrapped roll of arrows, now spilled on the leather, a flight arrow, and this, to my admiration, he fitted to the bow and drew it to the very pile itself.

He held the arrow up, pointing it into the sky, at an angle of some fifty degrees.

Then there came the clean, swift, singing flash of the bowstring and the flight arrow was aloft.

There were cries from all, of wonder and astonishment, for they would not have believed such a thing possible.

The arrow seemed lost, as though among the clouds, and so far was it that it seemed vanished in its falling.

The group was silent.

Ho-Hak unstrung the bow. "It is with this," he said, "that peasants defend their holdings."

He looked from face to face. Then he replaced the bow, putting it with its arrows, on the leather spread upon the mat of woven rence that was the surface of the island.

Ho-Hak regarded me. "Are you skilled with this bow?" he asked.

"Yes," I said.

"See that he does not escape," said Ho-Hak.

I felt the prongs of two marsh spears in my back. "He will not escape," said the girl, putting her fingers in the ropes that held my throat. I could feel her knuckles in the side of my neck. She shook the ropes. She irritated me. She acted as though it were she herself who had taken me.

"Are you of the peasants?" asked Ho-Hak of me.

"No," I said. "I am of the Warriors."

"This bow, though," said one of the men holding my neck ropes, "is of the peasants."

"I am not of the Peasants," I said.

Ho-Hak looked at the man who wore the headband of pearls of the Vosk sorp.

"With such a bow," he said to that man, "we might live free in the marsh, free of those of Port Kar."

"It is a weapon of peasants," said the man with the headband, he who had been unable to bend the bow.

"So?" asked Ho-Hak.

"I," said the man, "am of the Growers of Rence. I, for one, am not a Peasant."

"Nor am I!" cried the girl.

The others, too, cried their assent.

"Besides," said another man, "we do not have metal for the heads of arrows, nor arrowwood, and Ka-la-na does not grow in the marsh. And we do not have cords of strength enough to draw such bows."

"And we do not have leather," added another.

"We could kill tharlarion," said Ho-Hak, "and obtain leather. And perhaps the teeth of the marsh shark might be fashioned in such a way as to tip arrows."

"There is no Ka-la-na, no cord, no arrowwood," said another.

"We might trade for such things," said Ho-Hak. "There are peasants who live along the edges of the delta, particularly to the east."

The man with the headband, he who had not been able to bend the bow, laughed. "You, Ho-Hak," said he, "were not born to the rence."

"No," said Ho-Hak. "That is true."

"But we were," said the man. "We are Growers of the Rence."

There was a murmur of assent, grunts and shiftings in the group.

"We are not Peasants," said the man with the headband. "We are Growers of the Rence!"

There was an angry cry of confirmation from the group, mutterings, shouts of agreement.

Ho-Hak once again sat down on the curved shell of the great Vosk sorp, that shell that served him as throne in this his domain, an island of rence in the delta of the Vosk.

"What is to be done with me?" I asked.

"Torture him for festival," suggested the fellow with the headband of the pearls of the Vosk sorp.

Ho-Hak's ears lay flat against the side of his head. He looked evenly at the fellow. "We are not of Port Kar," said he.

The man with the headband shrugged, looking about. He saw that his suggestion had not met with much enthusiasm. This, naturally, did not displease me. He shrugged again, and looked down at the woven surface of the island.

"So," I asked, "what is to be my fate?"

"We did not ask you here," said Ho-Hak. "We did not invite you to cross the line of the blood mark."

"Return to me my belongings," I said, "and I shall be on my way and trouble you no longer."

Ho-Hak smiled.

The girl beside me laughed, and so, too, did the man with the headband, he who had not been able to bend the bow. Several of the others laughed as well.

"Of custom," said Ho-Hak, "we give those we capture who are of Port Kar a choice."

"What is the choice?" I asked.

"You will be thrown bound to marsh tharlarion, of course," said Ho-Hak.

I paled.

"The choice," said Ho-Hak, "is simple." He regarded me. "Either you will be thrown alive to the marsh tharlarion or, if you wish, we will kill you first."

I struggled wildly against the marsh vine, futilely. The rence growers, without emotion, watched me. I fought the vine for perhaps a full Ehn. Then I stopped. The vine was tight. I knew I had been perfectly secured. I was theirs. The girl beside me laughed, as did the man with the headband, and certain of the others.

"There is never any trace of the body," said Ho-Hak.

I looked at him.

"Never," he said.

Again I struggled against the vine, but again futilely.

"It seems too easy that he should die so swiftly," said the girl. "He is of Port Kar, or would be of that city."

"True," said the fellow with the headband, he who had been unable to bend the bow. "Let us torture him for festival."

"No," said the girl. She looked at me with fury. "Let us rather keep him as a miserable slave."

Ho-Hak looked up at her.

"Is that not a sweeter vengeance?" hissed she. "That rightless he should serve the Growers of Rence as a beast of burden?"

"Let us rather throw him to tharlarion," said the man with the headband of the pearls of the Vosk sorp. "That way we shall be rid of him."

"I say," said the blondish girl, "let us rather shame him and Port Kar as well. Let him be worked and beaten by day and tethered by night. Each hour with labors, and whips and thongs, let us show him our hatred for Port Kar and those of that city!"

"How is it," I asked the girl, "that you so hate those of Port Kar?"

"Silence, Slave!" she cried and thrust her fingers into the ropes about my neck, twisting her hand. I could not swallow, nor breathe. The faces about me began to blacken. I fought to retain consciousness.

Then she withdrew her hand.

I gasped for breath, choking. I threw up on the mat. There were cries of disgust, and derision. I felt the prongs of marsh spears in my back.

"I say," said he with the headband, "let it be the marsh tharlarion."

"No," I said numbly. "No."

Ho-Hak looked at me. He seemed surprised.

I, too, found myself stunned. It had seemed the words had scarcely been mine.

"No, No," I said again, the words again seeming almost those of another.

I began to sweat, and I was afraid.

Ho-Hak looked at me, curiously. His large ears leaned toward me, almost inquisitively.

I did not want to die.

I shook my head, clearing my eyes, fighting for breath, and looked into his eyes.

"You are of the warriors," said Ho-Hak.

"Yes," I said. "I know, yes."

I found I desperately wanted the respect of this calm, strong man, he most of all, he once a slave, who sat before me on the throne, that shell of the giant Vosk sorp.

"The teeth of the tharlarion," said he, "are swift, Warrior."

"I know," I said.

"If you wish," said he, "we will slay you first."

"I," I said, "I do not want to die."

I lowered my head, burning with shame. In my eyes in that moment it seemed I had lost myself, that my codes had been betrayed, Ko-ro-ba my city dishonored, even the blade I had carried soiled. I could not look Ho-Hak again in the eyes. In their eyes, and in mine, I could now be nothing, only slave.

"I had thought the better of you," said Ho-Hak. "I had thought you were of the warriors."

I could not speak to him.

"I see now," said Ho-Hak, "you are indeed of Port Kar."

I could not raise my head, so shamed I was. It seemed I could never lift my head again.

"Do you beg to be a slave?" asked Ho-Hak. The question was cruel, but fair.

I looked at Ho-Hak, tears in my eyes. I saw only contempt on that broad, calm face.

I lowered my head. "Yes," I said. "I beg to be a slave."

There was a great laugh from those gathered about, and, too, in those peals of merriment I heard the laugh of he who wore the headband of the pearls of the Vosk sorp, and most bitter to me of all, the laugh of contempt of the girl who stood beside me, her thigh at my cheek.

"Slave," said Ho-Hak.

"Yes," said I, "—Master." The word came bitterly to me. But a Gorean slave addresses all free men as Master, all free women as Mistress, though, of course, normally but one would own him.

There was further laughter.

"Perhaps now," said Ho-Hak, "we shall throw you to tharlarion."

I put down my head.

There was more laughter.

To me, at that moment, it seemed I cared not whether they chose to throw me to tharlarion or not. It seemed to me that I had lost what might be more precious than life itself. How could I face myself, or anyone? I had chosen ignominious bondage to the freedom of honorable death.

I was sick. I was shamed. It was true that they might now throw me to tharlarion. According to Gorean custom a slave is an animal, and may be disposed of as an animal, in whatever way the master might wish, whenever he might please. But I was sick, and I was shamed, and I could not now, somehow, care. I had chosen ignominious bondage to the freedom of honorable death.

"Is there anyone who wants this slave?" I heard Ho-Hak asking.

"Give him to me, Ho-Hak," I heard. It was the clear, ringing voice of the girl who stood beside me.

There was a great laughter, and rich in that humiliating thunder was the snort of the fellow who wore the headband, that formed of the pearls of the Vosk sorp.

Strangely I felt small and nothing beside the girl, only chattel. How straight she stood, each inch of her body alive and splendid in her vigor and freedom. And how worthless and miserable was the beast, the slave, that knelt, naked and bound, at her feet.

"He is yours," I heard Ho-Hak say.

I burned with shame.

"Bring the paste of rence!" cried the girl. "Unbind his ankles. Take these ropes from his neck."

A woman left the group to bring some rence paste, and two men removed the marsh vine from my neck and ankles. My wrists were still bound behind my back.

In a moment the woman had returned with a double handful of wet rence paste. When fried on flat stones it makes a kind of cake, often sprinkled with rence seeds.

"Open your mouth, Slave," said the girl.

I did so and, to the amusement of those watching, she forced the wet paste into my mouth.

"Eat it," she said. "Swallow it."

Painfully, almost retching, I did so.

"You have been fed by your Mistress," she said.

"I have been fed by my Mistress," I said.

"What is your name, Slave?" asked she.

"Tarl," said I.

She struck me savagely across the mouth, flinging my head to one side.

"A slave has no name," she said.

"I have no name," I said.

She walked about me. "Your back is broad," she said. "You are strong, but stupid." She laughed. "I shall call you Bosk," she said.

The Bosk is a large, horned, shambling ruminant of the Gorean plains. It is herded below the Gorean equator by the Wagon Peoples, but there are Bosk herds on ranches in the north as well, and peasants often keep some of the animals.

"I am Bosk," I said.

There was laughter.

"My Bosk!" she laughed.

"I should have thought," said he with the headband, formed of the pearls of the Vosk sorp, "that you might have preferred a man for a slave, one who is proud and does not fear death."

The girl thrust her hands into my hair and threw back my head. Then she spat in my face. "Coward and slave!" she hissed.

I dropped my head. It was true what she had said. I had feared death. I had chosen slavery. I could not be a true man. I had lost myself.

"You are worthy only to be the slave of a woman," said Ho-Hak.

"Do you know what I am going to do with you?" asked the girl.

"No," I said.

She laughed. "In two days," she said, "at festival, I will put you at stake as a prize for girls."

There was laughter at this, and shouts of pleasure.

My shoulders and head fell forward and, bound, I shook with shame.

The girl turned. "Follow me, Slave," said she, imperiously.

I struggled to my feet and, to the jeers of the rence growers, and blows, stumbled after the girl, she who owned me, my mistress.

The Hut

In the stem of the girl's rence craft, she poling the craft from its stern, I knelt, cutting rence. It was late in the year to cut rence but some quantities of the rence are cut during the fall and winter and stored on covered rence rafts until the spring. These stores of rence are not used in the making of rence paper, but in the weaving of mats, for adding to the surface of the island, and for the pith, used as a food.

"Cut there," said the girl, moving the rush craft into a thicket of rence.

One holds the stem of the plant in the left hand and, with the right, with a small, curved, two-inch knife makes a diagonal upward stroke.

We were towing a small rence raft and there was already much rence upon it.

We had been cutting since before dawn. It was now late in the afternoon.

I cut again, dropping the tufted, flowered head of the rence stem into the water, and then I tossed the stem onto the raft of rence, with the piles of others.

I could sense the rence craft move as the girl shifted her weight in it, balancing it and maintaining it in position.

I cut more.

She had not seen fit to give her slave clothing.

About my neck she had coiled and tied a length of marsh vine.

I knew her to be barefoot behind me, in the brief-skirted tunic of yellowish-brown rence cloth, cut away at the shoulders to give her freedom of movement. She wore a golden armlet. Her hair was bound back with the bit of purple rep-cloth. She had, as the girls do in rence craft, tied her skirt high about her thighs, for ease in moving and poling. I was terribly conscious of her. Her rather thick ankles seemed to me strong and lovely, and her legs sturdy and fine. Her hips were sweet, her belly a rhythm made for the touch of a man, and her breasts, full and

27

beautiful, magnificent, tormenting me, strained against the
brittle rence cloth of her tunic with an insolence of soft-
ness, as though, insistent, they would make clear their
contempt for any subterfuge of concealment.

"Slave," had cried the girl once, "do you dare to look
upon your mistress!"

I had turned away.

I was hungry. In the morning, before dawn, she had
placed in my mouth a handful of rence paste. At noon, in
the marshes, with the sun burning at meridian, she had
taken another handful of rence paste from a wallet worn
at her waist and thrust it in my mouth, again not permitting me the dignity of feeding myself. Though it was now
late in the afternoon and I was hungry I would not ask
to be fed again from the wallet at her side.

I cut another rence stem, cut away the tufted, flowered
head, and threw the stem onto the raft.

"Over there," she said, moving the rence craft to a new
location.

She had made little attempt to conceal her beauty from
me. Indeed, she used it to torment and shame me, using
it, like blows and abuse, to increase my miseries.

This morning, before dawn, she had affixed my collar.

I had spent the night in the open, a foot or two from
her tiny hut on the rence island, my wrists tied to my
ankles, my neck tethered to an oar pole thrust deep
through the rence of the island.

Before dawn her foot awakened me.

"Awake, Slave," she had said.

Then, as casually as one might untether an animal,
fearing nothing, she unbound me.

"Follow me, Slave," she had said.

At the edge of the rence island, where her rence craft
was drawn up on the shore, as well as several others,
together with some rafts for transporting cut rence, she
stopped, and turned, and faced me. She looked up into
my eyes.

"Kneel," she had said.

I had done so, and she had drawn out a handful of
rence paste from the wallet at her side, and she had fed
me.

"Stand," she had said.

I did so.

"In the cities," she asked, "they have slave collars, do they not?"

"Yes," I said.

Then she had taken a length of marsh vine from a packet on her rence craft.

Then, looking up into my eyes, smiling, close to me, her arms about my neck, she insolently wound the vine five times about my neck, and knotted it in front.

"Now," she said, "you have a collar."

"Yes," I said. "I have a collar."

"Say," said she, her arms still about my neck, "I am your collared slave."

My fists clenched. She stood within my grasp, her arms on my neck, taunting me with her eyes.

"I am your collared slave," I said.

"Mistress," she taunted.

"Mistress," I said.

She smiled. "I see," said she, tauntingly, "that you find me beautiful." It was true.

Then she struck me suddenly, with savagery. I cried out with pain.

"Dare you aspire to me!" she cried. "I am a free woman!" Then she hissed out, "Kiss my feet, Slave."

In pain, on my knees, I did so, to her laughter.

"Put now the rence craft in the water," she said, "and attach to it a raft for cut rence, Slave. We must cut rence today, and be quick, be quick, My Slave!"

I cut another rence stem, lopping away the tufted head, and throwing it onto the rence craft. And then another, and another.

The sun, though it was late afternoon, was still hot, and it was humid in the delta of the Vosk, and my hands ached, and were blistered.

"If you do not obey me in all things, and swiftly," had said the girl, "I will have the men bind you and throw you to tharlarion. And there is no escape in the marshes. You will be hunted down by the men with marsh spears. You are my slave!"

"Over there," said the girl. "Cut there."

She moved the craft to a new thicket of rence, and I obeyed.

It was true what she had said. Naked, without weapons, alone in the delta, without aid, without food, I could not escape. It would not be hard for the men of the rence islands, in their hundreds, to cut off escape, to find me, if the tharlarion did not manage to do so first.

But most I was miserable in my heart. I had had an image of myself, a proud image, and the loss of this image had crushed me. I had lived a lie with myself and then, in my own eyes, and in those of others, I had been found out. I had chosen ignominious bondage to the freedom of honorable death. I now knew the sort of thing I was, and in my worthless heart it so sickened me that I did not much care now whether I lived or died. I did not even much care that I might spend the rest of my life as an abject slave, abused on a rence island, the sport of a girl or children, the butt of cruelty and jests of men. Such, doubtless, was deserved. How could I face free men again, when in my own heart I could not even face myself?"

It was hot, and the coils of marsh vine about my throat were hot. Beneath the coils my neck was red, and slippery with sweat and dirt. I put my finger in the collar, to pull it a bit from my throat.

"Do not touch your collar," she said.

I removed my hand from the collar.

"There, cut there," said she, and again I cut rence for my mistress.

"It is hot," she said.

I turned.

She had loosened the cord that laced the tunic, refastening it more loosely. In the narrow innuendo of the slightly parted tunic I sensed her perfection.

She laughed. "Cut rence, Slave."

Again I turned to my work.

"You are pretty in your collar," she said.

I did not turn to face her. It was the sort of remark one would address to a slave girl, a simple, comely wench in bondage. The rence knife flashed through a stem and then I cut the tufted, flowered head, it falling in the water, and threw the stem on the rence craft, with the numerous others.

"If you remove your collar," said she, "you will be destroyed."

I said nothing.

"Do you understand?" she asked.

"Yes," I said.

"Mistress," said she.

"Yes," I said, "I understand, Mistress."

"Good," said she, "Pretty Slave."

The rence knife flashed through another stem, and I cut away the flowered, tufted head, and threw the stem in the piles on the raft.

"Pretty Slave," she repeated.

I shook with fury. "Please," said I, "do not speak to me."

"I shall speak to you as I wish," said she, "Pretty Slave."

I trembled with fury, the rence knife in my hand. I shook with humiliation, with the degradation of her scorn. I considered turning upon her and seizing her.

"Cut rence," said she, "Pretty Slave."

I turned again to the rence, trembling with fury, with shame, and again, stem by stem, began to cut.

I heard her laughter behind me.

Stem by stem, and pile by pile, the time was marked in strokes of rence.

The sun was low now and insects moved in the sedge. The water glistened in the dusk, moving in small bright circles about the stems of rushes.

Neither of us had spoken for a long time.

"May I speak?" I asked.

"Yes," she said.

"How is it," I asked, "that so many of the rence islands are now gathered together?" I had wondered about this.

"It is near the festival of Se'Kara," said she.

Indeed, I knew that tomorrow was festival for the rence islands.

"But so many?" I asked. "Surely that is unusual?"

"You are curious for a slave," she said. "Curiosity is not always becoming in a slave."

I said nothing.

"Ho-Hak," said she, "has called the nearby islands to a council."

"How many are there?" I asked.

"Five," said she, "in the general area. There are others, of course, elsewhere in the delta."

"What is the purpose of the council?" I asked.

She would feel free to speak to me. I was confined by the marsh, and only slave.

"He thinks to unite the rence growers," said she, a certain amused skepticism in her voice.

"For purposes of trade?" I asked.

"In a way," she said. "It would be useful to have similar standards for rence paper, to sometimes harvest in common, to sometimes, in times of need, share crops, and, of course, to obtain a better price for our paper than we might if we bargained as isolated islands with the rence merchants."

"Those of Port Kar," I said, "would doubtless not be pleased by such news."

She laughed. "Doubtless not," said she.

"Perhaps also," I suggested, "in uniting the islands there might be some measure of protection gained from the officials of Port Kar."

"Officials?" she asked. "Ah, yes, the collectors of the taxes, in the names of various Ubars, who may or may not have a current ascendency in the city."

"And would there not be some measure of protection against," I asked, "the simple slavers of Port Kar?"

"Perhaps," she said. She spoke bitterly. "The difference between the collector of taxes and the slaver is sometimes less than clear."

"It would doubtless be desirable, from the point of view of the rence islands," I suggested, "if they should, in certain matters, act in unanimity."

"We Rencers," she said, "are independent people. We, each of us, have our own island."

"You do not think," I asked, "that the plan of Ho-Hak will be successful?"

"No," she said, "I do not think it will be successful."

She had now turned the stem of the craft toward the rence island, which lay some pasang or two through the swamp, and, as I cut rence here and there, began to pole homeward.

"May I speak?" I asked.

"Yes," she said.

"You wear on your left arm," I said, "a golden armlet. How is it that a girl of rence islands has such an armlet?"

"You may not speak," she said, irritably.

I was silent.

"In there," she said, indicating the small, round hole that gave access to her tiny rence hut.

I was surprised. I had expected her to bind me, as she

had the night before, then tethering me to the oar pole thrust through the rence behind the hut.

We had returned her rence craft to the shore of the rence island, fastening it there, along with the rence raft. I had carried the rence, in many trips, to a covered area, where it was stored.

"In there," she repeated.

I fell to my hands and knees and, lowering my head, crawled through the small hole, the edges of the woven rence scratching at my shoulders.

She followed me into the hut. It was eight feet long and five feet wide. Its ceiling was continuous with its walls, and, in its curve, stood not more than four feet from the rence surface of the island. The rence hut is commonly used for little else than sleeping. She struck together, over a copper bowl, a bit of steel and flint, the sparks falling into some dried petals of the rence. A small flame was kindled into which she thrust a bit of rence stem, like a match. The bit of stem took the fire and with it she lit a tiny lamp, also sitting in a shallow copper bowl, which burned tharlarion oil. She set the lamp to one side.

Her few belongings were in the tiny hut. There was a bundle of clothing and a small box for odds and ends. There were two throwing sticks near the wall, where her sleeping mat, of woven rence, was rolled. There was another bowl and a cup or two, and two or three gourds. Some utensils were in the bowl, a wooden stirring stick and a wooden ladle, both carved from rence root. The rence knife, with which I had cut rence, she had left in the packet in her rence craft. There were also, in one corner, some coils of marsh vine.

"Tomorrow is Festival," she said.

She looked at me. I could see the side of her face and her hair, and the outline of the left side of her body in the light of the tiny lamp.

She put her hands behind the back of her head to untie the purple fillet of rep-cloth.

We knelt facing one another, but inches apart.

"Touch me and you will die," she said. She laughed.

She disengaged the fillet and shook her hair free. It fell about her shoulders.

"I am going to put you up at stake at festival," she said. "You will be a prize for girls—Pretty Slave."

My fists clenched.

"Turn," she said, sharply.

I did so, and she laughed.

"Cross your wrists," she ordered.

I did so, and with one of the coils of marsh vine, she lashed my wrists together, tightly, with the strong hands of a rence girl.

"There, Pretty Slave," she said. And then she said, "Turn," and I did so, and faced her.

"My," she said, "you are a pretty, pretty slave. It will be a lucky girl who wins you at festival."

I said nothing.

"Is Pretty Slave hungry?" she asked, solicitously.

I would not respond.

She laughed and reached into the wallet at her side and drew forth two handsful of rence paste and thrust them in my mouth. She herself nibbled on a rence cake, watching me, and then on some dried fish which she drew also from the wallet. Then she took a long draught of water from a yellow, curved gourd, and then, thrusting the neck of the gourd into my mouth, gave me a swallow, then drawing it away again and laughing, but then giving it to me again, that I might drink. When I had drunk, she put the plug, carved from gourd stem, back in the gourd, and replaced it in the corner.

"It is time to sleep," she said. "Pretty Slave must sleep, for tomorrow he will have many things to do. He will be very busy."

She indicated that I should lie on my left side, facing her.

Then, with another coil of marsh vine, she tied my ankles together.

She unrolled her sleeping mat.

She looked at me, and laughed.

Then, as I lay there, bound, she unlaced her tunic, opening it. Her beauty, and it was considerable, was now but ill concealed.

Again she looked on me, and, to my amazement, insolently, with a liquid motion, slipped the tunic off, over her head.

She sat on the mat and regarded me.

She had undressed herself before me as casually as though I had been an animal.

"I see," said she, "that you must again be punished."

Involuntarily, instinctively, I tried to withdraw but, bound, I could not.

She struck me with savagery, four times.

Inwardly I screamed with agony.

Then, sitting on the mat, forgetting me, she turned to the repair of a small sack, woven of rence, which had hung in the corner of the hut. She used thin strips of rence, breaking them and biting them, weaving them in and out. She worked carefully, attentively.

I had been a warrior of Ko-ro-ba.

Then on an island of rence in the delta of the Vosk I had learned myself, that I was, in the core of myself, ignoble and craven, worthless and fearing, only coward.

I had been a warrior of Ko-ro-ba.

Now I was only a girl's slave.

"May I speak?" I asked.

"Yes," she said, not looking up.

"Mistress has not honored me," said I, "even by telling me her name. May I not know the name of my mistress?"

"Telima," she said, finishing the work in which she had been engaged. She hung the sack again in the corner, putting the scraps and strips of rence left over from her work at the foot of her sleeping mat. Then, kneeling on the mat, she bent to the small lamp in its copper bowl on the flooring of the hut. Before she blew it out she said, "My name is Telima. The name of your mistress is Telima." Then she blew it out.

We lay in the darkness for a long time.

Then I heard her roll over to me. I could sense her lying near me, on her elbows, looking down at me.

Her hair brushed me.

Then I felt her hand on my belly. "Are you asleep, Pretty Slave?" she asked.

"No," I said.

Then I cried out, involuntarily.

"I will not hurt Pretty Slave," she said.

"Please," said I, "do not speak so to me."

"Be silent," said she, "Pretty Slave."

Then she touched me again.

"Ah," said she, "it seems a slave finds his mistress beautiful."

"Yes," I said.

"Ah," chided she, "it seems a slave has not yet learned his lesson."

"Please," I said, "do not strike me again."

"Perhaps," said she, "a slave should again be punished."

"Please," I said, "do not strike me again."

"Do you find me truly beautiful?" she asked. She had one finger inside my collar of marsh vine, idly playing with the side of my neck.

"Yes," I whispered. "Yes."

"Know you not," asked she, with sudden insolence and coldness, "that I am a free woman?"

I said nothing.

"Dare you aspire to a free woman?" she demanded.

"No," I said.

"Dare you aspire to your mistress, Slave!" she demanded.

"No," I said, "no!"

"Why not?" she demanded.

"I am a slave," I said. "Only a slave."

"That is true," she said. "You are only a slave."

Then, suddenly, holding my head in her hands, she pressed her lips savagely down on mine.

I tried to twist my head away, but could not.

Then she drew back her head, and, in the darkness I could sense her, and her lips, but an inch from my own.

Beams and timbers of misery and wanting clashed within me. It was she who had fastened coils of marsh vine about my neck, and knotted them, putting me in the collar of a slave. It was she who had placed her arms about my neck at dawn, on the shore of the rence island. It was she who had beaten me. It was she whom I must obey, she for whom I had cut rence, she who had fed me as one feeds an animal. It was she who had last night, and this night, bound me as a slave. It was she who had tortured me with her beauty, tormenting and tantalizing me, with a cruelty all the keener for its being so off-hand and casual. I found myself fearing her, and desperately wanting her, though knowing her immeasurably above me. I feared that she might hurt me, it was true, but the hurts I feared most were those of her insolence and contempt, those that more degraded me than bonds and blows. And I wanted her, for she was beautiful, and vital, maddening, ravishing. But she was free, and I only slave. She could move as she wished. I lay bound.

I wore besides my bonds only a collar of marsh vine. She wore her swiftness, and her freedom, and an armlet of gold.

But most perhaps, incredible as it might seem, I feared that if I asked for a kindness, even a word or a gesture, it would be refused. Alone and slave, beaten and degraded, I found myself desperately in need of something, be it almost nothing, to indicate that I was a man, a human being, something that might, to some extent or degree, be worthy of respect or understanding. I think that if she, this proud woman, before whom I felt myself nothing, she my mistress, if she had but cared to speak a word of simple kindness to me I might have cried out with gladness, willingly serving her in all things she asked. But if I should but beg a kindness, humbly, I feared it might be refused, that she might reject me in this as she had in all other things, my manhood and my humanity. And fused with this, excruciating in the pain of it, was my desire for her, the crying out of my blood that she had so, and deliberately, aroused.

In the darkness I sensed her, and her lips, but an inch from my own.

She had not deigned to move.

To my horror, timidly, fearing and hesitant, I felt my lips lift then to those of my beautiful mistress, and, in the darkness, touch them.

"Slave," said she, with contempt.

I put my head back to the woven rence that formed the floor of the hut.

"Yes," I said, "I am a slave."

"Whose?" she queried.

"Telima's," I said.

"I am your slave," I said.

She laughed. "Tomorrow," she said, "I will put you up at stake, to be a prize for girls."

I said nothing.

"Say, I am pleased," she said.

"Please!" I said.

"Say it," she said.

"I am pleased," I said.

"Say now," said she, "I am a pretty slave."

My wrists and ankles fought the marsh vine.

She laughed. "Do not struggle," she said. "Also," she added, "there is no point. Telima ties well."

It was true.

"Say it," said she.

"I cannot," I begged.

"Say it," said she.

"I—I am a pretty slave," I said.

I threw back my head and cried out with misery.

I heard her soft laugh. In the darkness I could see the outline of her head, could feel her hair on my shoulder. Her lips, still, were but an inch from mine.

"I will now teach you the fate of a pretty slave," she said.

Suddenly, her hands in my hair, she thrust her lips savagely down on mine and, to my horror, my lips met hers, but could not withstand them and I felt her head forcing mine down and I felt her teeth cut into my lips and I tasted blood, my own, in my mouth, and then, insolently, her tongue thrust into my mouth, possessively, forcing mine, as it would, from its path, and then, after some Ehn, withdrawing her tongue, she bit me, as I cried out in pain, diagonally across the mouth and lips, that, on the morrow, when I stood at stake in festival, the marks of my mistress's teeth, evidence of her conquest of me, would be visible in my body.

I was shattered.

I had been given the kiss of the Mistress to the male slave.

"You will move as I direct," she said.

In the darkness, shattered, bound, mouth swollen, I heard her with horror.

Then she mounted me, and used me for her pleasure.

Festival

"I think I shall win you," said a lithe, dark-haired girl, holding my chin and pushing up my head, that she might better see my face. She was dark-eyed, and slender, and vital. Her legs were marvelous, accentuated by the incredibly brief tunic of the rence girl.

"I shall win him," said another girl, a tall, blond girl, gray-eyed, who carried a coil of marsh vine in her right hand.

Another girl, dark-haired, carrying a folded net over her left shoulder, said, "No, he will be mine."

"No, mine!" said yet another.

"Mine!" cried yet another, and another.

They gathered about me, examining me, walking about me, regarding me as one might an animal, or slave.

"Teeth," said the first girl, the lithe, dark-haired girl. I opened my mouth that she might examine my teeth. Others looked as well.

Then she felt of my muscles, and thighs, and slapped my side two or three times.

"Sturdy," said one of the girls.

"But much used," said another.

She laughed, with others. They referred to my mouth. On the right side it was black, and cut, and swollen. Diagonally it wore the marks of the teeth of Telima.

"Yes," said the first girl, laughing, "much used."

"But good for all that!" laughed another.

"Yes," said the first girl, "good for all that." She stepped back and regarded me. "Yes," she said to the others, "all things considered, this is a good slave, a quite good slave."

They laughed.

Then the lithe girl stepped close to me.

I stood with an oar pole at my back, bound to it for their inspection. The pole, thrust deep in the rence of the island, stood in a clearing near the shore of the island. My wrists were bound behind the pole with marsh vine. My ankles were also fastened to the pole. Two other coils of marsh vine bound my stomach and neck to the pole. On my head my Mistress, Telima, had placed a woven garland of rence flowers.

The lithe, dark-haired girl, standing close to me, traced a pattern on my left shoulder, idly. It was the first letter of the Gorean expression for slave.

She looked up at me. "Would you like to be my slave?" she asked. "Would you like to serve me?"

I said nothing.

"I might even be kind to you," said the girl.

I looked away.

She laughed.

Then the other girls, too, came close to me, each to taunt me, with whether or not I would not rather serve them.

"Clear away there," called a man's voice. It was Ho-Hak.

"It is time for contests," called another voice, which I recognized as that of Telima, my mistress. She wore the golden armlet, and the purple fillet tying back her hair. She wore the brief tunic of the rence girl. She was exceedingly well pleased with herself today, and was stunning in her beauty. She walked, head back, as though she might own the earth. In her hand she carried a throwing stick.

"Come, come away," said Ho-Hak, gesturing for the girls to go down to the shore of the rence island.

I wanted Ho-Hak to look at me, to meet my eyes. I respected him, I wanted him to look upon me, to deign to recognize that I might exist.

But he did not look upon me, nor notice me in any way, and, followed by Telima, and the other girls, made his way to the shore of the rence island.

I was left alone, tied at the pole.

I had been aroused at dawn by Telima, and unbound, that I might help in the preparations for festival.

In the early morning the other rence islands, four of them, which had been tethered close by, were poled to the one on which I was kept, and now, joined by flat rence rafts, acting as bridges, they had been tied to one another, now forming, for most practical purposes, a large single island.

I had been used in the fastening of the bridges, and in the drawing up and tying of rence craft on the shore,

as other rencers, from distant islands, arrived for festival.
I had also been used to carry heavy kettles of rence beer.
from the various islands to the place of feasting, as well as
strings of water gourds, poles of fish, plucked gants,
slaughtered tarsks, and baskets of the pith of rence.

Then, about the eighth Gorean hour, Telima had
ordered me to the pole, where she bound me and placed
on my head the garland of rence flowers.

I had stood at the pole the long morning, subject to
the examination, the stares, and the blows and abuse of
those who passed by.

Around the tenth Gorean hour, the Gorean noon, the
rencers ate small rence cakes, dotted with seeds, drank
water, and nibbled on scraps of fish. The great feast would
be in the evening.

Around this time a small boy had come to stare at me,
a half-eaten rence cake in his hand.

"Are you hungry?" he had asked.

"Yes," I had told him.

He had held the rence cake up to me and I bit at it,
eating it.

"Thank you," I had said to him.

But he had just stood there, staring up at me. Then
his mother ran to him and struck him across the side of
the head, scolding him, dragging him away.

The morning was spent variously by the rencers. The
men had sat in council with Ho-Hak, and there had been
much discussion, much argument, even shouting. The
women who had men were busied with the preparation of
the feast. The younger men and women formed opposite
lines, shouting and jeering at one another delightedly. And
sometimes one or the other boy, or girl, would rush to the
opposite line to strike at someone, laughing, and run back
to the other line. Objects were thrown at the opposite line,
as well as jocose abuse. The smaller children played together, the boys playing games with small nets and reed
marsh spears, the girls with rence dolls, or some of the
older ones sporting with throwing sticks, competing
against one another.

After the council had broken up one of the men who
had been seated there came to regard me. It was he who
wore the headband of the pearls of Vosk sorp about his
forehead, who had been unable to bend the bow.

Strangely, to my mind, he carried over his left shoulder a large, white, silken scarf.

He did not speak to me, but he laughed, and passed on. I looked away, burning with shame.

It was now about the twelfth Gorean hour, well past noon.

I had been examined earlier by the girls who would compete for me.

Ho-Hak, with Telima, had summoned them away for the contests.

Most of these took place in the marsh. From where I was bound, over the low rence huts and between them, I could see something of what went on. There was much laughter and shouting, and cheering and crying out. There were races, poling rence craft, and skill contests maneuvering the small light craft, and contests with net and throwing stick. It was indeed festival.

At last, after an Ahn or so, the group, the girls, the men watching, the judges, turned their several rence craft toward the island, beaching them and fastening them on the woven-mat shore.

Then the entire group came to my pole, with the exception of Ho-Hak, who went rather to speak with some men carving rence root and talking, on the other side of the island.

The girls, perhaps more than forty or fifty of them, stood about me, laughing, looking from one to the other, giggling.

I looked at them, with agony.

"You have been won," said Telima.

The girls looked at one another, saying nothing, but laughing and poking one another.

I pulled at the marsh vine, helpless.

"Who has won you?" asked Telima.

The girls giggled.

Then the lithe, dark-haired girl, slender-legged and provocative, stepped quite close to me.

"Perhaps," she whispered, "you are my slave."

"Am I your slave?" I asked.

"Perhaps you are mine," whispered the tall, blond girl, gray-eyed, in my ear. She pressed a coil of marsh vine against my left arm.

"Whose slave am I?" I cried.

The girls gathered about, each one to touch me, to caress me as might a mistress, to whisper in my ear that it might be she to whom I belonged, she whom I must now serve as slave.

"Whose slave am I?" I cried, in agony.

"You will find out," said Telima, "at the feast, then, at the height of festival."

The girls laughed, and the men behind them.

I stood numb at the pole, while Telima unbound me. "Do not remove the garland of rence flowers," said she.

Then I stood free at the pole, save that I wore the collar of marsh vine she had fastened on my neck, and a garland of rence flowers.

"What am I to do?" I asked.

"Go help the women prepare the feast," said she.

All laughed as I turned away.

"Wait!" called she.

I stopped.

"At feast," she said, "you will, of course, serve us." She laughed. "And since you do not know which of us is your mistress, you will serve each, every one of us, as slave. And you will serve well. If she who is your mistress is not well satisfied, doubtless you will be severely punished."

There was much laughter.

"Now go," said she, "and help the women with the food."

I turned to face the girl. "Who," I begged, "is my mistress?"

"You will find out at feast," she said angrily, "at the height of festival! Now go and help the women to prepare the feast—Slave!"

I turned away, and, as they laughed, went to help the women in their work, preparing food for festival.

It was now late on the night of festival, and most of the feast had been consumed.

Torches, oiled coils of marsh vine wound about the prongs of marsh spears, thrust butt down in the rence of the island, burned in the marsh night.

The men sat cross-legged in the outer circles, and, in the inner circles, in the fashion of Gorean women, the women knelt. There were children about the periphery of the circles but many of them were already asleep on the rence. There had been much talking and singing. I gathered it was seldom the rencers, save for those on a given island, met one another. Festival was important to them.

Before the feast I had helped the women, cleaning fish and dressing marsh gants, and then, later, turning spits for the roasted tarsks, roasted over rence-root fires kept on metal pans, elevated above the rence of the island by metal racks, themselves resting on larger pans.

During most of the feast I had been used in the serving, particularly the serving of the girls who had competed for me, one of whom had won me, which one I did not know.

I had carried about bowls of cut, fried fish, and wooden trays of roasted tarsk meat, and roasted gants, threaded on sticks, and rence cakes and porridges, and gourd flagons, many times replenished, of rence beer.

Then, the rencers clapping their hands and singing, Telima approached me.

"To the pole," she said.

I had seen the pole. It was not unlike the one to which I had been bound earlier in the day. There was a circular clearing amidst the feasters, of some forty feet in diameter, about which their circles formed. The pole, barkless, narrow, upright, thrust deep in the rence of the island, stood at the very center of the clearing, surrounded by the circles of the feasting rencers.

I went to the pole, and stood by it.

She took my hands and, with marsh vine, lashed them behind it. Then, as she had in the morning, she fastened my ankles to the pole, and then, again as she had in the morning, she bound me to it as well by the stomach and neck. Then, throwing away the garland of rence flowers I had worn, she replaced it with a fresh garland.

While she was doing this the rencers were clapping their hands in time and singing.

She stood back, laughing.

I saw, in the crowd, Ho-Hak, clapping his hands and singing, and the others, and he who had worn the headband formed of the pearls of the Vosk sorp, who had been unable to bend the bow.

Then, suddenly, the crowd stopped clapping and singing.

There was silence.

Then there came a drumming sound, growing louder and louder, a man pounding on a hollowed drum of rence root with two sticks, and then, as suddenly as the singing and clapping, the drum, too, stopped.

And then to my astonishment the rence girls, squealing and laughing, some protesting and being pushed and shoved, rose to their feet and entered the clearing in the circle.

The young men shouted with pleasure.

One or two of the girls, giggling, tried to slip away, fleeing, but young men, laughing, caught them, and hurled them into the clearing of the circle.

Then the rence girls, vital, eyes shining, breathing deeply, barefoot, bare-armed, many with beads worn for festival, and hammered copper bracelets and armlets, stood all within the circle.

The young men shouted and clapped their hands.

I saw that more than one fellow, handsome, strong-faced, could not take his eyes from Telima.

She was, I noted, the only girl in the circle who wore an armlet of gold.

She paid the young men, if she noticed them, no attention.

The rence communities tend to be isolated. Young people seldom see one another, saving those from the same tiny community. I remembered the two lines, one of young men, the other of girls, jeering and laughing, and crying out at one another in the morning.

Then the man with the drum of hollow rence root began to drum, and I heard some others join in with reed flutes, and one fellow had bits of metal, strung on a circular wire, and another a notched stick, played by scraping it with a flat spoon of rence root.

It was Telima who began first to pound the woven rence mat that was the surface of the island with her right heel, lifting her hands, arms bent, over her head, her eyes closed.

Then the other girls, too, began to join her, and at last even the shiest among them moved pounding, and stamping and turning about the circle. The dances of rence girls are, as far as I know, unique on Gor. There is some savagery in them, but, too, they have sometimes, perhaps paradoxically, stately aspects, stylized aspects, movements reminiscent of casting nets or poling, of weaving rence or hunting gants. But, as I watched, and the young men shouted, the dances became less stylized, and became more universal to woman, whether she be a drunken house-wife in a suburb of a city of Earth or a jeweled slave in Port Kar, dances that spoke of them as women who want men, and will have them. To my astonishment, as the dances continued, even the shiest of the rence girls, those who had to have been forced to the circle, even those who had tried to flee, began to writhe in ecstasy, their hands lifted to the three moons of Gor.

It is often lonely on the rence islands, and festival comes but once a year.

The bantering of the young people in the morning, and the display of the girls in the evening, for in effect in the movements of the dance every woman is nude, have both, I expect, institutional roles to play in the life of the rence growers, significant roles analogous to the roles of dating, display and courtship in the more civilized environments of my native world, Earth.

It marks the end of a childhood when a girl is first sent to the circle.

Suddenly, before me, hands over her head, swaying to the music, I saw the dark-haired, lithe girl, she with such marvelous, slender legs in the brief rence skirt; her ankles were so close together that they might have been chained; and then she put her wrists together back to back over her head, palms out, as though she wore slave bracelets.

Then she said, "Slave," and spit in my face, whirling away.

I wondered if it might be she who was my mistress.

Then another girl, the tall, blond girl, she who had held the coil of marsh vine, stood before me, moving with ex-cruciating slowness, as though the music could be reflected only from moment to moment, in her breathing, in the beating of the heart.

"Perhaps it is I," she said, "who am your mistress."

She, like the other, spit then in my face and turned away, now moving fully, enveloped in the music's flame.

One after another of the girls so danced before me, and about me, taunting me, laughing at their power, then spitting upon me and turning away.

The rencers laughed and shouted, clapping, cheering the girls on in the dance.

But most of the time I was ignored, as much as the pole to which I was bound.

Mostly these girls, saving for a moment or two to humiliate me, danced their beauty for the young men of the circles, that they might be desired, that they might be much sought.

After a time I saw one girl leave the circle, her head back, hair flowing down her back, breathing deeply, and scarcely was she through the circles of rencers, but a young man followed her, joining her some yards beyond the circle. They stood facing one another in the darkness for an Ehn or two, and then I saw him, gently, she not protesting, drop his net over her, and then, by this net, she not protesting, he led her away. Together they disappeared in the darkness, going over one of the raft bridges to another island, one far from the firelight, the crowd, the noise, the dance.

Then, after some Ehn I saw another girl leave the circle of the dance, and she, too, was joined beyond the firelight by a young man and she, too, felt a net dropped over her, and she, too, was led away, his willing prize, to the secrecy of his hut.

The dance grew more frenzied.

The girls whirled and writhed, and the crowd clapped and shouted, and the music grew ever more wild, barbaric and fantastic.

And suddenly Telima danced before me.

I cried out, so startled was I by her beauty.

It seemed to me that she was the most beautiful woman I had ever seen, and before me, only slave, she danced her insolence and scorn. Her hands were over her head and, as she danced, she smiled, regarding me. She cut me with her beauty more painfully, more cruelly, than might have the knives of a torturer. It was her scorn, her contempt for me she danced. In me she aroused agonies of desire but in her eyes I read that I was but the object of her amusement and contempt.

And then she unbound me.

"Go to the hut," she said.

I stood there at the pole.

Torrents of barbaric music swept about us, and there was the clapping and the shouting, and the turning, and the twisting and swirling of rence girls, the passion of the dance burning in their bodies.

"Yes," she said. "I own you."

She spat up into my face.

"Go to the hut," she said.

I stumbled from the pole, making my way through the buffeting circle of dancers, through the laughing circles of rencers, shouting and clapping their hands, and made my way to Telima's hut.

I stood outside in the darkness.

I wiped her spittle from my face.

Then, falling to my hands and knees, lowering my head, I crawled into the hut.

I sat there in the darkness, my head in my hands.

Outside I could hear the music, the cries and clapping, the shouts of the rence girls dancing under the moons of Gor.

I sat for a long time in the darkness.

Then Telima entered, as one who owns the hut, as though I was not there.

"Light the lamp," she said to me.

I did so, fumbling in the darkness, striking together the flint and steel, sparks falling into the small bowl of dried petals of the rence. In this tiny flame I thrust a bit of rence stem, from a bundle of such, and, with it, lit the tiny tharlarion-oil lamp set in its copper bowl. I put the bit of rence stem back, as I had seen Telima do, in the small bowl of petals, where, with the flaming petals, it was soon extinguished. The tharlarion-oil lamp, now lit, flickering, illuminated the interior of the hut with a yellowish light.

She was eating a rence cake. Her mouth was half full. She looked at me. "I shall not bind you tonight," she said.

Holding half the rence cake in her mouth she unrolled her sleeping mat and then, as she had the night before, she unlaced her tunic and slipped it off over her head. She threw it to the corner of the hut, on her left, near her feet. She sat on the sleeping mat and finished the rence cake. Then she wiped her mouth with her arm, and slapped her hands together, freeing them of crumbs.

Then she unbound her hair, shaking it free.

Then she reclined on the mat, facing me, resting on her right elbow. Her left knee was raised. She looked at me.

"Serve my pleasure," she said.

"No," I said.

Startled, she looked at me.

Just then, from outside, there was the wild, high,

terrified scream of a girl, and suddenly the music stopped. Then I heard shouts, cries of fear, confusion, the clash of arms.

"Slavers!" I heard cry. "Slavers!"

Slavers

I was out of the hut.

My response had been instantaneous, that of the trained warrior, startling me.

The girl was but a moment behind me.

I saw torches in the night, moving at the periphery of the island.

A child ran past me. The circle of the dance was empty. The barkless pole stood alone. A woman was screaming among the refuse of the feast. The marsh torches burned as quietly as they had. There were shouts. I heard the clank of arms, overlapping shields. Two men, rencers, ran past us. I heard what might have been a marsh spear splinter against metal. One man, a rencer, staggered backward drunkenly toward us. Then he wheeled and I saw, protruding from his chest, the fins of a crossbow bolt. He fell almost at our feet, his fingers clutching the fins, his knees drawn to his chin. Somewhere an infant was crying.

In the light of the moving torches, beyond them, toward the marsh, I saw, dark, the high, curved prows of narrow marsh barges, of the sort rowed by slaves.

Telima threw her hands before her face, her eyes wild, and uttered a terrifying scream of fear.

My hand caught her right wrist and locked on it, like the manacle of a slave. I dragged her stumbling, screaming, toward the opposite side of the island, the darkness.

But we found rencers running toward us, men, and women, and children, their hands outstretched, stumbling, falling. We heard the shouts of men behind them, saw the movement of spears.

We ran with them toward yet another part of the island.

Then, from the darkness before us, we heard a trumpet, and we stopped, confused. Suddenly there fell among us a rain of crossbow bolts. There were screams. A man to the left of us cried out and fell.

We turned and ran again, stumbling in the torchlit

darkness, across the woven mat of rence that was the surface of the island.

Behind us we heard trumpets, and the beating of spears on shields, the shouts of men.

Then before us a woman screamed, stopping, pointing. "They have nets!" she cried.

We were being driven toward the nets.

I stopped, holding Telima to me. We were buffeted by the bodies of running rencers, plunging toward the nets.

"Stop!" I cried. "Stop! There are nets! Nets!" But most of those with us, heedless, fleeing the trumpets and beating of spears on shields, ran wildly toward the nets, which suddenly emerged before them, held by slaves. These were not the small capture nets but wall nets, to block a path of escape. Between their interstices, here and there, spears thrust, forcing back those who would tear at them. Then the long, wide net, held by slaves, began to advance.

I heard then from another side of the island as well the terrifying cry, "Nets, nets!"

Then, as we milled and ran, here and there among us were men of Port Kar, warriors, some with helmet and shield, sword and spear, others with club and knife, others with whips, some with capture loops, some with capture nets, all with binding fiber. Among them ran slaves, carrying torches, that they might see to their work.

I saw the rencer who had worn the headband of the pearls of the Vosk sorp, who had been unable to bend the bow. He now had the large, white, silken scarf tied over his left shoulder and across his body, fastened at his right hip. With him there stood a tall, bearded helmeted warrior of Port Kar, the golden slash of the officer across the temples of his helmet. The rencer was pointing here and there, and shouting to the men of Port Kar, crying orders to them. The tall, bearded officer, sword drawn, stood silently near him.

"It is Henrak!" cried Telima. "It is Henrak."

It was the first I had heard the name of the man of the headband.

In Henrak's hand there was clutched a wallet, perhaps of gold.

A man fell near us, his neck cut half through by the thrust of a spear.

My arm about Telima's shoulder I moved her away,

losing ourselves among the shouting rencers, the running men and women.

Some of the men of the rencers, with their small shields of rence wicker, fought, but their marsh spears were no match for the steel swords and the war spears of Gor. When they offered resistance they were cut down. Most, panic-stricken, knowing themselves no match for trained warriors, fled like animals, crying out in fear before the hunters of Port Kar.

I saw a girl stumbling, being dragged by the hair toward one of the narrow barges. Her wrists were bound behind her back. She had been the girl who, this morning, had carried a net over her left shoulder, one of those who had taunted me at the pole, one of those who had, at festival, danced her contempt of me. She had already been stripped.

I moved back further in the running, buffeting bodies, now again dragging Telima by the wrist. She was screaming, running and stumbling beside me.

I saw the nets on the two sides of the island had now advanced, the spears between their meshes herding terrified rencers before them.

Again we ran back toward the center of the island.

I heard a girl screaming. It was the tall, gray-eyed blond girl, whom I remembered from the morning, who had carried a coil of marsh vine, holding it against my arm, she who had danced, with excruciating slowness, before me at festival, who had, like the others, shown her contempt of me with her spittle.

She struggled, snared in two leather capture loops, held by warriors, tight about her waist. Another warrior approached her from behind, with a whip, and with four fierce strokes had cut the rence tunic from her body and she knelt on the rence matting that was the surface of the island, crying out in pain, begging to be bound. I saw her thrown forward on her stomach, one warrior binding her wrists behind her back, another crossing and binding her ankles.

A girl bumped into us, screaming. It was the lithe, dark-haired girl, the slender girl, who had been so marvelously legged in the brief rence tunic. I remembered her well from the pole, and the dance. It was she who had danced before me with her ankles so close together that they might have been chained, who had put her wrists together back to back over her head, palms out, as though she might have worn slave bracelets, and who had then said "Slave," and spat in my face, then whirling away. After Telima I had found her the most insolent, and desirable, of my tormentors. She turned about wildly, screaming, and fled into the darkness. The rence tunic had been half torn from her right shoulder.

My arm about Telima I cast about for some means of escape.

Everywhere about us there were shouting men, screaming women, running, crying children, and everywhere, it seemed, the men of Port Kar, and their slaves, holding torches aloft, burning like the eyes of predators in the marsh night. A boy ran past. It was he who had given me a piece of rence cake in the morning, when I had been bound at the pole, who had been punished by his mother for so doing.

I heard cries and shouts and, dragging Telima by the hand, ran toward them.

There, under the light of marsh torches, I saw Ho-Hak, crying with rage, shouting, with an oar pole laying about himself wildly. More than one warrior of Port Kar lay sprawled on the matting about him, his head broken or his chest crushed. Now, just outside the circle of his swinging pole, there must have been ten or fifteen warriors of Port Kar, their swords drawn, the light of the marsh torches reflecting from them, surrounding him, fencing him in with their weapons. He could not have been more inclosed had he found himself in the jaws of the long-bodied, nine-gilled marsh shark.

"A fighter!" cried one of the men of Port Kar.

Ho-Hak, sweating, breathing deeply, wildly, his great ears flat against the sides of his head, the iron, riveted collar of the galley slave, with its broken, dangling chain, about his neck, clutching his oar pole, stood with his legs planted widely apart on the rence, at bay.

"Tharlarion!" he shouted at the men of Port Kar.

They laughed at him.

Then two capture nets, circular, strongly woven, weighted, dropped over him.

I saw warriors of Port Kar rushing forward, clubbing him senseless with the pommels of their swords, the butts of their spears.

Telima screamed and I pulled her away.

We ran again through the torches and the men.

We came to an edge of the island. In the marsh, some yards away, rence craft were burning on the water. There were none on the shore of the island. We saw one rencer screaming in the water, caught in the jaws of a marsh tharlarion.

"There are two!" I heard cry.

We turned and saw some four warriors, armed with nets and spears, running toward us.

We fled back toward the light, the torches, the center of the island, the screaming women and men.

Near the oar pole to which I had been bound, some yards from what had been the circle of the dance, a number of rencers, stripped, men and women, lay bound hand and foot. They would later be carried, or forced to walk, to the barges. From time to time a warrior would add further booty to this catch, dragging or throwing his capture rudely among the others. These rencers were guarded by two warriors with drawn swords. A scribe stood by with a tally sheet, marking the number of captures by each warrior. Among these I saw the tall, gray-eyed girl, weeping and pulling at her bonds. She looked at me. "Help," she cried. "Help me!"

I turned away with Telima.

"I don't want to be a slave. I don't want to be a slave!" she cried.

I moved my head aside as a torch, in the hands of a slave of the warriors of Port Kar, flashed by.

We were jostled by a bleeding rencer stumbling past.

We heard a girl scream.

Then I saw, under the light of the torches, fleet as the Tabuk, running, the dark-haired, lithe girl, she who was so marvelously legged in the brief rence tunic. A warrior of Port Kar leapt after her. I saw the swirl of the circular, closely woven, weighted capture net and saw her fall, snared. She screamed, rolling and fighting the mesh. Then the warrior threw her to her stomach, swiftly binding her wrists together behind her back, then binding her ankles. With a slave knife he cut the rence tunic from her and threw her, still partly tangled in the net, over his shoulder, and carried her toward one of the dark, high-prowed barges in the shadows at the edge of the island. He would take no chances of the loss of such a prize.

I expected that the girl might soon again dance, and

perhaps again with ankles in delicious proximity and wrists lifted again together back to back above her head, palms out. But this time I expected that her ankles would not be as though chained, her wrists as though braceleted; rather would they be truly chained and braceleted; she would wear the linked ankle rings, the three-linked slave bracelets of a Gorean master; and I did not think she would then conclude her dance by spitting upon him and whirling away. Rather might she almost die with terror hoping that he would find her pleasing.

"There!" cried Henrak, with the white scarf tied about his body, pointing towards us. "Get the girl! I want her!"

Telima looked at him with horror, shaking her head.

A warrior leapt toward us.

We were buffeted apart by some five or six rencers. Telima, buffeted, turned and began to run toward the darkness. I stumbled and fell, and regained my feet. I looked wildly about. I had lost her. Then something, probably a club or the butt of a spear, struck the side of my head and I fell to the matting of rence that was the island surface. I rose to my hands and knees, and shook my head. There was blood on its side. A warrior of Port Kar, in the light of a torch held by a slave, was binding a girl near me. It was not Telima. More men ran past. Then a child. Then another warrior of Port Kar, followed by his slave with the torch. A man to my right was suddenly caught in a capture net, crying out, and two warriors were on him, pounding him, beginning to bind him.

I ran in the direction that Telima had taken.

I heard a scream.

Suddenly in the darkness before me there reared up a warrior of Port Kar. He struck down at me with the double-edged sword. Had he known I was a warrior he might not have used his blade improperly. I caught his wrist, breaking it. He howled with pain. I seized up his sword. Another man thrust at me with a spear. I took it in my left hand and jerked him forward, at the same time moving my blade in a swift, easy arc, transversely and slightly upward, towards him. It passed through his throat, returning me to the on-guard position. He fell to the matting, his helmet rolling, lost in his own blood. It is an elementary stroke, one of the first taught a warrior.

The slave who held his torch looked at me, and stepped back away.

Suddenly I was aware of a net in the air. I crouched slashing upward in a wide circle and caught it before it could fall about me. I heard a man curse. Then he was running on me, knife high. My blade had partially cut the net but was tangled in it. I caught his wrist with my left hand and, with the right, thrust my blade, tangled in the net, through his body. A spear flashed towards me but tangled in the net in which my sword had been enmeshed. I immediately abandoned the weapon. Before the man who had thrust with the spear had his sword half from its sheath I was on him. I broke his neck.

I turned and again ran toward the darkness, toward which I had seen Telima run, from whence I had heard a girl's scream.

"Free me!" I heard.

In the darkness I found a girl, stripped, bound hand and foot.

"Free me!" she cried. "Free me!"

I lifted her to a sitting position. It was not Telima. I threw her weeping back to the rence.

Then, some twenty yards to my left, and ahead of me, I saw a single torch.

I ran toward it.

It was Telima!

She had been thrown to her stomach. Already, with binding fiber, her wrists had been tied tightly behind her. A warrior now crouched at her ankles. With a few swift motions he fastened them together.

I seized him and spun him about, breaking in his face with a blow. Spitting teeth, his face a mask of blood, he tried to draw his sword. I lifted him over my head and threw him screaming into the jaws of tharlarion churning the marsh at the edge of the island. They had feasted much that night, and would more.

The slave who had carried his torch ran back toward the light, crying out.

Telima had turned on her side and was watching me. "I don't want to be a slave," she wept.

In a moment warriors would be upon us.

I picked her up in my arms.

"I don't want to be a slave," she said. "I don't want to be a slave!"

"Be silent," I told her.

I looked about. For the instant we were alone. Then

the night began to burn to my left. One of the rence islands, tied in the group, had begun to burn.

I cast madly about, looking for some possibility of escape.

On one side there was the marsh, with its marsh sharks and its tharlarion.

Here and there, on the water, apart from the flaming rence island, I could see the flat, black keels of rence craft, which had earlier been cast off and burned to the water, to prevent them from being used for escape.

On the other side there were the lights and torches, the cries of men, the slavers of Port Kar.

In the distance I could see, across one of the bridges formed of rafts for transporting rence, one of those I had helped to place earlier that very morning, stripped rencers, men and women, being herded by spears toward our island. Their wrists had been bound behind their backs and ropes had been tied about their necks.

Then I saw another island take fire, one far to the right.

I heard shouts from the area of torches and confusion. Warriors were coming.

The rafts, the bridges, I thought, the rafts!

Carrying Telima in my arms I sped about the periphery of the rence island, meeting no one. The area had been cleared earlier by the sweep of the great nets, carried by slaves. There were no rencers there and, doubtless because of that, none of Port Kar, though I did see many torches going to the place on the island where we had shortly before stood; then the torches there divided, half going to the left, half coming to the right, our direction.

Somewhere I heard the voice of Henrak crying out. "Get the girl! I want the girl!"

I came to one of the raft bridges I had helped to fasten in place that morning, shortly after dawn. I placed Telima in the center of the raft. Then I began to tear loose the rence-rope fastenings, fixed to stakes thrust through the rence.

The torches were moving towards us, coming from the right, around the periphery of the island.

There were eight fastenings, four on a side. I had torn loose six when I heard the shout, "Stop!"

The nearby island was now burning ever more rapidly

and wildly in the night and soon the entire area would be illuminated.

It was only one man who had called out, a guard perhaps, one patrolling this supposedly cleared area.

His spear fell near me, dropping through the rence of the raft. Then he was running forward, sword at the ready. It was his own spear that met him. It passed well through his body.

I turned madly about. No one else, it seemed, had yet seen us.

My leg slipped from the island into the water and suddenly a tiny tharlarion struck it, seizing his bit of flesh and backing, tail whipping, away. My leg was out of the water, but now the water seemed yellow with the flashing bodies of tiny tharlarion, and, beyond them, I heard the hoarse grunting of the great marsh tharlarion, some of which grow to be more than thirty feet in length, weighing more than half a hundred men. Beyond them would be the almost eel-like, long-bodied, nine-gilled Gorean marsh sharks.

I jerked loose the last two fastenings, and tore rence from the edge of the island, heaping it on the raft, covering Telima.

The torches were nearer now.

I heaped more rence on the craft and then, with one foot, thrust off from the islands between which the raft had been fastened. I slipped beneath the rence on the raft, next to the girl. I put my hand over her mouth, tightly, that she might be unable to cry out. She struggled slightly, pulling against the bonds that constrained her. I saw her eyes looking at me, frightened, over my hand.

The torches passed.

Unnoticed, the raft, with its heaped rence, drifted away from between the islands.

I Will Hunt

Lost among the rushes and sedge, out in the darkness of the marsh, some hundred yards from the rence islands, two of which were burning, Telima, bound, and I, a garland of rence flowers bloodied in my hair, watched the movement of torches, listened to the shouts of men, the screams of women, the cries of children.

The men of Port Kar had set fire to the two islands, beginning at the farther edges, to drive any who might be concealed on them, perhaps having cut burrows into the rence or hiding in the center oar wells, across the bridges toward the central island, on which had been the pole of the dance, Telima's hut. Those who had so concealed themselves must then choose between the fire, the marsh, and the nets of slavers. We saw several running across the bridges, crying out, being whipped toward the torches by those of Port Kar. Then the tetherings on the two burning islands were cut away with swords and they floated away, free, afire into the marsh.

Later, about an Ahn before dawn, the two other rence islands, tethered to the central island, were similarly set afire, their fugitives, too, being driven to the nets and binding fiber of the men of Port Kar. Then these two islands, too, were cut free and floated burning into the marsh.

By the time that dawn's gray knife had touched the waters of the marsh the work of the men of Port Kar was mostly done.

Their slaves, their torches extinguished, were loading the narrow, high-prowed barges, treading long, narrow planks extending from the barges to the matting of the island. Some of them carried rolls of rence paper, tied together by marsh vine, others the human booty of the raid. I gathered that much rence paper had been taken from the four islands, before they had been set afire. Surely there was more being loaded than could have been on the central island alone. The rence paper was loaded

forward, carefully, in stacks, like corded wood, that it not
be damaged. The slaves, like fish, were thrown between
the rowers benches, and aft, forward of the tiller deck,
three and four deep. There were six ships. One beautiful
girl was tied to the prow of each ship that, in returning to Port Kar, others might see that the raid had been
successful. I was not surprised to see that it was the dark-
haired, lithe girl, who had been so marvelously legged
in the brief rence tunic, that was bound to the prow of
the flagship of that small barge fleet. I supposed that had
Telima been taken, that place might have been hers. At
the prows of the second and third ships I saw two others
of my tormentors, the blond, gray-eyed girl, who had
carried marsh vine, and the shorter, dark-haired girl, who
had carried a net over her left shoulder.

As the barges, loading, sank deeper in the water, I
looked on Telima. She sat beside me, bound, my arm
about her shoulders. She stared at the distant barges. Her
eyes seemed vacant, empty. She was mine now.

On the island now, in its center, near the pole, there
stood, packed together, a miserable crowd of prisoners.
The two wall nets, tied together and passed twice around
the group, pressed in on them, holding them together,
standing. Many of them had their fingers in the meshes,
staring outward. Guards, with spears, stood about the net,
occasionally jabbing here and there, keeping the prisoners
quiet. Within the net there were men, and women and
children. Some guards, with crossbows, stood off a bit.
Near the net I saw Henrak, still with the white scarf tied
across his body, still clutching the heavy wallet, filled
perhaps with gold. He was conversing with the bearded
officer, tall and with the golden slashes on the temples
of his helmet. Within the net the rencers were clothed.
They were the last of the catch. There was perhaps a
hundred of them. One by one they were being taken from
the net, the net being tightened again by slaves, and
stripped and bound, hand and foot. The slaves who were
loading the barges would then gather up each new slave,
carrying him to the barges, adding him to the others.

About the island there was much litter, the garbage
from the feast, the remains of destroyed rence huts, brok-
en boxes, torn rence sacks, shattered marsh spears, gourds,
scattered marsh vine, spilled rence reeds, bodies.

Two wild gants alighted on the island, away from the

men and their prisoners, and began pecking about the ruins of one of the rence huts, probably after seeds or b.. c ke.

A small domesticated tarsk, grunting and snuffling, pattered across rence matting that was the surface of the island. One of the slavers, a man with a conical helmet, called the animal to him. He scratched it behind the ears and then threw it squealing out into the marsh. There was a rapid movement in the water and it was gone.

I saw an Ul, the winged tharlarion, high overhead, beating its lonely way eastward over the marsh.

Then, after a time, the last of the slaves had been secured and placed on the barges. The slaves of the men of Port Kar then separated the nets, rolling them, then folding them, then placing them on the barges. They then drew up the planks and took their seats at the rowers' benches, to which, unprotesting, one by one, they were shackled. The last two aboard had been Henrak, with his white scarf, and the tall, bearded officer, he with the golden slashes on the temples of his helmet. Henrak, I gathered, would be a rich man in Port Kar. The slavers of Port Kar, being in their way wise men, seldom betray and enslave those such as Henrak, who have served them so well. Did they so, they would find fewer Henraks in the marshes.

The high-prowed marsh barge is anchored at both stem and stern. Soon, each drawn by two warriors, the anchor-hooks, curved and three-pronged, not unlike large grappling irons, emerged dripping from the mud of the marsh. These anchor-hooks, incidentally, are a great deal lighter than the anchors used in the long galleys, and the round ships.

The officer, standing on the tiller deck of the flagship, lifted his arm. In marsh barges there is no time-beater, or keleustes, but the count to the oarsmen is given by mouth, by one spoken of as the oar-master. He sits somewhat above the level of the rowers, but below the level of the tiller deck. He, facing the rowers, faces toward the ship's bow, they, of course, in their rowing facing the stern.

The officer on the tiller deck, Henrak at his side, let fall his hand.

I heard the oar-master cry out and I saw the oars, with a sliding of wood, emerge from the thole ports. They

stood poised, parallel, over the water, the early-morning
sun illuminating their upper surfaces. I noted that they
were no more than a foot above the water, so heavily
laden was the barge. Then, as the oar-master again cried
out, they entered as one into the water; and then, as he
cried out again, each oar drew slowly in the water, and
then turned and lifted, the water falling in the light from
the blades like silver chains.

The barge, deep in the water, began to back away
from the island. Then, some fifty yards away, it turned
slowly, prow now facing away from the island, toward
Port Kar. I heard the oar-master call his time again and
again, not hurrying his men, each time more faintly than
the last. Then the second barge backed away from the
island, turned and followed the first, and then so, too,
did the others.

I stood up on the raft of rence reed, and looked after
the barges. At my feet, half covered with the rence reeds
with which we had concealed ourselves, lay Telima. I
reached to my head and drew away the garland of rence
flowers which I had worn at festival. There was some
blood on it, from the blow I had received during the raid.
I looked down at Telima, who turned her head away, and
then I threw the bloodied garland of rence flowers into
the marsh.

I stood on the surface of the rence island. I looked
about myself. I had taken some of the reeds which had
been heaped on the raft and, bundling them, had used
them, paddling, to move the raft back to the island. I
had not wished to place a limb in the marsh, particularly in
this area, though, to be sure, it seemed clearer now. I
had tethered the raft at the island's shore. Telima still
lay upon the raft.

I climbed the curve of the matted shore until I came
to the higher surface of the island.

It was quiet.

A flock of marsh gants, wild, took flight, circled, and
then, seeing I meant them no harm, returned to the island, though to its farther shore.

I saw the pole to which I had been tied, the circle of
the feast, the ruins of huts, the litter and the broken
things, and the scattered things, and the bodies.

I returned to the raft and picked up Telima in my

arms, carrying her to the high surface of the island where, near the pole, I placed her on the matting.

I bent to her, and she drew away, but I turned her and unbound her.

"Free me," I told her.

Unsteadily she stood up and, with fumbling fingers, untied the knot that bound the five coils of the collar of marsh vine about my neck.

"You are free," she whispered.

I turned away from her. There would be something edible on the island, if only the pith of rence. I hoped there would be water.

I saw the remains of a tunic which had been cut from a rencer, doubtless before his binding. I took what was left of it and, with its lacing, bound it about my waist.

I kept the sun behind me that I might follow, in the shadows on the rence matting before me, the movements of the girl. I saw, thus, her bending down and taking up of the broken shaft of a marsh spear, about a yard long, its three prongs intact.

I turned to face her, and looked at her.

She was startled. Then, holding the pronged spear before her, crouching down, she threatened me. She moved about me. I stood easily, turning when necessary to face her. I knew the distance involved and what she might do. Then as, with a cry of rage, she thrust at me I took the spear from her grasp, disarming her, tossing it to one side.

She backed away, her hand before her mouth.

"Do not attempt again to kill me," I said.

She shook her head.

I looked at her. "It seemed to me," I said, "last night that you much feared slavery."

I indicated that she should approach me.

Only when I had unbound her had I noticed, on her left thigh, the tiny mark, which had been burned into her flesh long ago, the small letter in cursive script which was the initial letter of Kajira, which is Gorean for a female slave. Always before, in the lighted hut, she had kept that side from me; in the day it had been covered by her tunic; in the night, in the darkness and tumult, I had not noticed it; on the raft it had been concealed in the reeds of the rence plant, with which I had covered her.

She had now come closer to me, as I had indicated she should, and stood now where, if I wished, I might take her in my grasp.

"You were once slave," I told her.

She fell to her knees, covering her eyes with her hands, weeping.

"But I gather," said I, "you somehow made your escape."

She nodded, weeping. "On beams bound together," she said, "poling into the marsh from the canals."

It was said that never had a slave girl escaped from Port Kar, but this, doubtless like many such sayings, was not true. Still, the escape of a slave girl, or of a male slave, must indeed be rare from canaled Port Kar, protected as it is on one side by the Tambar Gulf and gleaming Thassa, and on the other by the interminable marshes, with their sharks and tharlarion. Had Telima not been a rence girl she would, I supposed, most likely, have died in the marshes. I knew that Ho-Hak, too, had escaped from Port Kar. There were doubtless others.

"You must be very brave," I said.

She lifted her eyes, red with weeping, to me.

"And your master," I said, "you must have hated him very much."

Her eyes blazed.

"What was your slave name?" I asked. "By what name did he choose to call you?"

She looked down, shaking her head. She refused to speak.

"It was Pretty Slave," I told her.

She looked up at me, red-eyed, and cried out with grief. Then she put her head down to the rence, shoulders shaking, and wept. "Yes," she said. "Yes, yes."

I left her and went to look further about. I went to the remains of her hut. There, though the hut itself was destroyed, I found much of what had been in it. Most pleased I was to find the water gourd, which was still half filled. I also took the wallet of food, that which she had once tied about her waist. Before I left I noted, among the broken rence and other paraphernalia, some throwing sticks and such, the tunic of rence cloth which she had slipped off before me the night previously, before commanding me to serve her pleasure, before we had heard the cry "Slavers!" I picked it up and carried it, with the other things, to where she still knelt, near the pole, head down, weeping.

I tossed the tunic of rence cloth before her.

She looked at it, unbelievingly. Then she looked up at me, stunned.

"Clothe yourself," I said.

"Am I not your slave?" she asked.

"No," I said.

She drew on the garment, fumbling with the laces. I handed the water gourd to her, and she drank. Then I shook out what food lay in the wallet, some dried rence paste from the day before yesterday, some dried flakes of fish, a piece of rence cake.

We shared this food.

She said nothing, but knelt across from me, across from where I sat cross-legged.

"Will you stay with me?" she asked.

"No," I said.

"You are going to Port Kar?" she asked.

"Yes," I said.

"But why?" she asked. "I do not think you are of Port Kar," she said.

"I have business there," I said.

"May I ask your name?"

"My name is Bosk," I told her.

Tears formed in her eyes.

I saw no reason to tell her my name was Tarl Cabot. It was a name not unknown in certain cities of Gor. The fewer who knew that Tarl Cabot sought entry to Port Kar the better.

I would take rence from the island, and marsh vine, and make myself a rence craft. There were oar poles left on the island. I would then make my way to Port Kar. The girl would be all right. She was intelligent, and brave, a strong girl, as well as beautiful, a rence girl. She, too, would make a craft, take a pole, and find her way deeper into the delta, doubtless to be accepted by another of the small rence communities.

Before I had finished the bit of food we shared Telima had risen to her feet and was looking about the island. I was chewing on the last bit of fish.

I saw her take one of the bodies by an arm and drag it toward the shore.

I rose, wiping my hands on the bit of rence tunic I wore, and went to her.

"What are you doing?" I asked.

"We are of the marsh," she said, woodenly. "The rence growers," she said, "rose from the marsh, and they must return to the marsh."

I nodded.

She tumbled the body from the island into the water. Under the water I saw a tharlarion move toward it.

I helped her in her task. Many times we went to the shore of the island.

Then, turning over the slashed side of some broken matting, that had been part of the side of a rence hut, I found another body, that of a child.

I knelt beside it, and wept.

Telima was standing behind me. "He is the last one," she said.

I said nothing.

"His name," she said, "was Eechius."

She reached to take him. I thrust her hand away.

"He is of the rence growers," she said. "He arose from the marsh, and he must return to the marsh."

I took the child in my arms and walked down to the shore of the rence island.

I looked westward, the direction that had been taken by the heavily laden barges of the slavers of Port Kar.

I kissed the child.

"Did you know him?" asked Telima.

I threw the body into the marsh.

"Yes," I said. "He was once kind to me."

It was the boy who had brought me the bit of rence cake when I had been bound at the pole, he who had been punished for doing this by his mother.

I looked at Telima. "Bring me my weapons," I said to her.

She looked at me.

"It will take long, will it not," I asked, "for barges so heavily laden to reach Port Kar?"

"Yes," she said, startled, "it will take long."

"Bring me my weapons," I said.

"There are more than a hundred warriors," she said, her voice suddenly leaping.

"And among my weapons," I said, "bring me the great bow, with its arrows."

She cried out with joy and sped from my side.

I looked again westward, after the long barges, and looked again into the marsh, where it was now quiet.

Then I began to gather rence, drawing it from the surface of the island itself, long strips, with which a boat might be made.

What Occurred

in the Marshes

I had gathered the rence and Telima, with marsh vine, and her strong hands and skill, had made the craft.

While she worked I examined my weapons.

She had concealed them in the rence, far from her hut, weaving the reeds again over them. They had been protected.

I had again my sword, that wine-tempered blade of fine, double-edged Gorean steel, carried even at the siege of Ar, so long ago, with its scabbard; and the rounded shield of layered boskhide, with its double sling, riveted with pegs of iron and bound with hoops of brass; and the simple helmet, innocent of insignia, with empty crest plate, of curved iron with its "Y"-like opening, and cushioned with rolls of leather. I had even, folded and stained from the salt of the marsh, the warrior's tunic, which had been taken from me even in the marsh, before I had been brought bound before Ho-Hak on the island.

And there was, too, the great bow, of yellow, supple Ka-la-na, tipped with notched bosk horn, with its cord of hemp, whipped with silk, and the roll of sheaf and flight arrows.

I counted the arrows. There were seventy arrows, fifty of which were sheaf arrows, twenty flight arrows. The Gorean sheaf arrow is slightly over a yard long, the flight arrow is about forty inches in length. Both are metal piled and fletched with three half-feathers, from the wings of the Vosk gulls. Mixed in with the arrows were the leather tab, with its two openings for the right forefinger and the middle finger, and the leather bracer, to shield the left forearm from the flashing string.

I had told Telima to make the rence craft sturdy, wider than usual, stabler. I was not a rencer and, when possible, when using the bow, I intended to stand; indeed, it is difficult to draw the bow cleanly in any but a standing position; it is not the small, straight bow used in hunting light game, Tabuk, slaves and such.

I was pleased with the craft, and, not more than an Ahn after we had returned to the island from our concealment in the marsh, Telima poled us away from its shore, setting our course in the wake of the narrow, high-prowed marsh barges of the slavers of Port Kar.

The arrows lay before me, loose in the leather wrapper opened before me on the reeds of the rence craft.

In my hand was the great bow. I had not yet strung it.

The oar-master of the sixth barge was doubtless angry. He had had to stop calling his time.

The barges in line before him, too, had slowed, then stopped, their oars half inboard, waiting.

It is sometimes difficult for even a small rence craft to make its way through the tangles of rushes and sedge in the delta.

A punt, from the flagship, moved ahead. Two slaves stood aft in the small, square-ended, flat-bottomed boat, poling. Two other slaves stood forward with glaves, lighter poles, bladed, with which they cut a path for the following barges. That path must needs be wide enough for the beam of the barges, and the width of the stroke of the oars.

The sixth barge began to drift to leeward, a slow half circle, aimless, like a finger drawing in the water.

The oar-master cried out angrily and turned to the helmsman, he who held the tiller beam.

The helmsman stood at the tiller, not moving. He had removed his helmet in the noon heat of the delta. Insects undistracted, hovered about his head, moving in his hair.

The oar-master, crying out, leaped up the stairs to the tiller deck, and angrily seized the helmsman by the shoulders, shaking him, then saw the eyes.

He released the man, who fell from the tiller.

The oar-master cried out in fear, summoning warriors who gathered on the tiller deck.

The arrow from the great yellow bow, that of supple Ka-la-na, had passed through the head of the man, losing itself a hundred yards distant, dropping unseen into the marsh.

I do not think the men of Port Kar, at that time, realized the nature of the weapon that had slain their helmsman.

They knew only that he had been alive, and then dead, and that his head now bore two unaccountable wounds, deep, opposed, centerless circles, each mounted at the scarlet apex of a stained triangle.

Uncertain, fearing, they looked about.

The marsh was quiet. They heard only, from somewhere, far off, the piping cry of a marsh gant.

Silently, swiftly, with the stamina and skill of the rence girl, Telima, unerringly taking advantage of every break in the marsh growth, never making a false thrust or motion, brought our small craft soon into the vicinity of the heavy, slowed barges, hampered not only by their weight but by the natural impediments of the marsh. I marveled at her, as she moved the craft, keeping us constantly moving, yet concealed behind high thickets of rush and sedge. At times we were but yards from the barges. I could hear the creak of the oars in the thole ports, hear the calling of the oar-master, the conversation of warriors at their leisure, the moans of bound slaves, soon silenced with the lash and blows.

Telima poled us skillfully about a large, floating tangle of marsh vine, it shifting with the movements of the marsh water.

We passed the fifth barge, and the fourth and third. I heard the shouts being passed from barge to barge, the confusion.

Soon, shielded by rushes and sedge, we had the first of the narrow, high-prowed barges abeam. This was their flagship. The warriors in the craft, climbing on the rowing benches, were crowded amidships and aft, even on the tiller deck, looking back at the barge line behind them, trying to make out the shouting, the confusion. Some of the slaves, chained at their benches, were trying to stand and see what might be the matter. On the small foredeck of the barge, beneath the high, curved prow, stood the officer and Henrak, both looking aft. The officer, angrily, was shouting the length of the barge to its oar-master, who now stood on the tiller deck, looking back toward the other barges, his hands on the sternrail. On the high, curved prow, to which was bound, naked, the lithe, dark-haired girl, there stood a lookout, he, too, looking back-ward, shielding his eyes. Below the prow, in the marsh water, the slaves in the punt stopped cutting at the sedge and marsh vine that blocked their way.

I stood in the small craft, shielded by rushes and sedge. My feet were spread; my heels were aligned with the target; my feet and body stood at right angles to the target line; my head was sharply turned to my left; I drew the sheaf arrow to its pile, until the three half-feathers of the Vosk gull lay at my jawbone; I took breath and then held it, sighting over the pile; there must be no movement; then I released the string.

The shaft, at the distance, passed completely through his body, flashing beyond him and vanishing among the rushes and sedges in the distance.

The man himself did not cry out but the girl, bound near him, screamed.

There was a splash in the water.

The slaves standing in the punt, the two with their poles, the other two with their glaves, cried out in fear. I heard a thrashing in the water on the other side of the barge, the hoarse grunting of a suddenly emerged marsh tharlarion. The man had not cried out. Doubtless he had been dead before he struck the water. The girl bound to the prow, however, startled, hysterical, seeing the tumult of tharlarion below her, each tearing for a part of the unexpected prize, began to scream uncontrollably. The slaves in the punt, too, striking down with their glaves, shoving away tharlarion, began to cry out. There was much shouting. The officer, bearded and tall, with the two golden slashes on the temples of his helmet, followed by Henrak, still with the scarf bound about his body, ran to the rail. Telima, silently, poled us back further among the rushes, skillfully turning the small craft and moving again toward the last barge. As we silently moved among the growths of the marsh we heard the wild cries of men, and the screaming of the girl bound to the prow, until, by a whip slave, she was lashed to silence.

"Cut! Cut! Cut!" I heard the officer cry out to the slaves in the punt and, immediately, almost frenzied, they began to hack away at the tangles of marsh vine with their bladed poles.

Throughout the afternoon and evening, unhurried, Telima and I, like a prowling sleen, circled the barges, and, when it pleased us, loosed another of the long shafts of the great bow.

I struck first their helmsmen, and soon none would ascend to the tiller deck.

Then warriors climbed down to the punt, to help the slaves cut marsh vine and sedge, to clear the way, but these warriors, exposed, fell easy prey to the birds of the bow. Then more slaves were put in the punt, and ordered to cut, and cut more.

And when some growth had been cleared and an oarmaster would dare to take his seat to call the time for rowers he, too, like the helmsmen, would taste in his heart the touch of the metal-piled shaft.

And then none would dare take the place of the oarmaster.

As darkness fell in the marsh the men of Port Kar lit torches on the sides of the barges.

But by the light of these torches the great bow found the enjoyment of various victories.

Then the torches were extinguished and, in the darkness, fearing, the men of Port Kar waited.

We had struck from various sides, at various times. And Telima had often raised the piping cry of the marsh gant. The men of Port Kar knew, as I had not, that rencers communicate in the marshes by the means of such signals. The fact, delightful to me, that Telima's skill was such that actual marsh gants frequently responded to her cries was, I expect, less delightful to those of Port Kar. In the darkness, peering out, not seeing, they had no way of knowing which was a marsh gant and which an enemy. For all they knew, they were encircled by rencers, somehow masters of the great bow. That the great bow was used they understood from the time I struck the second helmsman, pinning him to his tiller beam.

Occasionally they would fire back, and the bolts of crossbows would drop into the marshes about us, but harmlessly. Usually they fell far wide of our true position, for, following each of my fired shafts, Telima would pole us to a new point of vantage, whence I might again, when ready, pick a target and loose yet another of the winged shafts. Sometimes merely the movement of a tharlarion or the flutter of a marsh gant, something com-

pletely unrelated to us, would summon a great falling and
hissing of bolts into the marsh.

In the darkness, Telima and I finished some rence
cake we had brought from the island, and drank some
water.

"How many arrows have you left?" she asked.

"Ten," I said.

"It is not enough," she said.

"That is true," I said, "but now we have the cover of
darkness."

I had cut some marsh vine and had, from this, formed
a loop.

"What can you do?" she asked.

"Pole me to the fourth barge," I said.

We had estimated that there had been more than a
hundred warriors on the six barges, but not, perhaps,
many more. Counting kills, and other men we had seen,
moving furtively, seldom lifting more than a head above
the barges' hulls, there might be some fifty men left,
spread over the six barges.

Silently Telima poled our small craft to the fourth
barge.

The most of the warriors, we had noted, were concentrated in the first and the last barges.

The barges, during the afternoon, had been eased into
a closer line, the stem of one lying abeam of the stern of
the next, being made fast there by lines. This was to prevent given barges from being boarded separately, where
the warriors on one could not come to the aid of the
other. They had no way of knowing how many rencers
might be in the marshes. With this arrangement they had
greater mobility of their forces, for men might leap, say,
from the foredeck of one barge to the tiller deck of the
other. If boarding were attempted toward the center of
the line, the boarding party could thus be crushed on both
flanks by warriors pouring in from adjacent barges. This
arrangement, in effect, transformed the formerly isolated
barges into what was now, for all practical purposes, a
long, single, narrow, wooden-walled fort.

These defensive conditions dictated that the offense,
putatively the male population of one or perhaps two
rence communities, say, some seventy or eighty men,
would most likely attack at either the first or the last of

the barges, where they would have but one front on which to attack and little, or nothing, to fear from the rear. That the punt might be used to bring men behind attacking rencers was quite improbable; further, had it been used, presumably it would have encountered rencers in their several rence craft and been thereby neutralized or destroyed.

In this situation, then, it was natural, expecting an attack on either the first or the last barge, that the officer, he of the golden slashes on the temples of his helmet, would concentrate his men in the first and last barges.

We had come now to the hull of the fourth barge, and we had come to her as silently as a rence flower might have drifted to her side.

Having no large number of men at my disposal, it seemed best to me to let the men of Port Kar themselves do most of my fighting.

Standing below the hull, quite close, in the shifting rence craft, I made a small clicking noise, a sound that meant nothing but, in the darkness, meaning nothing, would be startling, terrifying in its uncomprehended import.

I heard the sudden intake of breath which marked the position of a man.

With the noose of marsh vine I dragged him over the side of the hull, lowering him into the marsh, holding him until I felt the tharlarion take him from me, drawing him away.

Slaves chained at the benches began to cry out with fear.

I heard men running, from both sides toward the place from which came the cries of the slaves.

In the darkness they met one another, shouting, brandishing their weapons.

I heard two men, missing their step in the darkness, moving from one barge to the next, plunge screaming into the marsh.

There was much shouting.

Someone was calling for a torch.

Telima poled us backward, away from the hull of the fourth barge.

I picked up the bow and set to its string one of the ten remaining arrows.

When the torch first flickered I put the arrow into the

heart of the man who held it, and he and the torch, as
though struck by a fist, spun and reeled off the far side of
the barge. I then heard another man cry out, thrust in the
confusion over the side, and his screaming. There was
more shouting.

There were more cries for torches, but I did not see any
lit.

And then I heard the clash of sword steel, wildly,
blindly.

And then I heard one cry out "They are aboard! We
are boarded! Fight!"

Telima had poled us some thirty yards out into the
marsh, and I stood there, arrow to string, in case any
should bring another torch.

None did.

I heard men running on the gangway between the
rowers' benches.

I heard more cries of pain, the screams of terrified
slaves trying to crawl beneath their benches.

There was another splash.

I heard someone crying out, perhaps the officer, ordering more men aft to repell the boarders.

From the other direction I heard another voice ordering
men forward, commanding his warriors to take the boarders in the flank.

I whispered to Telima to bring the rence craft in again,
and put down my bow, taking out the steel sword. Again
at the side of the fourth barge I thrust over the side,
driving my blade into one of the milling bodies, then
withdrawing.

There were more cries and clashings of steel.

Again and again, on the fourth and the third barges, on
one side and then the other, we did this, each time returning to the marsh and waiting with the bow.

When it seemed to me there was enough screaming and
cursing on the barges, enough clashing of weapons and
cries, I said to Telima, "It is now time to sleep."

She seemed startled but, as I told her, poled the rence
craft away from the barges.

I unstrung the great bow.

When the rence craft was lost, some hundred yards
from the barges, among the reeds and sedge, I had her
secure the craft. She thrust the oar-pole deep into the

mud of the marsh, and fastened the rence craft to this mooring by a length of marsh vine.

In the darkness I felt her kneel on the reeds of the rence craft.

"How can you sleep now?" she asked.

We listened to the shouts and cries, the clash of weapons, the screams, carrying to us over the calm waters of the marsh.

"It is time to sleep," I told her. Then I said to her, "Approach me."

She hesitated, but then she did. I took a length of marsh vine and bound her wrists behind her back, and then, with another bit of marsh vine, crossed and bound her ankles. Then I placed her lengthwise in the craft, her head at the up-curved stern end of the vessel. With a last length of marsh vine, doubled and looped about her throat, its free ends tied about the up-curved stern, I secured her in place.

She, an intelligent, and proud girl, understanding the intention of these precautions, neither questioned me nor protested them. She was bound and secured in complete silence.

I myself was bitter.

I, Tarl Cabot, hating myself, no longer respected or trusted human beings. I had done what I had done that day for the sake of a child, one who had once been kind to me, but who no longer existed. I knew myself for one who had chosen ignominious slavery over the freedom of honorable death. I knew myself as coward. I had betrayed my codes. I had tasted humiliation and degradation, and most at my own hands, for I had been most by myself betrayed. I could no longer see myself as I had been. I had been a boy and now I had come to the seeings of manhood, and found within myself, disgusting me, something capable of cowardice, self-indulgence, selfishness, and cruelty. I was no longer worthy of the red of the warrior, no longer worthy of serving the Home Stone of my city, Ko-ro-ba, the Towers of the Morning; it seemed to me then that there were only winds and strengths, and the motions of bodies, the falling of rain, the movements of bacilli, the beating of hearts and the stopping of such beatings. I found myself alone.

And then, hearing still the cries, the alarms in the night, I fell asleep. My last thought before the sweet darkness of sleep was the remembrance that I was one who had chosen ignominious slavery to the freedom of honorable death, and that I was alone.

I awakened stiff in the cold of the marsh dawn, hearing the movement of the wind through the dim sedges, the cries of an occasional marsh gant darting among the rushes. Somewhere in the distance I heard the grunting of tharlarion. High overhead, passing, I heard the squeals of four Uls, beating their way eastward on webbed, scaled wings. I lay there for a time, feeling the rence beneath my back, staring up at the gray, empty sky.

Then I crawled to my knees.

Telima was awake, but lay, of course, where I had left her, bound.

I untied the girl and she, not speaking, painfully stretched, and rubbed her wrists and ankles. I gave her half of the food and water that we had left and, in silence, we ate.

She wiped the last of the crumbs of rence cake from her mouth with the back of her left hand. "You have only nine arrows left," she said.

"I do not think it matters," I said.

She looked at me, puzzled.

"Pole us to the barges," I said.

She unfastened the rence craft from the oar-pole which had served as a mooring and, slowly, drew up the pole from the mud of the marsh.

Then she poled us to the vicinity of the barges. They seemed lonely and gray in the morning light. Always keeping us shielded by thickets of rush and sedge, she circled the six barges, fastened together.

We waited for an Ahn or so and then I told her to move to the sixth barge.

I restrung the great bow, and put the nine arrows in my belt. In my scabbard was the short sword, carried even at the siege of Ar.

Very slowly we approached, almost drifting, the high, carved sternpost of the sixth barge.

We remained beneath it for several Ehn. Then, silently, I motioned Telima to scrape the oar-pole on the side of the barge, just touching the planks.

She did so.

There was no response.

I then took the helmet from my things on the rence craft, that without insignia, with empty crest plate, and lifted it until it cleared the side of the barge.

Nothing happened. I heard nothing.

I had Telima pole us back away from the barge and I stood regarding it, for some Ehn, the great bow quarter-drawn, arrow to string.

Then I motioned for her, silently, to move abeam of the prow of the sixth barge. There was a girl, naked, miserable, bound to the prow, but, tied as she was, she could not turn to see us. I do not even think she was aware of our presence.

I put the bow back on the reeds of the rence craft, and removed the arrows from my belt.

I did not take up the shield for in climbing it would have encumbered me.

I did place over my features the curved helmet, with its "Y"-like opening, of the Gorean warrior.

Then, slowly, making no sound, I lifted no more than my eyes over the side of the barge, and scanned the interior. Shielding myself from the fifth barge by the back of the prow of the sixth I climbed aboard. I looked about. I was its master.

"Make no sound," I said to the girl at the prow.

She almost cried out, terrified, and struggled to turn and see who stood behind her, but could not, bound, do so.

She was silent.

Slaves, chained at the benches, haggard, wild-eyed, looked up at me.

"Be silent," said I to them.

There was only a rustle of chain.

The slaves from the rence islands, lying between the rowers' benches, like fish, bound hand and foot, had their heads to the stern of the vessel.

"Who is there?" asked one.

"Be silent," I said.

I looked over the side to Telima, and indicated that she should hand me my shield, and, with difficulty, she did so.

I looked about more. Then I placed the shield by the rail, and extended my hand for the great bow, with its nine arrows.

Telima gave them to me.

Then I motioned that she should come aboard and,

tying the rence craft fast to the small mooring cleat just abaft of the prow, she did so.

She now stood beside me on the foredeck of the sixth barge.

"The punt is gone," she said.

I did not respond to her. I had seen that the punt had been gone. Why else would I have come as early as I had to the barges?

I unstrung the great bow and handed it, with its arrows, to Telima.

I took up my shield. "Follow me," I told her.

I knew she could not string the bow. I knew, further, that she could not, even were the weapon strung, draw it to the half, but further I knew that, at the range she might fire, the arrow, drawn even to the quarter, might penetrate my back. Accordingly she would follow me bearing the weapon unstrung.

I looked upon her, evenly and for a long time, but she did not drop her head, but met my gaze fully, and fearlessly.

I turned.

There were no men of Port Kar on the sixth barge, but, as I stepped from the foredeck of the sixth barge to the tiller deck of the fifth, I saw some of their bodies. In some were the arrows of the great bow. But many had apparently died of wounds inflicted with spear and sword. A number of others had doubtless been, in the darkness and confusion, thrust overboard.

I indicated those who had met the arrows of the great bow.

"Get the arrows," I told Telima.

I had used simple-pile arrows, which may be withdrawn from a wound. The simple pile gives greater penetration. Had I used a broad-headed arrow, or the Tuchuk barbed arrow, one would, in removing it, commonly thrust the arrow completely through the wound, drawing it out feathers last. One is, accordingly, in such cases, less likely to lose the point in the body.

Telima, one by one, as we passed those that had fallen to the great bow, drew from their bodies the arrows, adding them to those she carried.

And so I, with my shield and sword, helmeted, followed by Telima, a rence girl, carrying the great bow, with its arrows, many of them now bloodied, taken from the bodies of those of Port Kar, moved from barge to barge.

On none of them did we find a living man of Port Kar.

Those that had lived had doubtless fled in the punt. In the darkness, presumably, they had seized upon it and, either amidst the shouting and the blind fighting, or perhaps afterwards, in a terrifying quiet, the prelude perhaps to yet another putative attack, had climbed over the side and, poling away desperately, had made their escape. It was also possible that they had eventually realized that boarders were not among them or, if they had been, were no longer, but they did not wish to remain trapped in the marsh, to fall victim to thirst, or the string-flung arrows of the yellow bow. I supposed the punt could not carry many men, perhaps eight or ten, if dangerously crowded. I was not much concerned with how those of Port Kar had determined who would be passenger on that fugitive vessel. I expected that some of those dead on the barges had been, by their own kind, denied such a place.

We now stood on the foredeck of the first barge.

"They are all dead," said Telima, her voice almost breaking. "They are all dead!"

"Go to the tiller deck," I told her.

She went, carrying the great bow, with its arrows.

I stood on the foredeck, looking out over the marsh.

Above me, her back to the front of the curved prow of the barge, was bound the lithe, dark-haired girl, whom I well remembered, she who had been so marvelously legged in the brief rence tunic. She was curved over the prow nude, her wrists cruelly bound behind it, and was further held tightly in place by binding fiber at her ankles, her stomach and throat. I recalled I had been bound rather similarly at the pole, when she had danced her contempt of me.

"Please," she begged, trying to turn her head, "who is it?"

I did not answer her, but turned, and left the foredeck, walking back along the gangway between the rowers' benches. She heard my footsteps retreating. The slaves at the benches did not stir as I passed between them.

I ascended the steps of the tiller deck.

There I looked down into Telima's eyes.

She looked up at me, joy on her face. "Thank you, Warrior," she whispered.

"Bring me binding fiber," I said.

She looked at me.

I indicated a coil of binding fiber that lay near the foot of the rail, below the tiller deck, on my left.

She put down the great bow, with its arrows, on the tiller deck. She brought me the coil of binding fiber.

I cut three lengths.

"Turn and cross your wrists," I told her.

With the first length of binding fiber I tied her wrists behind her back; I then carried her and placed her, on her knees, on the second of the broad steps leading up to the tiller deck, two steps below that in which is fixed the chair of the oar-master; she now knelt below that chair, and to its left; there, with the second length of fiber, I tied together her ankles; with the third length I ran a leash from her throat to the mooring cleat on the aft larboard side of the barge, that some five yards forward of the sternpost.

I then sat down cross-legged on the tiller deck. I counted the arrows. I now had twenty-five. Several of the warriors struck by the arrows had plunged into the water; others had been thrown overboard by their fellows. Of the twenty-five arrows, eighteen were sheaf arrows and the remaining seven were flight arrows. I put the bow beside me, and laid the arrows out on the planking of the tiller deck.

I then rose to my feet and began to make my way, barge by barge, to the sixth barge.

Again the slaves, chained at their benches, facing the stern of each barge, did not so much as move as I passed among them.

"Give me water," whispered a bound rencer.

I continued on my way.

As I walked from barge to barge I passed, at each prow, tied above my head, a bound, nude girl. On the second prow of the six barges, only a few feet from the tiller deck of the first barge, it had been the tall, gray-eyed girl, who had held marsh vine against my arm, she who had danced with such excruciating slowness before me at the pole. On the third prow it had been the shorter, dark-haired girl, she who had carried the net over her left shoulder. I remembered that she, too, had danced before me, and, as had the others, spit upon me.

Bound as they were to the curved prows of the barges

these captives could see only the sky over the marsh. They could hear only my footsteps passing beneath them, and perhaps the small movement of the Gorean blade in its sheath.

As I walked back, from barge to barge, I walked as well among bound rencers, heaped and tied like fish among the benches of slaves.

I wore the heavy Gorean helmet, concealing my features. None recognized the warrior who walked among them. The helmet bore no insignia. Its crest plate was empty.

No one spoke. I heard not even the rattle of a chain. I heard only my footsteps, and the occasional sounds of the morning in the marsh, and the movement of the Gorean blade in my sheath.

When I reached the tiller deck of the sixth barge I looked back, surveying the barges.

They were mine now.

Somewhere I heard a child crying.

I went forward to the foredeck of the sixth barge and there freed the rence craft of its tether to the mooring cleat and climbed over the side, dropping into the small craft. I pulled the oar-pole from the mud at its side, and then, standing on the wide, sturdy little craft which Telima had fashioned from the rence I had gathered, I poled my way back to the first barge.

The slaves, those at the benches, and those who lay bound between them, as I passed the barges, were silent.

I refastened the rence craft at the first barge, to the starboard mooring cleat just abaft of the prow.

I then climbed aboard and walked back to the tiller deck, where I took my seat on the chair of the oarmaster.

Telima, haltered, bound hand and foot, kneeling on the second broad step of the stairs leading up to the tiller deck, looked up at me.

"I hate rencers," I told her.

"Is that why you have saved them," she asked, "from the men of Port Kar?"

I looked at her in fury.

"There was a child," I said, "one who was once kind to me."

"You have done all this," she asked, "because a child was once kind to you?"

"Yes," I said.

"And yet now," she said, "you are being cruel to a child, one who is bound and hungry, or thirsty."

It was true. I could hear a child crying. I now could place that the sound came from the second barge.

I rose from the chair of the oar-master, angrily. "I have you all," I told her, "and the slaves at the benches as well! If I wish, I will take you all to Port Kar, as you are, and sell you. I am one man armed and strong among many chained and bound. I am master here!"

"The child," she said, "is bound. It is in pain. It is doubtless thirsty and hungry."

I turned and made my way to the second barge. I found the child, a boy, perhaps of five years of age, blond like many of the rencers, and blue-eyed. I cut him free, and took him in my arms.

I found his mother and cut her free, telling her to feed the child and give water to it.

She did, and then I ordered them both back to the tiller deck of the first barge, making them stand on the rowing deck, below the steps of the tiller deck, to my left near the rail, where I might see them, where they might not, unnoticed, attempt to free others.

I sat again on the chair of the oar-master.

"Thank you," said Telima.

I did not deign to respond to her.

In my heart there was hatred for the rencers, for they had made me slave. More than this they had been my teachers, who had brought me to cruelly learn myself as I had no wish to know myself. They had cost me the concept that I had taken for my reality; they had torn from me a bright image, an illusion, precious and treasured, an unwarranted reflection of suppositions and wishes, not examined, which I had taken to be the truth of my identity. They had torn me from myself. I had begged to be a slave. I had chosen ignominious slavery over the freedom of honorable death. In the marshes of the delta of the Vosk I had lost Tarl Cabot. I had learned that I was, in my heart, of Port Kar.

I drew forth the Gorean blade from its scabbard and, sitting on the chair of the oar-master, laid it across my knees.

"I am Ubar here," I said.

"Yes," said Telima, "here you are Ubar."

I looked down to the slave at the starboard side, he at the first thwart, who would be first oar.

As I, in the chair of the oar-master, faced the bow of the vessel, he, as slave at the benches, faced its stern, and the chair of the oar-master, that which now served me as Ubar's throne, in this small wooden country lost in the marshes of the Vosk's delta.

We looked upon one another.

Both of his ankles were shackled to a beam running lengthwise of the ship and bolted to the deck; the chain on the shackles ran through the beam itself, through a circular hole cut in the beam and lined with an iron tube; the slaves behind him, as the beam, or beams, passed beneath their thwarts, were similarly secured. The arrangements for the slaves on the larboard side of the barge were, of course, identical.

The man was barefoot, and wore only a rag. His hair was tangled and matted; it had been sheared at the base of his neck. About his neck was hammered an iron collar.

"Master?" he asked.

I looked upon him for some time. And then I said, "How long have you been slave?"

He looked at me, puzzled. "Six years," he said.

"What were you before?" I asked.

"An eel fisher," he said.

"What city?"

"The Isle of Cos," he said.

I looked to another man.

"What is your caste?" I asked.

"I am of the peasants," he said proudly. It was a large, broad man, with yellow, shaggy hair. His hair, too, was sheared at the base of his neck; he, too, wore a collar of hammered iron.

"Do you have a city?" I asked.

"I had a free holding," he said proudly.

"A Home Stone?" I asked.

"Mine own," he said. "In my hut."

"Near what city," I asked, "did your holding lie?"

"Near Ar," said he.

"I have been in Ar," I said.

I looked out, over the marsh. Then I again regarded the eel fisher, who was first oar.

"Were you a good fisherman?" I asked.

"Yes," he said. "I was."

Again I regarded the yellow-haired giant, of the peasants.

"Where is the key to your shackles kept?" I asked.

"It hangs," said he, "in the arm of the chair of the oarmaster."

I examined the broad arm of the chair, and, in the right arm, I found a sliding piece of wood, which I slid forward, it extending beyond the chair arm. Inside was a cavity, containing some rags, and binding fiber, and, on a hook, a heavy metal key.

I took the key and unlocked the shackles of the eel fisher and the peasant.

"You are free men," I told them.

They did not get up for a long time, but sat there, looking at me.

"You are free men," I said, "no longer slaves."

Suddenly, with a great laugh, the yellow-haired giant, the peasant, leaped to his feet. He struck himself on the chest. "I am Thurnock!" he cried. "Of the Peasants!"

"You are, I expect," I said, "a master of the great bow."

"Thurnock," he said, "draws the great bow well."

"I knew it would be so," said I.

The other man had now stood easily, stepping from the bench.

"My name is Clitus," he said. "I am a fisherman. I can guide ships by the stars. I know the net and trident."

"You are free," I said.

"I am your man," cried the giant.

"I, too," said the fisherman. "I, too, am your man."

"Find among the bound slaves, the rencers," I said, "the one who is called Ho-Hak."

"We shall," said they.

"And bring him before me," I said.

"We shall," said they.

I would hold court.

Telima, kneeling bound below me, on the left, the binding fiber on her throat, tethered to the mooring cleat, looked up at me. "What will be the pleasure of my Ubar with his captives?" she asked.

"I will sell you all in Port Kar," I said.

She smiled. "Of course," she said, "you may do what you please with us."

I looked upon her in fury.

I held the blade of the short sword at her throat. Her head was up. She did not flinch.

"Do I so displease my Ubar?" she asked.

I slammed the blade back in the sheath.

I seized her by the arms and lifted her, bound, to face me. I looked down into her eyes. "I could kill you," I said. "I hate you." How could I tell her that it had been by her instrumentality that I had been destroyed in the marshes. I felt myself suddenly transformed with utter fury. It was she who had done this to me, who had cost me myself, teaching me my ignobility and my cowardice, who had broken the image, casting it into the mud of the marsh, that I had for so many years, so foolishly, taken as the substance and truth of my own person. I had been emptied; I was now a void, into which I could feel the pourings, the dark flowings, of resentment and degradation, of bitterness and self-recrimination, of self-hatred. "You have destroyed me!" I hissed to her, and flung her from me down the steps of the tiller deck. The woman with the child screamed, and the boy cried out. Telima rolled and then, jerked up short, half choked, by the tether, she lay at the foot of the stairs. She struggled again to her knees. There were now tears in her eyes.

She looked up at me. She shook her head. "You have not been destroyed," said she, "my Ubar."

Angrily I took again my seat on the chair of the oar-master.

"If any has been destroyed," said she, "it was surely I."

"Do not speak foolishly," I commanded her, angrily. "Be silent!"

She dropped her head. "I am at the pleasure of my Ubar," she said.

I was ashamed that I had been brutal with her, but I would not show it. I knew, in my heart, that it had been I, I myself, who had betrayed me, I who had fallen short of the warrior codes, I who had dishonored my own Home Stone, and the blade I bore. It was I who was guilty. Not she. But everything in me cried out to blame some other for the treacheries and the defections that were my own. And surely she had most degraded me of all. Surely, of all, she had been the most cruel, the one before whom I had groveled most slave. It was in my mouth, black and swollen, that she had put the kiss of the Mistress.

I dismissed her from my mind.

Thurnock, the peasant, and Clitus, the fisherman, approached, holding between them Ho-Hak, bound hand and foot, the heavy collar of the galley slave, with its dangling chain, still riveted about his neck.

They placed him on his knees, on the rowing deck, before me.

I removed my helmet.

"I knew it would be you," he said.

I did not speak.

"There were more than a hundred men," said Ho-Hak.

"You fought well, Ho-Hak," said I, "on the rence island, with only an oar-pole."

"Not well enough," said he. He looked up at me, from his bonds. His great ears leaned a bit forward. "Were you alone?" he asked.

"No," I said. I nodded to Telima, who, head down, knelt at the foot of the stairs.

"You did well, Woman," said Ho-Hak.

She lifted her head, tears still in her eyes. She smiled at him.

"Why is it," asked Ho-Hak, "that she who aided you kneels bound at your feet?"

"I do not trust her," I said, "nor any of you."

"What are you going to do with us?" asked Ho-Hak.

"Do you not fear that I will throw you bound to tharlarion?" I asked.

"No," said Ho-Hak.

"You are a brave man," I said. I admired him, so calm and strong, though before me naked and bound, at my mercy.

Ho-Hak looked up at me. "It is not," he said, "that I am a particularly brave man. It is rather that I know you will not throw me to tharlarion."

"How can you know that?" I asked.

"No man who fights a hundred," said he, "with only a girl at his side, could act so."

"I shall sell you all in Port Kar!" I cried.

"Perhaps," said Ho-Hak, "but I do not think so."

"But I have won you and your people, and all these slaves," I told him, "that I might have my vengeance on you, for making me slave, and come rich with cargo to Port Kar!"

"I expect that is not true," said Ho-Hak.

"He did it for Eechius," said Telima.

"Eechius was killed on the island," said Ho-Hak.

"Eechius had given him rence cake when he was bound at the pole," said Telima. "It was for him that he did this."

Ho-Hak looked at me. There were tears in his eyes. "I am grateful, Warrior," said he.

I did not understand his emotion.

"Take him away!" I ordered Thurnock and Clitus, and they dragged Ho-Hak from my presence, taking him back somewhere on the second barge, among other bound slaves.

I was angry.

Ho-Hak had not begged for mercy. He had not demeaned himself. He had shown himself a dozen times more man than me.

I hated rencers, and all men, saving perhaps the two who served me.

Ho-Hak had been bred a slave, a degraded and distorted exotic, and had served even in the darkness of the stinking rowing holds of the cargo vessels of Port Kar, and yet, before me, he had shown himself a dozen times more man than me.

I hated him, and rencers.

I looked at the slaves chained at the benches. Any of them, in rags, sheared and shackled, beaten and half-starved, was greater than I.

I was no longer worthy of the love of two women I had known, Talena, who had once foolishly consented to be the Free Companion of one now proved to be ignoble and coward, and Vella, Elizabeth Cardwell, once of Earth, who had mistakenly granted her love to one worthy rather only of her contempt and scorn. And, too, I was no longer worthy of the respect of my father, Matthew Cabot, Administrator of Ko-ro-ba, and of my teacher at arms, the Older Tarl, nor of he who had been my small friend, Torm, the Scribe. I could never again face those I had known, Kron of Tharna, Andreas of Tor, Kamchak of the Tuchuks, Relius and Ho-Sorl of Ar, none of them. All would despise me now.

I looked down on Telima.

"What will you do with us, my Ubar?" she asked.

Did she mock me?

"You have taught me," I said, "that I am of Port Kar."

"You have perhaps, my Ubar," said she, "misunderstood the lesson."

"Be silent!" I cried.

She put down her head. "If any here," she said, "is of Port Kar, it is surely Telima."

Furious at her mockery I leaped from the chair of the oar-master and struck her with the back of my hand, snapping her head to one side.

I felt shamed, agonized, but I would show nothing. I returned to my seat.

There was a streak of blood across her face where her lip had been cut by her teeth.

She put down her head again. "If any," she whispered, "surely Telima."

"Be silent!" I cried.

She looked up. "Telima," she whispered, "is at her Ubar's pleasure."

I looked at Thurnock and Clitus.

"I am going to Port Kar," I said.

Thurnock crossed his great arms on his chest, and nodded his head. Clitus, too, gave assent to this.

"You are free men," I said. "You need not accompany me."

"I," said Thurnock, in a booming voice, "would follow you even to the Cities of Dust."

"And I," said Clitus, "I, too."

Thurnock was blue-eyed, Clitus gray-eyed. Thurnock was a huge man, with arms like the oars of the great galleys; Clitus was slighter, but he had been first oar; he would have great strength, beyond what it might seem.

"Build a raft," I said, "large enough for food and water, and more than two men, and what we might find here that we might wish to take with us."

They set about their work.

I sat, alone, on the great chair of the oar-master. I put my head in my hands.

I was Ubar here, but I found the throne a bitter one. I would have exchanged it all for Tarl Cabot, the myth, and the dream, that had been taken from me.

When I raised my head from my hands I felt hard and cruel.

I was alone, but I had my arm, and its strength, and the Gorean blade.

Here, on this wooden land lost in the delta marshes, I was Ubar.

I knew now, as I had not before, what men were. I had in misery learned this in myself. And I now saw myself a fool for having espoused codes, for having set above myself ideals.

What could there be that could stand above the steel blade?

Was not honor a sham, loyalty and courage a deceit, an illusion of the ignorant, a dream of fools?

Was not the only wise man he who observed carefully and when he might took what he could?

The determinants of the wise man could not be such phantoms.

There was only gold, and power, and the bodies of women, and steel.

I was a strong man.

I was such that might make a place for himself in a city such as Port Kar.

"The raft is ready," said Thurnock, his body gleaming sweat, wiping a great forearm across his face.

"We found food and water," said Clitus, "and some weapons, and gold."

"Good," I said.

"There is much rence paper," said Thurnock. "Did you want us to put some on board?"

"No," I said. "I do not want rence paper."

"What of slaves?" asked Thurnock.

I looked to the prow of the first barge, where was bound the lithe, dark-haired beauty, she who had been so marvelously legged in the brief rence tunic. Then I looked to the second prow, and the third, where were tied the large girl, blond and gray-eyed, who had held marsh vine against my arm, and the shorter girl, dark-haired, who had carried a net over her left shoulder. These had danced their insolence, their contempt of me. They had spat upon me, when I had been bound helpless, and then whirled away laughing into the circle of the dance.

I laughed.

They had earned for themselves the chains and brands of slave girls.

Thurnock and Clitus regarded me.

"Bring the girls at second and third prow," I told them.

A grin broke across the face of Thurnock. "They are beauties," he said, shaking that great shaggy head of yellow hair, sheared at the base of his neck. "Beauties!"

He and Clitus went to fetch the slaves.

I myself turned and walked slowly down the gangway between the rowers' benches, and then climbed the stairs to the foredeck of the barge.

The girl, her back bound over the curved prow, facing forward, heard me, but could not see me. My head, as I stood on the foredeck, was about a foot below her fastened ankles. Her wrists, facing me, had been bound cruelly behind the prow.

"Who is it?" she asked.

I said nothing.

"Please," she begged. "Who is it?"

"Be silent," said I, "Slave."

A small cry of anguish escaped her.

With a movement of the Gorean blade I cut the fiber at her ankles.

Then, standing on the rail of the foredeck, my left hand on the prow, I cut first the fiber binding her at the throat, and then that binding her at the waist. Then, resheathing my sword, I eased her, wrists still bound, down the prow, until her feet at last stood on the rail, on which, beside her, I stood.

I turned her about.

She saw me, the black, swollen mouth, the eyes, and screamed helplessly.

"Yes," I said, "it is I."

Then, cruelly, I took her head in my hands and pressed my lips upon hers.

Never had I seen a woman so overcome with utter terror.

I laughed at her misery.

Then, contemptuously, I removed my blade from the sheath. I put the point under her chin, lifting her head. Once, when I had been bound at the pole, she had pushed up my head, that she might better assess the features of a slave. "You are a beauty, aren't you?" I commented.

Her eyes looked at me with terror.

I dropped the point to her throat, and she turned away her head, shutting her eyes. For a moment I let her feel the point in the delicacy of her throat, then I dropped the blade and slashed the binding fiber that fastened her wrists together about the prow.

She fell to the foredeck, on her hands and knees.

I leapt to the deck before her.

She struggled to her feet, half crouching, half mad with fear, and the pain from being bound at the prow.

With the point of my blade I pointed to the deck.

She shook her head, and turned, and ran to the rail, and held it, looking over.

A huge tharlarion, seeing the image on the water, half rose from the marsh, jaws clashing, and then dropped back into the water. Two or three more tharlarion then churned there beneath her.

She threw back her head and screamed.

She turned and faced me, shaking her head.

The tip of my blade still pointed inexorably to a place on the deck.

"Please!" she wept.

The blade did not move.

She came and stood before me, and then dropped to her knees, resting back on her heels. She lowered her head and extended her arms, wrists crossed, the submission of the Gorean female. I did not immediately bind her, but walked about her, examining her as prize. I had not hitherto understood her as so beautiful, and desirable. At last, after I had well satisfied myself as to her quality, I took a bit of binding fiber that had fastened her ankles at the prow, and lashed her wrists together.

She raised her head and looked up at me, her eyes searching mine, pleading.

I spat down into her face, and she lowered her head, shoulders shaking, sobbing.

I turned away and descended the foredeck, and returned between the slaves to the steps below the tiller deck.

The girl followed me, unbidden.

Once I turned, and saw that she wiped, with the back of her right wrist, my spittle from her face. She lowered her bound hands and stood on the planking, head down.

I took again my chair, that of the oar-master, in this my domain.

The large, blond, gray-eyed girl and the shorter girl, dark-haired, who had carried the net, knelt before the chair on the rowing deck.

My girl then knelt to one side, head down.

I surveyed the two girls, the blond one and the shorter one, and looked to Thurnock and Clitus.

"Do you like them?" I asked.

"Beauties!" said Thurnock. "Beauties!"

The girls trembled.

"Yes," said Clitus, "though they are rence girls, they would bring a high price."

"Please!" said the blond girl.

I looked at Thurnock and Clitus. "They are yours." I said.

"Ha!" cried Thurnock. And then he seized up a length of binding fiber. "Submit!" he boomed at the large, blond girl and, terrified, almost leaping, she lowered her head, thrusting forward her hands, wrists crossed. In an instant, with peasant knots, Thurnock had lashed them together. Clitus bent easily to pick up a length of binding fiber. He looked at the shorter girl, who looked up at him with hate. "Submit," he said to her, quietly. Sullenly, she did so. Then, startled, she looked up at him, her wrists bound, having felt the strength of his hands. I smiled to myself. I had seen that look in the eyes of girls before. Clitus, I expected, would have little difficulty with his short rence girl.

"What will masters do with us?" asked the lithe girl, lifting her head.

"You will be taken as slave girls to Port Kar," I said.

"No, no!" cried the lithe girl.

The blond girl screamed, and the shorter girl, dark-haired, began to sob, putting her head to the deck.

"Is the raft fully ready?" I asked.

"It is," boomed Thurnock. "It is."

"We have tied it with the rence craft," said Clitus, "abeam of the starboard bow of this barge."

I picked up the long coil of binding fiber from which I had, earlier, cut three lengths, to bind Telima. I tied one end about the throat of the lithe girl.

"What is your name?" I asked.

"Midice," said she, "if it pleases Master."

"It does not displease me," I said. "I am content to call you by that name."

I found it a rather beautiful name. It was pronounced in three syllables, the first accented.

Thurnock then took the same long length of binding

fiber, one end of which I had fastened about Midice's neck, and, without cutting it, looped and knotted it about the neck of the large, blond, gray-eyed girl, handing the coil then to Clitus, who indicated that the short rence girl should take her place in the coffle.

"What is your name?" boomed Thurnock to the large girl, who flinched.

"Thura," said she, "—if it pleases Master."

"Thura!" he cried, slapping his thigh. "I am Thurnock!"

The girl did not seem much pleased by this coincidence.

"I am of the peasants," Thurnock told her.

She looked at him, rather in horror. "Only of the peasants?" she whispered.

"The Peasants," cried out Thurnock, his voice thundering over the marsh, "are the ox on which the Home Stone rests!"

"But I am of the Rencers!" she wailed.

The Rencers are often thought to be a higher caste than the Peasants.

"No," boomed Thurnock. "You are only Slave!"

The large girl wailed with misery, pulling at her bound wrists.

Clitus had already fastened the short rence girl in the coffle, the binding fiber looped and knotted about her neck, the remainder of the coil fallen to the deck behind her.

"What is your name?" he asked the girl.

She looked up at him, shyly. "Ula," she said, "—if it pleases Master."

"I do not care what I call you," he said.

She lowered her head.

I turned to the woman and the child I had freed earlier, and had made to stand to one side.

Telima, haltered, bound hand and foot at the bottom of the stairs to the tiller deck, addressed herself to me. "As I recall," she said, "you are going to take us all to Port Kar, to be sold as slaves."

"Be silent," I told her.

"If not," she said, "I expect you will have the barges sunk in the marsh, that we may all be fed to tharlarion."

I looked upon her in irritation.

She smiled at me.

"That," she said, "is what one would do who is of Port Kar."

"Be silent!" I said.

"Very well," said she, "my Ubar."

I turned again to the woman, and the child. "When we have gone," I said, "free your people. Tell Ho-Hak that I have taken some of his women. It is little enough for what was done to me."

"A Ubar," pointed out Telima, "need give no accounting, no explanation."

I seized her by the arms, lifting her up and holding her before me.

She did not seem frightened.

"This time," she asked, "will you perhaps throw me up the stairs?"

"The mouths of rence girls," commented Clitus, "are said to be as large as the delta itself."

"It is true,' said Telima.

I lowered her to her knees again.

I turned to the woman and the child. "I am also going to free the slaves at the benches," I said.

"Such slaves are dangerous men," said the woman, looking at them with fear.

"All men are dangerous," I said.

I took the key to the shackles of the barge slaves. I tossed it to one of the men. "When we have left, and not before," I told him, "free yourself, and your fellows, on all the barges."

Numbly he held the key, not believing that it was in his hand, staring down at it. "Yes," he said.

The slaves, as one man, stared at me.

"The Rencers," I said, "will doubtless help you live in the marsh, should you wish it. If not, they will guide you to freedom, away from Port Kar."

None of the slaves spoke.

I turned to leave.

"My Ubar," I heard.

I turned to look on Telima.

"Am I your slave?" she asked.

"I told you on the island," I said, "that you are not."

"Why then will you not unbind me?" she asked.

Angrily I went to her and slipped the Gorean blade between her throat and the halter, cutting it, freeing her from its tether. I then slashed away the fiber that had confined her wrists and ankles. She stood up in the brief rence tunic, and stretched.

She maddened me in the doing of it.

Then she yawned and shook her head, and rubbed her wrists.

"I am not a man," she said, "but I expect that a man would find Midice a not unpleasing wench."

Midice, bound, leading the coffle, lifted her head.

"But," said Telima, "is not Telima much better than Midice?"

Midice, to my surprise, shook with anger and, bound, tethered, turned to face Telima. I gathered that she had regarded herself as the beauty of the rence islands.

"I was first prow," said Midice to Telima.

"Had I been taken," said Telima, "doubtless I would have been first prow."

"No!" shouted Midice.

"But I did not permit myself to be netted like a little fool," said Telima.

Midice was speechless with fury.

"When I found you," I reminded Telima, "you were lying on your stomach, bound hand and foot."

Midice threw back her head and laughed.

"Nonetheless," said Telima, "I am surely, in all respects, superior to Midice."

Midice lifted her bound wrists to Telima. "Look!" she cried. "It is Midice whom he has made his slave! Not you! That shows you who is most beautiful!"

Telima looked at Midice in irritation.

"You are too fat," I said to Telima.

Midice laughed.

"When I was your Mistress," she reminded me, "you did not find me too fat."

"I do now," I said.

Midice laughed again.

"I learned long ago," said Telima, loftily, "never to believe anything a man says."

"As large as the delta itself," commented Clitus.

Telima was now walking about the three girls. "Yes," she was saying, "not a bad catch." She stopped in front of Midice, who led the coffle. Midice stood very straight, disdainfully, under her inspection. Then Telima, to Midice's horror, felt her arm, and slapped her side and leg. "This one is a little skinny," said Telima.

"Master!" cried Midice, to me.

"Open your mouth, Slave," ordered Telima.

In tears, Midice did so, and Telima examined her, casually, turning her head this way and that.

"Master!" protested Midice, to me.

"A slave," I informed her, "will take whatever abuse a free person chooses to inflict upon them."

Telima stepped back, regarding Midice.

"Yes, Midice," she said, "all things considered, I think you will make an excellent slave."

Midice wept, pulling at the binding fiber on her wrists.

"Let us be off," I said.

I turned to go. Already, Thurnock and Clitus, in loading the raft, had placed on it my helmet, and shield, and the great bow, with its arrows.

"Wait," said Telima.

I turned to face her.

To my amazement she slipped out of her rence cloth tunic and took a place behind the third girl in the coffle, the shorter rence girl, Ula.

She shook her hair back over her shoulders.

"I am fourth girl," she said.

"No," I said, "you are not."

She looked at me with irritation. "You are going to Port Kar, are you not?" she asked.

"Yes," I said.

"That is interesting," she said. "I, too, am going to Port Kar."

"No, you are not," I said.

"Add me to the coffle," she said. "I am fourth girl."

"No," I said, "you are not."

Again she regarded me with irritation. "Very well," she said. And then, angrily, loftily, she walked to the deck before me and then, movement by movement, to my fury, knelt before me, back on her heels, head down, arms extended, wrists crossed, as though for binding.

"You are a fool!" I told her.

She lifted her head, and smiled. "You may simply leave me here if you wish," she said.

"It is not in the codes," I said.

"I thought," said she, "you no longer kept the codes."

"Perhaps I should slay you!" I hissed.

"One of Port Kar might do such," she said.

"Or," I said, "take you and show you well the meaning of a collar!"

"Yes," she smiled, "or that."

"I do not want you!" I said.

"Then slay me," she said.

I seized her by the arms, lifting her up. "I should take you," I said, "and break your spirit!"

"Yes," she said, "I expect you could do that, if you wished."

I threw her down, away from me.

She looked up at me, angrily, tears in her eyes. "I am fourth girl," she hissed.

"Go to the coffle," said I, "Slave."

"Yes," said she, "—Master."

She stood there proudly, straightly, behind the short rence girl, Ula, and, wrists bound, and tethered by the neck, was added to the slave coffle, as fourth girl.

I looked upon my former Mistress, nude, bound in my coffle.

I found myself not displeased to own her. There were sweet vengeances which were mine to exact, and hers to pay. I had not asked for her as slave. But she had, for some unaccountable reason, submitted herself. All my former hatreds of her began to rear within me, the wrongs which she had done me, and the degradation and humiliation to which she had submitted me. I would see that she abided well by her decision of submission. I was angry only that I myself had not stripped her and beaten her, and made her a miserable slave as soon as we had come to the barges.

She did not seem particularly disturbed at the plight in which she found herself.

"Why do you not leave her here?" demanded Midice.

"Be silent, Slave," said Telima, to her.

"You, too, are a Slave!" cried Midice. Then Midice looked at me. She drew a deep breath, there were tears in her eyes. "Leave her here," she begged. "I—I will serve you better."

Thurnock gave a great laugh. The large, blond girl, Thura, gray-eyed, and the shorter rence girl, Ula, gasped.

"We shall see," remarked Telima.

"What do you want her for?" asked Midice, of me.

"You are stupid, aren't you?" asked Telima, of the girl.

Midice cried out with rage. "I," she cried, "—I will serve him better!'

Telima shrugged. "We shall see," she said.

"We will need one," said Clitus, "to cook, and clean, and run errands."

Telima cast him a dark look.

"Yes," I said, "that is true."

"Telima," said Telima, "is not a serving slave."

"Kettle Girl," I said.

She sniffed.

"I would say," laughed Thurnock, grinning, "kettle and mat!" He had one tooth missing on the upper right.

I held Telima by the chin, regarding her. "Yes," I said, "doubtless both kettle and mat."

"As Master wishes," said the girl, smiling.

"I think I will call you—" I said, "—Pretty Slave." She did not seem, to my amazement, much distressed nor displeased.

"Beautiful Slave would be more appropriate," she said.

"You are a strange woman," said I, "Telima."

She shrugged.

"Do you think your life with me will be easy?" I asked.

She looked at me, frankly. "No," she said, "I do not."

"I thought you would never wish to go again to Port Kar," I said.

"I would follow you," she said, "—even to Port Kar." I did not understand this.

"Fear me," I said.

She looked up at me, but did not seem afraid.

"I am of Port Kar," I told her.

She looked at me. "Are we not both," she asked, "of Port Kar?"

I remembered her cruelties, her treatment of me. "Yes," I said, "I suppose we are."

"Then, Master," said she, "let us go to our city."

Port Kar

I watched the dancing girl of Port Kar writhing on the square of sand between the tables, under the whips of masters, in a Paga tavern of Port Kar.

"Your paga," said the nude slave girl, who served me, her wrists chained. "It is warmed as you wished."

I took it from her, not even glancing upon her, and drained the goblet.

She knelt beside the low table, at which I sat cross-legged.

"More," I said, handing her back the goblet, again not deigning to even glance upon her.

"Yes, Master," she said, rising, taking the goblet.

I liked paga warm. One felt it so much the sooner.

It is called the Whip Dance, the dance the girl upon the sand danced.

She wore a delicate vest and belt of chains and jewels, with shimmering metal droplets attached. And she wore ankle rings, and linked slave bracelets, again with shimmering droplets pendant upon them; and a locked collar, matching.

She danced under ships' lanterns, hanging from the ceiling of the paga tavern, it located near the wharves bounding the great arsenal.

I heard the snapping of the whip, her cries.

The dancing girls of Port Kar are said to be the best of all Gor. They are sought eagerly in the many cities of the planet. They are slave to the core, vicious, treacherous, cunning, seductive, sensuous, dangerous, desirable, excruciatingly desirable.

"Your paga," said the girl, who served me.

I took it from her, again not seeing her. "Go, Slave," said I.

"Yes, Master," she said and, with a rustle of chain, left my side.

I drank more paga.

So I had come to Port Kar.

Four days ago, in the afternoon, after two days in the marshes, my party had reached the canals of the city.

We had come to one of the canals bordering on the delta.

We had seen that the canal was guarded by heavy metal gates, of strong bars, half submerged in the water.

Telima had looked at the gates, frightened. "When I escaped from Port Kar," she said, "there were no such gates."

"Could you have escaped then," asked I, "as you did, had there been such gates?"

"No," she whispered, frightened, "I could not have."

The gates had closed behind us.

Our girls, our slaves, wept at the poles, guiding the raft into the canal.

As we passed beneath windows lining the canals men had, upon occasion, leaned out, calling us prices for them.

I did not blame them. They were beautiful. And each poled well, as could only one from the marshes themselves. We might well have congratulated ourselves on our catch of rence girls.

Midice, Thura, Ula, Telima.

We no longer kept them in throat coffle. But we had, about the throat of each, wrapped, five times, a length of binding fiber, and knotted it, that this, serving as collar, might mark them as slave. Aside from this they were not, at the time we had entered the city, secured, save that a long length of binding fiber, knotted about the right ankle of each, tied them together. Telima had been branded long ago, but the thighs of Midice, Thura and Ula had never yet felt the iron.

I watched the girl from Port Kar dance.

We could, tomorrow, brand the three girls, and purchase collars.

There was something of an uproar as a large, fierce-looking fellow, narrow-eyed, ugly, missing an ear, followed by some twenty or thirty sailors, burst into the tavern.

"Paga! Paga!" they cried, throwing over some tables they wished, driving men from them, who had sat there, then righting the tables and sitting about them, pounding on them and shouting.

Girls ran to serve them paga.

"It is Surbus," said a man near me, to another.

The fierce fellow, bearded, narrow-eyed, missing an ear,

who seemed to be the leader of these men, seized one of the paga girls, twisting her arm, dragging her toward one of the alcoves. I thought it was the girl who had served me, but I was not certain.

Another girl ran to him, bearing a cup of paga. He took the cup in one hand, threw it down his throat, and carried the girl he had seized, screaming, into one of the alcoves. The girl had stopped dancing the Whip Dance, and cowered on the sand. Other men, of those with Surbus, seized what paga girls they could, and what vessels of the beverage, and dragged their prizes toward the alcoves, sometimes driving out those who occupied them. Most, however, remained at the tables, pounding on them, demanding drink.

I had heard the name of Surbus. It was well known among the pirate captains of Port Kar, scourge of gleaming Thassa.

I threw down another burning swallow of the Paga.

He was pirate indeed, and slaver, and murderer and thief, a cruel and worthless man, abominable, truly of Port Kar. I felt little but disgust.

And then I reminded myself of my own ignobility, my own cruelties and my own cowardice.

I, too, was of Port Kar.

I had learned that beneath the hide of men burned the hearts of sleen and tharlarion, and that their moralities and ideals were so many cloaks to conceal the claw and the tooth. Greed and selfishness I now, for the first time, understood. There is more honesty in Port Kar, I thought, than in all the cities of Gor. Here men scorn to sheath the claws of their heart in the pretenses of their mouth. Here, in this city, alone of all the cities of Gor, men did not stoop to cant and prattle. Here they knew, and would acknowledge, the dark truths of human life, that, in the end, there was only gold, and power, and the bodies of women, and the steel of weapons. Here they concerned themselves only with themselves. Here they behaved as what they were, cruelly and with ruthlessness, as men, despising, and taking what they might, should it please them to do so. And it was in this city, now mine, that I belonged, I who had lost myself, who had chosen ignominious slavery to the freedom of honorable death.

I took yet another swallow of paga.

There was a girl's scream and, from the alcove into

which Surbus had dragged her, the girl, bleeding, fled among the tables, he plunging drunken after her.

"Protect me!" she cried, to anyone who would listen. But there was only laughter, and men reaching out to seize her.

She ran to my table and fell to her knees before me. I saw now she was the one who had served me earlier.

"Please," she wept, her mouth bloody, "protect me." She extended her chained wrists to me.

"No," I said.

Then Surbus was on her, his hand in her hair, and he bent her backwards.

He scowled at me.

I took another sip of paga. It was no business of mine.

I saw the tears in the eyes of the girl, her outstretched hands, and then, with a cry of pain, she was dragged back to the alcove by the hair.

Several men laughed.

I turned again to my paga.

"You did well," said a man next to me, half-shaven. "That was Surbus."

"One of the finest swords in Port Kar," said another.

"Oh," I said.

Port Kar, squalid, malignant Port Kar, scourge of gleaming Thassa, Tarn of the Sea, is a vast, disjointed mass of holdings, each almost a fortress, piled almost upon one another, divided and crossed by hundreds of canals. It is, in effect, walled, though it has few walls as one normally thinks of them. Those buildings which face outwards, say, either at the delta or along the shallow Tamber Gulf, have no windows on the outward side, and the outward walls of them are several feet thick, and they are surmounted, on the roofs, with crenelated parapets. The canals which open into the delta of the Tamber were, in the last few years, fitted with heavy, half-submerged gates of bars. We had entered the city through one such pair of gates. In Port Kar, incidentally, there are none of the towers often encountered in the northern cities of Gor. The men of Port Kar had not chosen to build towers. It is the only city on Gor I know of which was built not by free men, but by slaves, under the lash of masters. Commonly, on Gor, slaves are not permitted to build, that being regarded as a privilege to be reserved for free men.

Politically, Port Kar is a chaos, ruled by several conflicting Ubars, each with his own following, each attempting to terrorize, to govern and tax to the extent of his power. Nominally beneath these Ubars, but in fact much independent of them, is an oligarchy of merchant princes, Captains, as they call themselves, who, in council, maintain and manage the great arsenal, building and renting ships and fittings, themselves controlling the grain fleet, the oil fleet, the slave fleet, and others.

Samos, First Slaver of Port Kar, said to be an agent of Priest-Kings, was, I knew, a member of this council. I had been supposed to contact him. Now, of course, I would not do so.

There is even, in Port Kar, a recognized caste of Thieves, the only such I know of on Gor, which, in the lower canals and perimeters of the city, has much power, that of the threat and the knife. They are recognized by the Thiefs Scar, which they wear as caste mark, a tiny, three-pronged brand burned into the face in back of and below the eye, over the right cheekbone.

One might think that Port Kar, divided as she is, a city in which are raised the thrones of anarchy, would fall easy prey to either the imperialisms or the calculated retaliations of other cities, but it is not true. When threatened from the outside the men of Port Kar have, desperately and with the viciousness of cornered urts, well defended themselves. Further, of course, it is next to impossible to bring large bodies of armed men through the delta of the Vosk, or, under the conditions of the marsh, to supply them or maintain them in a protracted siege.

The delta itself is Port Kar's strongest wall.

The nearest solid land, other than occasional bars in the marshes, to Port Kar lies to her north, some one hundred pasangs distant. This area, I supposed, might theoretically be used as a staging area, for the storing of supplies and the embarkation of an attacking force on barges, but the military prospects of such a venture were decidedly not promising. It lay hundreds of pasangs from the nearest Gorean city other, of course, than Port Kar. It was open territory. It was subject to attack by forces beached to the west from the tarn fleets of Port Kar, through the marsh itself by the barges of Port Kar, or from the east or north, depending on the marches following the disembarkation of Port Kar forces. Further, it was open to attack from the air by means of the cavalries of mercenary tarnsmen of Port Kar, of which she has several. I knew one of these mercenary captains, Ha-Keel, murderer, once of Ar, whom I had met in Turia, in the house of Saphrar, a merchant. Ha-Keel alone commanded a thousand men, tarnsmen all. And even if an attacking force could be brought into the marsh, it was not clear that it would, days later, make its way to the walls of Port Kar. It might be destroyed in the marshes. And if it should come to the walls, there was little likelihood of its being effective. The supply lines of such a force, given the barges of Port Kar and her tarn cavalries, might be easily cut.

I took another drink of paga.

The men who had come to the tavern were roistering but order, to some extent, had been restored. Two of the ship's lanterns had been broken. There was glass, and spilled paga about, and two broken tables. But the musicians were again playing and again, in the square of sand, the girl performed, though not now the Whip Dance. Nude slave girls, wrists chained, hurried about. The proprietor, sweating, aproned, was tipping yet another great bottle of paga in its sling, filling cups, that they might be borne to the drinkers. There was an occasional scream from the alcoves, bringing laughter from the tables. I heard the flash of a whip somewhere, and the cries of a girl.

I wondered if, now that the canals were barred, slaves escaped from Port Kar.

The nearest solid land was about one hundred pasangs to the north, but it was open land, and, there, on the edges of the delta, there were log outposts of Port Kar, where slave hunters and trained sleen, together, patrolled the marshes' edges.

The vicious, six-legged sleen, large-eyed, sinuous, mammalian but resembling a furred, serpentine lizard, was a reliable, indefatigable hunter. He could follow a scent days old with ease, and then, perhaps hundreds of pasangs, and days, later, be unleashed for the sport of the hunters, to tear his victim to pieces.

I expected there was not likely to be escape for slaves to the north.

That left the delta, with its interminable marshes, and the thirst, and the tharlarion.

Hunting sleen are trained to scent out and destroy escaped slaves.

Their senses are unusually keen.

Tuchuks, in the south, as I recalled, had also used sleen to hunt slaves, and, of course, to protect their herds.

I was becoming drunk, my thoughts less connected.

The sea, I thought, the sea.

Could not Port Kar be attacked from the sea?

The music of the musicians began to beat in my blood, reeling there.

I looked at the girls serving paga.

"More paga!" I cried, and another wench ran lightly to serve me.

But only Cos and Tyros had fleets to match those of Port Kar.

There were the northern islands, of course, and they were numerous, but small, extending in an archipelago like a scimitar northeastward from Cos, which lay some four hundred pasangs west of Port Kar. But these islands were not united, and, indeed, the government of them was usually no more than a village council. They usually possessed no vessels more noteworthy than clinker-built skiffs and coasters.

The girl in the sand, the dancing girl, was now performing the Belt Dance. I had seen it done once before, in Ar, in the house of Cernus, a slaver.

Only Cos and Tyros had fleets to match those of Port Kar. And they, almost of tradition, did not care to engage their fleets with hers. Doubtless all sides, including Port Kar, regarded the risks as too great; doubtless all sides, including Port Kar, were content with the stable, often profitable, situation of constant but small-scale warfare, interspersed with some trading and smuggling, which had for so long characterized their relations. Raids of one upon the other, involving a few dozen ships, were not infrequent, whether on the shipping of Port Kar, or beaching on Cos or Tyros, but major actions, those which might involve the hundreds of galleys possessed by these redoubtable maritime powers, the two island Ubarates and Port Kar, had not taken place in more than a century.

No, I said to myself, Port Kar is safe from the sea.

And then I laughed, for I was considering how Port Kar might fall, and yet she was my own, my own city.

"More paga!" I cried.

Tarnsmen, aflight, might annoy her with arrows or fire, but it did not seem they could seriously harm her, not unless they come in thousands upon thousands, and not even Ar, Glorious Ar, possessed tarn cavalries so great. And how, even then, could Port Kar fall, for she was a mass of holdings, each individually defensible, room to room, each separated from the others by the canals which, in their hundreds, crossed and divided the city?

No, I said to myself, Port Kar could be held a hundred years.

And even should she, somehow, fall, her men need only take ship, and then, when it pleased them, return, ordering slaves again to build in the delta a city called Port Kar.

On Gor, I told myself, and perhaps on all worlds, there will always be a Port Kar.

I found the girl on the sand seductive, and beautiful. The girls of Port Kar, I told myself, are the best on Gor.

Tarnsmen, I thought, tarnsmen.

Off to my right a table was overturned and two men of the crew of Surbus were rolling about, brawling. Others were calling for Whip Knives to be brought.

I remembered, with fondness, my own tarn, the sable monster, Ubar of the Skies.

I extended my hand and the goblet was again refilled.

And I remembered, too, with bitterness, the girl, Elizabeth Cardwell, Vella of Gor, who had so helped me in my work in Ar on behalf of Priest-Kings. While returning her to the Sardar I had thought long on the matter of her safety. I surely could not permit her, though I then loved her, as I could not now, being unworthy to love, to remain longer in the dangers of Gor. Already she would doubtless be known to the Others, not Priest-Kings, who would challenge Priest-Kings for this world, and Earth. Her life would surely be in jeopardy. She had undertaken great risks with me, which I, foolishly, had permitted. When at last I had brought her safely back to the Sardar I had thus told her I would arrange with Misk, the Priest-King, that she be returned to Earth.

"No!" she had cried.

"I have made my decision," I told her. "You will be,

for your own good, for your own safety and well-being, returned to the planet Earth, where you will no longer have to fear the perils of this world."

"But this is my world!" she had cried. "It is mine as much as yours! I love it and you cannot send me from it!"

"You will be returned to the planet Earth," I had informed her.

"But I love you," she said.

"I am sorry," I said. "It is not easy for me to do what I must do." There had been tears in my eyes. "You must forget me," I said. "And you must forget this world."

"You do not want me!" she cried.

"That is not true," I said. "I love you."

"You have no right," said she, "to take me from this world. It is mine, as much as yours!"

It would be hard, certainly, for her to leave this world, beautiful, bright and green, but perilous, for the cities of Earth, to breathe again its air, to live in its cubicles, to move jostled among her uncaring crowds, to lose herself again in its mercantile grayness, its insensibilities and tediums, but it was better for her to do so. There she could be anonymous, and safe, perhaps contract a desirable marriage, and live well in a large house, perhaps with servants, and conveniences, and devices.

"You will not take this world from me!" she cried.

"I have made my decision," I told her.

"You have no right," said she, "to make such a decision for me."

"I have made it," I told her. "I am sorry."

She looked up at me.

"It is done," I said. "Tomorrow you will be returned to Earth. Your work here is done."

I attempted to kiss her, but she had turned and, not crying, left me.

My thoughts turned again to the great saddlebird, the War Tarn, Ubar of the Skies.

He had slain men who had attempted to climb to his saddle.

Yet, that night, he had permitted Elizabeth Cardwell, only a girl, to saddle him, to fly him from the Sardar.

He, alone, had returned four days later.

In fury I had driven the bird away.

I who had sought to protect her, had lost her.

And Talena, too, who had once been my Free Companion, years ago, I had lost.

I had loved two women, and I had lost them both.

I wept at the table, foolishly.

I drank more paga, and my senses reeled.

Port Kar seemed sovereign on Thassa.

Her seamen were surely the match for any who might sail against them.

They were perhaps the finest on all Gor.

It angered me, suddenly, drunkenly, that those of Port Kar, wicked as they were, should possess so superbly the skills of seamanship.

But then I laughed, for I should be proud. For was I not myself of Port Kar?

Could we not do what we wished, taking what we wanted, as we had rence girls that pleased us, simply binding them and making them our slaves?

I laughed, for I had been considering, aforetime, how Port Kar might fall, and yet she was my own, my own city!

The two drunken seamen were now cutting away, wildly, at one another, with whip knives. They fought in the square of sand among the tables. The girl, who had danced there, she who had worn the delicate vest and belt of chains and jewels, with shimmering metal droplets attached, with the musicians, had withdrawn to one side. Men were calling odds in betting.

The whip knife is a delicate weapon, and can be used with elegance, with finesse; it is, as far as I know, unique to Port Kar.

In the shouts, under the ship's lanterns, I saw the flesh leap from the cheek of one of the seamen. The girl, the dancer, eyes blazing with delight, fists clenched, was screaming encouragement to one of the contestants.

But these men were drunk and stumbling, and their brutal striking about, it seemed, was offensive to many at the tables, who disdained so crude an employment of a weapon of such subtlety.

Then one of the men was down, vomiting in his blood, on his hands and knees.

"Kill him!" screamed the girl. "Kill him!"

But the other fellow, drunk and bleeding, to great laughter among the tables, stumbled backwards, turned, and fell unconscious.

"Kill him!" screamed the girl, in her vest and belt of chains and jewels, to the unconscious man. "Kill him!"

But the other man, bleeding, shaking his head, had now crawled from the patch of sand and now, some yards off, had collapsed among the tables, quite as unconscious as the first.

"Kill him!" shrieked the girl to the first man. "Kill him!"

Then she screamed with pain, throwing back her head, as the lash of the five-strap Gorean slave whip cut into her back.

"Dance, Slave!" commanded the proprietor, her Master.

She, terrified, fled to the sand, with a jangling of her chains, and jewels and metal droplets, and stood there, tears in her eyes, knees flexed, arms lifted over her head.

"Play!" cried the proprietor to the musicians. He cracked the whip once again.

They began to play, and the girl, once more, danced.

I looked upon her, and looked, as well, from face to face in that crowded, noisy, poorly lit room, filled with men laughing and drinking. There was not a face there that I saw that did not seem to me the face of an animal.

And I, whoever or whatever I might be, sat with them, at the same tables.

I joined in their laughter. "More paga!" I cried.

And then I wept, for I had loved two women, and had lost them both.

And, as I watched, on that square of sand between the tables in a paga tavern in Port Kar, under the ship's lanterns, the movements of the body of a slave girl, the lights reflected in her chains, the rubies, the shimmering golden droplets, I grew slowly furious.

Then she was among the tables, her slave body glistening, sensuous and swaying.

I vowed that I would never again lose a woman.

Woman, I told myself, as many said, was natural slave.

Then she was before my very table. "Master," she whispered.

Our eyes met.

She wore a collar. I was free. Her garment was an ornament. At my side I wore a sword of steel.

In the instant that our glances had met I had seen that she, whom I took as woman, would, if she had had the power, make men slaves, but in that same instant she had seen, in my eyes, that it was men who were the stronger, who held the power, and that it would be she, if any, who would be the slave.

"Begone," I said, releasing her from my will.

She whirled away, angrily, frightened, moving to another table.

I watched her. "That," I said to myself, "is woman."

I watched her moving, noted the glistening of the ornament she wore, remarked its sound.

I observed her, vicious, seductive, sinuous, desirable, excruciatingly desirable, owned.

She was tormenting, the collared she of her, and beautiful, but I laughed, for these things were not truly hers, but his, her master's, who had but shortly before put the whip to her back, for she was but a wench in bondage, one owned by a man, in all things his.

I laughed.

The men of Port Kar, I said, know well how to treat women.

The men of Port Kar, I said to myself, know well how to keep women.

As slaves, and slaves alone!

Worthless are they for aught else!

I had loved two women, and I had lost them both. I vowed I would never lose another.

I rose drunkenly to my feet and kicked the table away.

I do not recall as clearly as I might what occurred during that night, but certain things have remained with me.

I do recall that I was incredibly drunk, and furious, and miserable, and filled with hate.

"I am of Port Kar!" I cried.

I threw a silver tarsk, taken from what we had obtained from the slavers in the marsh, to the proprietor of the paga tavern, and took in return one of the huge bottles of paga, of the sort put in the pouring sling, and reeled out of the tavern, making my way along the narrow walkway lining the canal, toward the quarters taken by my men, Thurnock and Clitus, with our slaves.

I had pounded on the beamed door of our quarters. "Paga!" I had cried. "I bring paga!"

Thurnock took down the beams from the door, and swung it open.

"Paga!" he shouted, pleased, seeing the great bottle.

Midice, startled, looked up from where she knelt, polishing the hoops of brass upon my shield. About her throat were the five coils of binding fiber, knotted there in token of her slavery. I had given her a brief tunic of silk, briefer even than had been the rence tunic she had worn when she had taunted me at the pole, and when she had danced before me, which had been taken from her by the slaver after she had been netted on the island.

"Good, my Captain," said Clitus, from one side, where he sat working on a net, reinforcing its knots one by one. He grinned at the sight of the bottle. "I could use some paga," said he. He had purchased the net in the morning, with a trident, the traditional weapons of the fisherman of the western shore and the western islands. Kneeling quite near him, holding cord for him, fiber on her throat serving as collar, knelt short, dark-haired Ula. She, too, wore a slight bit of silk.

Thura, the large, blond girl, gray-eyed, knelt near a pile of wood shavings. Thurnock, though in Port Kar, had found a piece of Ka-la-na stock, and had been carving a great bow, the long bow. I knew he had also found some bits of bosk horn, and some leather, and some hemp and silk. In two or three days, I expected, he, too, would have a bow. Piles he had already commissioned from a smith; and Thura, on his command, this afternoon, with a bit of stick, had struck down a Vosk gull, that the shafts he fashioned, whether from Ka-la-na or tem-wood, would be well fletched. She had been watching him make the bow, apparently, for most of the afternoon and evening. When I entered she dropped her head, saying "Greetings, my Master's Captain." She, too, wore binding fiber on her throat, and a bit of silk. I saw that Thurnock had had her put a flower in her hair, a talender. Kneeling, she looked up at him, and he gave her head a rough shake, getting shavings in her hair. She put her head down, smiling.

"Where is the Kettle Slave!" I cried.

"Here, Master," said Telima, not pleasantly, entering the room and dropping to her knees before me.

On her throat as well were wound the five coils of binding fiber, declaring her slave.

Of the four girls only she did not wear silk, for she was only a Kettle Slave. She wore a brief tunic only of rep-cloth, already stained with grease and the spatterings of the kitchen. Her hair was not combed, and there was dirt on her knees and face. Her face was tired, and strained, and red, flushed from the heat of the cooking fires. Her hands had been blistered from scrubbing and burned from the cooking, roughened and reddened from the cleaning and the washing of the bowls and goblets. I found great pleasure in seeing the proud Telima, who had been my Mistress, as mere Kettle Slave.

"Master?" she asked.

"Make a feast," I said, "Kettle Slave."

"Yes, Master," she said.

"Thurnock," cried I, "secure the slaves."

"Yes, my Captain," he boomed.

Midice stood up, timidly. Her hand was before her mouth. "What are you going to do, Master?" she asked.

"We are taking you out," I cried, "to be marked and collared!"

The three girls looked at one another in fear.

Already Thurnock was putting them in coffle, binding the right wrist of each.

Before we set out we broke open the great bottle of paga, and Thurnock, Clitus and I clashed goblets and emptied them of their swirling fires. Then we forced each of the girls, choking and sputtering, to themselves upturn a goblet, swilling down as best they could the fiery draught. I recall Midice standing there in her silk, the leather on her wrist, shaking, coughing, paga on her mouth, looking at me with fear.

"And then," I cried, "we will return and make a feast!"

Thurnock, Clitus and I once more clashed and emptied goblets, and then, leading Midice, first in the coffle, by the lead end of the binding fiber, I stumbled through the door, finding my way down the stairs, with the others, hunting for a smithy.

My memories are confused of the night, but we did find a smithy, and we had the girls marked, and purchased collars for them, lock collars, which we had suitably engraved. Ula's collar read I AM THE PROPERTY OF CLITUS; Thurnock had his slave's engraved THURA, SLAVE OF THURNOCK; I had two collars engraved, one for Midice and one for Telima; both read simply I BELONG TO BOSK.

I remember Midice, who had already been branded, standing with her back to me and my standing behind her,

quite close, with the collar, and placing it about her
throat, then, decisively, closing it.

Holding her thus I kissed her on the throat.

She turned to face me, tears in her eyes, fingering
the gleaming band of steel.

She had been branded, and doubtless her thigh still
stung from the fire of the iron. She knew herself then
animal and slave, and so marked.

Now, about her throat, she wore as well the graceful
badge of servitude.

There were tears in her eyes as she extended her arms
to me, and I took her into my arms and lifted her from
her feet, turning and carrying her back to our quarters.
As we walked, Thurnock following, carrying Thura, and
Clitus then, Ula weeping in his arms, Midice put her head
against my left shoulder, and I felt her tears through my
tunic.

"It seems," said I, "Midice, I have won you."

"Yes," she said, "you have won me. I am your slave."

I threw back my head and laughed.

She had taunted me at the pole. Now she was my slave.
The girl wept.

That night, the girls in our arms, we feasted, lifting
many cups of paga.

Clitus, after returning to our quarters, had left and
returned with four musicians, bleary-eyed, routed from
their mats well past the Twentieth Hour, but, lured by
the jingling of a pair of silver tarsks, ready to play for us,
past the dawn if need be. We soon had them drunk as
well and though it did not improve their playing, I was
pleased to see them join with us in our festivities, helping
us to make our feast. Clitus, too, had brought two bottles
of Ka-la-na wine, a string of eels, cheese of the Verr,
and a sack of red olives from the groves of Tyros.

We greeted him with cheers.

Telima had prepared a roast tarsk, stuffed with suls
and peppers from Tor.

There were great quantities of the yellow Sa-Tarna
bread, in its rounded, six-part loaves.

We were served by the Kettle Slave, Telima. She
poured paga for the men, and Ka-la-na for the women.
She tore the bread for us, broke the cheese, ribboned
the eels and cut the tarsk. She hurried from one to the
other, and the musicians as well, scarcely serving one

before being summoned to another. The girls commanded her as well as the men. She was only Kettle Slave and thus, they were of a higher sort than she. Further, I gathered, on the islands, Telima, with her beauty, her skills and arrogance, had not been popular, and it pleased them no little that she should be, in effect, slave for them as well as their masters.

I sat cross-legged at the low table, quaffing paga, my left arm about the shoulders of Midice, who, kneeling, snuggled against me.

Once, as Telima served me, I caught her wrist. She looked at me.

"How is it," I asked, "that a Kettle Slave has an armlet of gold?"

Midice lifted her head and kissed me on the neck, "Give Midice the armlet," she wheedled.

Tears appeared in the eyes of Telima.

"Perhaps later," I told Midice, "if you well please me."

She kissed me. "I will well please you, Master," she said. Then she threw a look of contempt at Telima. "Give me wine," said she, "Slave."

As Midice kissed me again, lingeringly, holding my head in her hands, Telima, tears in her eyes, filled her cup.

Across the table I saw Ula, eyes timid, lift her lips to Clitus. He did not refuse her, and they began to kiss, and touch. Thurnock then seized Thura, pressing his lips upon hers. Helpless in his great arms she struggled, but then, as I laughed, she cried out as though in misery and began to yield to him, and then, moments later, her lips eagerly were seeking his.

"Master," said Midice, looking at me, eyes bright.

"Do you recall," I asked pleasantly, looking down into her eyes, "how some days ago you taunted me when I was bound at the pole?"

"Master?" she asked, her eyes timid.

"Have you forgotten," I asked, "how you danced before me?"

She drew back. "Please, Master," she whispered, her eyes terrified.

I turned to the musicians. "Do you know," I asked, "the Love Dance of the Newly Collared Slave Girl?"

"Port Kar's?" asked the leader of the musicians.

"Yes," I said.

"Of course," said he.

I had purchased more than marking and collars at the smithy.

"On your feet," boomed Thurnock to Thura, and she leaped frightened to her feet, standing ankle deep in the thick pile rug.

At a gesture from Clitus, Ula, too, leaped to her feet.

I put ankle rings on Midice, and then slave bracelets. And tore from her the bit of silk she wore. She looked at me with terror.

I lifted her to her feet, and stood before her.

"Play," I told the musicians.

The Love Dance of the Newly Collared Slave Girl has many variations, in the different cities of Gor, but the common theme is that the girl dances her joy that she will soon lie in the arms of a strong master.

The musicians began to play, and to the clappings and cries of Thurnock and Clitus, Thura and Ula danced before them.

"Dance," said I to Midice.

In terror the dark-haired girl, lithe, tears in her eyes, she so marvelously legged, lifted her wrists.

Now again Midice danced, her ankles in delicious proximity and wrists lifted again together back to back above her head, palms out. But this time her ankles were not as though chained, nor her wrists as though braceleted; rather they were truly chained and braceleted; she wore the linked ankle rings, the three-linked slave bracelets of a Gorean master; and I did not think she would now conclude her dance by spitting upon me and whirling away.

She trembled. "Find me pleasing," she begged.

"Do not afflict her so," said Telima to me.

"Go to the kitchen," said I, "Kettle Slave."

Telima turned and, in the stained tunic of rep-cloth, left the room, as she had been commanded.

The music grew more wild.

"Where now," I demanded of Midice, "is your insolence, your contempt!"

"Be kind!" she cried. "Be kind to Midice!"

The music grew even more wild.

And then Ula, boldly before Clitus, tore from her own body the silk she wore and danced, her arms extended to him.

He leaped to his feet and carried her from the room. I laughed.

Then Thura, to my amazement, though a rence girl, dancing, revealed herself similarly to the great Thurnock, he only of the peasants, and he, with a great laugh, swept her from her feet and carried her from the room.

"Do I dance for my life?" begged Midice.

I drew the Gorean blade. "Yes," I said, "you do."

And she danced superbly for me, every fiber of her beautiful body straining to please me, her eyes, each instant, pleading, trying to read in mine her fate. At last, when she could dance no more, she fell at my feet, and put her head to my sandals.

"Find me pleasing," she begged. "Find me pleasing, my Master!"

I had had my sport.

I sheathed the blade.

"Light the lamp of love," I said.

She looked up at me, gratefully, but saw then my eyes. Her test was not yet done.

Trembling she fumbled with the flint and steel, to strike sparks into the moss bowl, whence by means of a Ka-la-na shaving the lamp might be lit.

I myself threw down, in one corner, near a slave ring, the Furs of Love.

The musicians, one by one, each with a silver tarsk, stole from the room.

An Ahn later, perhaps a bit more than an Ahn before dawn, the oil in the lamp of love had burned low.

Midice lay against me, in my arms. She looked up at me, and whispered, "Did Midice do well? Is Master pleased with Midice?"

"Yes," I said, wearily, looking at the ceiling. "I am pleased with Midice."

I felt empty.

For a long time then we did not speak.

Then she said, "You are well pleased with Midice, are you not?"

"Yes," I said, "I am well pleased."

"Midice is first girl, is she not?"

"Yes," I said. "Midice is first girl."

Midice looked at me, and whispered. "Telima is only Kettle Slave. Why should she have an armlet of gold?"

I looked at her. Then, wearily, I rose to my feet. I

drew on my tunic, and looked down at Midice, who lay there with her legs drawn up, looking at me. I could see the glow of the dim lamp on her collar.

I buckled about me the Gorean blade, with its belt and scabbard.

I went into the kitchen.

There I found Telima sitting against the wall, her knees drawn up, her head down. She raised her head and looked at me. I could see her barely in the light of the coals of the cooking fire, now a flat, reticulated pattern of red and black.

I slipped the golden armlet from her arm.

There were tears in her eyes, but she did not protest.

I unknotted the binding fiber about her throat, and took from my pouch her collar.

I showed it to her.

In the dim light she read the engraving. "I belong to Bosk," she said.

"I did not know you could read," I said. Midice, Thura, Ula were all, as is common with rence girls, illiterate.

Telima looked down.

I snapped the collar about her throat.

She looked up at me. "It is a long time since I have worn a steel collar," she said.

I wondered how she had, whether in her escape or afterwards in the islands, removed her first collar. Ho-Hak, I recalled, still wore the heavy collar of the galley slave. The rencers had not had the tools to remove it. Telima, a clever girl, had probably discovered and stolen the key to her collar. Ho-Hak's collar had been riveted about his throat.

"Telima," said I, thinking of Ho-Hak, "why was Ho-Hak so moved, when together we spoke of the boy Eechius?"

She said nothing.

"He would know him, of course," said I, "from the island."

"He was his father," said Telima.

"Oh," I said.

I looked down at the golden armlet I held in my hand. I put it on the floor and then, with the pair of slave bracelets I had removed from Midice, following her dance, I secured Telima to the kitchen's slave ring, fastened in its floor. I braceleted the left wrist first, passed the chain through the ring, and then braceleted the right wrist. I then picked up the golden armlet, and again regarded it.

"It is strange," I said, "that a rence girl should have a golden armlet."

Telima said nothing.

"Rest," said I, "Kettle Slave, for tomorrow you will doubtless have much to do."

At the door of the kitchen I turned again to face her. For a long time, not speaking, we looked at one another. Then she asked, "—Is Master pleased?"

I did not respond.

In the other room I tossed the golden armlet to Midice, who caught it and slipped it on her arm with a squeal of delight, holding up her arm, showing the armlet.

"Do not chain me," she wheedled.

But, with the ankle rings, taken from her following the dance, I secured her. I put one ring about the slave ring near which she had served me, and the other ring about her left ankle.

"Sleep, Midice," I said, covering her with the love furs.

"Master?" she asked.

"Rest," I said, "Sleep."

"I have pleased you?" she asked.

"Yes," I told her, "you have pleased me." Then I touched her head, moving back some of the dark hair. "Now sleep," said I, "now sleep, lovely Midice."

She snuggled down in the love furs.

I left the room, going down the stairs.

I found myself alone in the darkness. It was about an Ahn, I conjectured, before daylight. I trod the narrow walkway lining the canal. Then, suddenly, falling to my hands and knees, I threw up into the dark waters. I heard one of the giant canal urts twist in the water somewhere beneath me. I threw up again, and then stood up, shaking my head. I had had too much paga, I told myself.

I could smell the sea, but I had not yet seen her.

The buildings lining the canals on each side were dark, but, here and there, in the side of one, near a window, was a torch. I looked at the brick, the stone, watched the patterns and shadows playing on the walls of the buildings of Port Kar.

Somewhere I heard the squealing and thrashing of two

of the giant urts fighting in the water, among the floating garbage.

My steps took me again to the paga tavern where I had begun this night.

I was alone, and miserable. I was cold. There was nothing of worth in Port Kar, nor in all the worlds of all the suns.

I pushed open the doors of the paga tavern.

The musicians, and the dancer, had gone, long ago I supposed.

There were not so many men in the paga tavern now, and those there were seemed mostly lost in stupor. Here and there some lay among the tables, their tunics soiled with paga. Others lay, wrapped in ship's cloaks, against the wall. Some two or three still sat groggily at the tables, staring at goblets half-filled with paga. The girls, saving those who served still in the curtained alcoves, must have been somewhere chained for the night, probably in a slave room off the kitchen. The proprietor, when I entered, lifted his head from the counter, behind which hung a great bottle of paga in its pouring sling.

I threw down a copper tarn disk and he tilted the great bottle.

I took my goblet of paga to a table and sat down, cross-legged, behind it.

I did not want to drink. I wanted only to be alone. I did not even want to think. I wanted only to be alone.

I heard weeping from one of the alcoves.

It irritated me. I did not wish to be disturbed. I put my head in my hands and leaned forward, elbows on the table.

I hated Port Kar, and all that was of it. And I hated myself, for I, too, was of Port Kar. That I had learned this night. I would never forget this night. All that was in Port Kar was rotten and worthless. There was no good in her.

The curtain from one of the alcoves was flung apart. There stood there, framed in its conical threshold, Surbus, he who was a captain of Port Kar. I looked upon him with loathing, despising him. How ugly he was, with his fierce beard, the narrow eyes, the ear gone from the right side of his face. I had heard of him, and well. I knew him to be pirate; and I knew him to be slaver, and murderer, and thief; I knew him to be a cruel and worthless man, abominable, truly of Port Kar and, as I looked upon him, the filth and rottenness, I felt nothing but disgust.

In his arms he held, stripped, the bound body of a slave girl. It was she who had served me the night before, before Surbus, and his cutthroats and pirates, had entered the tavern. I had not much noticed her. She was thin, and not very pretty. She had blond hair, and, as I recalled, blue eyes. She was not much of a slave. I had not paid her much attention. I remembered that she had begged me to protect her and that I, of course, had refused.

Surbus threw the girl over his shoulder and went to the counter.

"I am not pleased with her," he said to the proprietor.

"I am sorry, Noble Surbus," said the man. "I shall have her beaten."

"I am not pleased with her!" cried Surbus.

"You wish her destroyed?" asked the man.

"Yes," said Surbus, "destroyed."

"Her price," said the proprietor, "is five silver tarsks."

From his pouch Surbus placed five silver tarsks, one after the other, on the counter.

"I will give you six," I said to the proprietor.

Surbus scowled at me.

"I have sold her for five," said the proprietor, "to this noble gentleman. Do not interfere, Stranger, this man is Surbus."

Surbus threw back his head and laughed. "Yes," he said, "I am Surbus."

"I am Bosk," I said, "from the Marshes."

Surbus looked at me, and then laughed. He turned away from the counter now, taking the girl from his shoulder and holding her, bound, in his arms. I saw that she was conscious, and her eyes red from weeping. But she seemed numb, beyond feeling.

"What are you going to do with her?" I asked.

"I am going to throw her to the urts," said Surbus.

"Please," she whispered, "please, Surbus."

"To the urts!" laughed Surbus, looking down at her. She closed her eyes.

The giant urts, silken and blazing-eyed, living mostly on the garbage in the canals, are not stranger to bodies, both living and dead, found cast into their waters.

"To the urts!" laughed Surbus.

I looked upon him, Surbus, slaver, pirate, thief, murderer. This man was totally evil. I felt nothing but hatred, and an ugly, irrepressible disgust of him.

"No," I said.

He looked at me, startled.

"No," I said, and moved the blade from the sheath.

"She is mine," he said.

"Surbus often," said the proprietor, "thus destroys a girl who has not pleased him."

I regarded them both.

"I own her," said Surbus.

"That is true," said the proprietor hastily. "You saw yourself her sale. She is truly his slave, his to do with as he wishes, duly purchased."

"She is mine," said Surbus. "What right have you to interfere?"

"The right of one of Port Kar," I said, "to do what pleases him."

Surbus threw the girl from him and, with a swift, clean motion, unsheathed his blade.

"You are a fool, Stranger," said the proprietor. "That is Surbus, one of the finest swords in Port Kar."

Our discourse with steel was brief.

Then, with a cry of hatred and elation, my blade, parallel to the ground, that it not wedge itself between the ribs of its target, passed through his body. I kicked him from the blade and withdrew the bloodied steel.

The proprietor was looking at me, wide-eyed.

"Who are you?" he asked.

"Bosk," I told him. "Bosk from the Marshes."

Several of the men around the tables, roused by the flash of steel, had awakened.

They sat there, startled.

I moved the blade in a semicircle, facing them. None of them moved against me.

I tore off some of his tunic and cleaned the blade on it.

He lay there on his back, blood moving from his mouth, the chest of his tunic scarlet, fighting for breath.

I looked down on him. I had been of the warriors. I knew he would not live long.

I felt no compunction. He was totally evil.

I went to the slave girl and cut the binding fiber that

fastened her ankles and wrists. The chains which she
had worn while serving paga, and when she had asked for
my protection, had been removed, doubtless while she had
been in the alcove, sometime after I had left the tavern,
that she might have better rendered Surbus, Captain of
Port Kar, the dues of the slave girl. They had been
serving bracelets, with two lengths of chain, each about a
foot long, which linked them.

I looked about the room. The proprietor stood back,
behind his counter. None of the men had arisen from the
tables, though many were of the crew of Surbus himself.

I looked at him.

His eyes were on me, and his hand, weakly, lifted.
His eyes were agonized. He coughed blood. He seemed to
want to speak, but could not do so.

I looked away from him.

I resheathed the blade.

It was good that Surbus lay dying. He was evil.

I looked upon the slave girl. She was a poor sort.
She was scrawny, and thin faced, with narrow shoulders.
Her blue eyes were pale. The hair was thin, stringy.
She was a poor slave.

To my surprise she went and knelt next to Surbus,
and held his head. He was looking at me. Again he
tried to speak.

"Please," said the girl to me, looking up at me, holding
the head of the dying man.

I looked upon them both, puzzled. He was evil. She,
perhaps, was mad. Did she not understand that he would
have hurled her bound to the urts in the canals?

His hand lifted again, even more weakly, extended to
me. There was agony in his eyes. His lips moved, but
there was no sound.

The girl looked up at me, and said, "Please, I am too
weak."

"What does he want?" I asked, impatient. He was
pirate, slaver, thief, murderer. He was evil, totally evil,
and I felt for him only disgust.

"He wants to see the sea," she said.

I said nothing.

"Please," she said, "I am too weak."

I bent and put the arm of the dying man about my
shoulders and, lifting him, with the girl's help, went back

through the kitchen of the tavern and, one by one, climbed the high, narrow stairs to the top of the building.

We came to the roof, and there, near its edge, holding Surbus between us, we waited. The morning was cold, and damp. It was about daybreak.

And then the dawn came and, over the buildings of Port Kar, beyond them, and beyond the shallow, muddy Tamber, where the Vosk empties, we saw, I for the first time, gleaming Thassa, the Sea.

The right hand of Surbus reached across his body and touched me. He nodded his head. His eyes did not seem pained to me, nor unhappy. His lips moved, but then he coughed, and there was more blood, and he stiffened, and then, his head falling to one side, he was only weight in our arms.

We lowered him to the roof.

"What did he say?" I asked.

The girl smiled at me. "Thank you," she said. "He said Thank you."

I stood up, wearily, and looked out over the sea, gleaming Thassa.

"She is very beautiful," I said.

"Yes," said the girl, "yes."

"Do the men of Port Kar love the sea?" I asked.

"Yes," she said, "they do."

I looked on her.

"What will you do now?" I asked. "Where will you go?"

"I do not know," she said. She dropped her head. "I will go away."

I put out my hand and touched her cheek. "Do not do that," I said. "Follow me."

There were tears in her eyes. "Thank you," she said.

"What is your name?" I asked.

"Luma," she said.

I, followed by the slave Luma, left the roof, descended the long, narrow stairs.

In the kitchen we met the proprietor. "Surbus is dead," I told him. He nodded. The body, I knew, would be disposed of in the canals.

I pointed to Luma's collar. "Key," I said.

The proprietor brought a key and removed his steel from her throat.

She fingered her throat, now bare, perhaps for the first time in years, of the encircling collar.

I would buy her another, when it was convenient, suitably engraved, proclaiming her mine.

We left the kitchen.

In the large central room of the tavern, we stopped. I thrust the girl behind me.

There, waiting for us, standing, armed, were seventy or eighty men. They were seamen of Port Kar. I recognized many of them. They had come with Surbus to the tavern the night before. They were portions of his crews.

I unsheathed my blade.

One of the men stood forward, a tall man, lean, young, but with a face that showed the marks of Thassa. He had gray eyes, large, rope-rough hands.

"I am Tab," he said. "I was second to Surbus."

I said nothing, but watched them.

"You let him see the sea?" said Tab.

"Yes," I said.

"Then," said Tab, "we are your men."

The Council of Captains

I took my seat in the Council of the Captains of Port Kar.

It was now near the end of the first passage hand, that following En'Kara, in which occurs the Spring Equinox. The Spring Equinox, in Port Kar as well as in most other Gorean cities, marks the New Year. In the chronology of Ar it was now the year 10,120. I had been in Port Kar for some seven Gorean months.

None had disputed my right to the seat of Surbus. His men had declared themselves mine.

Accordingly I, who had been Tarl Cabot, once a warrior of Ko-ro-ba, the Towers of the Morning, sat now in the council of these captains, merchant and pirate princes, the high oligarchs of squalid, malignant Port Kar, Scourge of Gleaming Thassa.

In the council, in effect, was vested the stability and administration of Port Kar.

Above it, nominally, stood five Ubars, each refusing to recognize the authority of the others, Chung, Eteocles, Nigel, Sullius Maximus and Henrius Sevarius, claiming to be the fifth of his line.

The Ubars were represented on the council, to which they belonged as being themselves Captains, by five empty thrones, sitting before the semicircles of curule chairs on which reposed the captains. Beside each empty throne there was a stool from which a Scribe, speaking in the name of his Ubar, participated in the proceedings of the council. The Ubars themselves remained aloof, seldom showing themselves for fear of assassination.

A scribe, at a large table before the five thrones, was droning the record of the last meeting of the council.

There are commonly about one hundred and twenty captains who form the council, sometimes a few more, sometimes a few less.

Admittance to the council is based on being master of at least five ships. Surbus had not been a particularly important captain, but he had been the master of a fleet of seven, now mine. These five ships, pertinent to council membership, may be either the round ships, with deep holds for merchandise, or the long ships, ram-ships, ships of war. Both are predominantly oared vessels, but the round ship carries a heavier, permanent rigging, and supports more sail, being generally two-masted. The round ship, of course, is not round, but it does have a much wider beam to its length of keel, say, about one to six, whereas the ratios of the war galleys are about one to eight.

The five ships, it might be added, must be of at least medium class. In a round ship this means she would be able, in Earth figures, to freight between approximately one hundred and one hundred and fifty tons below decks. I have calculated this figure from the Weight, a Gorean unit of measurement based on the Stone, which is about four Earth pounds. A Weight is ten Stone. A medium-class round ship should be able to carry from 5,000 to 7,500 Gorean Weight. The Weight and the Stone, incidentally, are standardized throughout the Gorean cities by Merchant Law, the only common body of law existing among the cities. The official "Stone," actually a solid metal cylinder, is kept, by the the way, near the Sardar. Four times a year, on a given day in each of the four great fairs held annually near the Sardar, it is brought forth with scales, that merchants from whatever city may test their own standard "Stone" against it. The "Stone" of Port Kar, tested against the official "Stone" at the Sardar, reposed in a special fortified building in the great arsenal, which complex was administered by agents of the Council of Captains.

Medium class for a long ship, or ram-ship, is determined not by freight capacity but by keel length and width of beam; a medium-class long ship, or ram-ship, will have a keel length of from eighty to one hundred and twenty feet Gorean; and a width of beam of from ten to fifteen feet Gorean. The Gorean foot, interestingly, is almost identical to the Earth foot. Both measures doubtless bear some distant relation to the length of the foot of an adult human male. The Gorean foot is, in my estimation, just slightly longer than the Earth foot; based on the supposition that each of its ten Horts is roughly one and one-quarter inches long, I would give the Gorean foot a length of roughly twelve and one-half inches, Earth measure. Normally, incidentally, in giving measures, the Earth foot, unless otherwise specified, should be understood. It seems pertinent, however, in this instance, to state the ratios in Gorean feet, rather than translate into English measures, where the harmony of the proportions would be obscured. As in the case of the official "Stone," so, too, at the Sardar is a metal rod, which determines the Merchant Foot, or Gorean foot, as I have called it. Port Kar's Merchant Foot, like her "Stone," is kept in the arsenal, in the same building as her "Stone."

Not only the ships of Surbus had become mine, his men having declared for me, but his holding as well, and his assets, his treasures and equipments, and his slaves. His holding was a fortified palace. It lay on the eastern edge of Port Kar, backing on the marshes; it opened, by means of a huge barred gate, to the canals of the city; in its courtyard were wharved his seven ships; when journeying to Thassa the great gate was opened and they were rowed through the city to the sea.

It was a strong holding, protected on the one side by its walls and the marshes, and on its others by walls, the gate, and the canals.

When Clitus, Thurnock and I, and our slaves, had first come to Port Kar, we had taken quarters not far from that holding. Indeed its nearest paga tavern was that at which Surbus and I had met, and had crossed steel.

The voice of the scribe droned on, reading the records of the council's last meeting.

I looked about myself, at the semicircles of curule chairs, at the five thrones. Although there were some one hundred and twenty captains in the council, seldom more than seventy or eighty, either in person or by proxy, made an appearance at its meetings. Many were at sea, and many saw fit to employ their time otherwise.

On one chair, some fifteen yards away, somewhat lower and closer the thrones of the Ubars, sat an officer, whom I recognized. He was the one who had come to the rence islands, who had had upon his helmet the two golden slashes. I had not seen Henrak, who had betrayed the rencers, in Port Kar. I did not know if he had perished in the marshes or not.

I smiled to myself, looking upon the bearded, dour

countenance of the officer, his long hair tied behind his head with scarlet string.

His name was Lysias.

He had been a captain for only four months, having acquired the fifth ship, medium class, required.

He was rather well known now in Port Kar, having lost six barges, with their slaves and cargo, and most of his crews, in the marshes. The story was that they had been attacked by more than a thousand rencers, abetted by a conjectured five hundred mercenaries, trained warriors, and had barely escaped with their lives. I was ready to grant him part of this story. But still, even in the face of such reputed odds as he had faced, there were those in Port Kar who smiled behind his back, thinking to themselves how he had gone forth with so fine a showing and had returned with little more than his life, a handful of terrified men, and a narrow wooden punt.

Though his helmet still bore the two golden slashes, it now bore as well a crest of sleen hair, permitted only to captains.

He had received his fifth ship as a gift from the Ubar Henrius Sevarius, claiming to be the fifth of his line. Henrius Sevarius was said to be a mere boy, and his Ubarate one which was administered by his regent, Claudius, once of Tyros. Lysias had been client to the house of Sevarius, it was said, for five years, a period coterminous with the regency of Claudius, who had assumed the power of the house following the assassination of Henrius Sevarius the Fourth.

Many of the captains, incidentally, were client to one Ubar or another.

I myself did not choose to apply for clienthood with a Ubar of Port Kar. I did not expect to need their might, nor did I wish to extend them my service.

I noted that Lysias was looking at me.

Something in his face seemed puzzled.

He may have seen me that night, among the rencers on the island, but he did not place me, one who now sat on the Council of the Captains of Port Kar.

He looked away.

I had seen Samos, First Slaver of Port Kar, only once at the meeting of the council. He was said to be an agent of Priest-Kings. Originally I had intended to come to Port

Kar to contact him, but I had, of course, now chosen not to do so.

He had not seen me before, though I had seen him, at the Curulean Auction House in Ar, something less than a year ago.

I had done well in Port Kar, since I had come to the city some seven months ago.

I was now through with the service of Priest-Kings. They might find others to fight their battles and risk their lives for them. My battles now would be my own; my risks would be undertaken only for my own gain.

For the first time in my life I was rich.

I despised, I discovered, neither power nor wealth.

What else might motivate an intelligent man, other perhaps than the bodies of his women, or those he would decide to make his women, which might serve him for recreation?

In these days, in myself, I found little that I could respect, but I did find that I had come, in my way, to love the sea, as is not uncommon with those of Port Kar.

I had seen her first at dawn, from the high roof of a paga tavern, holding in my arms the body of a man dying of a wound, one which I had inflicted.

I had found her beautiful then, and I had never ceased to do so.

When Tab, young, lean, gray-eyed, who had been second to Surbus, asked me what I would have him do, I had looked upon him and said, "Teach me the Sea."

I had raised my own flag in Port Kar, for there is no single flag for the city. There are the five flags of the Ubars, and many flags for many captains. My own flag bore the design of the head of a black bosk against a background of vertical green bars on a white field. I took the green bars to symbolize the rence of the marshes, and the flag, thus, became that of Bosk, a Captain, who had come from the marshes.

I had discovered, to my pleasure, that the girl Luma, whom I had saved from Surbus, was of the Scribes. Her city had been Tor.

Being of the Scribes she could, of course, read and write.

"Can you keep accounts?" I had asked her.

"Yes, Master," she had responded.

I had made her the chief scribe and accountant of my house.

Each night, in my hall, before my master's chair, she would kneel with her tablets and give me an accounting of the day's business, with reports on the progress of various investments and ventures, often making suggestions and recommendations for further actions.

This plain, thin girl, I found, had an excellent mind for the complicated business transactions of a large house.

She was a most valuable slave.

She much increased my fortunes.

I permitted her, of course, but a single garment, but I allowed it to be opaque, and of the blue of the Scribes. It was sleeveless and fell to just above her knees. Her collar, however, that she might not grow pretentious, was of simple steel. It read, as I wished, I BELONG TO BOSK.

Some of the free men in the house, particularly of the scribes, resented that the girl should have a position of such authority. Accordingly, when receiving their reports and transmitting her instructions to them, I had informed her that she would do so humbly, as a slave girl, and kneeling at their feet. This mollified the men a good deal, though some remained disgruntled. All, I think, feared that her quick stylus and keen mind would discover the slightest discrepancies in their columns and tally sheets, and, indeed, they seemed to do so. I think they feared her, because of the excellence of her work and because, behind her, stood the power of the house, its Captain, Bosk from the Marshes.

Midice now possessed a hundred pleasure silks, and rings and beads, which she might twine in her now-jeweled collar.

The dark-haired, lithe girl, so marvelously legged, I discovered, made an excellent slave.

Once I had discovered her gazing upon Tab, and I had beaten her. I did not kill him. He was a valuable man to me.

Thurnock and Clitus seemed pleased with Thura and Ula, who now wore expensive silks and jeweled collars. They were wise to have made themselves my men. They had much advanced themselves in doing so.

Telima I kept mostly in the kitchens, with the other Kettle Slaves, with instructions to the Kitchen Master

that the simplest and least pleasant tasks be hers, and
that she be worked the hardest of all. I did, however,
specify that it would be she who must personally wait my
table and serve my food each night, that I might each
night renew my pleasure at finding my former Mistress,
weary from her day's labors, soiled and uncombed, in her
brief, miserable, stained rep-cloth garment, serving me
as Kettle Slave. Following the meal she would retire to
my quarters which, on hands and knees, with brush and
bucket, she would scrub to the satisfaction of a Whip
Slave, with strap, standing over her. Then she would retire
again to the kitchens for the work there that would have
been left for her, after which, when finished, she would
be chained for the night.

Generally in the evening I ate with Thurnock and Clitus, with their slaves, and Midice. Sometimes we were
joined by Tab.

Captains, commonly, do not eat with their men.

My attention was returned now to the meeting of the
Council of the Captains of Port Kar.

A seaman, reportedly escaped from Cos, was telling
of the preparation of a great fleet intending to sail against
Port Kar, a fleet that would be enlarged by the forces
of Tyros as well.

There was little interest in this report. Cos and Tyros,
when not at one another's throats, are always threatening
to join their forces for an onslaught on Port Kar. The
rumor was a persistent one, a common one. But not in
over a hundred years had the united fleets of Cos and
Tyros challenged Port Kar, and at that time, because of
storms, they had been scattered and beaten off. As I
have mentioned, the warfare between Cos and Tyros and
Port Kar had been, for years, small-scale, seldom involving more than a few dozen galleys on a side. All
parties had apparently slipped into an arrangement which
was now almost sanctioned by tradition, an arrangement
characterized by almost constant conflict but few, or no,
extensive commitments. The risks of engaging fleets was
doubtless, by all, thought to be too great. Further, raids,
interspersed with smuggling and trading, had become a
fairly profitable way of life, apparently for all. Doubtless,
in Cos and Tyros as well there were rumors of fleets being
prepared to be sent against them. The seaman, to his
chagrin, was dismissed by a vote of the council.

We then turned our attention to matters of greater importance, the need for more covered docks in the arsenal, beneath which additional galleys could be caulked for the grain fleet, else how could a hundred vessels be ready for the voyage north to the grain fields before the sixth passage hand?

It is perhaps worth remarking, briefly, on the power of Port Kar, with it being understood that the forces of both Cos and Tyros, the other two significant maritime Ubarates in known Thassa, are quite comparable.

The following figures pertain to medium class or larger vessels:

The five Ubars of Port Kar, Chung, Eteocles, Nigel, Sullius Maximus and Henrius Sevarius, control among themselves some four hundred ships. The approximately one hundred and twenty captains of the Council of the Captains of Port Kar have, pledged to their personal service, some thousand ships. They further control another thousand ships, as executor, through the council, which ships comprise the members of the grain fleet, the oil fleet, the slave fleet, and others, as well as numerous patrol and escort ships. Beyond these ships there are some twenty-five hundred ships which are owned by some fifteen or sixteen hundred minor captains of the city, not wealthy enough to sit on the Council of Captains. The figures I have listed would give us some forty-nine hundred ships. To get a better figure, particularly since the above figures are themselves approximations, let us say that Port Kar houses in the neighborhood of five thousand ships. As mentioned above, the naval strengths of Cos and Tyros are, individually, comparable. It is, of course, true that not all of these some five thousand ships are war ships. My estimation would be that approximately fifteen hundred only are the long ships, the ram-ships, those of war. On the other hand, whereas the round ships do not carry rams and are much slower and less maneuverable than the long ships, they are not inconsequential in a naval battle, for their deck areas and deck castles can accommodate springals, small catapults, and chain-sling onagers, not to mention numerous bowmen, all of which can provide a most discouraging and vicious barrage, consisting normally of javelins, burning pitch, fiery rocks and crossbow quarrels. A war ship going into battle, incidentally, always takes its mast down and stores its sail below decks. The bulwarks and deck of the ship are often covered with wet hides.

It was voted that another dozen covered docks be raised within the confines of the arsenal, that the caulking schedules of the grain fleet might be met. The vote was unanimous.

The next matter for consideration was the negotiation of a dispute between the sail-makers and the rope-makers in the arsenal with respect to priority in the annual Procession to the Sea, which takes place on the first of En'Kara, the Gorean New Year. There had been a riot this year. It was resolved that henceforth both groups would walk abreast. I smiled to myself. I expected there would be a riot next year as well.

The rumor of the seaman, that Cos and Tyros were preparing fleets against Port Kar, again entered my mind, but again I dismissed it.

The next item on the agenda dealt with the demand of the pulley-makers to receive the same wage per Ahn as the oar-makers. I voted for this measure, but it did not pass.

A Captain next to me snorted, "Give the pulley-makers the wage of oar-makers, and sawyers will want the wages of carpenters, and carpenters of shipwrights!"

All who do skilled work in the arsenal, incidentally, are free men. The men of Port Kar may permit slaves to build their houses and their walls, but they do not permit them to build their ships. The wages of a sail-maker, incidentally, are four copper tarn disks per day, those of a fine shipwright, hired by the Council of Captains, as much as a golden tarn disk per day. The average working day is ten Ahn, or about twelve Earth hours. The amount of time spent in actual work, however, is far less. The work day of a free man in the arsenal is likely to be, on the whole, a rather leisurely one. Free Goreans do not like to be pressed in their tasks. Two Ahn for lunch and stopping an Ahn early for paga and talk in the late afternoon are not uncommon. Layoffs occur, but, because of the amount of work, not frequently. The organizations, such as the sail-makers, almost guildlike, not castes, have dues, and these dues tend to be applied to a number of purposes, such as support of those injured or their families, loans, payments when men are out of work, and pensions. The organizations have also, upon occasion, functioned as collective bargaining agencies. I suspected that the sail-makers would, threatening desertion of the arsenal, this year or the next obtain their desired increase in wages. Brutal repressions of organization have never character-ized the arsenal. The Council of Captains respects those who build and outfit ships. On the other hand, the wages tend to be so slight that an organization seldom has the means to mount a long strike; the arsenal can normally be patient, and can usually choose to build a ship a month from now rather than now, but one cannot well arrange to eat a month from now, and not today, or tomorrow, or until a month from now. But most importantly the men of the arsenal regard themselves as just that, the men of the arsenal, and would be unhappy apart from their work. For all their threats of desertion of the arsenal there are few of them who would want to leave it. Building fine and beautiful ships gives them great pleasure.

Beyond this, lastly, it might be mentioned that Gorean society, on the whole, tends to be tradition bound, and that there is little questioning of the wisdom of one's fathers; in such a society individuals usually have an iden-tity satisfactory to themselves, and a place in which they feel comfortable; accordingly they are less susceptible to the social confusions attendant upon a society in which greater mobility is encouraged and traditional prestige considerations replaced with materialistic ones. A society in which each is expected to succeed, and is placed under conditions where most must fail, would be incomprehensi-ble, irrational, to most Goreans. This will sound strange, I suppose, but the workers of the arsenal, as long as they make enough to live reasonably well, are more concerned with their work, as craftsmen, than they are with con-siderably and indefinitely improving their economic status. This is not to say that they would have any objection to being rich; it is only to remark, in effect, that it has never occurred to them, no more than to most Goreans, to take very seriously the pursuit of wealth as their universal and compelling motivation; being ignorant, it seems, they, like most other Goreans, are more concerned with other things, such as, as I have earlier noted, the building of fine and beautiful ships. I make no pronouncements on these matters, but report them as I find them. I would note, of course, that these weaknesses, or virtues, of the men of the arsenal are, of tradition, welcomed by the Council of

Captains; without them the arsenal could not be as efficiently and economically managed as it is. Again I make no pronouncements on these matters, but report them as I find them. My thinking on these matters is mixed.

Why, I asked myself, should Cos and Tyros consider bringing their fleets against Port Kar? What had changed? But then I recalled that nothing had changed. It was only a rumor, one which, it seemed, recurred at least every year in Port Kar. Doubtless there were similar rumors raising their small stirs, in the councils of Cos and Tyros. I recalled that the words of the seaman had been dismissed.

Now, crying to come before the council, was the mad, half-blind shipwright Tersites, a scroll of drawings in his hand, and calculations.

At a word from the scribe at the long table before the thrones of the Ubars, two men put Tersites from the chamber, dragging him away.

Once before he had been permitted to present plans to the council, but they had been too fantastic to be taken seriously. He had dared to suggest a redesign of the standard tarn ship. He had wanted to deepen the keel, to add a foremast, to change the rowing to great oars, each handled by several men, rather than one man to an oar; he had wanted even to raise the ram above the waterline.

I would have been curious to hear the arguments of Tersites pertinent to these recommendations, but before, when it had become clear how radical and, I gather, absurd were his proposals, he had been hooted from the chamber.

I recall men shouting, "Many men could not all sit through the stroke of an oar! Would you have them stand?" "So great an oar could not even be held by the hands of a man!" "Two masts with their sails could not be quickly removed before battle!" "You will slow the ship if you deepen the keel!" "If many men sit a single oar, some will slack their work!" "What good is a ram that does not make its stroke below the waterline?"

Tersites had been permitted that once to address the council because he, though thought mad, had once been a skilled shipwright. Indeed, the galleys of Port Kar, medium and heavy class, carried shearing blades, which had been an invention of Tersites. These are huge quartermoons of steel, fixed forward of the oars, anchored into the frame of the ship itself. One of the most common of naval strategies, other than ramming, is oar shearing, in which one vessel, her oars suddenly shortened inboard, slides along the hull of another, whose oars are still outboard, splintering and breaking them off. The injured galley then is like a broken-winged bird, and at the mercy of the other ship's ram as she comes about, flutes playing and drums beating, and makes her strike amidships. Recent galleys of Cos and Tyros, and other maritime powers, it had been noted, were now also, most often, equipped with shearing blades.

Tersites had also, it might be mentioned, though he had not presented these ideas in his appearance before the council, argued for a rudder hung on the sternpost of the tarn ship, rather than the two side-hung rudders, and had championed a square rigging, as opposed to the beautiful lateen rigging common on the ships of Thassa. Perhaps this last proposal of Tersites' had been the most offensive of all to the men of Port Kar. The triangular lateen sail on its single sloping yard is incredibly beautiful.

Tersites had, some five years before, been removed from the arsenal. He had taken his ideas to Cos and Tyros, but there, too, he had met with only scorn. He had then returned to Port Kar, his fortunes exhausted, no place left to him in the arsenal. He now lived, it was said, on the garbage in the canals. A small pittance granted him by the shipwrights, of whom he had been one, was spent in the paga taverns of the city. I dismissed Tersites from my mind.

I had made, since coming to Port Kar, five voyages. Four of these had been commercial in nature. I had no quarrel with the shipping of others. Like the Bosk itself I would not seek for trouble, but, too, like the Bosk, I would not refuse to meet it. My four commercial voyages had been among the exchange islands, or free islands, in Thassa, administered as free ports by members of the Merchants. There were several such islands. Three, which I encountered frequently in my voyages, were Teletus, and, south of it, Tabor, named for the drum, which it resembles, and, to the north, among the northern islands, Scagnar. Others were Farnacium, Hulneth and Asperiche. I did not go as far south as Anango or Ianda, or as far north as Hunjer or Skjern, west of Torvaldsland. These islands, with occasional free ports on the coast, north and south of the Gorean equator, such as Lydius and Helmutsport, and Schendi and Bazi, make possible the commerce between Cos and Tyros, and the mainland, and its cities, such as Ko-ro-ba, Thentis, Tor, Ar, Turia, and many others.

On these voyages my cargos were varied. I did not, however, in this early period, because of the cost, purchase cargos of great value. Accordingly I did not carry, in these first voyages, any abundance of precious metals or jewels; nor did I carry rugs or tapestries, or medicines, or silks or ointments, or perfumes or prize slaves, or spices or cannisters of colored table salts. In these first voyages I was content, quite, to carry tools and stone, dried fruit, dried fish, bolts of rep-cloth, tem-wood, Turwood and Ka-la-na stock, and horn and hides. I did once carry, however, a hold of chained slaves, and, another time, a hold filled with the furs of the northern sea sleen. The latter cargo was the most valuable carried in these first four voyages. Each of these cargos I managed to sell at a considerable profit. Twice we had been scouted by pirates from Tyros, in their green ships, painted to resemble the sea, but neither of them had chosen to engage us. We gathered that, seeing how low we sat in the water, they assumed our cargo to be one of bulk goods and departed, doubtless having higher hopes for gain upon the sea. It is scarcely worth the risk of crew and ship, unless desperate, to win a hold filled with lumber or stone.

My men were mostly pirates and cutthroats. Doubtless many of them did not much care to ply an honest trade. Better, they would think, to lie in wait on the open sea for the slave galleys of Tyros or the treasure ships of Cos. But two who challenged me for the captaincy I slew within a dozen strokes, and the others, thus given pause, chose to confine their disgruntlement, if any, to their cups and conclaves. Any who did not wish to continue in my service were free to go. I instructed Luma to discharge any such with a gift of gold, of half a stone's weight. Surprisingly, few left my ships. I do not think they cared to forsake their piracies, but, too, I think they felt a pride in serving one who was said, now, after the incident of the paga tavern, to possess one of the finest blades in Port Kar.

"When do we sail against the ships of Cos and Tyros?" asked Tab of me.

"Cos and Tyros," I said, "have not injured me."

"They will," said he.

"Then," said I, "we will sail against them."

Ashore my crews were roisterous and brawling but on the ships, strange as it is to relate, they were serious and disciplined men.

I attempted to treat them fairly.

On land I did not see much of them, preferring it this way, remaining aloof.

But I did, of course, pay them well and, in my holding, knowing men, saw that they could have their pick of some of Port Kar's most beautiful slave girls.

I had purchased the girl whom I had seen dance in the Paga Tavern, for forty pieces of gold. I had called her Sandra, after a girl once known on Earth. I had put my collar on her and, after using her, had consigned her to my men, that she might please their senses.

My fifth voyage was one to satisfy my interest, and made in a light swift galley.

I had wanted to see both Tyros and Cos.

Both lie some four hundred pasangs west of Port Kar, Tyros to the south of Cos, separated by some hundred pasangs from her. Tyros is a rugged island, with mountains. She is famed for her vart caves, and indeed, on that island, trained varts, batlike creatures, some the size of small dogs, are used as weapons. Cos is also a lofty island, even loftier than Tyros, but she has level fields to her west. Cos had many terraces, on which the Ta grapes are grown. Near her, one night, lying off her shore, silently, I heard the mating whistles of the tiny, lovely Cosian wingfish. This is a small, delicate fish; it has three or four slender spines in its dorsal fin, which are poisonous. It is called the wingfish because it can, on its stiff pectoral fins, for short distances, glide through the air, usually in an attempt to flee small sea tharlarion, who are immune to the poison of the spines. It is also called a songfish, because, in their courtship rituals, males and females thrust their heads from the water, uttering a kind of whistle. Their livers are regarded as a delicacy. I recalled I had once tried one, but had not cared for it, at a banquet in Turia, in the house of a man named Saphrar, who had been a merchant. Saphrar, I recalled, had once been a perfumer from Tyros but, being exiled as a thief, had made his way to Port Kar, and thence had gone to Turia.

I had leaned on the rail of the light galley, and, in

the moonlight, had listened to the mating whistles of the small fish.

They seemed so small, and innocent.

"The moons are now full," had said Tab to me.

"Yes," I had said, "weigh the anchors."

Silently, oars scarcely touching the water, we had moved from Cos, leaving her behind in the moonlight.

While I made my five voyages my other six ships were engaged in commercial ventures similar to those which had occupied my first four voyages. I seldom returned to Port Kar without learning from Luma that my fortunes had been augmented even further in my absence. I had made, to date, only the five voyages mentioned. In the last two months, in my holding, I had been largely occupied with matters of business and management, mostly organizing and planning the voyages of others. I expected I would again, however, return to Thassa. She, as it is said, cannot be forgotten.

I had made one innovation in practices common to Port Kar. I used free men on the rowing benches of my round ships, of which I had four, not slaves, as is traditional. The fighting ship, incidentally, the long ship, the ram-ship, has never been, to my knowledge, in Port Kar, or Cos, or Tyros, or elsewhere on Gor, rowed by slaves; the Gorean fighting ship always has free men at the oars. The galley slaves I thought worth freeing, I freed, and found that many would stay with me, taking me for their captain. Those I did not wish, for one reason or another, to free, I sold to other captains, or exchanged them for slaves whom I might free, several of whom, when freed, also agreed to serve with me. Gaps on my benches were easily filled. I would purchase a strong man from the market chain on the slave wharf, and then, saying nothing, set him free. I think not once did such a man not follow me to my holding, asking to be my man. Not only did free men render more efficient service at the oars, but, when they were given the opportunity, I found them eager to train with arms, and so hired masters to teach them weapons. It was thus that the round ships of Bosk, the captain from the marshes, with their free crews, became in their own right dangerous, formidable ships. Merchants of Port Kar began to apply to me that they might transport their goods in my ships. I preferred, however, to buy and sell my own cargos. Certain other captains, I noted, were now also experimenting, on certain of their ships, with free crews.

My attention was then returned to the meeting of the council of captains.

A motion was on the floor that a new preserve in the northern forests be obtained, that more timber for the arsenal be available. In the northern forests Port Kar already had several such preserves. There is a ceremony in the establishment of such a preserve, involving proclamations and the soundings of trumpets. Such preserves are posted, and surrounded by ditches to keep out cattle and unlicensed wagoners. There are wardens who watch the trees, guarding against illegal cutting and pasturage, and inspectors who, each year, tally and examine them. The wardens are also responsible, incidentally, for managing and improving the woods. They do such work as thinning and planting, and trimming, and keeping the protective ditch in repair. They are also responsible for bending and fastening certain numbers of young trees so that they will grow into desired shapes, usually to be used for frames, and stem and sternposts. Individual trees, not in the preserves, which are claimed by Port Kar, are marked with the seal of the arsenal. The location of all such trees is kept in a book available to the Council of Captains. These preserves are usually located near rivers, in order to facilitate bringing cut trees to the sea. Trees may also be purchased from the Forest People, who will cut them in the winter, when they can be dragged on sleds to the sea. If there is a light snowfall in a given year, the price of timber is often higher. Port Kar is, incidentally, completely dependent on the northern timber. Tur wood is used for galley frames, and beams and clamps and posts, and for hull planking; Ka-la-na serves for capstans and mastheads; Tem-wood for rudders and oars; and the needle trees, the evergreens, for masts and spars, and cabin and deck planking.

The motion to obtain a new preserve carried. I abstained from voting, not having been convinced that a new preserve was needed. I supposed it might be, but I did not know; I had not been convinced; so I had abstained.

But why should Cos and Tyros come against Port Kar at this time? But it was a rumor, I reminded myself again, forcibly, a rumor, a baseless rumor. I was angry. I again forced the thought from my mind.

I now had the means whereby I might purchase yet two more ships for my fleet. They would be deep-keeled round ships, with mighty holds, and high, broad sails. I had already, to a great extent, selected crews. I had projected voyages for them to Ianda and to Torvaldsland. Each would be escorted by a medium galley. They would bring me, I conjectured, much riches.

I took the note from the boy, who appeared suddenly beside my chair. He had long hair, and wore a tunic of red and yellow silk. I recognized him, he being a page of the council.

The note, folded, was sealed with a disk of melted wax. The wax did not bear the imprint of a signet ring.

I opened it.

The message was simple. It read, printed in block letters: I WOULD SPEAK WITH YOU. It was signed, also in block printing, SAMOS.

I crumpled the paper in my fist.

"Who gave you this message?" I asked the boy.

"A man," he said. "I do not know him."

I saw Lysias, with his helmet, with the two golden slashes, with its captain's crest of sleen hair, on the arm of his curule chair. He was looking at me, curiously.

I did not know if the message truly came from Samos, or not.

If it did, doubtless he had come to learn that Tarl Cabot was now in Port Kar. But how would he have come to know this? And how could he have come to understand that Bosk, fighting man and merchant, was the same as he who once had been a warrior of the towered city of Ko-ro-ba, the Towers of the Morning?

Doubtless he wished to summon me to his presence, that he might recall me to the service of Priest-Kings.

But I no longer served Priest-Kings. I served now only myself.

I was angry.

I would ignore the message.

At that moment a man burst into the hall in which was sitting the Council of Captains.

His eyes were wild.

It was Henrak, who had worn the white scarf, who had betrayed the rencers.

"The arsenal!" he cried. "The arsenal is afire!"

The Crest of Sleen Hair

The Captains leaped from their chairs, crying out. Great chairs fell bounding down the tiers of the council chamber. The Scribe at the table before the thrones was on his feet shouting. Papers were scattering to the floor. Feet were pounding toward the great double door, leading to the hallway beyond, leading out to the tiled piazza fronting on the hall of the council. I saw pages scurrying about, in their red and yellow silk. Ink had spilled on the great table.

Then I saw that Lysias, with the captain's crest of sleen hair on his helmet, had not stirred from his chair.

And I saw, too, that the Scribe who normally sat his attendance at the right arm of the empty throne of Henrius Sevarius, the Fifth, in the council chamber was gone.

Outside, in the distance, through the great door, flung open, I heard cries of alarm, and the clash of weapons.

Then I saw Lysias, his hair tied behind his neck with the scarlet string, rise.

He placed on his head his helmet.

He unsheathed his weapon.

So, too, did my steel leave its sheath.

But Lysias then, weapon at the ready, backed away, and then turned and fled through a side door, leading from the council hall.

I looked about.

A small fire was burning to one side, where a lamp with candle had been knocked to the floor, in the rush toward the door.

Chairs lay knocked over, furniture was broken. The floor was covered with papers.

The scribe at the central table, that before the empty thrones, stood numb behind the table.

Other scribes came and stood with him, looking from one to the other. To one side, cowering, stood several of the page boys.

Then, staggering, bloody, the quarrel of a crossbow protruding from the emblem on his velvet tunic, a captain reeled into the room and fell, clutching at the arm of one of the curule chairs. Then, behind him, in groups of four and five, crying out, many bleeding from wounds, weapons brandished, and sometimes bloodied, there came those captains who could.

I went to the place before the thrones.

I indicated the small fire burning to one side, that which had been caused by the fallen lamp with candle. "Put it out," I told two of the frightened pages.

I resheathed my sword.

The two pages leapt to do my bidding.

"Gather up and guard the book of the Council," I told the Scribe who had been at the great table.

"Yes, Captain," said he, leaping to seize it up.

I then, throwing papers to the floor, scattering ink, lifted the great table over my head.

There were cries of astonishment.

I turned and, step by step, carrying the great table, advanced toward the large door leading to the hallway.

More captains, their back to the room, fighting, falling, were retreating through the door.

They were the last of the captains.

Over their heads into the doorway I flung the great table.

Its great weight, to screams of horror, fell crushing upon men who, with shields and swords, were closely pressing the captains.

I saw, wide with horror in the apertures of their helmets, the eyes of men pinned beneath its beams.

"Bring curule chairs!" I ordered the captains.

Though many were wounded, though all could scarcely stand, they leaped to gather up chairs and hurl them into the doorway.

Crossbow bolts flashed through the chairs, splintering their backs and sides.

"More tables!" I cried.

Men, and scribes, and pages, too, came forward, four and six men to a table, adding the tables to our barricade.

From the outside some men tried to climb the barricade, and break it down.

On its height they met Bosk, in his hands the wine-tempered steel of a Ko-ro-ban blade.

Four men fell reeling backward, tumbling down the chairs and tables.

Crossbow bolts flashed about my head.

I laughed, and leaped down. No more men were trying to climb the wood of the barricade.

"Can you hold this door?" I asked the captains, and the scribes and pages there.

"We will," they said.

I gestured to the side door, through which Lysias and, I assumed, he who had been scribe for Henrius Sevarius, had escaped. Several of the pages, incidentally, and some of the scribes had also fled through that door. "Secure that door," I told four of the captains.

Immediately they went to the door, calling scribes and pages to help them.

I myself, taking with me two captains, went to a rear corner of the great chamber, whence, via a spiraling stair-well, the roof of the hall of the council might be attained.

We soon found ourselves on the sloping roof of the hall of the council, shielded by turrets and decorative embrasures at its edge.

From there, in the late afternoon sun, we could see smoke from the wharves and arsenal to the west.

"There are no ships from Cos or Tyros in the harbor," said one of the captains standing near me.

I had seen this.

I indicated wharves. "Those wharves," I said, "are those of Chung and Eteocles?"

"Yes," said one of the captains.

"And those," I asked, indicating other wharves, farther to the south, "are those of Nigel and Sullius Maximus."

We could see burning ships.

"Yes," said the other captain.

"Doubtless there is fighting there," said the first captain.

"And along the wharves generally," said the second.

"It seems," I said, "that the holdings of Henrius Sevarius, patron of the captain Lysias, are untouched."

"It does indeed," said the first captain, through gritted teeth.

Below in the streets we heard trumpets. Men were shouting.

We saw some waving banners, bearing the design of the house of Sevarius.

They were trying to urge men into the streets to support them.

"Henrius Sevarius," they were crying, "Ubar of Port Kar."

"Sevarius is proclaiming himself Ubar," said the first captain.

"Or Claudius, his regent," said the other.

We were joined by another captain. "It is quiet now below," he said.

"Look there," I said. I pointed down to some of the canals, cutting between the buildings. Slowly, moving smoothly, their oars dipping in rhythm, from various sides, we saw tarn ships moving toward the hall of the council.

"And there!" cried another captain, pointing to the streets.

There we saw crossbowmen fleeing, in lines along the edges of the buildings. Some men-at-arms were joining them.

"It appears," said one of the captains at my side, "that Henrius Sevarius is not yet Ubar of Port Kar."

At the far edge of the piazza, in one of the bordering canals, nosing forward to take a berth between two tiled piers, we saw a ram-ship, medium class. Her mast, with its long yard, was lashed to the deck. Doubtless her sail was stored below. These are the arrangements when a galley moves through the city, or when she enters battle. On a line running from the forward starboard mooring cleat to the stem castle, furnishing cover for archers and spearmen, there flew a flag, snapping in the wind. It was white with vertical green stripes on its field and, over these, in black, the head of a Bosk.

I could see, even at the distance, leaping from the prow of the ship to the tiles of the piazza, running across the large, oblique-looking, colored squares toward the Hall of the Council of Captains, the great Thurnock, with his yellow bow, followed by Clitus, with his net and trident, and by Tab, with my men.

"Estimate for me," I said, "the damage to the arsenal."

"It appears," said one, "to be the lumber sheds and the dry docks."

"The warehouses of pitch and that of oars, too," said another.

"Yes," said the first. "I think so."

"There is little wind," said another.

I was not dissatisfied. I was confident that the men of the arsenal, in their hundreds, almost to the count of two thousand, would, given the opportunity, control the fire. Fire has always been regarded as the great hazard to the arsenal. Accordingly many of her warehouses, shops and foundries are built of stone, with slated or tinned roofs. Wooden structures, such as her numerous sheds and roofed storage areas tend to be separated from one another. Within the arsenal itself there are numerous basins, providing a plenitude of water. Many of these basins, near which, in red-painted wooden boxes, are stored large numbers of folded leather buckets, are expressly for the purpose of providing a means for fighting fires. Some of the other basins are large enough to float galleys; these large basins connect with the arsenal's canal system, by means of which heavy materials may be conveyed about the arsenal; the arsenal's canal system also gives access, at two points, to the canal system of the city and, at two other points, to the Tamber Gulf, beyond which lies gleaming Thassa. Each of these four points are guarded by great barred gates. The large basins, just mentioned, are of two types: the first, unroofed, is used for the underwater storage and seasoning of Tur wood; the second, roofed, serves for the heavier fittings and upper carpentry of ships, and for repairs that do not necessitate recourse to the roofed dry docks.

Already it seemed to me there was less smoke, less fire, from the area of the arsenal.

The wharves of Chung, Eteocles, Nigel and Sullius Maximus, I conjectured, from the blazings along the waterfront on the west and south, would not fare as well.

The fires at the arsenal, I supposed, may have been even, primarily, a diversion. They had surely served to draw the captains of Port Kar into the ambush prepared for them outside the hall of the council. I supposed Henrius Sevarius might not have wished to seriously harm the arsenal. Could he come to be the one Ubar of Port Kar, it would constitute a considerable element of his wealth, indeed, the major one.

I, and the three other captains, stood on the sloping roof of the hall of the council and watched the ships burning at the wharves.

"I am going to the arsenal," I said. I turned to one of the captains. "Have scribes investigate and prepare reports on the extent of the damage, wherever it exists. Also have captains ascertain the military situation in the city. And have patrols doubled, and extend their perimeters by fifty pasangs."

"But surely Cos and Tyros—" said one of the Captains.

"Have the patrols doubled, and extend their perimeters by fifty pasangs," I repeated.

"It will be done," he said.

I turned to another man.

"Tonight," I said, "the council must meet again."

"It cannot—" he protested.

"At the twentieth hour," I told him.

"I will send pages through the city with torches," he said.

I looked out over the city, at the arsenal, at the burning wharves on the west and south.

"And summon the four captains," I said, "who are Chung, Eteocles, Nigel and Sullius Maximus."

"The Ubars!" cried a captain.

"The captains," I said. "Send for them only a single page with guard, with his torch. Summon them as captains."

"But they are Ubars," the man whispered.

I pointed to the burning wharves.

"If they do not come," I told him, "tell them they will no longer be captains in the eyes of the council."

The captains looked at me.

"It is the council," I said, "that is now the first power in Port Kar."

The captains looked at one another, and nodded.

"It is true," said one of them.

The power of the captains had been little diminished. The coup intended to destroy them, swift as the falling of the assassin's blade, had failed. Escaping into and barricading themselves within the hall of the Council, most had saved themselves. Others, fortunately as it had turned out for them, had not even been in attendance at the meeting. The ships of the captains were usually moored, beyond this, within the city, in the mooring lakes fronting on their holdings and walled. And those who had used the open wharves did not seem to have suffered damage.

The only wharves fired were apparently those of the four Ubars.

I looked out over the harbor, and over the muddy Tamber to the gleaming vastness beyond, my Thassa.

At any given time most of the ships of Port Kar are at sea. Five of mine were, at present, at sea. Two were in the city, to be supplied. The ships of the captains, returning, would further guarantee their power in the city, their crews being applicable where the captains might choose. To be sure, many of the ships of the Ubars were similarly at sea, but men pretending to the Ubarate of Port Kar commonly keep a far larger percentage of their power in port than would a common captain. I expected the power of the four Ubars, Chung, Eteocles, Nigel and Sullius Maximus, might have been, at a stroke, diminished by a half. If so, they might control, among themselves, a force of about one hundred and fifty ships, most of which were still at sea. I did not expect the Ubars would cooperate with one another. Further, if necessary, the council of captains, with its power, might intercept and impound their ships, as they returned, one by one. I had long felt that five Ubars in Port Kar, and the attendant anarchy resulting from this division of power, was politically insufferable, with its competition of extortions, taxes and decrees, but more importantly, I felt that it jeopardized my own interests. I intended, in Port Kar, to accumulate fortunes and power. As my projects developed I had no wish to suffer for not having applied for clienthood to one Ubar or another. I did not wish to have to sue for the protection of a strong man. I preferred to be my own. Accordingly I wished for the council to consolidate its power in the city. It seemed that now, with the failure of the coup of Henrius Sevarius, and the diminishment of the power of the other Ubars, she might well do so. The council, I expected, itself composed of captains, men much like myself, would provide a political structure within which my ambitions and projects might well prosper. Nominally beneath its aegis, I might, for all practical purposes, be free to augment my house as I saw fit, the House of Bosk, of Port Kar.

I, for one, would champion the council.

I expected that there would be support for this position, both from men like myself, self-seeking men, wise in political realities, and from the inevitable and useful fools, abundant even in Port Kar, hoping simply for a saner and more efficient governance of their city. It seemed the interests of wise men and fools lay for once conjoined.

I turned and faced the captains.

"Until the twentieth hour, Captains," said I.

Dismissed, they left the roof.

I stood alone on the roof, and watched the fires. A man such as I, I thought, might rise high in a city such as this, squalid, malignant Port Kar.

I then left the roof to go to the arsenal, to see for myself what might be the case there.

It was now the nineteenth hour.

Above us, in the chamber of the council of captains, I could hear feet moving about on the wooden floor, chairs scraping.

Each captain in Port Kar had come to the meeting, saving some of those most closely associated with the house of Sevarius.

It was said, even, that the four Ubars, Chung, Eteocles, Nigel and Sullius Maximus, sat now, or would soon sit, upon their thrones.

The man on the rack near me screamed in agony.

He was one of those who had been captured.

"We have the reports on the damage to the wharves of Chung," said a scribe, pressing into my hands the documents. I knew that the fires on the wharves of Chung still blazed, and that they had spread northward to the free wharves south of the arsenal. The reports, accordingly, would be incomplete.

I looked at the scribe.

"We will bring you further reports as soon as they arrive," he said.

I nodded, and he sped away.

The fires were now substantially out in the properties of Eteocles, Nigel and Sullius Maximus, though a warehouse of the latter, in which was stored tharlarion oil, still blazed. The city was heavy with the smell and smoke of it. As nearly as I could gather, Chung had been the most afflicted by the fire, losing perhaps thirty ships. The Ubars, it seemed, had not had their power halved, but it had been considerably reduced. The damage to the arsenal, which I had seen with my own eyes, and had taken statistical reports on from scribes, had not been particularly serious. It amounted to the destruction of one roofed area where Ka-la-na wood was stored, and the partial destruction of another; one small warehouse for the storage of pitch, one of several, had been destroyed; two dry docks had been lost, and the shop of the oar-makers, near the warehouse for oars, had been damaged; the warehouse itself, as it turned out, had escaped the fire.

Some of those who had started these fires, who had been apprehended, now, under the torches, screamed on the racks beneath the chamber of the council of Captains. Most, however, their retreat covered by crossbow-men, had escaped and fled to the holding of Henrius Sevarius.

The two slaves near me bent to the rack windlass. There was a creak of wood, the sound of the pawl, locking, dropping into a new notch on the ratchet, a hideous scream.

"Have the patrols been doubled?" I asked a captain nearby.

"Yes," he said, "and their perimeters extended by fifty pasangs."

The man on the rack screamed again.

"What," I asked a captain, "is the military situation?"

"The men of Henrius Sevarius," said he, "have with-drawn into his holdings. His ships and wharves are well defended. Men of the captains maintain their watch. Others are in reserve. Should the forces of Sevarius emerge from his holdings we shall meet them with steel."

"What of the city?" I asked.

"It has not rallied to Sevarius," said the captain. "In the streets men cry 'Power to the Council!' "

"Excellent," I commented.

A scribe came to my side. "An envoy from the House of Sevarius demands to speak before the council," he said.

"Is he a captain?" I asked.

"Yes," said the scribe. "Lysias."

I smiled. "Very well," I said, "send a page, and a man with a torch, to conduct him hither, and give him guard, that he may not be torn to death in the streets."

The scribe grinned. "Yes, Captain," said he.

A captain near me shook his head. "But Sevarius is a Ubar," he said.

"The council," I said, "will adjudicate his claims."

The captain looked at me, and smiled. "Good," he said. "Good."

I gestured for the two slaves at the rack windlass to again rotate the heavy wooden wheels, moving the heavy wooden pawl another notch in the beam ratchet. Again there was a creak of wood and the sound of the pawl, locking, dropping into its new notch. The thing fastened on the rack threw back its head on the cords, screaming only with his eyes. Another notch and the bones of its arms and legs would be torn from their sockets.

"What have you learned?" I asked the scribe, who stood with his tablet and stylus beside the rack.

"It is the same as the others," he said. "They were hired by the men of Henrius Sevarius, some to slay captains, some to fire the wharves and arsenal." The scribe looked up at me. "Tonight," he said, "Sevarius was to be Ubar in Port Kar, and each was to have a stone of gold."

"What of Cos and Tyros?" I asked.

The scribe looked at me, puzzled. "None have spoken of Cos and Tyros," he said.

This angered me, for I felt that there must be more in the coup than the work of one of Port Kar's five Ubars. I had expected, that very day, or this night, to receive word that the fleets of Cos and Tyros were approaching. Could it be, I asked myself, that Cos and Tyros were not implicated in the attempted coup?

"What of Cos and Tyros!" I demanded of the wretch fastened on the rack. He had been one who had, with his crossbow, fired on the captains as they had run from the council. His eyes had moved from his head; a large vein was livid on his forehead; his feet and hands were white; his wrists and ankles were bleeding; his body was little more than drawn suet; he was stained with his own excrement.

"Sevarius!" he whispered. "Sevarius!"

"Are not Cos and Tyros to attack?" I demanded.

"Yes! Yes!" he cried. "Yes!"

"And," I said, "what of Ar, and Ko-ro-ba, and Treve, and Thentis, and Turia, and Tharna and Tor!"

"Yes, yes, yes!" he whimpered.

"And," I said, "Teletus, Tabor, Scagnar!"

"Yes, yes!" he cried.

"And," I said, "Farnacium, and Hulneth and Asperiche! And Anango and Ianda, and Hunjer and Skjern and

Torvaldsland! And Lydius and Helmutsport, and Schendi and Bazi!"

"Yes," he cried. "All are going to attack."

"And Port Kar!" I cried.

"Yes," he raved, "Port Kar, too! Port Kar, too!"

With disgust I gestured for the slaves to pull the pins releasing the windlasses.

With a rattle of cord and chain the wheels spun back and the thing on the rack began to jabber and whimper and laugh.

By the time the slaves had unfastened him he had lost consciousness.

"There was little more to be learned from that one," said a voice near me. It might have been a larl that had spoken.

I turned.

There, facing me, his face expressionless, was one who was well known in Port Kar.

"You were not at the meeting of the council this afternoon," I said to him.

"No," he said.

The somnolent beast of a man regarded me.

He was a large man. About his left shoulder there were the two ropes of Port Kar. These are commonly worn only outside the city. His garment was closely woven, and had a hood, now thrown back. His face was wide, and heavy, and much lined; it, like many of those of Port Kar, showed the marks of Thassa, burned into it by wind and salt; he had gray eyes; his hair was white, and short-cropped; in his ears there were two small golden rings.

If a larl might have been transformed into a man, and yet retain its instincts, its heart and its cunning, I think it might look much like Samos, First Slaver of Port Kar.

"Greetings, noble Samos," I said.

"Greetings," said he.

It then occurred to me that this man could not serve Priest-Kings. It occurred to me then, with a shudder which I did not betray, that such a man could serve only the Others, not Priest-Kings, those Others, in the distant steel worlds, who surreptitiously and cruelly fought to gain this world and Earth for their own ends.

Samos looked about, gazing on the various racks, to many of which there were still fastened prisoners.

The torches lit the room with unusual shadows.

"Have Cos and Tyros been implicated?" he asked.

"These men will confess whatever we wish," I said dryly.

"But there seems nothing genuine?" he asked.

"No," I said.

"I suspect Cos and Tyros," he said, gazing at me, evenly.

"I, too," I said.

"But these minions," he said, "they will know nothing."

"It appears so," I said.

"Would you," asked Samos, "reveal your plans to such as these?"

"No," I said.

He nodded, and then turned, but stopped, and spoke over his shoulder. "You are the one who calls himself Bosk, are you not?"

"I am he," I told him.

"You are to be congratulated on taking the leadership this afternoon," he said. "You did the council good service."

I said nothing.

Then he turned. "Do you know who is senior captain of the council?" he asked.

"No," I said.

"I am," said Samos, of Port Kar.

I did not respond.

Then Samos addressed himself to the Scribe near the rack. He gestured toward the other racks. "Take down these men," he said, "and keep them chained. We may wish to question them further tomorrow."

"What do you expect to do with them eventually?" I asked.

"Our round ships," said Samos, "require oarsmen."

I nodded.

So they would be slaves.

"Noble Samos," I said.

"Yes," said he.

I recalled the note I had received before Henrak had burst in upon the council, crying that there was fire in the arsenal. I had thrust the note in the wallet I wore at my belt.

"Earlier today," I asked, "did Noble Samos send word to me that he wished to speak with me?"

Samos looked at me. "No," he said.

I bowed my head.

Then Samos, who was senior captain of the Council of Captains of Port Kar, turned and left.

"Samos," said one of the scribes nearby, "only made landfall in Port Kar this night, at the eighteenth hour, from Scagnar."

"I see," I said.

So who then, I asked myself, would write such a note? Apparently there were others then in Port Kar who would have business with me.

It was near the Twentieth Hour.

Lysias, captain, client of Henrius Sevarius, spoke before the council. He stood before the thrones of the Ubars, before even the large table, which now, on its upper face, was marked by sword cuts and the apertures splintered open by the passage of crossbow quarrels earlier this afternoon.

The Hall of the Council, this night, was surrounded by the men of the captains, who, too, patrolled the rooftops and the walks beside the canals for a full pasang on all sides.

The hall was lit by torches, and by many lamps with candles, set on tables between curule chairs.

As Lysias spoke he walked back and forth before the table, his cloak swirling behind him, his helmet, with its captain's crest of sleen hair, in the crook of his arm.

"And so," concluded Lysias, "I bring you all amnesty in the name of the Ubar of Port Kar, Henrius Sevarius!"

"Henrius Sevarius, the Captain," said Samos, speaking from his curule chair, in the name of the council, "is most kind."

Lysias dropped his head.

"Henrius Sevarius, the Captain," said Samos, in measured words, "may, however, find that the council is less inclined to lenience than he."

Lysias lifted his head in alarm.

"His power is greater than any of yours!" he cried. And then he spun about to face the Ubars, each, with men about him, on his throne. "Greater even than any of yours!" cried Lysias.

I gazed upon the Ubars, squat, brilliant Chung; narrow-faced, cunning Eteocles; tall, long-haired Nigel, like a warlord from Torvaldsland; and Sullius Maximus, who was said to write poetry and be a student of the properties of various poisons.

"How many ships has he?" asked Samos.

"One hundred and two!" said Lysias proudly.

"The captains of the council," said Samos, dryly, "have some one thousand ships pledged to their personal service. And further, the council is executor with respect to the disposition and application of the ships of the city, in the number of approximately another thousand."

Lysias stood scowling before Samos, his helmet in the crook of his arm, his long cloak falling behind him.

"The council commands," summarized Samos, "some two thousand ships."

"There are many other ships!" cried Lysias.

"Perhaps," asked Samos, "you refer to those of Chung, and Eteocles, and Nigel and Sullius Maximus?"

There was unpleasant laughter in the council.

"No!" cried Lysias. "I refer to the ships of the minor captains, in the number of better than twenty-five hundred!"

"In the streets," said Samos, "I have heard the cry 'Power to the council!' "

"Proclaim Henrius Sevarius sole Ubar," said Lysias numbly, "and your lives will be spared, and you will be granted amnesty."

"That is your proposal?" asked Samos.

"It is," said Lysias.

"Now hear," said Samos, "the proposal of the council, that Henrius Sevarius and his regent, Claudius, lay down their arms, and divest themselves of all ships, and men and holdings, and all properties and assets, and present themselves, stripped and in the chains of slaves, before the council, that its judgment may be passed on them."

Lysias, his body rigid with fury, his hand on the hilt of his sword, stood not speaking before Samos, First Slaver of Port Kar.

"Perhaps," said Samos, "their lives may be spared, that they may take their seat on the benches of the public round ships."

There was an angry cry of affirmation, and a shaking of fists, from those of the council.

Lysias looked about himself. "I claim the immunity of the herald!" he cried.

"It is yours," said Samos. Then he spoke to a page.

"Conduct Lysias, Captain, to the holdings of Henrius Sevarius," said Samos.

"Yes, Noble Samos," said the boy.

Lysias, looking about himself, his cloak swirling, followed the boy from the room.

Samos rose before his curule chair. "Is it true," he asked, "that in the eyes of the council Henrius Sevarius is no longer Ubar or Captain in Port Kar?"

"It is," cried the voices. "It is!"

And none, I think, cried louder than the other Ubars upon their thrones.

When the tumult had subsided, Samos faced the four thrones of the Ubars.

Uneasily they regarded him.

"Glorious Captains," said Samos.

"Ubars!" cried Sullius Maximus.

"Ubars," said Samos, bowing his head with a smile. The four men, Chung, Eteocles, Nigel and Sullius Maximus, rested back on their thrones.

"Be it known to you, Ubars," said he, "that Samos, First Slaver of Port Kar, now proposes to the council that it take into its own hands the full and sole governance of the city of Port Kar, with full powers, whether of policy and decree, of enforcement, of taxation and law, or other, pertinent to the administration thereof."

"No!" cried the Ubars, leaping to their feet.

"It will be civil war!" cried Eteocles.

"Power to the council," said Samos, bowing his head.

"Power to the council!" cried the men in the tiers. Even the page boys and the scribes, and minor captains, in the back of the room and about the sides, cried out these words. "Power to the council!"

I sat still in my curule chair, smiling.

"Further," said Samos, "I propose that the council decree that all bonds among clients and patrons in Port Kar be now dissolved, to be reestablished only on the basis of mutual consent and explicit contract on the part of the parties involved, which documents, in copy, are to be placed with the council."

Sullius Maximus shook his fist at Samos. "You will not shear us of our power!" he cried.

"Further," said Samos, "let the council decree that any who fail to abide by the resolutions of the council,

or act against it, be regarded, at the council's convenience,
subject to her pleasure."

There was much enthusiastic shouting from the tiers.

The Ubar Chung, throwing his cloak about his shoulders, followed by his men, left the chamber.

Then Nigel, with lofty disdain and measured tread, carrying his helmet, departed the chamber.

"I now ask the table scribe," said Samos, "to call the roll of Captains."

"Antisthenes," called the scribe.

"Antisthenes accepts the proposals," said a man in the third row, some yards from me.

In fury, with a shout of rage, Eteocles, cloak swirling, his hand on the hilt of his sword, strode to the table. He took his sword from its sheath and plunged it through the scribe's papers, pinning them to the table.

"There is the power in Port Kar," he cried.

Slowly Samos drew his own weapon and placed it across his knees. "Here, too," he said, "is power."

And almost every one of the captains in that council drew their weapon, as had Samos, and placed it across their knees.

I, too, unsheathed my weapon, and rose to my feet, regarding Eteocles.

He looked at me, and then, with a cry of anger, drew his blade from the papers and wood, slammed it back into its sheath, and turned and strode from the room.

I returned to my seat.

I saw that now, quietly, and with little show of emotion, Sullius Maximus had risen to his feet. A man behind him helped him adjust his cloak, so that it fell from its golden clasp, as he wished. Another man behind him held his helmet.

Sullius Maximus stopped before the table of the scribe, and regarded the council.

"I shall write a poem," he said, "lamenting the downfall of Ubars." Then he smiled, and turned and left.

He, I told myself, would be the most dangerous of the Ubars.

I resheathed my blade.

"Bejar," called the scribe.

"Bejar accepts the proposals of Samos," said a captain, a dark-skinned man with long, straight hair, who sat in the second row, some two chairs below me and to the right.

"Bosk," called the scribe.

"Bosk," I said, "abstains."

Samos, and many of the others, looked at me, quickly.

"Abstention," recorded the scribe.

I saw no reason, at the moment, to commit myself to the programs of Samos and the council. It seemed clear to me that his proposals would be accepted. Moreover, I regarded them as presumably in my best interest. But, by abstaining, my intentions and allegiances might perhaps remain usefully ambiguous. The abstention, it seemed to me, might well give me a wider eventual latitude of action. Besides, I told myself, it was still rather early to determine on which curule chairs the tarns of power might alight.

As I thought it would, the group of proposals set before the council by Samos passed overwhelmingly. There were some abstentions, and some nays, perhaps from those who feared the power of one or another of the Ubars, but the decision on the whole was clear, a devastating of the claims of the Ubars and the, in effect, enthronement of the council of captains as the sovereign of the city.

The council met late that night, and much business was conducted. Even before dawn walls were being raised about the holdings of Henrius Sevarius, and his wharves were being blockaded with ships of the arsenal, while large watches were being maintained on the holdings of the other four Ubars. Several committees were formed, usually headed by scribes but reporting to the council, to undertake various studies pertaining to the city, particularly of a military and commercial nature. One of these studies was to be a census of ships and captains, the results of which were to be private to the council. Other studies, the results of which would be kept similarly private to the council, dealt with the city defenses, and her stores of wood, grain, salt, stone and tharlarion oil. Also considered, though nothing was determined that night, were matters of taxation, the unification and revision of the codes of the five Ubars, the establishment of council courts, replacing those of the Ubars, and the acquisition of a sizable number of men-at-arms, who would be directly responsible to the council itself, in effect, a small council police or army. Such a body of men, it might be noted, though restricted in numbers and limited in jurisdiction, already existed in the arsenal. The arsenal guard, presumably, would become a branch of the newly formed council guard, if such became a reality. It is true, of course, that the council already controlled a large number of ships and crews, but it must be remembered that these forces were naval in nature; the council already had its navy; the events of the afternoon had demonstrated that it would be well if it had also at its disposal a small, permanent, dependable, rapidly deployable infantry. One might not always be able to count on the rallying of the men of individual captains to protect the council, as had been the case this afternoon. Besides, if the council were to become truly sovereign in Port Kar, as it had proclaimed itself, it seemed essential that it should soon have its own military forces within the city.

One other incident of that council meeting I shall mention.

It was shortly past daybreak, and the gray light of Port Kar's dawn was filtering in through the high, narrow windows of the council of captains. I had taken the note which I had received the preceding afternoon from my wallet, that which had purported to be from Samos, which he had denied sending. Bemused, I had burned it in the tiny flame of the candle on the table near me, now little more than a twig of wick in a puddle of clear, melted wax, and then I had, with the palm of my hand, snuffed out the tiny flame. It was day.

"I suspect," Samos was saying, "that Cos and Tyros are implicated in the attempted coup of the House of Sevarius."

I myself would not have been surprised if this had been true.

His words received grunts of affirmation from the assembled captains. It seemed they, too, had their suspicions. Surely it did not seem likely that Sevarius would have moved if he had not been assured, at some point, of the support of the power of Cos and Tyros.

"Myself," Samos went on, "I am weary of war with Cos and Tyros."

The captains looked at one another.

"Now that the council is sovereign in Port Kar," Samos said, his fist clenched on the arm of his curule chair, "might not peace be possible?"

This puzzled me.

I saw one or two of the captains raise their heads from the arms of their curule chairs.

One captain, leaning back in his curule chair, said, "There has always been war between Port Kar, and Cos and Tyros."

I did not expect these remarks from Samos. I was curious to know his motivation, his plan.

"As you know," said Samos, speaking evenly, "Port Kar is not the most loved, nor the most greatly respected nor highest honored among the cities of Gor."

There was rough laughter at this.

"Have we not been misunderstood?" he asked.

There was an unpleasant undercurrent of amusement which greeted his question. I myself smiled. Port Kar, I told myself, was only too well understood by the other cities of Gor.

"Consider our trade," said Samos. "Would it not be trebled if we were accounted, among Gorean cities, a city of love, of peace?"

There was a guffaw of laughter at this, and men pounded the arms of the curule chairs. There were none now in that room who were not awake. I saw even the pages and scribes laughed, poking one another.

When there was silence, it was suddenly, unexpectedly, broken by the voice of Dejai, the dark-skinned captain with the long, straight hair. He said simply, answering the question of Samos, "It would."

Then the room was very silent. And I think there were none then in that room who did not hold his breath for that moment, to hear the words of Samos.

"It is my proposal," said Samos, "that the council approach Cos and Tyros, offering terms of peace."

"No!" came the cry from the assembled captains. "No!"

When the tumult had subsided, Samos spoke, softly. "Of course," said Samos, "our terms will be rejected."

The captains looked at one another in puzzlement, and then they began to smile, and then several laughed.

I smiled to myself. Samos was indeed a shrewd man. The facade of magnanimity would indeed be a valuable possession for a maritime Ubarate. Further, men might be willing to believe Port Kar now other than she had been, that the coming to power of the council would have reformed her. And what better gesture than this

mission of peace to the hereditary enemies Cos and Tyros?
If the burden of maintaining the conflict were clearly on
them, it was possible that allies of theirs might be in-
fluenced to diminish or, perhaps, withdraw their support,
or, perhaps pledge it even to Port Kar. And there were
undeclared ports and cities to consider. Surely these might
then be dissuaded from becoming allies of Cos and Tyros, and perhaps might be inclined to offer their services
to Port Kar? At the very least, the ships of Port Kar
might, in such a situation, become suddenly welcome in
ports that had hitherto been closed to them. And who
knew what trading ships might make their way to Port
Kar, if they thought her a fair and honest city? The estimate of Samos, that such a gesture on Port Kar's part
might eventually result in a trebling of her trade, seemed
to me possibly conservative.

"What if the offer of peace is accepted?" I asked
Samos.

The captains looked at me, dumbfounded. Some
laughed. But most looked then to Samos.

"I do not think it likely," said Samos, smiling.

Several of the captains then laughed.

"But," I asked, "if it is?"

Samos scowled, and then his clear gray eyes met mine,
but without emotion. I could not read his heart. Then
he smiled, and spread his hands. "Then," said he, "it is
accepted."

"And," I asked, "do we abide by their acceptance?
Would there then be truly peace between Port Kar, and
Cos and Tyros?"

"That," smiled Samos, "may always be taken under
consideration at a future meeting of the council."

There was rough laughter at this.

"The time is opportune," said Samos, "to offer peace
to Cos and Tyros. For one thing, the Council has newly
come to power. For another, I have learned from spies
that this very week the Ubar of Tyros visits Cos."

The captains muttered angrily. It did not bode well
for Port Kar that the Ubar of Tyros should voyage to
Cos. More than ever it now seemed possible, or probable,
that the two island Ubarates might well be conspiring
against Port Kar. Why else should there be a meeting of
the two Ubars? Generally, there was almost as little

love lost between them as between them and the Ubars of Port Kar.

"Then," said one of the captains, "they must intend to bring their fleets against us."

"Perhaps," said Samos, "members of a mission of peace might learn such matters."

There was a grunt of agreement from the captains.

"What of your spies," I asked, "who seem so well informed? Surely, if they can learn the itineraries of the Ubar of Tyros, it must be difficult to conceal from them a gathering of the fleets of two such powers as Cos and Tyros?"

The hand of Samos went instinctively to the hilt of his weapon, but then he closed his hand and slowly placed the fist on the arm of his curule chair. "You speak quickly," he said, "for one who is new to the Council of Captains."

"More quickly than you choose to answer, it seems, Noble Samos," said I.

I wondered what the interests of Samos in Cos and Tyros might be.

Samos spoke slowly. I saw that he did not care to speak. "The fleets of Cos and Tyros," he said, "have not yet gathered."

I drew a deep breath. Several in the council chamber gasped.

"No," said Samos, shaking his head, "they have not yet gathered."

If he had known this, I asked myself, why had he not spoken before?

"Perhaps," I asked, "Samos will propose that we now withdraw our patrols from Thassa?"

Samos looked at me, and the look was as cold and hard as Gorean steel.

"No," he said, "I would not propose that."

"Excellent," I said.

The captains looked at one another.

"Let there be peace in the council," said the scribe behind the great table, that before the now-empty five thrones of the Ubars of Port Kar.

"I have less interest in piracy, I gather, than many of my colleagues," I said. "Since my interests are substantially in commerce I, for one, would welcome peace with Cos and Tyros. It seems not unlikely to me that these two

powers may well be weary of war, as Samos informs us
he is. If that is true, it seems they may well accept an
honorable peace. Such a peace would, I note, open the
ports of Tyros and Cos, and their allies and others, to my
ships, and, of course, to yours. Peace, my captains, might
well prove profitable." I regarded Samos. "If an offer
of peace is to be made to Cos and Tyros," I said, "it is
my hope that it would be genuine."

Samos looked at me strangely. "It would be genuine,"
he said.

The captains murmured among themselves. I myself
was taken aback.

"Bosk," said Samos to the group, "speaks well the ad-
vantages of peace. Let us consider his words with care,
and favorably. I think there are few of us here who are
not more fond of gold than blood."

There was some laughter at this.

"If peace was made," challenged Samos, "which of
you would not keep it?"

He looked from man to man. To my surprise none
denied that he would keep the peace, were it made.

It then seemed to me, so simply, that there was for
the first time the possibility of peace on Thassa, among
her three major Ubarates.

Somehow, suddenly, I believed Samos.

I was astonished but it was my sensing of the group
that, if peace were made, Port Kar would keep it.

There had been war for so long.

None laughed.

I sat numb in the great curule chair, that of a captain
of Port Kar.

I regarded Samos, wondering of him. He was a strange
man, that larl of a man. I could not read him.

"Of course," said Samos, "the offer of peace will be
rejected."

The captains looked at one another, and grinned. I
realized I was again in Port Kar.

"We will need one to carry the offer of peace to Cos,
where he may now find joint audience with the Ubars
of both Cos and Tyros," said Samos.

I was scarcely listening now.

"It should be one," Samos was saying, "who has the
rank of captain, and who is a member of the council it-

self, that the authenticity of the offer shall thus be made manifest."

I found myself in agreement with this.

"Further," said Samos, "it should be one who has proved that he can take action, and who has in the past well served the council."

I scratched with my fingernail in the wax, breaking up the bits of charred paper that had been the note I had burned in the candle flame. The wax was now yellow and hard. It was something past daybreak now, and I was tired. The gray light now filled the room.

"And," Samos was saying, "it must be one who is not afraid to speak, one who is a worthy representative of the council."

I wondered if Samos himself might be tired. It seemed to me he was saying very little now.

"And," Samos went on, "it should preferably be one who is not well known to Cos and Tyros, one who has not angered them, nor proven himself to them a blood enemy upon gleaming Thassa."

Suddenly I seemed awake, quite, and apprehensive. And then I smiled. Samos was no fool. He was senior captain of the Council of Captains. He had marked me, and would be done with me.

"And such a one," said Samos, "is Bosk—he who came from the marshes. Let it be he who carries peace on behalf of the council to Cos and Tyros. Let it be Bosk!"

There was silence.

I was pleased at the silence. I had not realized until then that I was valued in the council of captains.

Antisthenes spoke, who had been first on the roll of captains. "I do not think it should be a captain," he said. "To send a captain is equivalent to sentencing him to the bench of a slave on the round ships of Cos or Tyros."

There was some muttered assent to this.

"Further," said Antisthenes, "I would recommend that we do not even send one who wears the twin ropes of Port Kar. There are merchants of other cities, voyagers and captains, known to us, who will, for their fees, gladly conduct this business."

"Let it be so," said various voices throughout the chamber of the council.

Then all looked at me.

I smiled. "I am, of course, highly honored," I began, "that Noble Samos should think of me, that he should nominate me, doubtless the lowliest of the captains here assembled, for a post of such distinction, that of bearing the peace of Port Kar to her hereditary enemies Cos and Tyros."

The captains looked at one another, grinning.

"Then you decline?" asked Samos.

"It only seems to me," said I, "that so signal an honor, and a role so weighty, ought to be reserved for one more august than I, indeed, for he who is most prominent among us, one who could truly negotiate on equal footing with the Ubars of powers so mighty as those of Cos and Tyros."

"Do you have a nomination?" asked the scribe at the center table.

"Samos," I said.

There was laughter among the chairs.

"I am grateful for your nomination," said Samos, "but I scarcely think, in these troubled times, it behooves he who is senior captain of the council to leave the city, voyaging abroad in search of peace when war itself looms at home."

"He is right," said Bejar.

"Then you decline?" I asked Samos.

"Yes," said Samos, "I decline."

"Let us not send a captain," said Antisthenes. "Let us send one who is from Ar or Thentis, who can speak for us."

"Antisthenes is wise," I said, "and understands the risks involved, but many of the words Samos has addressed to us seem to me sound and true, and chief among them his assertion that it should be a captain who conducts this mission, for how else could we so easily prove the seriousness of our intentions, if not to Cos and Tyros, then to their allies and to undeclared ports and cities on the islands and coasts of gleaming Thassa, and to those communities inland as well, with whom we might well improve our trade?"

"But," said Bejar, "who among us will go?"

There was laughter in the council.

When it was silent, I said, "I, Bosk, might go."

The captains regarded one another.

"Did you not decline?" asked Samos.

"No," I smiled, "I only suggested that one more worthy than myself undertake so weighty a task."

"Do not go," said Antisthenes.

"What is your price?" asked Samos.

"A galley," I said, "a ram-ship, heavy class."

I had no such ship.

"It will be yours," said Samos.

"—if you can return to claim it," muttered a captain, darkly.

"Do not go," said Antisthenes.

"He will have, of course," said Samos, "the immunity of the herald."

The captains said nothing.

I smiled.

"Do not go, Bosk, Captain," said Antisthenes.

I already had a plan. Had I not had one, I should not have volunteered. The possibility of peace on Thassa was an attractive one to me, a merchant. If Cos and Tyros could be convinced to make peace, and it could be held, my fortunes would considerably increase. Cos and Tyros themselves are important markets, not to mention their allies, and the ports and cities either affiliated with Cos and Tyros, or favorable to them. Further, even if my mission failed, I would be richer by a galley, and that a ram-ship of heavy class, the most redoubtable naval weapon on gleaming Thassa. There were risks, of course, but I had taken them into account. I would not go as a fool to Cos and Tyros.

"And," I said, "as escort, I will require five ram-ships from the arsenal, of medium or heavy class, to be captained and crewed by men selected by myself."

"Which ships," asked Samos, "are returned to the arsenal upon the completion of your mission?"

"Of course," I said.

"You shall have them," said Samos.

We looked at one another. I asked myself if Samos thought he was so easily rid of me, one who might challenge him, senior captain, in the council of the captains of Port Kar. Yes, I said to myself, he thinks he is so easily rid of me. I smiled to myself. I myself did not believe he was.

"Do not go, Bosk, Captain," pleaded Antisthenes.

I rose to my feet. "Antisthenes, Captain," I said, "I am grateful for your concern." I shook my head, and stretched. And then I turned to the captains on the tiers. "You may continue your business now without me," I said. "I am going to return to my holding. The night has been long, and I have lost much sleep."

I gathered up my cloak, and my helmet, it with the captain's crest of sleen hair, and left the chamber.

Outside I was joined by Thurnock and Clitus, and many of my men.

I Fish in the Canal

It was late at night, two nights after the unsuccessful coup of Henrius Sevarius.

I was waiting for my ships, and those of the arsenal, to be made ready for my trip, my mission of peace, to Cos and Tyros.

In my role as captain I was often about the city, accompanied by Thurnock, and Clitus, and a squad of my men.

Until the formation of the council guard, the captains and their men would have for their responsibility the maintaining of watches throughout the city.

Even before the emergency session of the council, the night of the unsuccessful coup, had concluded, slaves, instructed by men of the arsenal, were raising walls about the various holdings of Henrius Sevarius. His wharves, moreover, were, with arsenal ships, almost immediately blockaded by sea.

Now, from the height of one of the investing walls, some hundred yards from the high bleak wall of one of the holdings of Sevarius, said to be his palace, I, with Thurnock, Clitus, and others, by the light of Gor's three moons, observed the opening of a postern gate. At the base of the wall, extending for some twenty yards, there was a tiled expanse, which suddenly dropped off, sheer, into a canal, itself some ninety feet wide; we had closed off the canal, where it might give access to the city or sea, by sea gates. We observed, in the light of the three Gorean moons, some five men emerging from the tiny iron gate. They were carrying something in a large, tied sack.

Slowly they made their way toward the edge of the canal.

"Stop, men of Henrius Sevarius!" I shouted. "Stop, Traitors!"

"Hurry!" cried one of them. I recognized his voice, and his frame. It was Lysias, friend of the regent Claudius, client of the Ubar Henrius Sevarius. I saw another man

169

look up in alarm. It was Henrak, he who had betrayed the rencers.

"Hurry!" I said to my men.

I, followed by Clitus and Thurnock, and others, leaped over the wall and ran toward the edge of the canal.

The men were now hastening forward, to hurl the sack into the dark waters.

Thurnock stopped long enough to draw his great bow. One of the men, hit by the arrow, spun away, rolling across the tiles, snapping the shaft.

The others, now at the edge of the canal, with a heave, flung the sack far out into the water.

A crossbow bolt slipped through the air, passing between myself and Clitus.

The four men now turned and began to run back toward the postern gate.

Before they could reach the gate Thurnock's great bow had struck twice more.

Lysias and Henrak, and no other, fled back through the gate.

One of the bodies Thurnock had struck lay dark, sprawled on the tiles, some fifteen yards from the gate; the other lay, inert and twisted in the shadows, at the very portal itself.

"Knife!" I said.

I was handed a knife.

"Do not, Captain!" cried Thurnock.

Already I could see the sleek, wet muzzles of urts, eyes like ovals of blazing copper, streaking through the dark waters toward the bag.

I leaped into the cold waters, the knife between my teeth.

The sack, filling with water, began to sink, and, as I reached it, it had slipped beneath the water. I cut it open and seized the bound arm of the body inside it.

I heard an arrow flash into the water near me and heard a high-pitched pain squeal from one of the web-footed canal urts. Then there was the sound of biting and tearing and thrashing in the water, as other urts attacked the injured one.

Knife again between my teeth, pulling the bound thing from the sack, I shoved its head above the water. It was gagged as well as bound, and I saw its eyes wild, inches over the murky waters of the canal. It was a boy, perhaps sixteen or seventeen years old.

I brought it to the edge of the canal and one of my men, lying on his stomach, extending his hand downward, caught him under the arm.

Then I saw Clitus' net flash over my head and heard the confused protesting squeal of another urt, and then Clitus, again and again, was thrusting into the dark waters with his trident.

I felt my leg then caught in the jaws of an urt, like triple bands of steel, set with needles, and was dragged beneath the surface. I thrust my thumbs in its ears and tore its head back from my leg. The mouth kept reaching for me, head turned to the side, trying for the throat. I let it free and as it snapped at me I knocked its jaws up and slipped behind it, my left arm locked about its broad, furred throat. I got the knife from between my teeth and, with it, sometimes half out of the water, sometimes beneath it, thrashing and twisting, thrust the blade a dozen times into its hide.

"It's dead!" cried Clitus.

I released it, kicking it back away from me.

It disappeared beneath the water, dragged under by other urts.

I felt the folded sweep of Clitus' net behind me and I thrust back my hand, and hooked my fingers into its mesh. Bleeding and choking, shivering with cold, I was drawn from the water. In moments, trembling, half supported by two men-at-arms, I was conducted back to the investing wall. There, in the heat of a watch fire, I stripped away my clothes and took a cloak from Thurnock. Someone gave me a swallow of paga from a leather bota.

Suddenly I laughed.

"Why do you laugh!" asked one of the men-at-arms.

"I am pleased to find myself alive," I said.

The men laughed. Thurnock clapped me on the shoulders. "So, too, are we, my captain," said Thurnock.

"What of your leg?" asked one of the men-at-arms.

"It is all right," I told him.

I took another swig of paga.

I had found that I could stand on the leg. It had been lacerated but none of the long, rough-edged wounds was deep. I would have it soon treated by a physician in my own holding.

"Where is our fish from the canal?" I asked.

"Follow me," said one of the men-at-arms, grinning.

I, and the others, followed him to another of the watch fires, one some fifty yards from the one at which I had warmed myself.

There, huddled against the inside of the investing wall, naked, wrapped in a warrior's cloak, near the watch fire, sat the boy. He had been ungagged, and unbound. He looked up at us. He had blond hair, and blue eyes. He was frightened.

"Who are you?" asked Thurnock.

The boy looked down, frightened.

"What is your name?" asked Clitus.

The boy did not respond.

"He should be beaten with a bow," said Thurnock.

The boy looked up, proudly, angrily.

"Hah!" said Thurnock.

The boy regarded me. "Are these men yours?" he asked.

"Yes," I said.

"Who are you?" he asked.

"Bosk," I told him.

"Of the Council of Captains?" he asked.

"Yes," I answered.

I thought I saw fear for a moment flicker in his blue eyes.

"Who are you?" I asked.

He looked down. "Only a slave," he said.

"Show me your hands," I said.

Reluctantly he did so. They were smooth.

"Is he branded?" I asked one of the men-at-arms who had been with the boy.

"No," said the man-at-arms.

"What is your name?" I asked.

He looked down again.

"Since we brought you from the canal," I said, "we will call you Fish." And I added, "And since you are a slave, you will be marked and collared, and taken to my holding."

He looked at me, angrily.

I gestured for one of the men-at-arms to take him up and carry him away, which he did.

I then dismissed the men who stood near me, except Thurnock and Clitus.

That boy, I thought, may well prove useful to me. If he

fell into the hands of the council he would doubtless be tortured and impaled, or, perhaps, condemned to a seat on the rowing benches of the arsenal round ships. In my holding, his identity could be kept secret. In time, I might find a use for him. There was surely little to be gained in turning him over to the council.

"Who is he?" asked Thurnock, looking after the boy, wrapped in the warrior's cloak, who was being carried away into the darkness.

"He is, of course," said I, "Henrius Sevarius."

How Bosk

Came To Be Pirate

"Paint my ships green," I had said.

It was now within the Fifth Passage Hand, some four months after the unsuccessful coup of Henrius Sevarius in the city of Port Kar.

By this time, the Fifth Passage Hand, the flag of Bosk, pirate, had come to be much feared on Thassa.

How this came about I shall now relate.

Some four months ago I, in my swiftest ram-ship, accompanied by my two other ram-ships, and escorted, as well, by five ram-ships of the arsenal, heavy class, had come to the vast, wall-encircled harbors of Telnus, which is the capitol city of the Ubarate of Cos. There are four major cities on Cos, of which Telnus is the largest. The others are Selnar, Temos and Jad.

I took a longboat ashore, and sent the boat back to my galley.

I would go before the thrones of the Ubars of Cos and Tyros alone.

This was my wish, and a part of my plan.

I recalled standing before the thrones, in the towering throne room of Cos.

I put to them, the Ubars of Cos and Tyros, as well as I could, the proposals of the Council of Captains of Port Kar, that there would be concord, and doubtless an opening of commerce, between the two Ubarates and the maligned city in the Vosk's delta, my own Port Kar.

As I spoke, the Ubar of Cos, Lurius of Jad, and the Ubar of Tyros, Chenbar of Kasra, the Sea Sleen, who was visiting Lurius on matters of state, sat unspeaking upon their thrones. They asked no questions. They merely regarded me. Kasra is the capitol of Tyros; its only other major city is Tentium.

To one side, in a silken veil, richly robed and jeweled,

sat Vivina, the ward of Chenbar. It was not a coincidence that she was now in Cos. She had been brought to Cos that Lurius might look upon her and, should he find her pleasing, be proclaimed as his future companion of state. It was her body that would serve to link the two island Ubarates. Her veil was diaphanous, and I could see that she was very beautiful, though she was also very young. I looked from her to the corpulent, sagging Lurius of Jad, Ubar of Cos, who, like a great bag of meat, slouched swollen between the arms of his throne. Such, I thought to myself, are the affairs of state. Chenbar of Kasra, Ubar of Tyros, on the other hand, was a lean, large-eyed man, with nervous hands. I had little doubt that he would be highly intelligent, and skilled with weapons. Tyros, I told myself, has an efficient, and dangerous Ubar.

Lurius and Chenbar listened most patiently to my discourse.

When I had finished, Chenbar, with a look to Lurius, rose to his feet and said, "Seize his ships."

"I think you will find," I said, "that my ships have already withdrawn from the harbor of Telnus."

Corpulent Lurius sprang to his feet, paunch swinging. He shook his fist at me.

"Tharlarion!" he cried. "Tharlarion of Port Kar!"

"I gather," I said, smiling, "that our terms of peace are rejected."

Lurius sputtered.

"Your surmise is correct," said Chenbar, who had now sat again upon his throne.

"I shall then take my leave," I said.

"I think not," smiled Chenbar.

"Put him in chains!" screamed Lurius.

I regarded them. "I claim," I said, "the immunity of the herald."

"It is denied!" screamed Lurius, his wide, bloated face scarlet with rage.

I extended my wrists, to the sides, and felt manacles, with leashes, snapped on them.

"You have been offered peace," I told them.

"And we have refused it!" screamed Lurius.

I heard the laughter of the girl, Vivina, who seemed amused. Several of the others in the court laughed as well.

Lurius settled himself, breathing heavily, again in his throne.

"Put him in a market chain," said Lurius, "and sell him at the slaves' wharf."

The girl laughed.

"When," snarled Lurius, "you find yourself chained in the rowing hold of a round ship, you may, my fine captain of Port Kar, bethink yourself less brave and clever than now you do."

"We shall see," said I, "Ubar."

I felt a movement on the chains, and turned to leave the presence of the two Ubars.

"Wait," I heard. It was Chenbar, who had spoken.

I turned again to face the Ubars.

The hall was high about my head. Broad tiles lay beneath my feet.

"May I present," asked Chenbar, indicating the veiled, robed girl sitting to one side, "the Lady Vivina?"

"I do not wish to be presented to a tarsk of Port Kar," hissed the girl.

"Let us not forget our manners, my dear," smiled Chenbar.

She rose to her feet, and, small gloved hand in the hand of Chenbar, descended the steps of the dais on which sat the thrones of Lurius and Chenbar, and stood before me.

"May I present, Captain," said Chenbar, "the Lady Vivina?"

She dropped her head, and then lifted it.

"I am honored," I said.

"Tharlarion," she said.

The girl turned and was escorted, again by Chenbar, her gloved hand in his, to her seat on the dais.

When she had regained her seat, I said, "Your extraordinary beauty, High Lady, which, forgive me, your veil but scarcely conceals, is indeed worthy of a Ubar of Cos—"

Lurius grinned. The girl herself permitted herself the smallest of smiles.

"Or," I added, "a collar in Port Kar."

Lurius sprang to his feet, his fists clenched. The girl, eyes flashing, scarlet beneath the white silken veil, too sprang to her feet. She pointed her finger at me. "Slay him!" she cried.

I heard two swords leave their sheaths behind me.

But Chenbar laughed. He motioned the men behind me to resheath their weapons. Lurius, furious, returned to his throne. The girl, enraged, took again her seat on the dais.

"Doubtless, stripped," I said, "you would be even more beautiful."

"Slay him!" she hissed.

"No," said Chenbar, smiling.

"I meant only," I said, "that your beauty reminded me of that of girls, serving slaves, nude and double chained in the paga taverns of Port Kar. Many of them are very beautiful."

"Slay him! Slay him!" she begged.

"No, no," smiled Chenbar.

"Do not speak of me as though I were a slave girl," said the girl.

"Are you not?" I asked.

"The impudence!" she screamed.

I nodded my head toward Lurius, swollen in the chair of the Ubar of Cos.

"I own women," I said, "who are more free than you."

"Tharlarion!" she cried. "I will be Ubara!"

"I wish you happiness, High Lady," I said, dropping my head.

She could not speak, so furious was she.

"Here," I said, "you will be Ubara. In my house you would be Kettle Slave."

"Slay him!" she screamed.

"Be silent," said Chenbar.

The girl was silent.

"The Lady Vivina, as you doubtless know, is promised to Lurius, Ubar of Cos," said Chenbar.

"I did not know," I said, "that the promise had been given."

"Yes," said Chenbar, "this morning I gave my word."

Lurius grinned.

The girl looked at me with fury.

There was some polite striking of the left shoulder with the right hand in the room, which is a common Gorean applause, though not of the warriors, who clash weapons.

Chenbar smiled and lifted his hand, silencing the applause.

"This companionship," said Chenbar, "will link our two

Ubarates. Following the ceremony of the companionship there will be a conjoining of our fleets, that we may soon thereafter pay Port Kar a visit of state."

"I see," I said.

"Even now our fleets are being outfitted," said Chenbar.

"When will the gathering take place?" I asked.

"In the neighborhood of the sixth passage hand," he said.

"You are free with your information," I said.

"Well," said Chenbar, "we are all friends here."

"Or slaves," said the girl, looking pointedly at me.

"Or slaves," I said, looking at her very directly.

Her eyes flashed over her veil.

"You have had dealings," I asked, "with the Ubar Henrius Sevarius in Port Kar?"

Chenbar smiled. "We have dealt with his regent, Claudius," said Chenbar.

"What of Henrius Sevarius himself?" I asked.

"He is only a boy," said Chenbar.

"But what of him?" I asked.

"He is a boy," said Chenbar. "He has no power."

"Whom do his men follow?" I asked.

"Claudius," said Chenbar.

"I see," I said.

"Mark well the name of Claudius, Captain," said Chenbar, "for he is to become Ubar of Port Kar."

"As the agent of Cos and Tyros," I said.

"Assuredly," laughed Chenbar.

"As you may not know," I said, "Claudius and the various forces of Henrius Sevarius are scarcely in command of Port Kar."

"Our information is better than you seem to understand," smiled Chenbar. "Be assured," said he, "that we will free Claudius from his current predicaments."

"You seem," I said, "to be well aware of what transpires in Port Kar."

"Yes," said Chenbar. "Perhaps you would care to meet our principal courier, he who will, in time, lead our fleets to the harbor of Port Kar?"

"Yes," I said, "I would."

A man stepped from among a group of robed dignitaries, standing to one side of the Ubars' thrones. He had previously been standing in the shadows.

He had long black hair, tied behind his neck with a scarlet string.

He carried, in the crook of his left arm, a helmet, bearing that crest of sleen hair that marks a captain of Port Kar. The helmet, too, bore two golden slashes. A long cloak swirled behind him.

I had expected it to be Samos.

"I am Lysias," he said. "Bosk, you remember me."

I smiled to myself. He, with a handful of men, had managed to escape from the holding of Henrius Sevarius. It had occurred the night following my rescue of the boy from the canal. The guard had since been increased. I did not think more would escape.

"Yes," I said, "I remember you perhaps better than you know."

"What do you mean?" he asked.

"Are you not the one who, in the delta of the Vosk, was overcome by vast numbers of rencers, and forced to abandon your barges, and a treasure of rence paper and slaves?"

"This man is dangerous," said Lysias to Chenbar. "I recommend that he be slain."

"No, no," said Chenbar. "We will sell him and make a profit on him."

The girl, Lady Vivina, threw back her head and laughed merrily.

"He is dangerous," said Lysias.

Chenbar looked at me. "The money that we obtain from your sale," he said, "will be applied to the outfitting of our fleets. It will not be a great deal, but that way you can feel that you have not been left out, that you have done your small bit to augment the glories of Cos and Tyros."

I said nothing.

"I trust, too," said Chenbar, "that you will not be the last of the captains of Port Kar to pull an oar on the round ships of Cos or Tyros."

"Apparently I have business to attend to," I said. "If I may, I request your permission to withdraw."

"One thing more," said Chenbar.

"What is that?" I asked.

"Have you not forgotten," he asked, "to bid the Lady Vivina farewell?"

I looked at Chenbar.

"Doubtless," said he, "you will not see her again."

I turned to face her.

"I do not frequent the rowing holds of round ships," she said.

There was laughter in the room.

"Have you ever been in the hold of a round ship?" I asked.

"Of course not," she said.

High born ladies commonly sailed in cabins, located in the stern castle of the galleys.

"Perhaps someday," I said, "you shall have the opportunity."

"What do you mean by that?" she asked.

"It is a joke," said Chenbar.

"When," I asked, "High Lady, will you drink the wine of the Free Companionship with Lurius, noble Ubar of Cos?"

"I shall return first to Tyros," she said, "where I shall be made ready. Then, with treasure ships, we shall return in festive voyage to the harbor of Telnus, where I shall take the arm of Lurius and with him drink the cup of the Free Companionship."

"May I wish you, Lady," said I, "a safe and pleasant voyage, and much future happiness."

She nodded her head, and smiled.

"You spoke of treasure ships," I said.

"Of course," said she.

"It seems then," said I, "that your body alone is not enough for noble Lurius."

"Tarsk!" she said.

Chenbar laughed.

"Take him away," cried Lurius, leaning forward in the throne, fists clenched upon its arms.

I felt the chains at my wrists.

"Farewell, Lady," said I.

"Farewell," said she, "Slave."

I was spun about and dragged stumbling from the high throne room of Cos.

When, early the next morning, chained and under guard, I was taken from the palace of Lurius of Jad, Ubar of Cos, the streets were mostly deserted. It had rained the night before and, here and there, there were puddles among the stones of the street. The shops were shuttered with wood, and the wood was still stained dark from the night's rain. There were few lights in the windows. I recall seeing, crouched against the wall of a building near the postern gate of the palace of Lurius, a coarse-robed figure, foolishly come too early to sell his vegetables, suls and tur-pah, near the palace. He seemed asleep, and doubtless scarcely noticed us. He was a large man in the rough rain robes of the peasant. Near him, leaning against the wall behind him, wrapped in leather to protect it from the dampness, was a yellow bow, the long bow of the peasants. He had shaggy yellow hair. I smiled as I passed him.

On the slaves' wharf I was, with little ceremony, added to the market chain.

By the eighth hour various captains of round ships had arrived and begun to haggle with the slave master over the prices of the oarsmen. The slave master, in my opinion, wanted far too much for his merchandise, considering we were merely fodder for the benches of the round ships. Having no particular interest in being struck to silence I refrained from pointing this out to him. Besides, he doubtless had his instructions to receive as much pay as possible. Apparently Cos was outfitting her fleets and her treasury was currently strained. Every copper tarn disk, I told myself, in such a situation doubtless assumes greater importance than it normally would. I was a bit irritated at being slapped and punched, and told to exhibit my teeth, but, in all honesty, these indignities were no worse than those heaped upon my chain mates. Besides, I was not, considering that I was about to be sold to the galleys, in a particularly bad mood.

To one side, leaning against a heavy, roped post, supporting part of the structure of the slaves' wharf, cross-legged, there sat a fisherman. He was working carefully on a net spread across his knees, repairing it. Near him there lay a trident. He had long black hair, and gray eyes.

"Let me test your grip," said one of the captains. "I use only strong men on my ships."

He extended his hand.

In an instant he was screaming for mercy.

"Stop, Slave!" cried the slave master, striking me with the butt of his whip.

I released the man's hand, not having chosen to break it.

He stood unsteadily, half crouching over, looking at me with disbelief, his hand thrust into his left armpit.

"Forgive me, Master," said I, with concern.

Unsteadily he went elsewhere, to examine others farther along the market chain.

"Do that again," said the slave master, "and I will cut your throat."

"I doubt," said I, "that Chenbar and Lurius would much approve of that."

"Perhaps not," said the slave master, grinning.

"What do you want for that slave?" asked a captain, a tall man with a small, carefully trimmed beard.

"Fifty copper tarn disks," said the slave master.

"It is too much," said the captain.

I agreed, but it did not seem up to me to enter into the question.

"That is the price," said the slave master.

"Very well," said the captain, gesturing to a scribe near him, with a wallet of coins slung over his shoulder, to pay the slave master.

"May I ask," I asked, "the name of my master and his ship?"

"I am Tenrik," said he, "Tenrik of Temos. Your ship will be the Rena of Temos."

"And when do we sail?" I asked.

He laughed. "Slave," he said, "you ask questions like a passenger."

I smiled.

"With the evening's tide," he said.

I bowed my head. "Thank you, Master," said I.

Tenrik, followed by the scribe, turned and left. I noted that now the fisherman had finished with his net and that he, too, was preparing to depart. He folded the net carefully and dropped it over his left shoulder. He then picked up his trident in his right hand and, not looking back, took his way from the slaves' wharf.

The slave master was again counting the fifty copper tarn disks.

I shook my head. "Too much," I told him.

He shrugged and grinned. "Whatever the market will bear," he said.

"Yes," I said, "I guess you are right."

I was not displeased when I was conducted to the Rena of Temos. She was indeed a round ship. I noted with satisfaction the width of her beam and the depth of her keel. Such a ship would be slow.

I did not much care for the crusts, and the onions and peas, on which we fed, but I did not expect to be eating them long.

"You will not find this an easy ship to row," said the oar-master, chaining my ankles to the heavy footbrace.

"The lot of a slave is miserable," I told him.

"Further," he laughed, "you will not find me an easy master."

"The lot of a slave is indeed miserable," I lamented.

He turned the key in the locks and, laughing, turned about and went to his seat, facing us, in the stern of the rowing hold.

Before him, since this was a large ship, there sat a keleustes, a strong man, a time-beater, with leather-wrapped wrists. He would mark the rowing stroke with blows of wooden, leather-cushioned mallets on the head of a huge copper-covered drum.

"Out oars!" called the oar-master.

I, with the others, slid my oar outboard.

Above us, on the upper deck, I could hear the cries of the seamen, casting off mooring lines, shoving away from the dock with the traditional three long poles. The sails would not be dropped from the yards until the ship was clear of the harbor.

I heard the creak of the great side-rudders and felt the heavy, sweet, living movement of the caulked timbers of the ship.

We were now free of the land.

The eyes of the ship, painted on either side of the bow, would now have turned toward the opening of the harbor of Telnus. Ships of Gor, of whatever class or type, always have eyes painted on them, either in a head surmounting the prow, as in tarn ships, or, as in the Rena, as in round ships, on either side of the bow. It is the last thing that is done for the ship before it is first launched. The painting of the eyes reflects the Gorean seaman's belief that the ship is a living thing. She is accordingly given eyes, that she may see her way.

"Ready oars!" called the oar-master.

The oars were poised.

"Stroke!" called the oar-master.

The keleustes struck the great copper drum before him with the leather-cushioned mallet.

As one the oars entered the water, dipping and moving within it. My feet thrust against the footbrace and I drew on the oar.

Slowly the ship, like a sweet, fat bird, heavy and stately, began to move toward the opening between the two high, round towers that guard the entrance to the walled harbor of Telnus, capitol city of the island of Cos, seat of its Ubar's throne.

We had now been two days at sea.

I and the others, from our pans, were eating one of our four daily rations of bread, onions and peas. We were passing a water skin about among us.

The oars were inboard.

We had not rowed as much as normally we would have. We had had a fair wind for two days, which had slacked off yesterday evening.

The Rena of Temos, like most round ships, had two permanent masts, unlike the removable masts of the war galleys. The main mast was a bit forward of amidships, and the foremast was some four or five yards abaft of the ship's yoke. Both were lateen rigged, the yard of the foresail being about half the length of the yard of the mainsail. We had made good time for a heavy ship, but then the wind had slacked.

We had rowed for several Ahn this morning.

It was now something better than an Ahn past noon.

"I understand," said the oar-master, confronting me, "that you were a Captain in Port Kar."

"I am a captain," I said.

"But in Port Kar," he said.

"Yes," I said, "I am a Captain in Port Kar."

"But this is not Port Kar," he said.

I looked at him. "Port Kar," I said, "is wherever her power is."

He looked at me.

"I note," I said, "the wind has slackened."

His face turned white.

"Yes," I said.

At that moment, from far above, from the basket on the main mast, came the cry of the lookout, "Two ships off the port beam!"

"Out and ready oars!" cried the oar-master, running to his chair.

I put down my pan of bread, onions and peas, sliding it under the bench. I might want it later.

I slid the oar out of the thole port and readied it.

Above on the deck I could hear running feet, men shouting.

I heard the voice of the Captain, Tenrik, crying to his helmsmen, "Hard to starboard!"

The big ship began to swing to starboard.

But then another cry, wild, drifted down from the basket on the main mast, "Two more ships! Off the starboard bow!"

"Helm ahead!" cried Tenrik. "Full sail! Maximum beat!"

As soon as the Rena had swung to her original course, the oar-master cried "Stroke!" and the mallets of the keleustes began to strike, in great beats, the copper-covered drum.

Two seamen came down from the upper deck and seized whips from racks behind the oar-master.

I smiled.

Beaten or not, the oarsmen could only draw their oars so rapidly. And it would not be rapidly enough.

I heard another cry drifting down from the basket far above, "Two more ships astern!"

The heavy, leather-cushioned mallets of the keleustes struck again and again on the copper-covered drum.

I heard, about a half an Ahn later, Tenrik call up to the lookout.

The man carried a long glass of the builders.

"Can you make out their flag?" he cried.

"It is white," he cried, "with stripes of green. It bears on its field the head of a bosk!"

One of the slaves, chained before me, whispered over his shoulder. "What is your name, Captain?"

"Bosk," I told him, pulling on the oar.

"Aiii!" he cried.

"Row!" screamed the oar-master.

The seamen with whips rushed between the benches, but none, of all those there chained, slacked on the oars.

"They are gaining!" I heard a seaman cry from above.

"Faster!" someone cried from above decks.

But already the keleustes was pounding maximum beat. And doubtless that beat could not be long maintained.

About a quarter of an Ahn later I heard what I had been waiting for.

"Two more ships!" cried the lookout.

"Where?" cried Tenrik.

"Dead ahead!" cried the lookout. "Dead ahead!"

"Helm half to starboard!" cried Tenrik.

"Up oars!" cried the oar-master. "Port Oars! Stroke!"

We lifted our oars, and then those of the port side only entered the water and pressed against it. In a few strokes the heavy Rena had swung some eight points, by the Gorean compass, to starboard.

"Full oars!" cried the oar-master. "Stroke!"

"What shall we do?" whispered the slave before me.

"Row," I told him.

"Silence!" cried one of the seamen, and struck us each a stroke with the whip. Then, foolishly, they began to lash away at the sweating backs of the slaves. Two of the men lost the oars, and the free oars fouled those of other men.

The oar-master rushed between the benches and tore the whips away from the seamen, ordering them above decks.

He was a good oar-master.

The man then called out, "Up oars! Ready oars! Stroke!"

Again we found our rhythm, and again the Rena moved through the waters.

"Faster!" cried a man down into the rowing hold.

The oar-master judged his men. The beat was, even now, scarcely being made.

"Decrease the beat by five points," said the oar-master to the keleustes.

"Fool!" I heard.

And an officer rushed down the steps into the rowing hold, and struck the oar-master from his chair. "Maximum beat!" he screamed to the keleustes.

Again the rhythm was that of the maximum beat.

The officer, with a cry of rage, then turned and ran up the stairs to the main deck.

Maximum beat.

But, in less than an Ehn, one man failed to maintain it, and then two, and the oars began to foul. Relentlessly though the keleustes, under his orders, pounded the great drum.

Then the strokes of the drum were no longer coordinated with the oars. The men, many of them, could no longer maintain the beat of the keleustes, and they had no guide for a stroke they could draw.

The oar-master, his face bloody, climbed to his feet. "Up oars!" he cried. Then he spoke to the keleustes, wearily, "Ten from maximum beat."

We took up this beat, and again the Rena moved.

"Faster!" cried the officer from above. "Faster!"

"This is not a tarn ship!" cried the oar-master.

"You will die!" screamed the officer down into the hold. "You will die!"

As the keleustes kept his beat, the oar-master, trembling, mouth bloody, walked between the benches. He came toward me. He looked at me.

"I am in command here," I told him.

"I know," he said.

At that moment the officer again came down the steps, entering the rowing hold. His eyes were wild. He had a drawn sword in his hand.

"Which of these," he asked, "is the captain from Port Kar?"

"I am," I told him.

"You are the one they call Bosk?" he asked.

"I am he," I said.

"I am going to kill you," he said.

"I would not, if I were you," I said.

His hand hesitated.

"Should anything happen to me," I said, "I do not think my men would be much pleased."

His hand fell.

"Unchain me," I told him.

"Where is the key?" he asked the oar-master.

When I was unchained, I stepped from the oar. The rest of the men were startled, but they maintained the beat.

"Those of you who are with me," I said, "I will free."

There was a cheer from the slaves.

"I am in command here," I said. "You will do as I say."

There was another cheer.

I held out my hand and the officer placed his sword in it, hilt first.

I motioned that he might now take my oar.

In fury, he did so.

"They are going to shear!" came a cry from above board.

"Oars inboard!" cried the oar-master, instinctively.

The oars slid inboard.

"Oars outboard!" I commanded.

Obediently the oars slid outboard, and suddenly, all along the starboard side there was a great grinding, and the slaves screamed, and there was a sudden ripping of planks and a great snapping and splintering of wood, the sounds magnified, thunderous and deafening, within the wooden hold. Some of the oars were torn from the thole ports, others were snapped off or half broken, the inboard portions of their shafts, with their looms, snapping in a stemward arc, knocking slaves from the benches, cracking against the interior of the hull planking. I heard some men cry out in pain, ribs or arms broken. For an ugly moment the ship canted sharply to starboard and we shipped water through the thole ports, but then the other ship, with her shearing blade, passed, and the Rena righted herself, but rocked helplessly, lame in the water.

From my point of view the battle was now over.

I looked at the officer. "Take the key," I said, "and release the other slaves."

I heard Captain Tenrik above calling his men to arms to prepare to repel boarders.

The officer, obediently, one by one, began to release my fellow slaves.

I regarded the oar-master. "You are a good oar-master," I said. "But now there are injured men to attend to."

He turned away, to aid those who had been hurt in the shearing.

I reached under my rowing bench. There, dented, its contents half spilled, itself floating in an inch or two of sea water, not yet drained down to the cargo hold, I found my pan of bread, onions and peas.

I sat down on my bench and ate.

From time to time I glanced out of my thole port. The Rena was now hemmed in by the eight ships, and two, heavy-class galleys, from the arsenal, were drawing alongside. No missiles were being exchanged.

Then I heard Captain Tenrik, from above decks, call out not to offer resistance.

In a moment I heard someone board the Rena, and then two others, and then several more.

I put down the pan, having finished its contents. And I walked up the steps, carrying the officer's sword.

"Captain!" cried Thurnock.

Near him, grinning, were Clitus and Tab.

There were cheers from the clustered ships of Port Kar. I lifted my blade to them, acknowledging their salute.

I turned to Captain Tenrik.

"My thanks," said I, "Captain."

He nodded his head.

"You have impressed me," I said, "as being an excellent captain."

He looked at me, puzzled.

"And your crew seems skilled," I said, "and the ship is a good ship."

"What will you do with us?" he asked.

"The Rena," I said, "will need repairs. Doubtless you can give her the attention she will need either in Cos or Tyros."

"We are free?" he asked, disbelievingly.

"It would ill repay the hospitality of a captain," said I, "for his passenger to refuse churlishly to return to him his vessel."

"My thanks," said he, "Bosk, Captain of Port Kar."

"The slaves, of course," said I, "are freed. They come with us. Your crew, under sail, or oar, doubtless, will make do."

"We shall be all right," he said.

"Bring those who were slaves," I said, "whether injured or not, aboard our ships. Within the Ahn I wish to set course for Port Kar."

Clitus barked orders to my seamen.

"Captain," I heard a voice.

I turned, and saw at my side, the oar-master.

"You are worthy," said I, "of calling stroke on a ram-ship."

"I was your enemy," said he.

"If you wish," said I, "serve me."

"I do," said he. "And I will."

I turned to Thurnock and Tab.

"I carried peace to Cos and Tyros," I said, "and for this I was awarded the chains of a slave in the galleys."

"When," asked Tab, "do we sail against the ships of Cos and Tyros?"

I laughed.

"Surely now," laughed he, "Cos and Tyros have injured you."

"Yes," said I, "they have, and now we may sail against them!"

There were cheers from the men about, who felt that too long had the ships of Bosk surrendered the seas to those of Cos and Tyros.

"The Bosk," laughed Thurnock, "has been angered."

"It has," said I.

"Then let Cos and Tyros beware!" roared Thurnock.

"Yes," said I, turning to the captain, "let them beware."

Captain Tenrik nodded his head, curtly.

"What shall we do now, Captain," asked Clitus, of me.

"Return to Port Kar," I said. "As I recall, I have waiting for me there a galley, heavy class, for my work in Cos."

"True!" said Thurnock.

"And when we have come to Port Kar, what then?" asked Tab.

I looked at him evenly. "Then," said I, "paint my ships green."

Green, on Thassa, is the color of pirates. Green hulls, sails, oars, even ropes. In the bright sun reflecting off the water, green is a color most difficult to detect on gleaming Thassa. The green ship, in the bright sun, can be almost invisible.

"It will be done," cried Tab.

There were more cheers from the men about.

Seeing the officer whose sword I had, I laughed and flung the weapon into the deck at his feet. "Sir," I said, "your sword."

Then I vaulted over the rail of the Rena onto the deck of the heavy-class arsenal galley.

I was followed by my men, who loosened the grappling hooks and ropes that bound our ships to the Rena.

"Now," said I, "to Port Kar!"

"To Port Kar!" cheered my men. "To Port Kar!"

And thus it was that the ships of Bosk, he of Port Kar, came to be painted green.

Within the month, supplied and outfitted, the ramships of Bosk, a light galley, two of medium class, and one of heavy class, made their first strikes on Thassa.

By the end of the second month the flag of Bosk, carried by one ship or another, was known from Ianda to Torvaldsland, and from the delta of the Vosk to the throne rooms of Cos and Tyros.

My treasures were soon increased considerably, and the number of ships in my fleet, by captured prizes, was radically augmented, so much so that I could not begin to wharf them within the lakelike courtyard of my holding. With gold won by sword at sea I purchased extensive wharfage and several warehouses on the western edge of Port Kar. Even so I found myself pressed and, to ease the difficulties of wharfage and mooring rights, I sold many a round ship taken, and some of the inferior long ships. My round ships, as much as possible, I engaged in commerce, usually acting on the advice of Luma, the slave girl, my chief accountant; the ram-ships I sent against Cos and Tyros, usually in twos and threes; I myself commonly commanded a fleet of five ram-ships, and spent much time searching the seas for larger prey.

But in all this time I had not forgotten the treasure fleet which was due to sail from Tyros to Cos, bearing precious metals and jewels for her coffers, and a lovely lady, Vivina, to grace the couch of her Ubar.

I put spies in Tyros and Cos, and in many of the other ports of Thassa.

I think I knew the shipping, the cargos and the schedules of those two island Ubarates, and several of their allies, as well or better than many of the members of their own high councils.

It was, accordingly, no accident that I, Bosk, from the marshes, in the Fifth Passage Hand of the year 10,120 from the founding of the city of Ar, four months after the unsuccessful coup of Henrius Sevarius in the city of Port Kar, stood admiral on the stern castle of my flagship, the Dorna of Tharna, in command of my fleet, eighteen ships of my own and twelve consigned from the arsenal, at a given place at a given time on gleaming Thassa.

"Fleet off the port beam!" came the cry from the man in the basket, circling the masthead above.

I turned to Tab.

"Remove the mast," said I, "from the mast well. Lash it and its yard to the deck. Store the sail. We are going into battle."

How Bosk Conducted

Business Upon Thassa

It must be understood that the ship itself is the weapon. The Dorna, a tarn ship, is not untypical of her class. Accordingly I shall, in brief, describe her. I mention, however, in passing, that a great variety of ram-ships ply Thassa, many of which, in their dimensions, their lines, their rigging and their rowing arrangements, differ from her considerably. The major difference, I would suppose, is that between the singly-banked and the doubly- or trebly-banked vessel. The Dorna, like most other tarn ships, is single-banked; and yet her oar power is not inferior to even the trebly-banked vessels; how this is I shall soon note.

The Dorna, like most tarn ships, is a long, narrow vessel of shallow draft. She is carvel-built, and her planking is fastened with nails of bronze and iron; in places, wooden pegs are also used; her planking, depending on placement, varies from two to six inches in thickness; also, to strengthen her against the shock of ramming, four-inch-thick wales run longitudinally about her sides. She carries a single, removable mast, with its long yard. It is lateen rigged. Her keel, one hundred and twenty-eight feet Gorean, and her beam, sixteen feet Gorean, mark her as heavy class. Her freeboard area, that between the water line and the deck, is five feet Gorean. She is long, low and swift.

She has a rather straight keel, and this, with her shallow draft, even given her size, makes it possible to beach her at night, if one wishes. It is common among Gorean seamen to beach their craft in the evening, set watches, make camp, and launch again in the morning.

The Dorna's ram, a heavy projection in the shape of a tarn's beak, shod with iron, rides just below the water line. Behind the ram, to prevent it from going too deeply into an enemy ship, pinning the attacker, is, shaped like the spread crest of a tarn, the shield. The entire ship is built in such a way that the combined strength of the keel, stempost and strut-frames centers itself at the ram, or spur. The ship is, thus, itself the weapon.

The bow of the Dorna is concave, sloping down to meet the ram. Her stern describes what is almost a complete semicircle. She has two steering oars, or side rudders. The sternpost is high, and fanlike; it is carved to represent feathers; the actual tail feathers of a tarn, however, would be horizontal to the plane, not vertical; the prow of the tarn ship resembles the ram and shield, though it is made of painted wood; it is designed and painted to resemble the head of a tarn.

Tarn ships are painted in a variety of colors; the Dorna, of course, was green.

Besides her stem and stern castles the Dorna carried two movable turrets amidships, each about twenty feet high. She also carried, on leather-cushioned, swivel mounts, two light catapults, two chain-sling onagers, and eight springals. Shearing blades, too, of course, were a portion of her equipment. These blades, mentioned before, are fixed on each side of the hull, abaft of the bow and forward of the oars. They resemble quarter moons of steel and are fastened into the frames of the ship itself. They are an invention of Tersites of Port Kar. They are now, however, found on most recent ram-ships, of whatever port of origin.

Although the Dorna's true beam is sixteen feet Gorean, her deck width is twenty-one feet Gorean, due to the long rectangular rowing frame, which carries the thole ports; the rowing frame is slightly higher than the deck area and extends beyond it, two and one half feet Gorean on each side; it is supported by extensions of the hull beams; the rowing frame is placed somewhat nearer the stem than the sternpost; the extension of the rowing frame not only permits greater deck area but, because of the size of the oars used, is expedient because of matters of work space and leverage.

The size and weight of the oars used will doubtless seem surprising, but, in practice, they are effective and beautiful levers. The oars are set in groups of three, and three men sit a single bench. These benches are not perpendicular to the bulwarks but slant obliquely back toward the stern castle. Accordingly their inboard ends are farther aft than their outboard ends. This slanting makes it possible to have each of the three oars in an oar group parallel to the others. The three oars are sometimes of the same length, but often they are not. The Dorna used oars of varying lengths; her oars, like those of many tarn ships, varied by about one and one-half foot Gorean, oar to oar; the most inboard oar being the longest; the outboard oar being the shortest. The oars themselves usually weigh about one stone a foot, or roughly four pounds a foot. The length of those oars on a tarn ship commonly varies from twenty-seven to thirty foot Gorean. A thirty-foot Gorean oar, the most inboard oar, would commonly weigh thirty stone, or about one hundred and twenty pounds. The length and weight of these oars would make their operation impractical were it not for the fact that each of them, on its inboard end, is weighted with lead. Accordingly the rower is relieved of the weight of the oar and is responsible only for its work. This arrangement, one man to an oar, and oars in groups of three, and oars mounted in the rowing frame, long and beautiful sweeps, has been found extremely practical in the Gorean navies. It is almost universal on ram-ships. The rowing deck, further, is open to the air, thereby differing from the rowing holds of round ships. This brings many more free fighting men, the oarsmen, into any action which might be required. They, while rowing, are protected, incidentally, by a parapet fixed on the rowing frame. Between each pair of benches, behind the parapet, is one bowman. The thole ports in a given group of three are about ten inches apart and the groups themselves, center to center, are a bit less than four feet apart. The Dorna carried twenty groups of three to a side, and so used one hundred and twenty oarsmen.

From this account it may perhaps be conjectured why the oar power of a single-banked ram-ship is often comparable or superior to that of a doubly- or trebly-banked ship. The major questions involve the number and size of oars that can be practically mounted, balanced against the size of ship required for the differing arrangements. The use of the extended rowing frame, permitting the leverage necessary for the great oars, and the seating of several oarsmen, each with his own oar, on a given bench, conserving space, are important in this regard. If we suppose a trebly-banked ship with one hundred and twenty oarsmen, say, in three banks of twenty each to a side, I think we can see she would have to be a rather large ship, and a good deal heavier than the single-decked, three-men-to-a-bench type, also with one hundred and twenty oarsmen. She would thus, also, be slower. And this does not even take into consideration the longer, larger oar possible with the projecting rowing frame. To be sure, there are many factors involved here, and one might suppose triple banks following the model of the single-banked, three-men-three-oars-to-a-bench type, and so on, but, putting aside questions of the size of vessel required for such arrangements, we may simply note, without commenting further, that the single-banked, three-men-three-oars arrangement is almost universal in fighting ships on Thassa. The other type of ship, though found occasionally, does not seem, at least currently, to present a distinct challenge to the low, swift, single-banked ships. In questions of ramming, I suppose the heavier ship would deliver the heaviest blow, but, even this might be contested, for the lighter ship would, presumably, be moving more rapidly. Further, of course, the chances of being rammed by a lighter ship are greater than those of being rammed by a heavier ship, because of the greater speed and maneuverability of the former. Other disadvantages to the double- and triple banked systems, of course, are that valuable hold space is consumed by oarsmen; and that many of your oarsmen, if not all, are below decks and thus unable to enter into necessary actions as easily as they might otherwise do; further, in case of ramming or wreck, it is a good deal more dangerous to be below decks than above decks. At any rate, whatever the reasons or rationale, the single-banked tarn ship, of which the Dorna is an example, is the dominant type on Thassa.

I had, at my disposal, thirty ram-ships, eighteen of my own, and twelve on consignment from the arsenal. The treasure fleet, with her escort, consisted of seventy ships; forty were ram-ships and thirty round ships. Of the forty ram ships, twenty-five were heavy class, and fifteen medium class. Of my thirty ram-ships, twenty were heavy class, and ten medium class. There were no light galleys in either fleet.

I had made it a practice never to ram round ships,

and I had seen that this practice was well publicized. I had even had it observed by men at the various slave wharves, presumably inspecting the merchandise. Doubtless, from hold to hold, over the months, the word has spread that Bosk not only would not sink a round ship, but that, when he took one, he freed her slaves. I think, had it not been for this, my own actions against round ships of the past months would not have been as successful as they had been. Further, I had spread the rumor that I would be displeased should I discover, after capturing a round ship, that her slaves had been either mistreated or slain. Accordingly I thus, in effect, recruited tacit allies in the rowing holds of round ships. The slaves, eager for the capture of the vessel by one of my ships, could scarcely be expected to row with their full strength, and the masters, knowing full well the ship might be taken, feared, under the conditions obtaining, to seriously abuse or slay the chained oarsmen. The principal alternatives, under these conditions, open to the men of Cos and Tyros would then seem to be, first, to use free oarsmen, which was not, however, traditional on round ships, or, two, increase the ram-ship escort for round ships. It was this latter alternative, rather expensive, which the men of Cos and Tyros had apparently, almost invariably, selected. On the other hand, the treasure fleet, under any conditions, would have a heavy escort, which it did.

The prices of goods, I might note, carried on ships of Cos and Tyros and her allies, because of the need of paying for additional escort, had risen considerably. Accordingly, her goods, to the dismay of her merchants, were becoming less competitive in the markets of Thassa. Insurance rates on such shipments, even those with escort, I might add, had also soared.

Because of my practices in connection with round ships, I did not expect Cos and Tyros to enter them seriously into any naval engagement with my fleet. Thus, the odds, which might have been prohibitive under normal conditions, of seventy ships to thirty, I suspected I had reduced to something like forty, or perhaps fifty, to thirty. But even so, I did not regard it as rational to undertake odds of forty, or fifty, to thirty. I had no intention of engaging except under conditions of either equality or, preferably, superiority. The important thing, as I saw it, was not so much the absolute numbers of ships involved as the numbers of ships that could be applied at a given place and given time.

Accordingly I began to put my plan into effect.

With twelve ships I began to approach the treasure fleet from the southeast.

Although I had had the masts, with their yards, taken down and lashed to the decks, and the sails stored below, I had the flutists and drummers, not uncommon on the ram-ships of Thassa, strike up a martial air.

Then, rather bravely, the music drifting over the water, our oars at only half of maximum beat, we moved across the gleaming waters toward the large fleet.

Since the ram-ships of the enemy had not yet struck their masts, it would be only a matter of moments before we were sighted.

From the stern castle of the Dorna, then, with a long glass of the builders, I observed, far across the waters, the masts of the ram-ships, one by one, lowering. I could hear, moreover, their war trumpets, carrying from one ship to the other, signaling fleet movements. Message flags, doubtless repeating the message of the trumpets, were being run from the decks on their halyards to the heights of the stem castles. Although I could not yet see the decks, I had no doubt that there was a flurry of activity there. Bowmen were setting their weapons; helmets, weapons and shields were being brought up from below decks. Fires were being stoked to heat pitch and stones; bundles of tarred javelins would be shaken out near the springals and light catapults. In a few moments hides, soaked overside, would be spread over good portions of the decks and bulwarks; and bags of sea water, for putting out fires, would be drawn and placed about the ships. In about ten Ehn the decks of the treasure fleet, save for the paraphernalia of war, would be clear, and her hatches would be secured. Similar preparations, of course, were taking place on my own ships.

"Quarter of maximum!" I called down to the oar-master, some feet below me.

I did not wish to approach the fleet too rapidly.

The treasure fleet would have no way of knowing that I definitely knew her size and composition.

For all they knew I might be astonished at the force on which I had come.

I listened for a while, chuckling, to the brave tunes being put forth by my flutists and drummers.

Then, when I saw the perimeter ships of the treasure fleet swinging about toward me, I motioned for the musicians to discontinue their performance.

When they were silent, I could hear the flutes and drums from the enemy ships.

I called down to the oar-master to rest oars.

I wanted it to appear that I was suddenly undecided as to whether or not to attack, as though I was confused, startled.

I signaled my trumpeter to transmit the command "Rest oars." The same message was run up the halyard to the height of the stem castle.

Over the faint music coming from the distant ships, now approaching, I could hear her war trumpets and, with the glass, observe her flags. Whereas I did not know exactly the codes employed by the treasure fleet, I had little doubt that our hesitation was being signaled about the fleet, and then I heard other trumpets, and saw the round ships drawing apart, and tarn ships streaking between them, fanning out in our direction.

I slapped shut the glass of the builders and laughed. "Excellent!" I cried.

Thurnock, near me, the tooth missing on his upper right side, grinned.

"Helmsmen about," I said. "Oar-master, half beat."

I did not even, following my plan, signal this move to my other ships. I wished it to appear that we were turning, suddenly fearing, in flight. I wanted it to appear that the other ships must take their cue to action from our own, as though, in fear and confusion, we had not even signaled them. I heard more trumpets from across the water. Some of these were from the enemy fleet. Others, brief notes, interrogations, demands for clarification, were from my own ships. They had good commanders. I listened to the flutes and drums of the ram-ships of the treasure fleet. A javelin, with tarred, burning blade, fell hissing into the water, some hundred yards away.

I snapped open the builder's glass again.

I counted, clearly, some twenty ships, fanned out in a long enveloping line, moving towards us.

The Dorna had now come about and, at half beat, was moving southeast, directly away from the pursuing ships.

The other eleven ships with me were, not too gracefully, by intention, coming about to join me in my flight.

I ordered the trumpeter and the man on the flags to now signal flight to them.

These twelve ships, including the Dorna, incidentally, were my swiftest. It seemed probable, with a decent start, which we had, we could stay ahead of the pursuing ram-ships, if we chose, either indefinitely, or, if they were faster, which I doubted, as least for several Ahn.

We were now moving, of course, at only half beat.

I wished our pursuit to be tempting.

It was.

Another tarred, flaming javelin fell hissing into the water. This time it fell only fifty yards astern.

In another quarter of an Ahn I could count thirty ram-ships engaged in our pursuit. If there were more, I could not see them. The treasure fleet itself lay to.

I watched a burning javelin from the lead ship of the pursuers arc gracefully and smoking through the air and drop hissing into the water some fifteen yards to my right, abeam of the stern.

I smiled. "Three quarters beat," I recommended to our oar-master.

My vessels, as though in terror, were keeping no formation, but apparently scattering across the southeast. Each had picked up two or three pursuers. My own ship, perhaps recognized as the probable flagship, it having been first in the original formation, was honored by five pursuers. After two Ahn, sometimes increasing the beat, sometimes decreasing it, depending on whether or not we wished to avoid being actually overtaken or we wished to encourage our pursuers, we had spread them behind us in a long, straggling line, its spacing an index to the speed of their individual ships.

By this time, of course, the balance of my fleet, eighteen ram-ships, would have struck the treasure fleet, now protected only by some ten ram-ships, from the northwest.

I was puzzled somewhat, but not too much, that our pursuit had been so relentless.

I had flown the flag of Bosk, from the marshes, boldly, trusting that this incitement would encourage prompt and fierce pursuit. Doubtless in Cos and Tyros there was a high price indeed on my head. I was puzzled only that the pursuit had been as relentless and prolonged as it was. I had not realized my importance to the men of the two island Ubarates. I chuckled. Apparently I was more significant to them than I had fancied myself.

It was the twelfth Ahn before the commander of the first pursuing ship understood either that he had been tricked or that he was not likely to overtake our ships.

"Rest oars!" I called.

I watched the tarn ship heave to, then port oars, and turn away.

"How are the men?" I asked the oar-master.

It was he who had been oar-master on the Rena of Temos.

"They are strong," he said. "You did not even call maximum beat."

"Rest them now," I said.

There were trumpet signals now from the ship that had been pursuing us, and flags on her halyards. The ships behind her began turning about. Some of the ships to the sides, perhaps having seen the flags with glasses from their stem or stern castles, also ceased the pursuit. Others were out of visual range, scattered somewhere on Thassa.

As soon as I saw the tarn ship which had been pursuing us begin to move away, I gave my orders.

"Come about," I said, "and maximum beat."

There was a cheer from the oarsmen.

I had little doubt the Dorna was swifter than the ship that had pursued her.

She was now moving away, perhaps at half beat.

I did not think she would have time to turn about again.

We fired no missile, and gave no warning.

We were within fifty yards of her before a seaman on her stern castle, looking back, screamed the warning.

The iron-shod ram of the Dorna splintered into her stern a foot below the water line.

"Back oars!" came the cry from the oar-master, and the Dorna, rocking and shuddering from the impact, chopped her way backward.

"Helmsmen pass to starboard!" I called. "Stroke! Maximum beat!"

The stern of the enemy ship was already under water as we slipped past her.

Crossbow quarrels struck the reinforced parapet protecting my rowers.

There were no other missiles.

We heard screams, cries of alarm.

There were still four ships ahead of us. The nearest was not more than a hundred yards before the one we had just struck.

The noise of our strike and the cries of the men aboard the rammed ship carried over the water.

We saw the ship ahead of us trying to come about, but, before she could make four points of the Gorean compass, our ram struck the corner of her stern, skidding through and freeing itself, the ships, the Dorna's port oars inboard, grating together, and then the Dorna was clear, free, and we were driving toward the stern of the next ship.

We heard trumpets blaring behind us frantically, trying to warn the ship ahead of us.

It, too, began to come about, and we caught her amidships, the ram thrusting through the heavy planking like kindling, then stopped by the shield, like a spread tarn's crest, and we chopped our way back and free, and then knifed past her stern toward the next two ships.

By this time the two ships ahead of us were well aware of their danger and, given the distances involved, neither captain elected to chance the dangerous maneuver of coming about to meet us. Both were fleeing at maximum beat.

"Half of maximum beat," I told the oar-master.

The oar-master grinned, and went to the center of the rowing frame.

As the beat dropped, I took out the glass of the builders and scanned the horizon.

I could see few ships, but most of those I saw were green, my own. I could see the wreckage of two of the enemy tarn ships. I was quite content, of course, if each of my ships not in view were continuing to lead their pursuers a merry chase. If each of them could lure their two or three hounds astray, the odds of engagement at the truly critical points would be so much the more in my favor. I was willing to spend one ship to draw two or three enemy ships from the battle, if battle there was to be. And, of course, as soon as the enemy ships would turn back, they would be vulnerable to my own, presumably faster vessels. Of the twelve ships in my diversion, five were my fastest and seven were among the fastest in the arsenal.

I now turned the glass again to the ship fleeing me. As I had expected, he had now begun to draw substantially ahead, since I had reduced to half of maximum beat. In another four or five Ehn I expected he would regard his lead as sufficient to permit him the time to safely come about and engage. He would be assuming, of course, that I, in pursuing him, was at maximum beat, as he was. I had held my beat to half of maximum. My oar-master had been calling the beat, this time, by mouth from the center of the rowing frame.

When I saw the tarn ship ahead, its captain doubtless confident of his speeds and distances, lift her oars, preparing to come about, I called to the oar-master, "Now!"

Without the loss of a stroke he, at the center of the rowing frame, began to call maximum beat, "Stroke! Stroke! Stroke!"

The Dorna, stern low, ram almost lifted from the water, leapt ahead, as beautiful, as eager and vicious as an unleashed sleen.

We took the fourth ship amidships, as we had the third. Angrily the Dorna shook herself loose.

Then, in an Ehn, we were in pursuit of the last ship. It showed no sign of turning. It was now far in advance of us.

"Maximum beat," said the oar-master to his keleustes, and then came to stand beside me on the stern castle.

"Can we catch her?" I asked.

"Hand me your glass," he said.

I did so.

"Do you know the ship?" I asked.

"No," he said.

He looked at her for better than an Ehn, studying the rise and fall, the sweep, of the oars.

Then he said, "Yes, we can catch her."

He handed me back the glass.

He then went down the steps of the stern castle, to the helm deck, and then down to the chair of the oar-master.

"Three quarters beat," I heard him tell the keleustes.

I did not question him. I knew him to be a good oar-master.

From time to time I observed the distant ship growing farther and farther away.

But after about an Ahn and a half, when I again raised the glass, I saw that she was not much farther away than she had been when last I had looked. My own men were still drawing a strong three quarters beat.

The oar-master again joined me on the stern castle. He did not ask for the glass again.

"She carries one hundred and thirty-two oars," he said, "but she is a heavier ship, and her lines are not as good as those of the Dorna."

"Apparently," I said, "she has had to reduce her beat."

"She will be at three quarters now," he said, "as we are. One cannot maintain maximum beat that long. And, at three quarters we can overtake her."

"Thank you," said I, "Oar-master."

He returned to his chair.

Doubtless it would soon become evident to our enemy also that she could not outrun us. Accordingly, sooner or later, she would turn to fight.

After a quarter of an Ahn, in the distance, I could see her, at last, come about.

"Quarter of maximum," I called to the oar-master. Then, about four Ehn later, "Rest oars."

The two tarn ships, the Dorna and the other, faced one another, motionless, save for their response to the swells of Thassa.

We were separated by some four hundred yards.

Since the principal weapons of the ram-ship are the ram and shearing blades, she is most dangerous taken head on. Accordingly, in such a combat situation, involving only two ships at sea, both ships commonly described the broad starboard circle, prowling about one another like wary sleen, exchanging missiles, watchful for the opportunity to engage with ram and blades. I had little doubt that the Dorna, a somewhat lighter ship, with better lines and shorter keel, would be more responsive to her helm than the other ship and that, sooner or later, as the circles grew smaller, she would be able to wheel and take her foe in the stern quarter or amidships.

Doubtless this was reasonably clear, also, to the commander of the other vessel. He had surely refused to engage. Now it seemed he had no choice.

He did what I expected.

His oars took up maximum beat and his heavy ship, the crest of the ram dividing the water before the concave bow, the tarn's beak just below the water line, plunged toward us.

I laughed. I had caught the other ship. I had proved the Dorna, and her oar-master.

The other ship did not truly wish to fight.

"Helmsmen," said I, "take your course four points to starboard."

"Yes, Captain," said they.

"Oar-master," said I, "we have an appointment with the treasure fleet of Cos and Tyros."

He grinned up. "Yes, Captain!" said he. Then he called to his keleustes. "Maximum beat!"

The ram of the other ship did not find us. As it plunged through Thassa we had slipped, as swiftly as a sleen, from its path, knifing by a hundred yards past his port bow, and soon leaving him astern. He did not even fire missiles.

I laughed.

I saw him turn slowly toward Cos.

I had removed him from the battle, if battle there was to be.

"Helmsmen," said I, "take your course now for the treasure fleet of Cos and Tyros."

"Yes, Captain," said they.

"Half beat," said I to the oar-master.

"Yes, Captain," said he.

Matters had proceeded as I had expected at the treasure fleet. Of the forty tarn ships in her escort, thirty, lured away, had pursued my ships far from the critical points. I myself had damaged or destroyed four of these ships, and had removed a fifth from the theater of action. As my other eleven ships, one by one, began to return to the treasure fleet, the story was similar with them. Some of the enemy ships, however, in turning back from the chase, had been able to regroup and somewhere, abroad on Thassa, there was doubtless a fleet of some ten enemy tarn ships, still a possible threat. They had not yet returned to the treasure fleet. The others had been damaged or destroyed, or driven away. At the treasure fleet itself, while most of her escort pursued my diversionary ships, the other eighteen vessels in my fleet had fallen, suddenly, silently, on the ten tarn ships left behind with the treasure fleet. Using, on the whole, elementary triangle tactics, wherein an attack by two ships, from different quadrants, is made on a single ship, which can face but one of the attackers, my ships had, in a short time, less than an Ahn, destroyed seven of the ten ram-ships left behind at the treasure fleet. Two had been permitted to escape, and one lay, even now, penned in among the round ships. Some of the round ships, intelligently, had scattered, but, of the thirty originally in the fleet, there were now twenty-two ringed with our vessels. And another was soon herded in by one of my ram-ships, which, in returning to the fleet, had picked it up.

I was in no particular hurry to move against the captured round ships. They were mine.

I was more interested in the seven round ships that had fled.

Accordingly, as soon as a sufficient number of my ships had returned to the treasure fleet, I set about organizing a pursuit of the missing round ships. I communicated with my other ships by flag and trumpet, some of them conveying my messages to others more distant. I dispatched ten tarn ships abroad in search patterns, hoping to snare some of the seven missing round ships. Five of these search ships I sent in a net formation toward Cos, supposing this the most likely, if not the most wise, course that would soon be taken by the majority of the escaping round ships. My other five search ships I sent in sweeps away from Cos. If the endeavors of these various ships, after two days, were unsuccessful, they were to return to Port Kar. This left, after the last of my original eleven ships had returned, twenty of my ships with the treasure fleet, more than enough to counter any returning enemy tarn ships.

I ordered the mast raised on the Dorna. When the mast, with its sail fastened to its yard, had been set in the mast well, and stayed fore, aft and amidships, I climbed to the basket myself, carrying the glass of the builders.

I looked upon my twenty-three round ships, and was not unsatisfied.

Round ships, like ram-ships, differ among themselves considerably. But most are, as I may have mentioned, two masted, have permanent masts and, like the ram-ships, are lateen rigged. They, though they carry oarsmen, generally slaves, are more of a sailing ship than the

ram-ship. They can, generally, sail satisfactorily to windward, taking full advantage of their lateen rigging,
which is particularly suited to windward work. The ram-
ship, on the other hand, is difficult to sail to windward,
even with lateen rigging, because of its length, its narrow-
ness and its shallow draft. In tacking to windward her
leeward oars and rowing frame are likely to drag in the
water, cutting down speed considerably and not infre-
quently breaking oars. Accordingly the ram-ship most
commonly sails only with a fair wind. Further, she is less
seaworthy than the round ship, having a lower freeboard
area, being more easily washed with waves, and having
a higher keel-to-beam ratio, making the danger of
breaking apart in a high sea greater than it would be
with a round ship. There are in the building of ships, as
in other things, values to be weighed. The ram-ship is
not built for significant sail dependence or maximum
seaworthiness. She is built for speed, and the capacity to
destroy other shipping. She is not a rowboat but a racing
shell; she is not a club, but a rapier.

I, swaying in the basket at the masthead, with the
glass of the builders, smiled.

Penned in among the twenty-three round ships was a
long galley, a purple ship, flying the purple flag of Cos. It
was a beautiful ship. And the flag she flew was bordered
with gold, the admiral's flag, marking that vessel as the
flagship of the treasure fleet.

I snapped shut the glass of the builders and, by means
of a slender rope ladder fastened at the masthead and
anchored to a cleat near the mast well below, took my
way down to the deck.

"Thurnock," I said, "let the flags of division and acquisition be raised."

"Yes, Captain," said he.

There was a cheer from the men on the deck of the
Dorna.

I anticipated, and received, little resistance from the
round ships. There were various reasons for this. They
had been herded together and could not maneuver.
They were slower than the ram-ships and, under any
conditions, little match for them. And their rowing
slaves, by this time, were fully aware that the fleet
encircling them was that of Bosk, from the marshes.

Vessel by vessel my men boarded the round ships, commonly meeting no resistance.

The free crews of these ships, of course, were hopelessly outnumbered by my men. The round ship, although she often carries over one hundred, and sometimes over two hundred, chained slaves in her rowing hold, seldom, unless she intends to enter battle, carries a free crew of more than twenty to twenty-five men. Moreover, these twenty to twenty-five men are often largely simply sailors and their officers, and not fighting men. The Dorna, by contrast, carried a free crew of two hundred and fifteen men, most of whom were well trained with weapons.

In an Ahn I stepped across the plank thrown from the rail of the Dorna to that of the flagship of the treasure fleet. The ship itself, by my men, had already been subdued.

I was met by a tall bearded figure in a purple cloak. "I am Rencius Ho-Bar," said he, "of Telnus, Admiral of the Treasure Fleet of Cos and Tyros."

"Put him in chains," I told my men.

He looked at me in fury.

I turned to Clitus, who had been on the ship before me. "Do you have the master cargo lists?" I asked.

He presented a folio-sized book, bound with golden cord and sealed with wax, bearing the impress of the Ubar of Tyros, Chenbar.

The admiral, to one side, was being fitted with wrist and ankle irons, joined by a length of chain.

I broke the golden cord and the seal and opened the master cargo lists.

They were most excellent.

From time to time, as I scanned the lists, there was a cheer from one round ship or another as her slaves were freed. The free crewmen, of course, were placed in chains, men and officers alike. The distinction of man and officer does not exist on the benches of a galley.

"Admiral!" said the admiral of the treasure fleet to me.

I glanced to the gold-bordered, purple flag, the admiral's flag, flying from the halyard strung between the forward starboard mooring cleat and the height of the stem castle. "Strike that flag," I said, "and put there the flag of Bosk, from the marshes."

"Yes, Captain," said Thurnock.

"Admiral!" protested the admiral of the treasure fleet to me.

"Take him away," I told my men.

He was dragged from my presence.

I snapped shut the book. "If these figures are correct," I said to Clitus, "as doubtless they are, we and the Captains of Port Kar are today the masters of much treasure."

He laughed. "Surely enough," said he, "to make us all among the richest of men!"

"More wisely spent," said I, "these goods would go to increase the arsenal fleet of Port Kar."

"But surely," said he, "the arsenal does not require so much?"

I laughed. "The arsenal share," said I, "is eighteen shares of thirty." Eighteen of the ships in my fleet had been arsenal vessels.

I had, by agreement with the council, reserved to myself twelve shares of thirty divisions, as well as all slaves taken.

"Captain," said a voice.

"Yes," I said.

A seaman had approached me.

"The Lady Vivina," said he, "asks to be presented to you."

"Very well," said I. "Tell her that her request to present herself to me has been granted."

"Yes, Captain," said he.

I reopened the book of cargo lists.

When I lifted my head again I discovered that the Lady Vivina was, and had been, standing before me.

Seeing me, she started.

I smiled.

Her hand was before her veil. Her eyes were wide. She wore swirling, dazzling robes of concealment, of purple and golden cloths, brocades and silks. The veil itself was purple, and trimmed with gold.

Then she caught herself and presented herself before me, as a high-born lady.

"I am Vivina," said she, "of the city of Kasra of Tyros."

I nodded my head. "Call me Bosk," I said. "I am a captain in Port Kar."

Behind the girl, in robes almost as rich as hers, were two other high-born maidens.

"I gather," she said, "I am your prisoner."

I said nothing.

"You will, of course," she said, "be severely punished for what you have done."

I smiled.

"As you know," she said, "I am pledged to be the Free Companion of Lurius, Ubar of Cos. Accordingly, my ransom will be high."

I indicated the two girls behind Vivina. "How many of these are there?" I asked Clitus.

"Forty," he said.

"They did not appear," I said to him, "on the master cargo lists."

Clitus grinned.

The girls looked at one another uneasily.

"My maidens," said Vivina, "will also be ransomed, though their ransoms will be less than mine."

I regarded her.

"What makes you so certain," I asked, "that you will be held for ransom?"

She looked at me, stunned.

"Remove your veil," I told her.

"Never!" she cried. "Never!"

"Very well," said I. I returned my attention to the master cargo lists.

"What is to be done with us?" she asked.

I turned to Clitus. "The Lady Vivina," I said to him, "will of course grace the prow of this ship, the flagship of the treasure fleet."

"No!" she screamed.

"Yes, Captain," said Clitus.

Already two men held her arms.

"Take then those that were with her," I said, "and distribute them to the extent of their number among our other ships, the twenty most beautiful to our twenty tarn ships now with the fleet, and the most beautiful of that twenty to the prow of the Dorna, and the other twenty set at the prows of twenty of our prizes."

"Yes, Captain," said Clitus.

Men laid hands on the two girls behind the Lady Vivina, and they cried out with fear.

I again turned my attention to the master cargo lists.

"Captain!" said the Lady Vivina.

"Yes," I said, lifting my head and looking at her.

"I—I," she said, "will remove my veil."

"That will not be necessary," I said.

I handed Clitus the book of cargo lists and strode to the girl, jerking out the pins that held her veil, face-stripping her.

"Beast!" she cried.

I gestured that the seamen should remove the veils from the two girls who stood behind her.

They wept.

They were beauties, all.

I looked down into the face of the Lady Vivina, who was beautiful.

"Put her at the prow," I said to Clitus.

I turned away, taking the book of master cargo lists from Clitus, and again giving them my attention. The other two girls were taken from my presence. The Lady Vivina, to one side, was readied for the prow.

Within the Ahn we were ready to sail for Port Kar. I had the admiral of the treasure fleet, Rencius Ho-Bar of Telnus, in his chains, brought before me.

"I am returning one round ship to Cos," I said. "You, with certain of the seamen captured, will sit chained at her benches. Beyond this, I will give you, from among our prisoners, ten free men, six seamen, two helmsmen, an oar-master and a keleustes. The treasure from the ship, of course, will be placed aboard other ships, taken to Port Kar as prizes. On the other hand, your ship will be adequately provisioned and I do not doubt you will make port in Telnus within five days."

"You are generous," said the Admiral, dismally.

"I expect," I said, "when you return to Telnus, should you decide to do so, that you will make a reasonably full and accurate account of what has occurred here recently."

"Doubtless," smiled the Admiral, "I shall receive requests to that effect."

"In order that your information may be as accurate as possible, at least to this point, I inform you that seven of your treasure ships have, at least until now, eluded me. I expect to pick up some of them, however.

And, of tarn ships, I have one captured, your flagship, and, from the reports of my captains, some eighteen or twenty have been seriously damaged or sunk. That would leave you with some ten, or perhaps twelve, ships yet abroad on Thassa."

At that point, from the foremast of a nearby round ship, where I had placed a lookout, came the cry, "Twelve sail! Twelve sail abeam!"

"Ah," said I, "twelve ships, it seems."

"They will fight!" cried the admiral. "You have not yet won!"

"Doubtless they will strike their masts," I said, "but I do not think they will fight."

He looked at me, his fists clenched in his irons.

"Thurnock," said I, "signal seventeen of my twenty ships to present themselves to our approaching friends. Let two remain on the far side of the treasure fleet. The Dorna, for the time, will remain here. The seventeen ships are not to enter battle unless accompanied by the Dorna, and under no conditions, if battle ensues, are any of my ships to move more than four pasangs from the fleet."

"Yes, Captain," roared Thurnock, turning and crossing on the plank to the deck of the Dorna, then taking his way to the shielded flag racks at the foot of her stem castle.

Soon the flags were whipping from the halyards.

Battle preparations were underway on my ships. Seventeen soon began to move around the fleet, or come about, to face the approaching twelve vessels. Men sat ready at the oars of the Dorna, should I come aboard her. Others, with axes, stood ready to chop away the lines that now bound the Dorna to the flagship.

"They are striking their masts!" came the cry from the lookout.

In a quarter Ahn my vessels were aligned for battle. The enemy fleet, the twelve ships, was now, by estimate from the lookout, with his glass, some four pasangs distant.

If they came within two pasangs, I would board the Dorna.

I had the admiral freed of his leg irons and he and I, from the stem castle of his own ship, regarded the approaching ships.

"Do you wager," I asked him, "that they come within two pasangs?"

"They will fight!" he said.

The Lady Vivina, prepared for the prow, stood nearby, a sailor's hand on her arm, she, too, watching the approaching ships.

Then the admiral cried out with rage and the Lady Vivina, her hand at her breast, eyes horrified, cried out, "No, No!"

The twelve ships had put about, taking their course now for Cos.

"Take the admiral away," I said to Thurnock.

The admiral was dragged away.

I looked on the Lady Vivina. Our eyes met. "Put her at the prow," I said.

How Bosk Returned
in Triumph To Port Kar

The return to Port Kar was triumphal indeed.

I wore the purple of a fleet admiral, with a golden cap with tassel, and gold trim on the sleeves and borders of my robes, with cloak to match.

I wore at my side a jeweled sword, no longer the sword I had worn for the long years when I had served Priest-Kings. That sword, shortly after coming to Port Kar, I had put aside, and purchased others. I did not feel, somehow, that I should carry that old sword any longer. It stood for too many things, and its steel was deep with too many memories. It spoke to me of an old life, that of a fool, which I, now grown wise, had put from me. Besides, more importantly, it was insufficiently grand, with its plain pommel and unfigured blade, for one of my position, one of the most significant men in one of Gor's greatest ports. I was Bosk, a simple, but shrewd man, who had come from the marshes to startle Port Kar and dazzle and shake the cities of Gor with my cunning and my blade, and now my power and my wealth.

My ten search vessels had managed to bring in five of the seven missing round ships, four of which had been, foolishly, striking out directly for Telnus in Cos. The world, I thought, is filled with fools. There are the fools, and there are the wise, and I could now surely, perhaps for the first time, count myself securely among the latter.

I stood at the prow of the long, purple ship, which had been the flagship of the treasure fleet. The rooftops and the windows of the buildings were crowded with cheering throngs, and I lifted my arm to them and accepted their acclaim. The ships, in a splendid, long line, filing behind me, the Dorna first, then the tarn ships, then the round ships, under oars, moved slowly through the city, following the triumphal circuit of the great canal, passing even before the chamber of the Council of Captains.

Flowers had been scattered in the canal, and others were thrown on our ships as we passed.

The cheers and cries were deafening.

I had decreed that from my shares of the treasure, each worker in the arsenal would receive one gold piece, and each citizen of the city a silver tarsk.

I lifted my hand to the crowd, smiling and waving.

Near me, chief among my prizes, exposed to the crowds, their hootings and jeerings, bound on the prow, ankles and wrists, neck and belly, like a common slave girl, was the Lady Vivina, who was to have been the Ubara of Cos.

Few men, thought I, have enjoyed such triumph as this.

And, petty though it might seem, I was eager to present myself before Midice, my favored slave, with my new robes and treasures. I could now give her garments and jewels that would be the envy of Ubaras. I could well imagine the wonder in her eyes as she understood the greatness of her master, her joy, the eagerness with which she would now serve me.

I was well satisfied.

How simple it is, I thought, to become a true man, powerful and predatory, self-regarding and self-seeking. It requires only to put apart from oneself the hesitations and trammels which the weak and the fools would impose upon themselves, making themselves and their fortunes their own prisoners. In coming to Port Kar I had, for the first time, become free.

I lifted my hand to the crowds. Flowers fell about me. I looked at the girl bound on the prow, my prize. I accepted the acclaim of the wild throngs.

I was Bosk, who could do as he pleased, who could take what he wanted.

I laughed.

Had there ever been triumph such as this in Port Kar?

I brought with me fifty-eight ships: the flagship of the treasure fleet, Vivina bound at its prow, the Dorna, the other twenty-nine ships which had composed my original fleet, and, as prizes, laden with wealth which might have been the ransom of cities, a full twenty-seven of the thirty round ships of the fabulous treasure fleet of Cos and Tyros. And bound at the prow of the first forty ships, following the flagship, beginning with the Dorna, and then the tarn ships and the first ten and largest of the captured round ships, was a high-born beauty, once intended to be the maiden of Cos' Ubara, now, like herself, destined only for the brand and collar of a slave girl.

I raised my hand to the cheering crowds.

"This is Port Kar," I told Vivina.

She said nothing.

The wild crowds screamed and shouted, and threw flowers, and the flagship, oars dipping in stately fashion, took her regal path, ram's crest dividing flowers in the water, between the buildings lining the great canal.

I stood among the falling flowers, my hand lifted to the crowds.

"Should I put you in a public paga tavern," I said, "doubtless hundreds of these would crowd its doors, that they might be served by one once destined to be a Ubara in Cos."

"Slay me," she said.

I waved to the crowds.

"My maidens?" she asked.

"Slaves," I said.

"Myself?" she asked.

"Slave," said I.

She closed her eyes.

In the five days it had taken to reach Port Kar from the scene of the engagement with the treasure fleet, due to the slowness of the round ships, I had not kept Vivina, and her maidens, of course, at the prows of the ships. I had only placed them there in victory, and now again, for the entry to Port Kar.

I recalled, late the first night, under ship's torches, I had had Vivina brought down from the prow and brought before me.

I received her in the admiral's cabin, which was, of course, on the treasure fleet's flagship.

"If I remember correctly," I had said, behind the admiral's table, busied with papers, "in the hall of the Ubar of Cos you told me that you did not frequent the rowing holds of round ships."

She looked at me. There had been laughter from my

men present. High-born ladies commonly sail in cabins, located in the stern castles of either ram-ships or round ships. She had had, of course, a luxurious cabin in the flagship of the treasure fleet, this very ship.

"I asked you, as I recall," I had reminded her, "if you had ever been in the hold of a round ship?"

She said nothing.

"You responded that you had not, as I recall," I had said, "and then, I mentioned that perhaps someday you would have the opportunity."

"No," she said, "please no!"

I had then turned to some of my men. "Take this lady," said I to them, "in a long boat to the largest of the round ships, one rowed by captured officers of the treasure fleet, and chain her there, with other treasures, in the rowing hold."

"Please," she begged. "Please!"

"I trust you will find the accommodations satisfactory," I said.

She drew herself up to her full height. "I am sure I shall," said she.

"You may conduct the Lady Vivina to her quarters," I told the seaman responsible for her.

"Come along, Girl," said he to her.

Like a Ubara she turned and followed him.

But before she had left my cabin, she turned again at the door. "Only slave girls, I understand," said she, "are kept chained below decks in round ships."

"Yes," I said.

Angrily she turned, and left, following the seaman.

Now, in my triumphal entry and course through Port Kar, I looked again upon her.

I saw that she had again opened her eyes.

On the prow, she passed slowly beneath the men, and the women and children, on the rooftops, many of whom called out to her, hooting and jeering her.

I took two talenders which had fallen on my shoulder and fastened them in the ropes at her neck.

This delighted the crowds, who cried out with pleasure.

"No," she begged. "Not talenders."

"Yes," said I, "talenders."

The talender is a flower which, in the Gorean mind, is associated with beauty and passion. Free Companions, on the Feast of their Free Companionship, commonly wear a garland of talenders. Sometimes slave girls, having been subdued, but fearing to speak, will fix talenders in their hair, that their master may know that they have at last surrendered themselves to him as helpless love slaves. To put talenders in the neck ropes of the girl at the prow, of course, was only mockery, indicative of her probable disposition as pleasure slave.

"What are you going to do with me?" she asked.

"When the treasures have been checked, tallied, and appraised, which should take some four or five weeks," I told her, "you, with your maidens, in the chains of slave girls, will be displayed, together with samples of, and full accountings of, the other treasures, before the Council of Captains."

"We are booty?" she asked.

"Yes," I said.

"Apparently then, Captain," said she, icily, "you have perhaps a full month of triumph before you."

"Yes," I said, waving again to the crowds, "that is true."

"What will you do with us after we have been displayed before the Council of Captains?" she asked.

"That," I told her, "you may wait until then to find out."

"I see," she said, and turned her head away.

More flowers fell, and there was more cheering, and hootings and jeers for the bound girl.

Had there ever been triumph such as this in Port Kar, I asked myself, and answered, doubtless never, and smiled, for I knew that this was but the beginning. The climax would occur in some four or five weeks in the formal presentations before the Council, and in the receipt of its highest accolade as worthy captain of Port Kar.

"Hail Port Kar!" I cried to the crowds.

"Hail Port Kar!" they cried. "And hail Bosk, Admiral of Port Kar!"

"Hail Bosk!" cried my retainers. "Hail Bosk, Admiral of Port Kar!"

It was now five weeks after my triumphal entry into Port Kar.

In this very afternoon the formal presentations and accountings of the victory and its plunder had taken place in the chamber of the Council of Captains.

I rose to my feet and lifted my goblet of paga, acknowledging the cries of my retainers.

The goblets clashed and we drank.

It had been five weeks of entertainments, of fetes, of banquets and honors piled one upon another. The treasures taken were rich beyond our wildest expectations, beyond the most remote calculations of our most avaricious scribes. And now, in this very afternoon, my glories had been climaxed in the chamber of the Council of Captains, in which had taken place the formal presentations and accountings of the victory and its plunder, in which had taken place the commendation of the Council for my deeds and the awarding of its most coveted accolade, that of worthy captain of Port Kar.

Even now, in my feast of celebration, hours after the meeting of the council, I still wore about my neck the broad scarlet ribbon with its pendant medallion of gold, bearing the design of a lateen-rigged tarn ship, the initials in cursive Gorean script of Council of Captains of Port Kar in a half curve beneath it.

I threw down more paga.

I indeed was a worthy captain of Port Kar.

I smiled to myself. As the holds of the round ships, one by one, had been emptied, appraised and recorded, hundreds of men, most of them unknown to me, had applied to me for clientship. I had received dozens of offers of partnership in speculative and commercial ventures. Untold numbers of men had found their way to my holding to sell their various plans, proposals and ideas. My guards had even turned away the mad, half-blind shipwright, Tersites, with his fantastic recommendations for the improvement of tarn ships, as though ships so beautiful, so swift, and vicious, might be improved.

Meanwhile, while I had been plying the trade of pirate, the military and political ventures of the Council itself, within the city, had proceeded well. For one thing, they had now formed a Council Guard, with its distinct livery, that was now recognized as a force of the Council, and, in effect, as the police of the city. The Arsenal Guard, however, perhaps for traditional reasons, remained a separate body, concerned with the arsenal, and having jurisdiction within its walls. For another thing, the four Ubars, Chung, Eteocles, Nigel and Sullius Maximus, their powers considerably reduced during the time of the unsuccessful coup of Henrius Sevarius, had apparently resigned themselves to the supremacy of the Council in the city. At any rate, for the first time in several years, there was now a single, effective sovereign in Port Kar, the Council. Accordingly, its word, and, in effect, its word alone, was law. A similar consolidation and unification had taken place, of course, in the realm of inspections and taxations, penalties and enforcements, codes and courts. For the first time in several years one could count on the law being the same on both sides of a given canal. Lastly, the forces of Henrius Sevarius, under the regency of Claudius, once of Tyros, had been driven by the Council forces from all their holdings, save one, a huge fortress, its walls extending into the Tamber itself, sheltering the some two dozen ships left him. This fortress, it seems, might be taken by storm, but the effort would be costly. Accordingly the Council, ringing it with double walls on the land side and blockading it with arsenal ships by sea, chose to wait. The time that the fortress might still stand was now most adequately to be charted by the depth of its siege reservoir, and by the fish that might swim within her barred sea gates, and the mouthfuls of bread yet stored in her towers. The Council, for the most part, in her calculations, ignored the remaining fortress of Sevarius. It was, in effect, the prison of those penned within. One of those therein imprisoned, of course, in the opinion of the Council, was Henrius Sevarius, the boy, himself, the Ubar.

I looked up. The slave boy, Fish, had emerged from the kitchen, holding over his head on a large silver platter a whole roasted tarsk, steaming and crisped, basted, shining under the torchlight, a larma in its mouth, garnished with suls and Tur-pah.

The men cried out, summoning him to their table.

It had been on one side, a land side, of that last remaining fortress of Henrius Sevarius, that Lysias, Henrak, and others had emerged from a postern, carrying the heavy sack which they had hurled into the canal, that sack from which I had saved the boy.

Fish put down the whole roasted tarsk before the men. He was sweating. He wore a single, simple rep-cloth tunic. I had had a plate collar hammered about his neck. I had had him branded.

The men ordered him away again, that he might fetch yet another roasted tarsk from the spit which he had been turning slowly over the coal fires during the afternoon. He sped away.

He had not been an easy slave to break to his collar. The kitchen master had had to beat him often.

One day, after he had been three weeks slave in my house, the door to my audience chamber had suddenly burst open, and he had stumbled in, breathless, the kitchen master but two steps behind him, with a heavy switch.

"Forgive me!" cried the kitchen master.

"Captain!" demanded the boy.

The kitchen master, in fury, grabbed him by the hair and raised his arm to thrash him.

I gestured that he not do so.

The kitchen master stepped back, angry.

"What do you want?" I had asked the boy.

"To see you, Captain," said he.

"Master!" corrected the kitchen master.

"Captain!" cried the boy.

"Normally," I said to the boy, "a kitchen slave petitions to enter his master's presence through the kitchen master."

"I know," said the boy.

"Why did you not do so?" I asked.

"I have," said the boy defiantly, "many times."

"And I," said the kitchen master, "have refused him."

"What is his request?" I asked the kitchen master.

"He would not tell me," said the kitchen master.

"How then," I asked the boy, "did you expect the kitchen master to consider whether or not you should be permitted to enter my presence?"

The boy looked down. "I would speak with you alone," he said.

I had no objection to this, but, of course, as master of the house, I intended to respect the prerogatives of the kitchen master, who, in the kitchen, must speak with my own authority.

"If you speak," I said, "you will do so before Tellius."

The boy looked angrily at the kitchen master.

Then the boy looked down, and clenched his fists. Then, agonized, he looked up at me. "I would learn weapons," he whispered.

I was stunned. Even Tellius, the kitchen master, could say nothing.

"I would learn weapons," said the boy, again, this time boldly.

"Slaves are not taught weapons," I said.

"Your men," said he, "Thurnock, Clitus, and others, have said that they will teach me, should you give your permission." He looked down.

The kitchen master snorted with the absurdity of the idea. "You would do better," said he, "to learn the work of the kitchen."

"Does he do good work in the kitchen?" I asked.

"No," said the kitchen master. "He is lazy. He is slow and stupid. He must be beaten often."

The boy looked up angrily. "I am not stupid," he said.

I looked at the boy, absently, as though I could not place him.

"What is your name?" I asked.

He looked at me. Then he said, "—Fish."

I permitted myself to betray that I now remembered the name. "Yes," I said, "—Fish."

"Do you like your name?" I asked.

"No," he said.

"What would you call yourself," I asked, "if you had your choice of name?"

"Henrius," said he.

The kitchen master laughed.

"That is a proud name for a kitchen boy," I commented.

The boy looked at me proudly.

"It might," I said, "be the name of a Ubar."

The boy looked down angrily.

I knew that Thurnock and Clitus, and others, had taken a liking to the boy. He had often, I had heard, snuck away from the kitchen to observe the ships in the courtyard and the practices of men with weapons. The kitchen master had had his hands full with the boy, there was no doubting that. Tellius had, and deserved, my sympathies.

I looked at the boy, the blondish hair and the frank, earnest eyes, blue, pleading.

He was a spare, strong-limbed lad, and perhaps might, if trained, be able to handle a blade.

Only three in my holding, other than himself, knew his true identity. I knew him, and so, too, did Thurnock and Clitus. The boy himself, of course, did not know that we knew who he was. Indeed, he, a price on his head from the Council, had excellent reasons for concealing his true identity. And yet, in a sense, he had no true identity other than that of Fish, the slave boy, for he had been enslaved and a slave has no identity other than that which his master might care to give him. In Gorean law a slave is an animal; before the law he has no rights; he is dependent on his master not only for his name but for his very life; he may be disposed of by the master at any time and in any way the master pleases.

"The slave boy, Fish," I said to the kitchen master, "has come unbidden into my presence and he has not, in my opinion, shown sufficient respect for the master of my kitchen."

The boy looked at me, fighting back tears.

"Accordingly," I said, "he is to be beaten severely."

The boy looked down, his fists clenched.

"And beginning tomorrow," I said, "if his work in the kitchen improves to your satisfaction, and only under that condition, he is to be permitted one Ahn a day to train with weapons."

"Captain!" cried the boy.

"And that Ahn," I said, "is to be made up in extra work in the evening."

"Yes, Captain," said the kitchen master.

"I will work for you, Tellius," said the boy. "I will work better than any for you!"

"All right, Lad," said Tellius. "We shall see."

The boy looked at me. "Thank you," he said, "Captain."

"Master," corrected Tellius.

"May I not," asked the boy of me, "address you as Captain?"

"If you wish," I said.

"Thank you," said he, "Captain."

"Now begone, Slave," said I.

"Yes, Captain!" he cried and turned, followed by the kitchen master.

"Slave!" I called.

The boy turned.

"If you show skill with weapons," I said, "perhaps I shall change your name."

"Thank you, Captain," he said.

"Perhaps we could call you Publius," I suggested, "—or Tellius."

"Spare me!" cried Tellius.

"Or," I said, "Henrius."

"Thank you, Captain," said the boy.

"But," said I, "to have such a name, which is a proud name, one would have to handle weapons very well."

"I shall," he said. "I shall!"

Then the boy turned and ran joyfully from the room.

The kitchen master looked at me and grinned. "Never," said he, "Captain, did I see a slave run more eagerly to a beating."

"Nor did I," I admitted.

Now, at my victory feast, I drank more paga. That, I told myself, letting a boy train with weapons, had been a moment of weakness. I did not expect I would allow myself more such moments.

I observed the boy bringing in yet another roasted tarsk.

No, I told myself, I should not have showed such lenience to a slave.

I would not again allow myself such moments of weakness.

I fingered the broad scarlet ribbon and the medallion, pendant about my neck, bearing its tarn ship and initials, those of the Council of Captains of Port Kar.

I was Bosk, Pirate, Admiral of Port Kar, now perhaps one of the richest and most powerful men on Gor.

No, I would not again show such moments of weakness.

I thrust out the silver paga goblet, studded with rubies, and Telima, standing beside my thronelike chair, filled it. I did not look upon her.

I looked down the table, to where Thurnock, with his slave Thura, and Clitus, with his slave, Ula, were drinking and laughing. Thurnock and Clitus were good men, but they were fools. They were weak. I recalled how they had taken a fancy to the boy, Fish, and had helped him with his work in weapons. Such men were weak. They had not in themselves the stuff of captains.

I sat back on the great chair, paga goblet in hand, surveying the room.

It was crowded with the tables of my retainers, feasting.

To one side musicians played.

There was a clear space before my great table, in which, from time to time, during the evening, entertainments had been provided, simple things, which even I upon occasion found amusing, fire eaters and sword swallowers, jugglers and acrobats, and magicians, and slaves, riding on one another's shoulders, striking at one another with inflated tarsk bladders tied to poles.

"Drink!" I cried.

And again goblets were lifted and clashed.

I looked down the long table, and, far to my right, sitting alone at the end of the long bench behind the table, was Luma, my slave and chief scribe. Poor, scrawny, plain Luma, thought I, in her tunic of scribe's cloth, and collar! What a poor excuse for a paga slave she had been! Yet she had a brilliant mind for the accounts and business of a great house, and had much increased my fortunes. So indebted to her was I that I had, this night, permitted her to sit at one end of the great table. No free man, of course, would sit beside her. Moreover, that my other scribes and retainers not be angered, I had had her put in slave bracelets, and about her neck had had fastened a chain, which was bolted into the heavy table. And it was thus that Luma, she of perhaps greatest importance in my house, saving its master, with us, yet chained and alone, apart, shared my feast of victory.

"More paga," said I, putting out the goblet.

Telima poured me more paga.

"There is a singer," said one of my men.

This irritated me, but I had never much cared to interfere with the entertainments which were presented before me.

"It is truly a singer," said Telima, behind me.

It irritated me that she had spoken.

"Fetch Ta grapes from the kitchen," I told her.

"Please, my Ubar," said she, "let me stay."

"I am not your Ubar," I said. "I am your master."

"Please, Master," begged she, "let Telima stay."

"Very well," I said.

The tables grew quiet.

The man had been blinded, it was said, by Sullius Maximus, who believed that blinding improved the quality of a singer's songs. Sullius Maximus, who himself dabbled in poetry, and poisons, was a man of high culture, and his opinions in such matters were greatly respected. At any rate, whatever be the truth in these matters, the singer, in his darkness, was now alone with his songs. He had only them.

I looked upon him.

He wore the robes of his caste, the singers, and it was not known what city was his own. Many of the singers wander from place to place, selling their songs for bread and love. I had known, long ago, a singer, whose name was Andreas of Tor.

We could hear the torches crackle now, and the singer touched his lyre.

> I sing the siege of Ar
> of gleaming Ar.
> I sing the spears and walls of Ar
> of Glorious Ar.
> In the long years past of the siege of the city
> the siege of Ar
> of her spires and towers
> of undaunted Ar
> Glorious Ar
> I sing.

I did not care to hear his song. I looked down into the paga goblet. The singer continued.

> I sing of dark-haired Talena
> of the rage of Marlenus
> Ubar of Ar
> Glorious Ar.

I did not wish to hear this song. It infuriated me to see that the others in that room sat rapt, bestowing on the singer such attention for such trifles, the meaningless noises of a blind man's mouth.

> And of he I sing
> whose hair was like a larl from the sun
> of he who came once to the walls of Ar
> Glorious Ar
> he called Tarl of Bristol.

I glanced at Telima, who stood beside my great chair. Her eyes were moist, drinking in the song. She was only a rence girl, I reminded myself. Doubtless never before had she heard a singer. I thought of sending her to the kitchens, but did not do so. I felt her hand on my shoulder. I did not indicate that I was aware of it.

And, as the torches burned lower in the wall racks, the singer continued to sing, and sang of gray Pa-Kur, Master of the Assassins, leader of the hordes that fell on Ar after the theft of her Home Stone; and he sang, too, of banners and black helmets, of upraised standards, of the sun flashing on the lifted blades of spears, of high siege towers and deeds, of catapults of Ka-la-na and tem-wood, of the thunder of war tharlarion and the beatings of drums and the roars of trumpets, the clash of arms and the cries of men; and he sang, too, of the love of men for their city, and, foolishly, knowing so little of men, he sang, too, the bravery of men, and their loyalties and their courage; and he sang then, too, of duels; of duels fought even on the walls of Ar herself, even at the great gate; and of tarnsmen locked in duels to the death over the spires of Ar; and of yet another duel, one fought on the height of Ar's cylinder of justice, between Pa-Kur, and he, in the song, called Tarl of Bristol.

"Why does my Ubar weep?" asked Telima.

"Be silent, Slave," said I. Angrily I brushed her hand from my shoulder. She drew back her hand swiftly, as though she had not known it had lain there.

The singer had now finished his song.

"Singer," called I to him, "is there truly a man such as Tarl of Bristol?"

The singer turned his head to me, puzzled. "I do not know," he said. "Perhaps it is only a song."

I laughed.

I extended the paga goblet to Telima and, again, she filled it.

I rose to my feet, lifting the goblet, and my retainers, as well, rose to their feet, lifting their goblets.

"There is gold and steel!" I said.

"Gold and steel!" cried my retainers.

We drank.

"And songs," said the blind singer.

The room was quiet.

I looked upon the singer. "Yes," I said, lifting my goblet to him, "and songs."

There was a cry of pleasure from my retainers, and again we drank.

When again I sat down I said to the serving slaves, "Feast the singer well," and then I turned to Luma, slave and accountant of my house, braceleted and chained at the end of the long table, and said to her, "Tomorrow, the singer, before he is sent on his way, is to be given a cap of gold."

"Yes, Master," said the girl.

"Thank you, Captain!" cried the singer.

My retainers cried out with pleasure at my generosity, many of them striking their left shoulders with their right fists in Gorean applause.

Two slave girls helped the singer from the stool on which he had sat and conducted him to a table in a far corner of the room.

I drank more paga.

I was furious.

Tarl of Bristol lived only in songs. There was no such man. There were, in the end, only gold and steel, and perhaps the bodies of women, and perhaps songs, the meaningless noises that might sometimes be heard in the mouths of the blind.

Again I was Bosk, from the marshes, Pirate, Admiral of Port Kar.

I fingered the golden medallion with the lateen-rigged tarn ship, and the initials of the Council of Captains of Port Kar in its half-curve beneath it.

"Sandra!" I called. "Send for Sandra!"

There were cheers from the tables.

I looked about. It was indeed a feast of victory. I was only angered that Midice was not present with me. She had felt ill, and had begged to remain behind in my quarters, which leave I had given her. Tab, too, was not present.

Then there was a rustle of slave bells and Sandra, the dancing girl of Port Kar, whom I had first seen in a Paga tavern, and had purchased, primarily for my men, stood before me, her master.

I looked on her with amusement.

How desperate she was to please me.

She wanted to be first girl, but I had kept her primarily with my men. Beautiful, dark-haired, slender, marvelously-legged Midice was, in my house, first girl, my favored slave. As Tab was my first Captain.

But yet Sandra was of interest.

She had high cheekbones, and flashing black eyes, and coal-black hair, now worn high, pinned, over her head. She stood wrapped in an opaque sheet of shimmering yellow silk. As she had approached me I had heard the bells which had been locked on her ankles and wrists, and hung pendant from her collar.

It would not hurt, I thought, for Midice to have a bit of competition.

And so I smiled upon Sandra.

She looked at me, eagerness and pleasure transfusing her features.

"You may dance, Slave," I told her.

It was to be the dance of the six thongs.

She slipped the silk from her and knelt before the great table and chair, between the other tables, dropping her head. She wore five pieces of metal, her collar and locked rings on her wrists and ankles. Slave bells were attached to the collar and the rings. She lifted her head, and regarded me. The musicians, to one side, began to play. Six of my men, each with a length of binding fiber, approached her. She held her arms down, and a bit to the sides. The ends of six lengths of binding fiber, like slave snares, were fastened on her, one for each wrist and ankle, and two about her waist; the men, then, each holding the free end of a length of fiber, stood about her, some six or eight feet from her, three on a side. She was thus imprisoned among them, each holding a thong that bound her.

I glanced to Thura. I recalled that she had been caught in capture loops on the rence island, not unlike the two now about Sandra's waist. Thura was watching with eagerness.

So, too, were all.

Sandra then, luxuriously, catlike, like a woman awakening, stretched her arms.

There was laughter.

It was as though she did not know herself bound.

When she went to draw her arms back to her body there was just the briefest instant in which she could not do so, and she frowned, looked annoyed, puzzled, and then was permitted to move as she wished.

I laughed.

She was superb.

Then, still kneeling, she raised her hand, head back, insolently to her hair, to remove from it one of the ornate pins, its head carved from the horn of kailiauk, that bound it.

Again a thong, this time that on her right wrist, prohibited, but only for an instant, the movement, but inches from her hair.

She frowned. There was laughter.

At last, sometimes immediately permitted, sometimes not, she had removed the pins from her hair. Her hair was beautiful, rich, long and black. As she knelt, it fell back to her ankles.

Then, with her hands, she lifted the hair again back over her head, and then, suddenly, her hands, by the thongs were pulled apart and her hair fell again loose and rich over her body.

Now, angrily, struggling, she fought to lift her hair again but the thongs, holding apart her hands, did not permit her to do so. She fought them. The thongs would permit her only to wear her hair loosely.

Then, as though in terror and fury, as though she now first understood herself in the snares of a slave, she leaped to her feet, fighting, to the music, the thongs.

The dancing girls of Port Kar, I told myself, are the best on all Gor.

Dark and golden, shimmering, crying out, stamping, she danced, her thonged beauty incandescent in the light of the torches and the frenzy of the slave bells.

She turned and twisted and leaped, and sometimes seemed almost free, but was always, by the dark thongs, held complete prisoner. Sometimes she would rush upon one man or another, but the others would not permit her to reach him, keeping her always beautiful female slave snared in her web of thongs. She writhed and cried out, trying to force the thongs from her body, but could not do so.

At last, bit by bit, as her fear and terror mounted, the men, fist by fist, took up the slack in the thongs that tethered her, until suddenly, they swiftly bound her hand and foot and lifted her over their heads, captured female slave, displaying her bound arched body to the tables.

There were cries of pleasure from the tables, and much striking of the right fist on the left shoulder.

She had been truly superb.

Then the men carried her before my table and held her bound before me. "A slave," said one.

"Yes," cried the girl, "slave!"

The music finished with a clash.

The applause and cries were wild and loud.

I was much pleased.

"Cut her loose," I told the men.

They did so and, swiftly, like a cat, the girl ran to my chair, and knelt at my feet. She looked up, streaked with sweat, breathing heavily, her eyes shining.

"Your performance was not without interest," I said to her.

She put her cheek to my knee.

"Ka-la-na!" I called.

A cup was brought. And I took her by the hair and held back her head, pouring the wine down her throat, some of it running down her face and body, under the slave collar and its bells.

She looked up at me, her mouth stained with wine. "Did I please you?" she asked.

"Yes," I said.

"Do not send me back to your men," she begged. "Keep Sandra for yourself."

"We shall see," I said.

"Sandra wants much to please Master," she said.

Wily wench, I thought.

"You used Sandra only once," pouted the girl. "It is not fair." She looked up at me. "Sandra is better than Midice," she said.

"Midice," I said, "is very good."

"Sandra is better," wheedled the girl. "Try Sandra and see."

"Perhaps," I said. I gave her head a rough shake and permitted her to remain kneeling at the arm of my chair. I saw other slave girls, serving at the tables, cast looks of hatred and jealousy on her. Like a satisfied cat, she knelt beside my chair.

"The gold, Captain," said one of my treasure guards.

I had arranged a surprise for my retainers on this night of feasting and victory.

He lifted, heavily, to the dais on which my chair and

table sat a heavy leather sack filled with golden tarn disks of double weight, of Cos and Tyros, of Ar and Port Kar, even of distant Thentis and remote Turia, far to the south. He placed the sack beside my great chair. Few, saving those immediately near me, saw it there.

"Send for the slave girl from Tyros!" I called.

There was laughter from the tables.

I held out my paga goblet, but it was not filled. I looked about, angrily.

I called out to a passing slave girl. "Where is the slave Telima?" I demanded.

"She was here but a moment ago," said a slave girl.

"She went to the kitchens," said another.

I had not given her permission to leave.

"I will serve you paga," said Sandra.

"No," I said, holding the paga goblet away from her. I addressed myself to one of the slave girls. "Have Telima beaten," I said, "and sent to my side. I would be served."

"Yes, Master," said the girl, speeding away.

Sandra looked down, angrily, pouting.

"Do not fret," I said to her, "or I shall have you beaten as well."

"It is only, Master," said she, "that I wish to serve you."

I laughed. She was indeed a wily wench.

"Paga?" I asked.

She looked up at me, suddenly, her eyes bright, her lips slightly parted. "No," she said, "wine."

"I see," I said.

There was a rustle of chain and the Lady Vivina, to the pleasure of the tables, was conducted before me.

I heard a movement at my side and saw that Telima now stood again where she had before. There were tears in her eyes. I did not doubt that she now had four or five welts on her back from the switch of the kitchen master. The thin rep-cloth tunic provides little protection from the kitchen master's switch. I held out the paga goblet, and she refilled it.

I looked upon the Lady Vivina.

All attention was upon her. Even several of the slaves, about the edges of the room, behind the tables, had gathered to look upon her. I saw the slave boy, Fish, among them.

I regarded the girl before me. She had been chief among my prizes.

This afternoon I had presented her, with her maidens, in the chains of slave girls, together with portions of the treasures of the treasure fleet, and accountings of the balance thereof, before the Council of Captains of Port Kar. They had been beautiful, in silver throat coffle, their wrists bound behind their backs in golden slave bracelets, kneeling as pleasure slaves among the jewels, the piled gold, and the heaps of silk and kegs of spices. She who was to have been the Ubara of Cos was in the city of Port Kar only booty.

"Greetings, Lady Vivina," said I to her.

"Is that the name you will choose to know me by?" she asked.

This afternoon, after returning from the Council of Captains, I had had her marked and collared.

Now, aside from her collar and brand, standing before me, she wore only slave bracelets.

She was very beautiful.

"Remove the bracelets," I told the man who had conducted her before me.

He did so.

"Unbind her hair," I said.

He did so, and her hair fell about her shoulders, and there was a cry of pleasure from my men.

"Kneel," I told her.

She did so.

"You are Vina," I told her.

She dropped her head, acknowledging the name I had given her. Then she looked up. "I congratulate Master," said she. "It is an excellent name for a slave girl."

"Who are you?" I asked.

"I am Vina," she said.

"What are you?" I asked.

"Slave," she said.

"What are your duties, Slave?" I asked.

"Master has not yet informed me," she said.

I looked upon her. I had also had her maidens marked and collared, following the meeting of the Council of Captains. They were now chained within my holding. I had not yet decided on their disposition. Perhaps I should distribute them among my officers, or give them to my men. They might serve as prizes in games or as inducements to serve me better, that one might be received as gift in token of good service. Also I had toyed with the idea of opening a paga tavern in the center of the city, the most opulent in Port Kar, perhaps, called the Tavern of the Forty Maidens. There were few in Port Kar who would not be eager to patronize such an establishment, that they might be served by the high-born beauties of Tyros.

But now my attention was on the girl Vina, once the Lady Vivina, once to have been the Ubara of Cos, now only female slave in the house of Bosk, he of Port Kar.

"What garments shall be brought for you?" I asked.

She looked up at me.

"Shall it be the tunic of a house slave?" I asked.

She said nothing.

"Or," I asked, "should I call for the bells and the silk, and the perfumes, of a pleasure slave?"

She smiled. "I assume," she said icily, "that I will be used as a pleasure slave."

From the sack at the side of my chair, that filled muchly with gold, I drew forth a small piece of folded, wadded cloth. I threw it to the girl.

She caught it, and looked at it. "No!" she cried.

"Put it on," I told her.

"No, no!" she cried in fury, leaping to her feet, holding the piece of cloth.

She turned to flee, but was ringed by my men. She turned again to face me, holding the cloth, "No!" she said in rage, "No!"

"Put it on," I told her.

Furiously she drew on the garment.

There was great laughter from the tables.

The Lady Vivina stood before me clad in the garment of a Kettle Slave.

"In Cos," I told her, "you would have been Ubara. In my house you will be Kettle Slave."

Enraged, red with shame, her fists clenched, in the brief garment of the Kettle Slave, the Lady Vivina stood before us.

The room was convulsed with laughter.

"Kitchen Master!" I called.

"Here, Captain!" cried Tellius, from behind the tables.

"Come here!" I called.

The man approached the table.

"Here," I told him, gesturing to the girl, "is a new girl for the kitchens."

He laughed, and walked about her, his switch in his hand. "She is a beauty," he said.

"See that she is worked well," I said.

"She will be," he promised me.

The Lady Vivina looked on me with fury.

"Fish!" I called. "Where is the slave boy Fish!"

"Here!" he cried, and came forward, from behind the tables, where, with other slaves, for some time, he had been watching what had been going on.

I gestured to the girl. "Do you find this slave pleasing?" I asked.

He looked at me, puzzled.

"Yes," he said.

"Good," said I. Then I turned to the girl. "You please the slave boy Fish," I said to her. "Therefore your use will be his."

"No!" she cried. "No! No!"

"The use of her," I told the boy, "is yours."

"No," cried the girl. "No! No! No! No!"

She threw herself to her knees before me, weeping, extending her arms. "He is only a slave," she wept. "I was to have been Ubara! Ubara!"

"Your use is his," I said.

She held her face in her hands, bent over, weeping.

There was much laughter in the room. I looked about, well pleased. Of those I looked upon, only Luma did not laugh. There were tears in her eyes. This irritated me. Tomorrow, I thought, I will have her beaten.

Sandra, at my side, was laughing merrily. I gave her head a rough shake. She began to kiss my left arm, and I, with my right hand, brushed her away. But in a moment she again held her cheek to my left arm.

The boy, Fish, was looking on the girl, Vina, not without compassion. They were both quite young. He was perhaps seventeen, she perhaps fifteen or sixteen. Then he reached down and lifted her to her feet, turning her to face him.

"I am Fish," he said.

"You are only a slave boy!" she cried.

She would not meet his eyes.

He took her by the collar and turned it slightly upward in his large hands, forcing her head up to face his.

"Who are you?" he asked.

"I am the Lady Vivina of Kasra!" she cried.

"No," he said, "you are a slave."

"No!" she said, shaking her head.

"Yes," he said, "and I, too, am a slave."

And then, to our surprise, holding her head in his hands, he kissed her gently on the lips.

She looked at him, tears in her eyes.

Raised as she had been, in the sequestered quarters of high-born women in the palace of Tyros in Kasra, I supposed it was perhaps the first time that the lips of a man had touched hers. Doubtless she had expected to receive that kiss standing in the swirling love silks of the Free Companion, beneath golden love lamps, beside the couch of the Ubar of Cos; but it was not in the white, marbled palace of the Ubar of Cos that that kiss was to take place; and it was not to be received as a Ubara from the lips of a Ubar; that kiss was to take place in Port Kar, in the holding of her enemies, under barbaric torchlight, before the table of her master; and she was not to wear the love silks of a Free Companion and Ubara but the brief, wretched garment of a Kettle Slave, and a collar that proclaimed her slave girl; and the lips would be those of a slave which touched hers, those themselves of a slave.

To our surprise she had not resisted the boy's kiss. He held her by the arms. "I am a slave," he said.

To our astonishment, then, she, in all her friendlessness, in all her misery and loneliness, lifted her lips to his, with great timidity, that he might, should it please him to do so, again touch them.

Again he gently kissed her.

"I, too, am a slave," she said. "My name is Vina."

"You are worthy," he said, holding her head in his hands, "to be a Ubara."

"And you," she whispered, "to be a Ubar."

"I think you will find," I told her, "the arms of the boy Fish more welcome, though on the mat of a slave, than the arms of gross Lurius, on the furs of the Ubar's couch."

She looked at me, tears in her eyes.

I spoke to the kitchen master. "At night," I said, "chain them together."

"A single blanket?" he asked.

"Yes," I told him.

The girl collapsed weeping, but Fish, with great gentleness lifted her in his arms and carried her from the hall.

I laughed.

And there was great laughter.

How rich a joke it was, to have enslaved the girl who would have been Ubara of Cos, to have put her to work in my kitchens, to have given the use of her to a mere slave boy! This story would soon be told in all the ports of Thassa and all the cities of Gor! How shamed would be Tyros and Cos, enemies of my city, Port Kar! How delicious is the defeat of enemies! How glorious is power, success, triumph!

I reached drunkenly into the bag of gold beside my chair and grabbed up handfuls flinging them about the room. I stood and threw about me showers of the tarn disks of Ar, of Tyros, of Cos, Thentis, Turia and Port Kar! Men scrambled wildly laughing and fighting for the coins. Each was of double weight!

"Paga!" I cried and held back the goblet and Telima filled it.

I regretted only that Midice and Tab were not with me to share my triumph.

I stood drunkenly, holding to the table. I spilled paga. "Paga!" I cried, and Telima again filled the goblet. I drank again. And then, again, wildly, shouting, crying out, I threw gold to all the corners of the room, laughing as the men fought and leaped to seize it.

I drank and then threw more coins and more coins about the room.

There was laughter and delighted cries.

"Hail Bosk!" I heard. "Hail Bosk, Admiral of Port Kar!"

I threw more gold wildly about. I drank again, and again. "Yes," I cried. "Hail Bosk!"

"Hail Bosk!" they cried. "Hail Bosk, Admiral of Port Kar!"

"Yes," I cried. "Hail Bosk! Hail Bosk, Admiral of Port Kar! Hail Bosk, Admiral of Port Kar!"

I heard a cry, as of fear, from my right, and I turned to stare drunkenly toward the end of the table. There, Luma, chained at the table, in her bracelets, was looking at me. On her face there was a look of horror.

"Your face," she cried. "Your face!"

I looked at her, puzzled.

The room was suddenly quiet.

"No," she said, suddenly, shaking her head. "It is gone now."

"What is wrong?" I asked her.

"Your face," she said.

"What of it?" I asked.

"It is nothing," she said, looking down.

"What of it!" I demanded.

"For an instant," she said, "I thought—I thought it was the face of Surbus."

I cried out with rage and seized the great table, flinging it, scattering dishes and paga, from the dais. Thura and Ula screamed. Sandra screamed, darting away, her hands before her, with an incongruous clash of slave bells. Luma, fastened by the neck to the table, was jerked from the dais, and thrown over the table to the tiles of the hall. Slave girls fled from the room, screaming.

Enraged I took the bag of gold, what was left of it, and hurled it out into the hall, spilling a rain of golden tarn disks before it struck the tiles.

Then, furious, I turned about and, stumbling, left the hall.

"Admiral!" I heard behind me. "Admiral!"

I clutched the medallion about my neck, with its tarn ship and the initials of the Council of Captains.

Stumbling, crying out in rage, I staggered toward my quarters.

I could hear the consternation behind me.

In fury, I rushed on, sometimes falling, sometimes striking against the walls.

Then I burst open the doors of my quarters.

Midice and Tab leaped apart.

I howled with rage and turned about striking the walls with my fists and then, throwing off my cloak, spun weeping to face them, in the same instant drawing my blade.

"It is torture and impalement for you, Midice," I said.

"No," said Tab. "It is my fault. I forced myself upon her."

"No, No!" cried Midice. "It is my fault! My fault!"

"Torture and impalement," I said to her. Then I regarded Tab. "You have been a good man, Tab," said I, "so I will not save you for the torturers." I gestured with my blade. "Defend yourself," I said.

Tab shrugged. He did not draw his weapon. "I know you can kill me," he said.

"Defend yourself," I screamed to him.

"Very well," said Tab, and his weapon left its sheath.

Midice flung herself on her knees between us, weeping. "No!" she cried. "Kill Midice!"

"I shall slay you slowly before her," I said, "and then I shall deliver her to the torturers."

"Kill Midice!" wept the girl. "But let him go! Let him go!"

"Why have you done this to me!" I cried out to her weeping. "Why? Why?"

"I love him," she said, weeping. "I love him."

I laughed. "You cannot love," I told her. "You are Midice. You are small, and petty, and selfish, and vain! You cannot love!"

"I do love him," she whispered. "I do."

"Do you not love me?" I begged.

"No," she whispered, tears in her eyes. "No."

"But I have given you many things," I wept. "And have I not given you great pleasure?"

"Yes," she said, "you have given me many things."

"And have I not," I demanded, "given you great pleasure!"

"Yes," she said, "you have."

"Then why!" I cried out.

"I do not love you," she said.

"You love me!" I screamed at her.

"No," she said, "I do not love you. And I have never loved you."

I wept.

I returned my blade to its sheath.

"Take her," I said to Tab. "She is yours."

"I love her," he said.

"Take her away!" I screamed. "Leave my service! Leave my sight!"

"Midice," said Tab, hoarsely.

She fled to him and he put one arm about her. Then they turned and left the room, he still carrying the unsheathed sword.

I walked slowly about in the room, and then I sat on the edge of the stone couch, on the furs, and put my head in my hands.

How long I had sat thus I do not know.

I heard, after some time, a slight sound in the threshold of my quarters.

I looked up.

In the threshold stood Telima.

I looked at her.

"Have you come to scrub the tiles?" I asked, sternly. She smiled. "It was done earlier," she said, "that I might serve late at the feast."

"Does the kitchen master know you are here?" I asked. She shook her head. "No," she said.

"You will be beaten," I said.

I saw that, about her left arm, she wore again the armlet of gold, which I remembered from so long ago, that which I had taken from her to give to Midice.

"You have the armlet," I said.

"Yes," she said.

"How did you get it?" I asked.

"From Midice," she said.

"You stole it," I said.

"No," she said.

I met her eyes.

"Midice gave it back to me," she said.

"When?" I asked.

"More than a month ago," said Telima.

"She was kind to a Kettle Slave," I said.

Telima smiled, tears in her eyes. "Yes," she said.

"I have not seen you wear it," I said.

"I have kept it hidden in the straw of my mat," said Telima.

I looked on Telima. She stood in the doorway, rather timidly. She was barefoot. She wore the brief, stained, wretched garment of a Kettle Slave. About her throat, looked, was a simple, steel collar. But she wore on her left arm an armlet of gold.

"Why have you worn the armlet of gold?" I asked.

"It is all I have," she said.

"Why have you come here at this time?" I asked.

"Midice," she said.

I cried out and put my head in my hands, weeping.

Telima timidly came closer. "She did care for you," she said.

I shook my head.

"She cannot help it if she did not love you," whispered Telima.

"Go back to the kitchens!" I wept. "Go back now, or I will kill you,"

Telima knelt down, a few feet from me. There were tears in her eyes.

"Go away," I cried, "or I will kill you!"

She did not move, but knelt there, with tears in her eyes. She shook her head. "No," she said, "you would not. You could not."

"I am Bosk!" I cried, standing.

"Yes," she said, "you are Bosk." She smiled. "It was I who gave you that name."

"It was you," I cried, "who destroyed me!"

"If any was destroyed," said she, "it was not you, but I."

"You destroyed me!" I wept.

"You have not been destroyed, my Ubar," said she.

"You have destroyed me," I cried, "and now I shall destroy you!"

I leaped to my feet, whipping the sword from my sheath and stood over her, the blade raised to strike.

She, kneeling, looked up at me, tears in her eyes.

In rage I hurled the blade away and it struck the stones of the wall thirty feet across the room and clattered to the floor, and I sank to my knees weeping, my head in my hands.

"Midice," I wept. "Midice."

I had vowed once that I had lost two women, and would never lose another. And now Midice was gone. I had given her the richest of silks, the most precious of jewels. I had become famed. I had become powerful and rich. I had become great. But now she was gone. It had not mattered. Nothing had mattered. And now she was gone, fled away in the night, no longer mine. To me she had chosen another. I had lost her. I had lost her.

"Midice," I wept. "Midice!"

Then I rose to my feet, and stood there, and shook my head, and wiped the sleeve of my tunic across my eyes and then, catching my breath, I walked to the bottom of the stone couch and sat down, my head down.

"It is hard," I said to Telima, "to love, and not to be loved."

"I know," she said.

I looked at her. Her hair had been combed.

"Your hair is combed," I said.

She smiled. "One of the girls in the kitchen," she said, "has a broken comb, one that Ula threw away."

"She let you use it," I said.

"I did much work for her," said Telima, "that I might, one night, when I chose, use it."

"Perhaps the new girl," I said, "to please the boy Fish, will sometimes wish to use the comb."

Telima smiled. "Then she, too," said Telima, "will have to work."

I smiled.

"Come here," I said.

Obediently the girl rose to her feet and came and knelt before me.

I put out my hands and took her head in my hands. "My proud Telima," I said, "my former mistress." I looked on her, kneeling barefoot before me, my steel collar locked on her throat, in the scanty, miserable, stained garment of the Kettle Slave.

"My Ubar," she whispered.

"Master," I said.

"Master," she said.

I drew the golden armlet from her arm, and looked at it.

"How dare you, Slave," I asked, "wear this before me?"

She looked startled. "I wanted to please you," she whispered.

I threw the armlet to one side. "Kettle Slave," I said.

She looked down, and a tear ran down her cheek.

"You thought to win my favor," I said, "by coming here at this time."

She looked up. "No," she said.

"But your trick," I told her, "has not worked."

She shook her head, no.

I put my hands on her collar, forcing her to look directly at me. "You are well worthy of a collar," I said.

Her eyes flashed, the Telima of old. "You, too," she said, "wear a collar!"

I tore away from my throat the broad scarlet ribbon, with its pendant medallion, with the tarn ship and the initials of the Council of Captains. I flung it from me.

"Arrogant Slave!" I said.

She said nothing.

"You have come to torment me in my grief," I told her.

"No," she said, "no!"

I rose to my feet and flung her to the tiles of the bed chamber.

"You want to be first girl!" I cried.

She stood up, looking down. "It was not for that reason that I came here tonight," she said.

"You want to be first girl!" I cried. "You want to be first girl!"

She looked suddenly at me, angrily. "Yes," she cried, "I want to be first girl!"

I laughed, pleased that she had spoken her guilt out of her own mouth.

"You are only a Kettle Slave," I laughed. "First girl! I am going to send you back to the kitchens to be beaten, Kettle Slave!"

She looked at me, tears in her eyes. "Who will be first girl?" she asked.

"Doubtless Sandra," said I.

"She is very beautiful," said Telima.

"Perhaps," I asked, "you saw her dance?"

"Yes," said Telima, "she is very, very beautiful."

"Can you dance thus?" I asked her.

She smiled. "No," she said.

"Sandra," I said, "seems eager to please me."

Telima looked at me. "I, too," she whispered, "am eager to please you."

I laughed at her, that she, the proud Telima, would so demean herself.

"You resort well," I said, "to the wiles of the slave girl."

She dropped her head.

"Are the kitchens that unpleasant?" I taunted her.

She looked up at me, angrily. There were tears in her eyes. "You can be hateful," she said.

I turned away.

"You may return to the kitchens," I told her.

I sensed her turn and move toward the door.

"Wait!" I cried, turning, and she, too, in the doorway, turned.

And then the words that I spoke did not seem to come from me but from something within me that was deeper than the self I knew. Not since I had knelt bound before Ho-Hak on the rence island had such words come from me, so unbidden, so tortured. "I am unhappy," I said, "and I am lonely."

There were tears in her eyes. "I, too," she said, "am lonely."

We approached one another, and extended to one another our hands, and our hands touched, and I held her hands. And then, weeping, the two of us cried out, holding one another.

"I love you," I cried.

And she cried, "And I love you, my Ubar. I have loved you for so long!"

What Occurred One Night

in Port Kar

I held the sweet, loving, uncollared thing in my arms.

"My Ubar," whispered Telima.

"Master," I said, kissing her.

She drew back, reproachfully. "Would you not rather be my Ubar, than my Master?" she asked.

I looked at her. "Yes," I said, "I would."

"You are both," she pronounced, again kissing me.

"Ubara," I whispered to her.

"Yes," she whispered, "I am your Ubara—and your slave girl."

"You wear no collar," I pointed out.

"Master removed it," said she, "that he might more easily kiss my throat."

"Oh," I said.

"Oh!" she cried.

"What is wrong?" I asked.

"Nothing," she laughed.

I felt her back, and the five weals left there by the switch of the kitchen master.

"But a few hours ago," said she, "I displeased my master and he had me beaten."

"I am sorry," I said.

She laughed. "How silly you sometimes are, my Ubar. I left your side unbidden, and so, of course, I was beaten." She looked up at me, laughing. "I have richly deserved many beatings," she confided, "but I have not always received them."

Telima was Gorean to the core. I myself would always be, doubtless, at least partly, of Earth. I held her. There could never be, I told myself, any question of sending this woman to Earth. In that overcrowded desert of hypocracies and hysterical, meaningless violences, she would surely wither and blacken, like some rare and beautiful

244

plant of the marshes uprooted and thrust down among stones to die.

"Are you still sad, my Ubar?" she asked.

"No," I told her, kissing her. "No."

She looked at me, gently. And touched my cheek with her hand. "Do not be sad," she said.

I looked about and found the golden armlet. I slipped it once again on her arm.

She leaped to her feet, standing on the furs of the couch, and threw her left arm into the air. "I am a Ubara!" she cried.

"Commonly," I said, "a Ubara wears more than a golden armlet."

"On the couch of her Ubar?" asked Telima.

"Well," I admitted, "I do not know about that."

"I do not either," said Telima. She looked down at me, brightly. "I shall ask the new girl in the kitchens," she said.

"You wench!" I cried, grabbing for her ankle.

She stepped back swiftly, and then stood there, regally on the furs.

"How dare you address such a word to your Ubara, Slave!" demanded she.

"Slave!" I cried.

"Yes," she taunted, "Slave!"

I cast about for the slave collar I had taken from her throat.

"No, no!" she cried, laughing, almost losing her footing in the furs.

Then I had the collar.

"You will never collar me!" she cried.

She darted away, laughing. I, laughing, leaped from the couch, pursuing her. She ran this way and that, and dodged back and forth, laughing, but then I had her pinned in the corner of the room, her arms held down by the walls and my body, and snapped the collar again on her throat. I lifted her and carried her again to the furs and threw her down upon them.

She jerked at the collar and looked up at me, as though in fury.

I held her wrists down.

"You will never tame me!" she hissed.

I kissed her.

"Well," she said, "perhaps you will tame me."

I kissed her again.

"Ah," she said, looking up at me, "it is not unlikely that in the end I will succumb to you."

I laughed.

But then, as though infuriated by my laughter, she began to struggle viciously. "But, in the meantime," she hissed, between clenched teeth, "I shall resist you with all my might!"

I laughed again, and she laughed, and I permitted her to struggle until she had exhausted herself, and then, with lips and hands, and teeth and tongue, I touched her, until her body, caressed and loved, in all its loneliness and passion, yielded itself, moaning and crying out, to mine in our common ecstasy. And in the moments before she yielded, when I sensed her readiness, to her faint protest, then joy, I removed from her throat the slave collar that her yielding, our games ended, would be that of the free woman, glorious in the eager and willing, the joyous, bestowal of herself.

"I love you," she said.

"I love you, too," I said. "I love you, my Telima."

"But sometime," she said, teasingly, "you must love me as a slave girl."

"Women!" I cried, in exasperation.

"Every woman," said Telima, "sometimes wishes to be loved as a Ubara, and sometimes as a slave girl."

"Oh," I said.

For a long time we lay together in one another's arms.

"My Ubar," she said.

"Yes," I said.

"Why, at the feast, when the singer sang," she asked, "did you weep?"

"For no reason," I said.

We lay side by side, looking up at the ceiling.

"Years ago," she said, "when I was so much younger, I recall hearing sing of Tarl of Bristol."

"In the marshes?" I asked.

"Yes," she said, "sometimes a singer comes to the rence islands. But, too, when I was a slave in Port Kar I heard sing of Tarl of Bristol, in the house of my master."

Telima had never spoken much to me of her slavery in Port Kar. She had hated her master, I had known, and she had escaped. And, as I had sensed, her slavery had scarred her deeply. In the marshes I had been unfortunate

enough to taste something of the hatreds and frustrations
that had been built up within her. Her wounds had been
deep, and having been hurt by a man it had been her desire to hurt one in turn, and cruelly so, that in his suffering
her imagined vengeance on another would be the sweeter.
Telima was a strange woman. I wondered again how she
had come by an armlet of gold. And I recalled, now
puzzled again, that she, though a rence girl, had been
able to read the lettering on the collar I had placed on her
one night long ago.

But I did not speak to her of these things, for she was
speaking to me, dreamily, remembering.

"When I was a girl on the rence island," she said,
"and later, sometimes at night, when I was a slave, in
my cage in my master's house, I would lie awake and
think of the songs, and of heroes."

I touched her hand.

"And sometimes," she said, "even often, I would think
of the hero Tarl of Bristol."

I said nothing.

"Do you think there is such a man?" she asked.

"No," I said.

"Could not such a man exist?" she asked. She had
rolled over on her stomach, and was looking at me. I was
lying on my back, looking at the ceiling.

"In songs," I said. "Such a man might exist in songs."

She laughed. "Are there no heroes?" she asked.

"No," I told her. "There are no heroes."

She said nothing.

"There are only human beings," I told her.

I lay looking for a long time at the ceiling.

"Human beings," I told her, "are weak. They are capable
of cruelty. They are selfish, and greedy, and vain and
petty. They can be vicious, and there is much in them that
is ugly and worthy only of contempt." I looked at her.
"All men," I told her, "are corruptible. There are no
heroes, no Tarls of Bristol."

She smiled at me. "There is gold and steel," she said.

"And the bodies of women," I said.

"And songs," she said.

"Yes," I said, "and songs."

She laid her head on my shoulder.

Dimly, far off, I heard the ringing of a great bar.
Though it was early I heard noises in the house. Some

men, down one or another of the corridors, were shouting.

I sat up on the couch, and drew about myself my robes.

I heard feet running in the corridor, approaching.

"The blade," I said to Telima.

She leaped up, and picked up the sword, which lay near the wall, where I had thrown it some hours before, when I had not slain her.

I put the blade in my scabbard, and wrapped the straps about the scabbard.

The steps were close now, and then I heard a pounding at my door.

"Captain!" I heard.

It was Thurnock.

"Enter!" I called.

Thurnock burst in. He stood there, within the room, his eyes wild, his hair wild, holding a torch. "Patrol ships have returned," he cried. "The joint fleets of Cos and Tyros are but hours from us!"

"Outfit my ships," I said.

"There is no time!" he cried. "And captains are fleeing! All who can are leaving Port Kar!"

I looked at him.

"Flee, my Captain!" he said. "Flee!"

"You may go," said I, "Thurnock."

He looked at me, confused, and then turned and stumbled away down the hall. Somewhere I heard a girl screaming in fear.

I dressed, and slung the sword over my left shoulder.

"Take your ships and what men are left to you," said Telima. "Fill your ships with treasure and fly, my Ubar."

I regarded her. How beautiful she was.

"Let Port Kar die!" she cried.

I picked up the broad scarlet ribbon, with its medallion, that with the tarn ship and the initials of the Council of Captains.

I put it in my pouch.

"Let Port Kar burn," said Telima. "Let Port Kar die!"

"You are very beautiful, my love," I told her.

"Let Port Kar die!" she cried.

"It is my city," I said. "I must defend it."

I heard her weeping as I left the room.

Strangely there was little in my mind as I walked to

the great hall, where the feast had been held. I walked as though I might be another, not knowing myself.

I knew what I would do, and yet I knew not why I would do it.

To my surprise, in the great hall, I found gathered the officers of my men.

I think there was not one that was not there.

I looked from face to face, the great Thurnock, now calm, swift, strong Clitus, the shrewd oar-master, the others. Many of these men were cutthroats, killers, pirates. I wondered why they were in this room.

A door at the side opened and Tab strode in, his sword over his left shoulder. "I am sorry, Captain," said he, "I was attending to my ship."

We regarded one another evenly. And then I smiled. "I am fortunate," I said, "to have one so diligent in my service."

"Captain," said he.

"Thurnock," I said, "I gave orders, did I not, to have my ships outfitted."

Thurnock grinned, the tooth missing on his upper right side. "It is being done," he said.

"What are we to do?" asked one of my captains.

What could one say to them? If the joint fleets of Cos and Tyros were indeed almost upon us, there was little to do but flee, or fight. We were truly ready to do neither. Even had the fortunes I had brought from the treasure fleet been applied immediately after my return to the city, we could not, in the time, have outfitted a fleet to match that which must be descending upon us.

"What would be your estimate of the size of the fleet of Cos and Tyros," I asked Tab.

He did not hesitate. "Four thousand ships," he said.

"Tarn ships?" I asked.

"All," he said.

His surmise agreed closely with the reports of my spies. The fleet would consist, according to my information, of forty-two hundred ships, twenty-five hundred from Cos and seventeen hundred from Tyros. Of the forty-two hundred, fifteen hundred would be galleys heavy class, two thousand medium-class galleys, and seven hundred light galleys. A net, a hundred pasangs wide, was closing on Port Kar.

It seemed that only the departure date of the fleet

had eluded my spies. I laughed, yet I could not blame them. One scarcely advertises such matters. And ships may be swiftly outfitted and launched, if materials and crews are at hand. The council and I had apparently miscalculated the damage done by the capture of the treasure fleet to the war plans of Cos and Tyros. We had not expected the launching of the fleet to take place until the spring. Besides, it was now in Se'Kara, late in the season to launch tarn ships. Most sailing, save by round ships, is done in the spring and summer. In Se'Kara, particularly later in the month, there are often high seas on Thassa. We had been taken totally unprepared. It was dangerous to attack us now. In this bold stroke I saw not the hand of Lurius, Ubar of Cos, but of the brilliant Chenbar of Kasra, Ubar of Tyros, the Sea Sleen.

I admired him. He was a good captain.

"What shall we do, Captain?" asked the officer once more.

"What do you propose?" I asked him, smiling.

He looked at me, startled. "There is only one thing to do," he said, "and that is to ready our ships, take our treasure and slaves aboard, and flee. We are strong, and may take an island for our own, one of the northern islands. There you can be Ubar and we can be your men."

"Many of the captains," said another officer, "are already weighing anchor for the northern islands."

"And others," said another, "for the southern ports."

"Thassa is broad," said another officer. "There are many islands, many ports."

"And what of Port Kar?" I asked.

"She has no Home Stone," said one of the men.

I smiled. It was true. Port Kar, of all the cities on Gor, was the only one that had no Home Stone. I did not know if men did not love her because she had no Home Stone, or that she had no Home Stone because men did not love her.

The officer had proposed, as clearly as one might, that the city be abandoned to the flames, and to the ravaging seamen of Cos and Tyros.

Port Kar had no Home Stone.

"How many of you think," I asked, "that Port Kar has no Home Stone?"

The men looked at one another, puzzled. All knew, of course, that she had no Home Stone.

There was silence.

Then, after a time, Tab said, "I think that she might have one."

"But," said I, "she does not yet have one."

"No," said Tab.

"I," said one of the men, "wonder what it would be like to live in a city where there was a Home Stone."

"How does a city obtain a Home Stone?" I asked.

"Men decide that she shall have one," said Tab.

"Yes," I said, "that is how it is that a city obtains a Home Stone."

The men looked at one another.

"Send the slave boy Fish before me," I said.

The men looked at one another, not understanding, but one went to fetch the boy.

I knew that none of the slaves would have fled. They would not have been able to. The alarm had come in the night, and, at night, in a Gorean household, it is common for the slaves to be confined; certainly in my house, as a wise precaution, I kept my slaves well secured; even Midice, when she had snuggled against me in the love furs, when I had finished with her, was always chained by the right ankle to the slave ring set in the bottom of my couch. Fish would have been chained in the kitchen, side by side with Vina.

The boy, white-faced, alarmed, was shoved into my presence.

"Go outside," I told him, "and find a rock, and bring it to me."

He looked at me.

"Hurry!" I said.

He turned about and ran from the room.

We waited quietly, not speaking, until he had returned. He held in his hand a sizable rock, somewhat bigger than my fist. It was a common rock, not very large, and gray and heavy, granular in texture.

I took the rock.

"A knife," I said.

I was handed a knife.

I cut in the rock the initials, in block Gorean script, of Port Kar.

Then I held out in my hand the rock.

I held it up so that the men could see.

"What have I here?" I asked.

Tab said it, and quietly, "The Home Stone of Port Kar."

"Now," said I, facing the man who had told me there was but one choice, that of flight, "shall we fly?"

He looked at the simple rock, wonderingly. "I have never had a Home Stone before," he said.

"Shall we fly?" I asked.

"Not if we have a Home Stone," he said.

I held up the rock. "Do we have a Home Stone?" I asked the men.

"I will accept it as my Home Stone," said the slave boy, Fish. None of the men laughed. The first to accept the Home Stone of Port Kar was only a boy, and a slave. But he had spoken as a Ubar.

"And I!" cried Thurnock, in his great, booming voice.

"And I!" said Clitus.

"And I!" said Tab.

"And I!" cried the men in the room. And, suddenly, the room was filled with cheers and more than a hundred weapons left their sheaths and saluted the Home Stone of Port Kar. I saw weathered seamen weep and cry out, brandishing their swords. There was joy in that room then such as I had never before seen it. And there was a belonging, and a victory, and a meaningfulness, and cries, and the clashing of weapons, and tears and, in that instant, love.

I cried to Thurnock. "Release all the slaves! Send them throughout the city, to the wharves, the taverns, the arsenal, the piazzas, the markets, everywhere! Tell them to cry out the news! Tell them to tell everyone that there is a Home Stone in Port Kar!"

Men ran from the room to carry out my orders.

"Officers," I cried, "to your ships! Form your lines beyond the harbor four pasangs west of the wharves of Sevarius!"

"Thurnock and Clitus," I said, "remain in the holding."

"No!" they cried together.

"Remain!" I ordered.

They looked at one another in dismay.

I could not send them to their deaths. I had no hopes that Port Kar could muster enough ships to fend off the joint fleet of Cos and Tyros.

I turned away from them, and, with the stone, strode from the room.

Outside the holding, on the broad promenade before the holding, bordering on the lakelike courtyard, with the canal gate beyond, I ordered a swift, tharlarion-prowed longboat made ready.

Even from where I was I could hear, beyond the holding, the cries that there was a Home Stone in Port Kar, and could see torches being borne along the narrow walks which, in most places, line the canals.

"Ubar," I heard, and I turned to take Telima in my arms.

"Will you not fly?" she begged, tears in her eyes.

"Listen," I told her. "Hear them? Hear what they are crying outside?"

"They are crying that there is a Home Stone in Port Kar," she said, "but there is no Home Stone in Port Kar. Everyone knows that."

"If men will that there be a Home Stone in Port Kar," I said, "then in Port Kar there will be a Home Stone."

"Fly," she wept.

I kissed her and leaped down into the longboat, which was now beside the promenade.

The men shoved off with the oars.

"To the Council of Captains," I told them.

The tharlarion head of the craft turned toward the canal gate.

I turned to lift my hand in farewell to Telima. I saw her standing there, near the entryway to my holding, in the garment of the Kettle Slave, under the torches. She lifted her hand.

Then I took my seat in the longboat.

I noted that at one of the oars sat the slave boy Fish.

"It is a man's work that must now be done, Boy," I said to him.

He drew on the oar. "I am a man," he said, "Captain."

I saw the girl Vina standing beside Telima.

But Fish did not look back.

The ship nosed through the canals of Port Kar toward the hall of the Council of Captains.

There were torches everywhere, and lights in the windows.

We heard the cry about us sweeping the city, like a

spark igniting the hearts of men into flame, that now in Port Kar there was a Home Stone.

A man stood on a narrow walk, a bundle on his back, tied over a spear. "Is it true, Admiral?" he cried. "Is it true?

"If you will have it true," I told him, "it will be true."

He looked at me, wonderingly, and then the tharlarion-prowed longboat glided past him in the canal, leaving him behind.

I looked once behind, and saw that he had thrown the bundle from his spear, and was following us, afoot.

"There is a Home Stone in Port Kar!" he cried.

I saw others stop, and then follow him.

The canals we traversed were crowded, mostly with small tharlarion boats, loaded with goods, moving this way and that. All who could, it seemed, were fleeing the city.

I had heard already that men with larger ships, hundreds of them, had put out to sea, and that the wharves were packed with throngs, bidding exorbitant amounts of gold for a passage from Port Kar. Many fortunes, I thought, would be made this night in Port Kar.

"Make way for the Admiral!" cried the man in the bow of the longboat. "Make way for the admiral!"

We saw frightened faces looking out from the windows. Men were hurrying along the narrow walks lining the canals. I could see the shining eyes of urts, their noses and heads dividing the torchlit waters silently, their pointed, silken ears laid back against the sides of their heads.

"Make way for the Admiral!" cried the man in the bow of the longboat.

Our boat mixed oars with another, and then we shoved apart and continued on our way.

Children were crying. I heard a woman scream. Men were shouting. Everywhere dark figures, bundles on their backs, were scurrying along the sides of the canals. Many of the boats we passed were crowded with frightened people and goods.

Many of those we passed asked me, "Is it true, Admiral, that there is a Home Stone in Port Kar," and I responded to them, as I had to the man before, "If you will have it true, it will be true."

I saw the man at the tiller of one of the boats put about.

There were now torches on both sides of the canals, in long lines, following us, and boats, too, began to follow us.

"Where are you going?" asked a man from a window of the passing throng.

"I think to the Council of Captains," said one of the men on the walk. "It is said that there is now a Home Stone in Port Kar."

And I heard men behind him cry, "There is a Home Stone in Port Kar! There is a Home Stone in Port Kar!" This cry was taken up by thousands, and everywhere I saw men pause in their flight, and boats put about, and men pour from the entryways of their buildings onto the walks lining the canals. I saw bundles thrown down and arms unsheathed, and behind us, in throngs of thousands now, came the people of Port Kar, following us to the great piazza before the hall of the Council of Captains.

Even before the man in the bow had tied the thar-larion-prowed longboat to a mooring post at the piazza, I had leaped up to the tiles and was striding, robes swirling, across the squares of the broad piazza toward the great door of the hall of the Council of Captains.

Four members of the Council Guard, beneath the two great braziers set at the entrance, leaped to attention, the butts of their pikes striking on the tiles.

I swept past them and into the hall.

Candles were lit on several of the tables. Papers were strewn about. There were few scribes or pages there. Of the usual seventy or eighty, or so, captains of the approximately one hundred and twenty entitled to sit in the council, only some thirty or forty were present.

And even as I entered some two or three left the hall.

The scribe, haggard behind the great table, sitting before the book of the council, looked up at me.

I glanced about.

The captains sat silently. Samos was there, and I saw that short-cropped white hair buried in his rough hands, his elbows on his knees.

Two more captains rose to their feet and left the room.

One of them stopped beside Samos. "Make your ships ready," he said. "There is not much time to flee."

Samos shook him away.

I took my chair. "I petition," said I to the scribe,

as though it might be an ordinary meeting, "to address the council."

The scribe was puzzled.

The captains looked up.

"Speak," said the Scribe.

"How many of you," asked I of the captains, "stand ready to undertake the defense of your city?"

Dark, long-haired Bejar was there. "Do not jest," said he, "Captain." He spoke irritably. "Most of the captains have already fled. And hundreds of the lesser captains. The round ships and the long ships leave the harbor of Port Kar. The people, as they can, flee. Panic has swept the city. We cannot find ships to fight."

"The people," said Antisthenes, "flee. They will not fight. They are truly of Port Kar."

"Who knows what it is to be truly of Port Kar?" I asked Antisthenes.

Samos lifted his head and regarded me.

"The people flee," said Bejar.

"Listen!" I cried. "Hear them! They are outside!"

The men of the council lifted their heads. Through the thick walls, and the high, narrow windows of the hall of the Council of Captains, there came a great, rumbling cry, the thunderous mixture of roiling shouts.

Bejar swept his sword from his sheath. "They have come to kill us!" he cried.

Samos lifted his hand. "No," he said, "listen."

"What is it they are saying?" asked a man.

A page rushed into the hall. "The people!" he cried. "They crowd the piazza. Torches! Thousands!"

"What is it that they cry!" demanded Bejar.

"They cry," said the boy, in his silk and velvet, "that in Port Kar there is a Home Stone!"

"There is no Home Stone in Port Kar," said Antisthenes.

"There is," I said.

The captains looked at me.

Samos threw back his head and roared with laughter, pounding the arms of his curule chair.

Then the other captains, too, laughed.

"There is no Home Stone in Port Kar!" laughed Samos.

"I have seen it," said a voice near me. I was startled. I looked about and, to my wonder, saw, standing near me, the slave boy Fish. Slaves are not permitted in the hall of the captains. He had followed me in, through the guards, in the darkness.

"Bind that slave and beat him!" cried the scribe.

Samos, with a gesture, silenced the scribe.

"Who are you?" asked Samos.

"A slave," said the boy. "My name is Fish."

The men laughed.

"But," said the boy, "I have seen the Home Stone of Port Kar."

"There is no Home Stone of Port Kar, Boy," said Samos.

Then, slowly, from my robes, I removed the object which I had hidden there. No one spoke. All eyes were upon me. I slowly unwrapped the silk.

"It is the Home Stone of Port Kar," said the boy.

The men were silent.

Then Samos said, "Port Kar has no Home Stone."

"Captains," said I, "accompany me to the steps of the hall."

They followed me, and I left the chamber of the council, and, in a few moments, stood on the top of the broad marbled steps leading up to the hall of the Council of Captains.

"It is Bosk," cried the people. "It is Bosk, Admiral!"

I looked out into the thousands of faces, the hundreds of torches.

I could see the canals far away, over the heads of the people, crowded even to the distant waters bordering the great piazza. And in those waters beyond there were crowded hundreds of boats, filled with men, many of them holding torches, the flames' reflection flickering on the walls of the buildings and on the water.

I said nothing, but faced the crowd for a long moment.

And then, suddenly, I lifted my right arm, and held in my right hand, high over my head, was the stone.

"I have seen it!" cried a man, weeping. "I have seen it! The Home Stone of Port Kar!"

"The Home Stone of Port Kar!" cried thousands. "The stone!"

There were great cheers, and cries, and shouts, and the lifting of torches and weapons. I saw men weep. And women. And I saw fathers lift their sons upon their shoulders that they might see the stone.

I think the cries of joy in the piazza might have carried even to the moons of Gor.

"I see," said Samos, standing near to me, his voice indistinct in the wild cries of the crowd, "that there is indeed a Home Stone in Port Kar."

"You did not flee," I said, "nor did the others, nor have these people."

He looked at me, puzzled.

"I think," I said, "that there has always been a Home Stone in Port Kar. It is only that until this night it had not been found."

We looked out over the vast throng, shaken in its jubilation and its tears.

Samos smiled. "I think," said he, "Captain, you are right."

Near to me, tears in his eyes, shouting, was the slave boy Fish. And I saw tears, too, in the eyes of the vast crowds, with their torches, before me.

There was much shouting, and a great crying out.

"Yes, Captain," said Samos, "I think that you are right."

How Bosk Conducted the

Affairs of Port Kar

Upon Thassa

I stood in the swaying basket at the height of the mast of the Dorna, the glass of the builders in hand.

It was a very beautiful sight, the great lines of ships in the distance, extending to the ends of the horizons, the sails like yellow and purple flags, in their thousands, in the sun of the ninth Gorean hour, an Ahn before noon.

Port Kar had mustered what ships she could.

In the hurrying of our formations and the drawing of battle plans, I was not even certain of the numbers of ships engaged in our various ventures. The nearest estimations I could make were that we were bringing, at the time of the engagement, in the neighborhood of twenty-five hundred ships, fourteen hundred of them only round ships, against the joint fleet of Cos and Tyros, of some forty-two hundred ships, all tarn ships, now approaching from the west. We had all of the arsenal ships that were available, some seven hundred out of an approximate thousand. So many were in the arsenal because of the lateness of the season. As I may have mentioned, most Gorean sailing, particularly by tarn ships, is done in the spring and summer. Of the seven hundred arsenal ships, three hundred and forty were tarn ships, and three hundred and sixty were round ships. Our fleet was further supplemented by some fourteen hundred ships furnished by private captains, minor captains of Port Kar, most of which were round ships. Beyond this, we had three hundred and fifty ships furnished by the captains of the council who had not, prior to the time of the showing of the Home Stone, fled. Of these three hundred and fifty ships, approximately two hundred, happily, were tarn

ships. My own ships counted in with these of the captains
of the council. Lastly, I was pleased, though astonished,
to accept the service of thirty-five ships of two of Port
Kar's Ubars, twenty from the squat, brilliant Chung, and
fifteen from tall, long-haired Nigel, like a war lord from
Torvaldsland. These were all the ships that were left to
these two Ubars after the fires of En'Kara. None of the
ships of the Ubars Eteocles or Sullius Maximus had
been pledged to the fleet, nor, of course, none of those
of Henrius Sevarius, under the command of his regent,
Claudius, once of Tyros.

Had it not been for the finding of the Home Stone of
Port Kar, if one may so speak, I doubt that we could have
brought more than four or five hundred ships against Cos
and Tyros.

I snapped shut the glass of the builders and descended
the narrow rope ladder to the deck of the Dorna.

I had scarcely set foot on the deck when I saw, near
the mast well, the boy Fish.

"I told you," I cried, "to remain ashore!"

"Beat me later," said he, "Captain."

I turned to an officer. "Give him a sword," I said.

"Thank you, Captain," said the boy.

I strode to the stern castle of the Dorna.

"Greetings, Oar-master," said I.

"Greetings, Captain," said he.

I climbed the stairs past the helm deck to the captain's deck of the stern castle.

I looked out.

Astern there were, each separated by about one hundred yards, four tarn ships of Port Kar, and behind this
four, there was another, and behind that another, and
behind that another. The Dorna was thus leading a rela-
tively close formation of sixteen tarn ships. This was one
of fifty such task forces, consisting altogether of eight
hundred tarn ships. The attacking fleet, in order to provide
its net to prevent escape from Port Kar, had overextended
its lines. Their ships were only four deep and widely
spaced. Our sets of sixteen ships, each in a position not
to interfere with but support one another, could cut such
a line easily. We would cut it in fifty places. As soon as
the ships broke through the line they would spread in
predesignated pairs, attacking where possible from the
rear, but always conjointly. Each pair would single out a

given ship by signals and as it maneuvered to meet one the other could make its strike. The balance, the great majority of ships in the joint fleet, thus, would remain, at least for the time, unengaged, apart from the battles. Once more it would not be so much a question of absolute numbers of ships as concentrating superior numbers at strategic points. With their lines cut in fifty places, for no extended handful of tarn ships, part of a great line, could resist a close-set formation of sixteen tarn ships, I hoped that many of the ships would turn to face the attackers, now in their rear. Each of my fifty sets of attacking tarn ships would be followed, by some half of an Ahn, by another pair of my tarn ships, which, hopefully, would be able to take a number of these come-about ships of Cos and Tyros from the rear. I recalled the Dorna, under similar circumstances, had done great damage. The original pairs, of the fifty sets of sixteen tarn ships, after cutting the line and fighting, would, if possible, regroup with their sixteen and recut the line again, this time moving toward Port Kar, and repeat these tactics. I had, however, little hope that we could successfully, in many cases, cut the line more than once. By that time the ships of Cos and Tyros would have concentrated in their numbers and shortened their lines. After the first cutting I expected a free combat, except insofar as the designated pairs of ships could continue to work together. The predesignation of fighting pairs, incidentally, and my injunctions to refuse to engage singly if possible, even withdrawing from equal odds, I am told, was now in Gorean naval warfare, though the pairing principle, on a more informal basis, is as old as the triangle tactic, which may be remembered from the engagement of my nondiversion ships with the ships which had been left behind to guard the treasure fleet. I had also arranged signals whereby my ships, those of my task forces and others, might, if the pairs became separated, switch partners, thus retaining the possibility of pair-attacks on single ships even if the members of the original pairs should become separated.

The first two waves of my attack consisted, thus, of fifty task forces of sixteen tarn ships apiece and, following each of the task forces, at an interval of half an Ahn, another pair of tarn ships. This meant the first wave consisted of eight hundred ships, and the second of one hundred.

This left me approximately one hundred and eighty-five tarn ships, and the large numbers, fourteen hundred, of round ships.

I signaled that the sixteen tarn ships with me should proceed. They pulled away, acknowledging with flags my message. The Dorna dropped back.

I would have preferred to go with them, but, as a commander, I could not.

My third wave, following the second by an Ahn, would consist of a long extended line of round ships, the full fourteen hundred. It was my hope that by the time they arrived at the engagement the fleet of Cos and Tyros, responding to my first two waves, would have shortened their lines and concentrated their ships. Thus the fourteen hundred round ships might, hopefully, be able to envelop their formation, surround it, and attack on the flanks, with their not inconsiderable barrage of flaming javelins, heated stones, burning pitch and showers of crossbow bolts. Further, when the ships of Cos and Tyros turned upon these round ships I did not think they would find them common foes. Each was rowed either by citizens of Port Kar or by eager slaves, armed and unchained, that they might, if they chose, fight for their freedom and the Home Stone of a city. Only slaves whose origin was of Cos or Tyros, or their allies, had been taken from the ships and left behind, chained in the warehouses of Port Kar. Besides having large numbers of unchained, armed men in their rowing holds, these round ships, moreover, were, below decks, and in the turrets and the stem and stern castles, crowded with armed, able-bodied men, citizens of Port Kar who had swarmed aboard, that they might fight. There were crews on these ships armed with grappling irons and each of the ships carried two or more of the spiked planks. These are actually like gangplanks, some five feet in width, to be fastened at one end to the round ship and intended to be dropped, with their heavy spiked ends, into the deck of an enemy ship. The round ship has a substantially higher freeboard area than the ram-ship, which is lower, and so the spiked plank is feasible. Commonly, of course, it is the round ship, with her normally small, free crews, which attempts to evade boarding. But now I expected, to the surprise of attacking ram-ships which might attempt to board them, they would find themselves boarded, and their decks overwhelmed with swarms of armed, free men. We had crowded far more armed men into each of these round ships than would be carried even in the normal crew of a heavy-class tarn ship. The common strategy with a round ship is to shear and board, because, normally, one wishes not to sink the ship but take it as a prize. This strategy, however, we expected would work, under the present conditions, to our advantage. And if the tarn ships of Cos and Tyros should use their rams, we hoped that, in the moments it would take to disengage the ram, the grappling irons and the spiked planks might be brought into play. Meanwhile, of course, the numerous bowmen, and the men at the springals, catapults and onagers would be keeping up a heavy fire, the more devastating, the closer the distance. It was my hope that my round ships, with their large, free crews, and their artillery, and their boarding potentialities, might be a match for even heavy-class tarn ships. In effect, rather than do sea battle, they would attempt to close with the enemy and, via the rails and the spiked planks, board her and fight what would be, for most practical purposes, a land engagement at sea.

My fourth wave consisted of fifty tarn ships, instructed not to lower their masts, which would follow the round ships by an Ahn. Coming on the heels of the round ships, with their masts high, these, I assumed, might well be taken for more round ships, for the mast of a tarn ship is always lowered before battle. Accordingly I hoped the tarn ships of Cos and Tyros, seeing the sails, would think their new enemies were single-masted round ships, of which there are some types, and either misjudge their speeds or rush on them unwarily, finding out, too late, that they were plunging headlong toward swift, maneuverable, deadly, ram carrying tarn ships. These ships would then, when free to do so, support the round ships in their battle, destroying tarn ships which might, unaware of the new danger, be attempting to close with them.

My fifth wave, following the fourth by half an Ahn, consisted of two fleets of forty tarn ships apiece, one attacking from the north and the other from the south. I did not think I had the ships to make this pincer attack truly devastating, but, in the turmoil of a battle at sea, without the clearest understanding of the position and numbers of the enemy, such flanking attacks might have unusual psychological value. The Admiral of Cos and Tyros, Chenbar I supposed, could not know the exact numbers and disposition of our forces. Indeed, we ourselves, until early this morning, had not a full comprehension of our plans, or, indeed, even the ships we would have to carry them out. I hoped that Chenbar might assume that many of the ships which had fled from Port Kar might have come about and decided to join the battle, or he might infer that he had, before he could ascertain the ships involved in the flanking attacks, seriously misjudged our numbers. The flanking attack, of course, was mounted as late as it was because, until the fleet of Cos and Tyros had shortened their lines and concentrated their ships, to meet our earlier moves, it would have been impractical. Hopefully, the terror of being taken in the flank might cause many captains, or even Chenbar himself, to have the fleet put about, and, if so, this would make their ships the most vulnerable to our own.

We saw my second-wave ships sweep past, the pairs scattering themselves, each pair following its assigned task force.

The Dorna rested, rocking on the waters, her oars inboard.

I kept in reserve one hundred and five tarn ships, which, simultaneously with the fifth wave, that of the flanking fleets, would draw within signal distance of the Dorna.

"Shall I lower our mast, Captain?" asked one of my officers.

"No," I told him.

I would wish to use its height to observe, as well as I might, the battle.

It was fall, and the wind was cold whipping across the water. Clouds scudded across the sky. In the north there was a darkness lying like a line against the horizon. We had had a frost in the morning.

"Furl the sail," I told an officer.

He began to cry orders to the seamen.

Soon seamen were clambering out on the long sloping yard and, assisted by others on the deck, hauling on brail ropes, were tying in the long triangular sail.

I studied the surface of the water to windward.

"What shall we do now?" asked an officer.

"Lay to," I told him.

"What will you do now?" he asked.

"I am going to sleep," I told him. "Call me in half an Ahn."

After some sleep I felt much refreshed.

Upon awakening I was served some bread and cheese in my cabin.

I came out on the deck.

The wind was very cold now, and the Dorna shook in it, the windward waters striking at her hull. We had both the stem and stern anchors down.

I was given my Admiral's cloak and I flung this over my shoulder, my left, that to which the strap carrying the glass of the builders was attached. I then thrust some strips of dried tarsk meat in my belt. I called the lookout down from the basket, that I might climb to his place. In the basket I wrapped the admiral's cloak about me, began to chew on a piece of tarsk meat, as much against the cold as the hunger, and took out the glass of the builders.

I examined the state of the battle.

Tarsk meat tends to be salty. There is usually a water gourd kept at the masthead, for the lookout. I uncorked the gourd and took some of the water. There had been a light film of ice in it. Some of the crystals melted in my mouth.

The line of darkness in the north was now a margin of darkness.

I turned my attention again to the battle.

As I watched, the long, strung-out line of round ships of Port Kar moved past, tacking, scarcely using their oars, their small, triangular storm sails beaten from the north. The lateen-rigged galley, whether a round ship or a ram-ship, although it can furl its sail, cannot well let out and take in sail; it is not a square-rigged craft; accordingly she carries different sails for different conditions; the yard itself, from the mast, is lowered and hoisted, sails being removed or attached; the three main types of sail used are all lateens, and differ largely in their size; there is a large, fair-weather sail, used with light winds; there is a smaller sail, used with strong winds astern; and yet a smaller sail, a storm sail, used most often in riding out storms. It was the latter sail which, although it was unusual, the round ships were using for tacking; had they used either of the larger sails, with the sharp wind, they would have heeled dangerously toward the water, perhaps shipping water through the leeward thole ports.

I smiled as the ships swept past. Their decks were almost deserted. But I knew that, crowded in the stem and stern castles, in the turrets, below decks, in the rowing and cargo holds, there were hundreds of men.

I resumed my watch, lifting again the glass of the builders toward the west.

The ships of my first wave had now struck the lines of the fleet of Cos and Tyros.

It was cold in the basket.

Behind them, scattered across the cold waters of Thassa, I could see the pairs of the second wave proceeding, swiftly gliding, oars dipping, toward the long lines of yellow and purple sails in the distance, yellow for Tyros, purple for Cos.

I wondered how many men would die.

I pulled the admiral's cloak more closely about me.

I asked myself who I was, and I told myself, I did not know. I knew only that I was cold, and that I was alone, and that, far in the distance, men were fighting, and so, too, would others.

I wondered if my plans had been good ones, and I told myself I did not know that, either. There were so many thousands of factors, impossible to foresee, so much that might alter, or shift unaccountably.

I knew Chenbar to be a brilliant Ubar and captain, but even he, the brilliant Chenbar, could not well have understood our plans, our dispositions and our ventures, for we ourselves, until hours before, had not known with what we might work and how it might be used.

I did not expect to win the day.

It seemed to me a fool's choice that I had not, when it had been possible, fled Port Kar. Surely many captains, of the council and otherwise, had done so, their holds filled with their chained slaves and secured treasures. Why had I not fled? Why had not these others? Were all men fools? Now men would die. Is anything worth so much as a human life? Is not the most abject surrender preferable to the risk of its loss? Is it not better to grovel as a slave, begging the favor of life from a master, than to risk the loss of even one life? I recalled that I, once, in the far marshes of the delta of the Vosk, had whined and groveled that I might live, and now, I, that same coward, wrapped in the robes of an admiral, watched the locking of the lines of battle, watched men move to fates and destructions, or victories, to which I had sent them, knowing as little as I did of life, or war, or fortunes.

Surely there must be others more fitted than I to assume the responsibilities of such words, sending men forth to fight, to die or live. What would they think of me as they fell beneath the cold waters of Thassa or reeled from the blows of sword blades, their death's blood in their mouths? Would they sing me then? And what guilt must I bear for each of those deaths, for it had been my words, those of an ignorant fool, which had sent them to the waters and the blades?

I should have told them all to flee. Instead I had given them a Home Stone.

"Admiral!" cried a voice below. "Look!" The voice came from a seaman, he, too, with a glass, high on the prow of the Dorna. "The Venna!" he cried. "She has broken through!"

I lifted the glass to the west. There, far off, I could see my tarn ship, the Venna. She had struck the line of Cos and Tyros, had torn her way through, and was now coming about, to strike again. With her was her sister ship, the Tela. I saw two of the tarn ships of Cos and Tyros, one heeled over in the water, the other slipping stern first beneath the waves. There was wreckage in the water.

The Venna was under the command of the incomparable Tab.

There was a cheer from the men below me.

Well done, I thought, well done.

Several of the ships in the lines near the point where my task force had struck were now coming about to meet their enemy.

But, behind them, low in the water, no masts, came the second wave of my attack.

I saw the lines of Cos and Tyros shortening, compressing their formations to bring more ships into play at given points. As they deepened their lines I could now see the borders of their fleet, as I had not been able to before.

Behind my second-wave ships, I saw, scattered in its

long enveloping line stretching from horizon to horizon across Thassa, their small storm sails pounded by the wind, the third wave, that of the round ships.

I glanced back.

Astern of the Dorna, not hurrying, at half beat, came fifty tarn ships, their masts high, storm sails bound to their long, sloping yards. In the turmoil of the battle I had little doubt that they would be taken, at first, and perhaps until it was too late, as a second wave of round ships.

Following the fourth wave, its own attack timed to occur half an Ahn after that of the fourth wave, would come the fifth wave, the two small fleets of tarn ships, of forty ships apiece, masts down, who would initiate their pincers attack from the north and the south.

And simultaneously with the initiation of the pincers attack the balance of my fleet, the reserves, one hundred and five tarn ships, should draw within signal distance of the Dorna.

With the reserves would come ten more round ships, wide-beamed lumber ships from the arsenal. Their cargoes were unknown even to my highest officers.

All the factors which had entered into my calculations were now in motion.

But there would be other factors, always others.

I glanced to the north. Then I opened the glass and studied the waters to the north. I snapped shut the glass. Above the waters to the north there was now a towering blackness. Overhead the white clouds swept past, like white, leaping Tabuk fleeing from the jaws of the black-maned larl.

It was late in the season.

I had not counted on Thassa herself, her swiftness and her moods.

I was cold in the basket, and I chewed on another piece of dried tarsk meat. The water had now frozen in the gourd, splitting it.

I reopened the glass of the builders, turning it again to the west.

For better than three Ahn I had sat in the basket at the masthead of the Dorna, whipped by the wind, my fingers numb on the glass of the builders, observing the battle.

I had watched my first wave break in dozens of places the long lines of Cos and Tyros, and had seen the ships of the great fleet turn to face them, and had witnessed their vulnerability to the slender second wave of ships, each wreaking destruction beyond what might be expected of their sizes and weights. Then, as the lines of Cos and Tyros had closed and deepened, to match formations with my task forces, the great encircling line of round ships had cast its net about them. Hundreds of ships had turned to destroy these clumsy intruders, but, of these hundreds, great numbers discovered, too late, that they fought not common round ships but floating fortresses jammed with armed men, eager to engage. And then I had seen fleet ships, in their fifties, come about to move against what they had taken to be a new wave of round ships, only to be taken off guard by the rams and shearing blades of ships as swift and terrible as their own. I was proud of my men and their ships. I think they did well. And I did not feel my strategies were negligible. And yet, as I sat there, I felt that in time the weight of ships and numbers would be felt. I had only some twenty-five hundred ships, most of them round ships, to bring against a fleet of prime vessels, some forty-two hundred in strength, each a tarn ship, with fierce ram and shearing blades.

I could see numerous ships burning in the dark, wind-swept afternoon. Sparks and flames were carried from one ship to another. In places ships were crowded together, in tens and twelves, like floating wooden islands in the sea.

The sea was now growing high, and the darkness in the north was now half the sky, looming like a beast with wild fur rooting and sniffing for its prey.

The fifth wave was late.

The Dorna fought her anchors. We had lifted them that she might swing into the wind, and had then dropped them once more, but still she shook and reared, lifted and dropped into the waters. Her timbers groaned, and I could hear the creaking of the bolts, the irons and great chains that, in places, reinforced her beams.

My fifth wave was divided into two portions, the pincer blade striking from the north under the command of the tall, long-haired Nigel, with his fifteen ships, supplemented by twenty-five of the arsenal, and the pincer blade from the south under the command of Chung, with

his twenty ships, supplemented by another twenty, from
the arsenal. All of these ships were tarn ships.

But I did not see the fifth wave.

I could see, now, approaching the Dorna, from the
east, the reserves, the hundred and five tarn ships, and
the ten wide-beamed round ships, lumber ships from the
arsenal, whose cargoes were unknown even to my highest
officers.

I wondered if I should have trusted the Ubars Nigel
and Chung.

The command ship of the reserves heaved to within
hailing distance of the Dorna.

With the glass I saw, on her stern castle, Antisthenes,
that captain of the council whose name had been always
first on her rolls.

The other ships took their places in four lines behind
the command ship of the reserves.

And between them, heavy, their hulls buffeted by the
wind, even their small storm sails now furled to their
yards, came the ten round ships, the lumber ships from
the arsenal. Even they, broad-beamed and deep-keeled,
pitched and bucked in the roiling waters of late Se'Kara
on Thassa.

I turned the glass again to the west, to the smoke in
the distance.

I saw now that the tarn ships of Cos and Tyros were,
where possible, not engaging the round ships, but concentrating their superior numbers on my tarn ships. The
round ships, slow, much at the mercy of the wind, were
now being abandoned as antagonists.

I smiled. Chenbar was an excellent admiral. He chose
to fight wars in which he was most familiar. He would
use his superior numbers on my tarn ships, leaving the
round ships for later, when they might be struck by as
many as four or five tarn ships simultaneously. The round
ships, of course, were too slow to offer the swift, decisive
support to my tarn ships which they would surely need
shortly.

I closed the glass, and blew on my fingers. It was very
cold, and it now seemed to me that the outcome of the
battle was written on that great board, the width of the
horizon, the pieces ships and men, which lay burning and
smoking in the distance.

The wind whipped past.

Then I heard a cry from below me, and a cheer. The man on the height of the prow, his builders' glass slung about his shoulder, standing, his feet fixed in ropes, was waving his cap in the air. The oarsmen below were crying out and waving their caps.

I snapped open the glass of the builders. From both the north and the south, like distant black slivers knifing through the cold waters of Thassa, masts down, came the fleets of the fifth wave.

I grinned.

Chung had been forced to beat his way northward against the wind. Nigel, wise in the ways of sea war, had held back his ships, the wind pounding behind them, that the blades of the pincers might strike simultaneously, as though wielded by a single hand and will.

I let the builders' glass, attached to the strap about my shoulder, fall to my side. I crammed the last of the tarsk meat into my mouth and, chewing, climbed down the narrow rope ladder, fastened to the deck near the mast well.

I leaped from the ladder to the deck of the Dorna and waved my hand to Antisthenes, some hundred yards away on the stern castle of the command ship of the reserves. He, in turn, ran a flag up the halyard running to the height of the stem turret.

I climbed to my own stern castle.

To cries of wonder from my men, and those of other ships nearby, the deck planking of the ten round ships was lifted and thrown aside.

The tarn is a land bird, generally of mountainous origin, though there are brightly-plumaged jungle tarns. The tarns crowded into the holds of the round ships were hooded. Feeling the wind and the cold suddenly strike them they threw back their heads and beat their wings, pulled against the chains that bound them to the keel timbers.

One was unhooded, the straps that bound its beak unbuckled.

It uttered its scream, that pierced even the freezing winds of Thassa.

Men shook with fear.

It is extremely difficult to take a tarn far out over the water.

I did not know if they could be controlled at sea.

Generally even tarn goads cannot drive them from the sight of land.

I took the glass of the builders, and its strap, from my shoulder. I handed them to a seaman.

"Lower a longboat," I told an officer.

"In this sea?"

"Hurry!" I cried.

The boat was lowered to the water. At one of the oars, as though he belonged there, was the slave boy Fish. The oar-master took the longboat's tiller.

We approached the first of the round ships on its leeward side.

Soon I stood on the deck of the round ship.

"You are Terence," I asked, "mercenary captain of Treve?"

The man nodded.

Treve is a bandit city, high among the crags of the larl-prowled Voltai. Most men do not even know its location. Once the tarnsmen of Treve had withstood the tarn cavalries of even Ar. In Treve they do not grow their own food but, in the fall, raid the harvests of others. They live by rapine and plunder. The men of Treve are said to be among the proudest and most ruthless on Gor. They are most fond of danger and free women, whom they bind and steal from civilized cities to carry to their mountain lair as slave girls. It is said the city can be reached only on tarnback. I had once known a girl from Treve. Her name had been Vika.

"You have, in the ten round ships," I said, "one hundred tarns, with riders."

"Yes," said he, "and, as you asked, with each tarn a knotted rope and five of the seamen of Port Kar."

I looked down into the open hold of the round ship. The wicked, curved, scimitarlike beak of the unhooded tarn lifted itself. Its eyes blazed. It looked like a good bird. I regretted that it was not Ubar of the Skies. It was a reddish brown tarn, a fairly common coloring for the great birds. Mine own had been black-plumaged, a giant tarn, glossy, his great talons shod with steel, a bird bred for speed and war, a bird who had been, in his primitive, wild way, my friend. I had driven him from the Sardar.

"I will have a hundred stone of gold for the use of these birds and my men," said Terence of Treve.

"You shall have it," I said.

"I wish payment now," said the captain of Treve.

I whipped my blade from its sheath, angrily, and held it to his throat.

"My pledge is steel," I said.

Terence smiled. "We of Treve," he said, "understand such a pledge."

I lowered the blade.

"Of all the tarnsmen in Port Kar," I said, "and of all the captains, you alone have accepted the risks of this venture, the use of tarns at sea."

There was one other who had been in Port Kar, whom I thought might, too, have undertaken the risks, but he, with his thousand men, had not been in the city for several weeks. I speak of lean, scarred Ha-Keel, who wore about his neck, on a golden chain, a worn tarn disk, set with diamonds, of the city of Ar. He had cut a throat for that coin, to buy silks and perfumes for a woman, but one who fled with another man; Ha-Keel had hunted them, slain in combat the man and sold the woman into slavery. He had been unable to return to Ar. His forces were now engaged, I had learned, by the city of Tor, to quell incursions by tarn-riding desert tribesmen. The services of Ha-Keel and his men were available to the highest bidder. I knew he had once, through agents, served the Others, not Priest-Kings, who contested surreptitiously for this world, and ours. I had met Ha-Keel at a house in Turia, the house of Saphrar, a Merchant.

"I will want the hundred stone," said Terence, "regardless of the outcome of your plan."

"Of course," I said. Then I regarded him. "A hundred stone," I said, "though a high price, seems small enough considering the risks you will encounter. It is hard for me to believe that you ride only for a hundred stone of gold. And I know that the Home Stone of Port Kar is not yours."

"We are of Treve," said Terence.

"Give me a tarn goad," I said.

He handed me one of the instruments.

I threw off the robes of the Admiral. I accepted a wind scarf from another man.

It had begun to sleet now.

The tarn can scarcely be taken from the sight of land. Even driven by tarn goads he will rebel. These tarns had been hooded. Whereas their instincts apparently tend to keep them within the sight of land, I did not know what would be the case if they were unhooded at sea, and there was no land to be found. Perhaps they would not leave the ship. Perhaps they would go mad with rage or fear. I knew tarns had destroyed riders who had attempted to ride them out over Thassa from the shore. But I hoped that the tarns, finding themselves out of the sight of land, might accommodate themselves to the experience. I was hoping that, in the strange intelligence of animals, it would be the departure from land, and not the mere positioning of being out of the sight of land, that would be counter-instinctual for the great birds.

Doubtless I would soon know.

I leaped down to the saddle of the unhooded tarn. It screamed as I fastened the broad purple safety strap. The tarn goad was looped about my right wrist. I wrapped the wind scarf about my face.

"If I can control the bird," I said, "follow me, and keep the instructions I have given you."

"Let me ride first," said Terence of Treve.

I smiled. Why would one who had been a tarnsman of Ko-ro-ba, the Towers of the Morning, let one of Treve, a traditional enemy, take the saddle of a tarn before him? It would not do, of course, to tell him this.

"No," I said.

There was a pair of slave manacles wrapped about the pommel of the saddle, also a length of rope. These things I thrust in my belt.

I gestured and the tarn hobble, fastening the right foot of the great bird to a huge bolt set in the ship's keel, was opened.

I drew on the one-strap.

To my delight the tarn, with a snap of its wings, leaped from the hold. He stood on the deck of the round ship, opening and closing his wings, looking about himself, and then threw back his head and screamed. The other tarns below in the hold, some ten of them, shifted and rattled their hobbles.

The sleet struck down cutting my face.

I drew again on the one-strap and again the bird's wings snapped, and he was on the long, sloping yard on the round ship's foremast.

His head was very high and every nerve in his body seemed alert, but puzzled. He looked about himself.

I did not hurry the bird.

I slapped the side of its neck, and spoke to it, gently, confidently.

I drew on the one-strap. The bird did not move. His talons clutched the sloping yard.

I did not use the tarn goad.

I waited for some time, stroking it, and talking to it.

And then, suddenly, I gave a cry and jerked on the one-strap and the bird, by training and instinct, flung itself into the sleeting wind and began to climb the dark, running sky.

I was again on tarnback!

The bird climbed until I released the one-strap and then it began to circle. Its movements were as sure and as swift as though it might have been over the familiar crags of the Voltai or the canals of Port Kar.

I tested its responses to the straps. They were immediate and eager. And suddenly I realized that the bird was trembling with excitement and pleasure, finding itself swift and alive and strong in a new world to his senses.

Already, below me, I saw tarns being unhooded, and the straps that bound their beaks being unbuckled, and cast aside. Riders were climbing into the saddles. I saw tarns leaping to the decks of the round ships, and I saw the knotted ropes being attached to the saddles, and picked seamen, experts with the sword, five to a rope, taking their positions. And besides these seamen, each tarnsman, tied to his saddle, carried a shielded, protected ship's lantern, lighted, and, in the pockets of leather aprons, tied together and thrown across the saddles, numerous clay flasks, corked with rags. These flasks, I knew, were filled with tharlarion oil, and the rags that corked them had been soaked in the same substance.

Soon, behind me, there were some hundred tarnsmen, and below each, dangling, hanging to the knotted ropes, were five picked men.

I saw that the fleets of my fifth wave, the two fleets of forty ships apiece, under the command of Chung and Nigel, were well engaged in their strikes on the flanks of the great fleet.

At this time, before their numbers could have been well ascertained by the enemy, before the enemy could be much aware of anything more than the unexpected flanking attacks, I, followed by the tarnsmen, with the picked seamen, darted through the sleeting, windy skies over the locked fleets.

In the turmoil below, primarily of tarn ships locked in battle, and the great round ships trying to close with enemy tarn ships, I saw, protected by ten tarn ships on each side, and ten before and ten behind, the flagship of Cos and Tyros. It was a great ship, painted in the yellow of Tyros, with more than two hundred oarsmen.

It was the ship of Chenbar.

It would carry, besides its oarsmen, who were all free, fighting men, some one hundred bowmen, and another hundred men, seamen, artillery men, auxiliary personnel and officers.

I drew on the four-strap.

Almost instantly the ship was the center of a great beating of wings and descending tarns.

My own tarn landed on the stern castle itself, and I leaped from its back.

I whipped the sword from its sheath.

Startled, Chenbar himself, Ubar of Tyros, the Sea Sleen, drew his blade.

I tore away the wind scarf from my face.

"You!" he cried.

"Bosk," I told him, "Captain of Port Kar."

Our blades met.

Behind us I could hear shouts and cries, and the sounds of men dropping from their ropes to the deck, and of weapons meeting weapons. I heard the hiss of crossbow quarrels.

As one set of birds hovered over the deck and their men dropped to its planks, the birds darted away, and another set took their place. And then, their fighters disembarked, the birds with their riders swept away, up into the black, vicious sleeting sky, to light the oily rags, one by one, in the clay flasks of tharlarion oil and hurl them, from the heights of the sky, down onto the decks of ships of Cos and Tyros. I did not expect a great deal of damage to be done by these shattering bombs of burning oil, but I was counting on the confluence of three factors: the psychological effect of such an attack, the fear of the outflanking fleets, whose numbers could not yet well have been ascertained, and, in the confusion and, hopefully, terror, the unexpected, sudden loss of their commander.

I slipped on the sleet-iced deck of the stern castle and parried Chenbar's blade from my throat.

I leaped to my feet and again we engaged.

Then we grappled, the sword wrist of each in the hand of the other.

I threw him against the sternpost and his back and head struck against the post. I heard someone behind me but whoever it was was met by one of my men. There were blades clashing at my back. I feared for the instant I might have broken Chenbar's back. I released the sword hand of the admiral of Tyros and struck him in the stomach with my left fist. As he sank forward I wrenched free my sword hand and, holding the sword still in my fist, struck him a heavy blow across the jaw with my fist. I spun about. My men were engaging those who would try to climb to the stern castle. Chenbar had sunk to his knees, stunned. I pulled the slave manacles from my belt and clapped them on Chenbar's wrists. Then, on his stomach, I dragged him to the talons of the tarn. With the rope, taken from my belt, I tied the slave manacles to the right foot of the bird.

Chenbar tried, groggily, to get up, but my foot on his neck held him in place.

I looked about.

My men were forcing the defenders of the ship over the side, into the cold waters. The defenders had not been prepared for such an attack. They had been taken unawares and resistance had been slight. Moreover, my men outnumbered them by some hundred swords.

The defenders were swimming across to the other tarn ships of Tyros, now swinging about to close with us and board.

Crossbow bolts from the other ships began to fall into the deck of the flagship.

"Hold the men of Tyros left aboard at the parapets!" I cried.

I heard a voice from across the water cry out. "Hold your fire!"

Then the first of the tarns returned to the flagship, having cast down its flaming bombs of burning oil.

Five of my men seized its rope, and, in an instant, they were lifted away from the ship.

"Fire the ship!" I called to my men.

They rushed below the decks to set fires in the hold.

More tarns returned and more of my men, sometimes six and seven to a rope, were carried away from the ship.

Smoke began to drift up through the planking of the deck.

One of the ships of Cos grated against the side of our own.

My men fought back boarders and then, with oars, thrust away the other ship.

Another ship struck our side, shearing oars.

My men rushed to repel boarders again.

"Look!" one cried.

They gave a cheer. The ship flew the flag of Bosk, with its green stripes on the white background.

"Tab!" they cried. "Tab!"

It was the Venna, thrust through to free us.

I briefly saw Tab, sweating even in the cold, in a torn tunic, a sword in his hand on the stern castle of the Venna.

Then, on the other side, was the Tela, the Venna's sister ship. The heavy, protective wales, the parallel beams protecting her hull, were fresh scarred and half cut away.

My men eagerly leaped aboard these two ships.

I waved away other tarnsmen, returning to the flagship to pick up men.

I could see ships burning in the distance.

Then flames shot up through the deck planking of the flagship.

The last of the men of Tyros aboard the ship leaped free to the cold waters to swim to their own ships. I could see some, a hundred yards away, climbing the wales of tarn ships, some clinging to their oars.

Chenbar and I remained alone on the deck of the stern castle of the flagship.

I climbed to the saddle.

A crossbow bolt dropped past me, striking into the burning deck.

Chenbar shook his head, and leaped to his feet, his wrists in manacles. "Fight!" he screamed to his distant ships. "Fight!"

I drew on the one-strap and the tarn, against the wind, took flight and Chenbar of Kasra, Ubar of Tyros, the Sea Sleen, in the manacles of a common slave, swung free below us, helpless and pendant in the furies of the wind and the sleeting rain, the captive of Bosk, a captain of Port Kar, admiral of her fleet.

How Bosk Returned

To His House

When we struck the icy, wind-driven decks of the Dorna my men rose at their benches and, cheering, waved their caps.

"Take this prisoner," I told an officer, "and chain him below decks. The council will decide what is to be done with him."

There was another cheer.

Chenbar stood facing me for an instant, his fists clenched, fury in his eyes, and then he was rudely turned about and, by two seamen, forced below decks.

"I expect," said the oar-master, "that in the rag of a slave he will eventually find his place at the bench of an arsenal round ship."

"Admiral!" cried the voice from the masthead. "The fleet of Cos and Tyros is putting about! They fly!"

I shook with emotion. I could not speak.

The men were cheering about me.

Then I said, "Recall our ships."

Men ran to signal ships among the reserves, that they might draw toward our engaged fleet, recalling it.

The Dorna now heaved and pitched like a snared sleen. She, like most tarn ships, was a narrow vessel, long and of shallow draft. I looked to the round ships. Even they leaped in the water. I did not think the Dorna would long live in such a sea unless she might run before it.

"Lift the anchors," I said. "Set the storm sail!"

Men hastened to do what I had told them, and, as they did so, I sent signals to reserve ships, to be conveyed to the balance of the fleet, that they might save themselves while they could. There could be no question of following up what had appeared to be the victory over the fleets of Cos and Tyros.

I stood on the icy, wind-struck deck of the Dorna, my

back turned to the storm. My admiral's cloak, brought with my returning men from the round ship, was given to me and I wrapped it about my shoulders. A vessel of hot paga was brought, too.

"The victory draught," said the oar-master.

I grinned. I did not feel victorious. I was cold. I was alive. I swallowed the hot paga.

The yard had been lowered and the small, triangular storm sail was attached to it. The anchors were raised and the yard, on its ropes and pulleys, began to climb toward the masthead. Meanwhile, the starboard oars, under the call of the oar-master, began swinging the vessel about, to bring her stern into the wind. The wind struck the side of the hull and the ship heeled to leeward. The deck was suddenly washed with cold waves, and then the waters had slipped back. The two helmsmen strained with their side rudders, bringing the ship about. Then the wind was at the stern and the oar-master began his count, easing the ship ahead until the storm sail was caught by the blasts. When it was it was like a fist striking the sail and the mast screamed, and the bow, for a terrible moment, dipped in the water and then, dripping the cold waters, the bow leaped up and tilted to the sky.

"Stroke!" called the oar-master, his cry almost lost in the sleet and wind. "Stroke! Stroke!"

The beating of the copper drum of the keleustes took up maximum beat.

The tiny storm sail, swollen with the black wind and sleet, tore at the yard and the brail ropes. The Dorna knifed ahead, leaping between the waves that rose towering on either side.

She would live.

I did not know if the victory we had won, for victory it surely seemed to be, was decisive or not, but I well knew that the twenty-fifth of Se'Kara, for that was the day on which this battle had been fought, would not be soon forgotten in Port Kar, that city once called squalid and malignant, but which had now found a Home Stone, that city once called the scourge of gleaming Thassa, but which might now be better spoken of, as she had been by some of her citizens aforetimes, as her jewel, the jewel of gleaming Thassa. I wondered how many men would claim to have fought on the twenty-fifth of Se'Kara, abroad on Thassa. I smiled. This day would doubt-

less be made holiday in Port Kar. And those who had
fought here would be, in years to come, as comrades
and brothers. I am English. And I recalled another victory, in another time, on a distant world. I supposed that
in time to come men might, on this holiday, show their
wounds to slaves and wondering children, saying to them,
"These I had in Se'Kara." Would this battle be sung as
had that one? Not in England, I knew. But on Gor, it
would. And yet songs, I told myself, are lies. And those
that had died this day did not sing. And yet, I asked
myself, had they lived, would they not have sung? And I
told myself, I thought yes. And so, then, I asked myself,
might we not then sing for them, and for ourselves as
well, and could there not be, in some way that was hard
to understand, but good, truth in songs?

I went to the tarn that I had ridden back to the Dorna.
I took off my Admiral's cloak and threw it over the shivering bird.

Standing near it was the slave boy Fish.

I looked into his eyes, and I saw, to my surprise, that
he understood what I must do.

"I am coming with you," he said.

I knew that the ships of Eteocles and Sullius Maximus
had not been added to our fleet. I also knew that the
blockade about the last major holding of Sevarius had
been lifted, that its ships, arsenal ships, might participate
in the day's battle. There had been, I knew, exchanges of
information between Claudius, regent for Henrius Sevarius, and Cos and Tyros. I was not disposed to think
that there had not been similar communications between
Cos and Tyros and Eteocles and Sullius Maximus. Doubtless there would be coordinated actions. The hall of the
council itself might now be in flames. The two Ubars, and
Claudius, regent for Henrius Sevarius, I supposed, might
already have claimed power, as a triumvirate, in Port
Kar. Their power, of course, would not last long. Port
Kar had not lost the battle. When the storm abated,
whether in hours or in one or two days, the fleet would
put about and return to Port Kar. But in the meantime
I knew that the two Ubars and Claudius, confident but
ignorant of the outcome of the battle, would be attempting
to rid the city of those who stood against them.

I wondered if my holding still stood.

I had meat brought for the tarn, great chunks of tarsk,

thighs and shoulders, which I had thrown before it, on the cold deck. It tore at them greedily. I had had the bones removed from the meat. If it had been bosk I would not, but the bones of the tarsk are thinner and splinter easily. Then I had water brought for the tarn, in a leather bucket, the ice broken through that coated the water like a lid. It drank.

"I am coming with you," said the boy.

In the belt of his tunic he had thrust the sword that I had had the officer give him before the battle.

I shook my head. "You are only a boy," I told him.

"No," he said, "I am a man."

I smiled at him.

"Why would you come to my holding?" I asked.

"It is to be done," he said.

"Does the girl Vina mean so much to you?" I asked.

He looked at me, and, flustered, looked down at the deck. He kicked at the deck. "She is a mere slave," he said.

"Of course," I said.

"And," said he, defiantly, "a man does not concern himself for a mere female slave."

"Of course not," I admitted.

"Even if it were not for her," he said, looking up, angrily, "I would accompany you."

"Why?" I asked.

"You are my captain," he said, puzzled.

"Remain here," I told him, gently.

He drew the sword I had had given him.

"Test me!" he demanded.

"Put away," I said, "the tools of men."

"Defend yourself!" he cried.

My blade leaped from its sheath and I parried his blow. He had come to me much more swiftly than I had expected.

Men gathered about. "It is sport," said one of them.

I moved the blade toward the boy and he parried it. I was impressed, for I had intended to touch him that time.

Then, moving about, on the pitching deck, in the sleet, we matched blades. After an Ehn or two I replaced my blade in its sheath. "At four times," I said, "I could have killed you."

He dropped his blade, and looked at me agonized.

"But," I said, "you have learned your lessons well. I have fought with warriors who were less swift than you."

He grinned. Some of the seamen pounded their left shoulders with their right fists.

The boy, Fish, was a favorite with them. How else, I asked myself, had he been able to take an oar on the longboat in the canals when I had gone to the hall of the Council of Captains, or been able to board the Dorna, or taken his place in the longboat that had ferried me to the round ship? I, too, was not unfond of the boy. I saw in him, in this boy, wearing a collar, branded, clad in the garment of a kitchen slave, as most others would not, a young Ubar.

"You may not come with me," I told him. "You are too young to die."

"At what age," asked he, "is a man ready for death?"

"To go where I am to go," I told him, "and do what I must do, is the action of a fool."

He grinned. I saw a tear in his eye.

"Yes," said he, "Captain."

"It is the action of a fool!" I told him.

"Each man," said the boy, "has the right, does he not, to perform, if he wishes, the act of a fool?"

"Yes," I said, "each man may, if he wishes, choose such acts."

"Then," said he, "Captain, the bird having rested, let us be on our way."

"Bring a woolen cloak for a young fool," I told a seaman. "And, too, bring a belt and scabbard."

"Yes, Captain," cried the man.

"Do you think you can cling," asked I, "to a knotted rope for hours."

"Of course, Captain," said he.

In a few moments the tarn spread his wings before the black wind and, caught in the blast, was hurled before the Dorna, and began, in dizzying circles, to climb in the wind and sleet. The boy, his feet braced on a knot in the swaying rope, his hands clenched on its fibers, swung below me. Far below I saw the Dorna, lifting and falling in the troughs of the waves, and, separated from her, the ships of the fleet, round ships and tarn ships, storm sails set, oars dipping, flying before the storm.

I did not see any of the ships of Cos or Tyros.

Terence of Treve, mercenary captain of the tarnsmen, had refused to return to Port Kar before the return of the fleet. The environs of Port Kar might now be filled with tarnsmen, other mercenaries, but in the hire of the rebellious Ubars, and Claudius, regent of Henrius Sevarius. "We men of Treve are brave," had said he, "but we are not mad."

The bird was buffeted by the storm, but it was a strong bird. I did not know the width of the storm, but I hoped its front would be only a few pasangs. The bird could not fly a direct line to Port Kar, because of the wind, and we managed an oblique path, cutting away from the fleet. From time to time the bird, tiring, its wings wet, cold, coated with sleet, would drop sickeningly downward, but then again it would beat its way on the level, half driven by the wind, half flying.

The boy, Fish, cold, numb, wet, his hair and clothing iced with sleet, clung to the rope dangling beneath the bird.

Once the bird fell so low that the boy's feet and the bottom of the rope on which he stood splashed a path in the churning waters, and then the bird, responding to my fierce pressures on the one-strap, beat its way up again and again flew, but then only yards over the black, rearing waves, the roaring sea.

And then the sleet became only pelting rain, and the rain became only a cruel wind, and then the cruelty of the wind yielded to only the cold rushing air at the fringe of the storm's garment.

And Thassa beneath us was suddenly streaked with the cold sunlight of Se'Kara, and the bird was across and through the storm. In the distance we could see rocky beaches, and grass and brushland beyond, and beyond that, a woodland, with Tur and Ka-la-na trees.

We took the shuddering bird down among the trees. Fish leaped free as I let the bird hover, then alight. I unsaddled it and let it shake the water from its wings and body. Then I threw over it the admiral's cloak. The boy and I built a fire, over which we might dry our clothes and by which we might warm ourselves.

We will return to Port Kar after the fall of darkness," I told him.

"Of course," he said.

The boy, Fish, and I now stood in the dimly lit great hall of my house, where, the night before, had been celebrated the feast of my victory.

The only light in the huge high-roofed hall was furnished by a single brazier, whose coals, through the iron basket, now glowed redly.

Our footsteps sounded hollow on the tiles of the great hall.

We had left the tarn outside on the promenade, fronting on the lakelike courtyard.

We had encountered no tarnsmen over the city.

The city itself was much darkened.

We had flown over the city, seeing below us the darkened buildings, the reflection of the three moons of Gor flickering in the dark canals.

Then we had come to my holding and now we stood, together, side by side, in the apparently deserted, almost darkened great hall of my holding.

Our blades were unsheathed, those of an admiral of the fleet and a slave boy.

We looked about ourselves.

We had encountered no one in the passageways, or the rooms into which we had come, making our way to the great hall.

We heard a muffled noise, coming from a corner of the almost darkened hall.

There, kneeling on the tiles, back to back, their wrists bound behind their backs to a slave ring, were two girls. We saw their eyes, wild, over their gags. They shook their heads.

They wore the miserable garments of kitchen slaves.

They were the girl Vina, and Telima.

Fish would have rushed forward, but my hand restrained him.

Not speaking, I motioned that he should take his place at the side of the entryway to the great hall, where he might not be seen.

I strode irritably to the two girls. I did not release them. They had permitted themselves to be taken, to be used as bait. Vina was very young, but Telima should have known better, and yet she, too, the proud Telima, knelt helplessly at the ring, her wrists bound behind her back, securely and expertly gagged, a young and beautiful woman, yet fastened as helplessly to a slave ring as a young girl.

I gave her head a shake. "Stupid wench," I said.

She was trying to tell me that there were men about, to attack me.

"The mouths of rence girls," I said, "are said to be as large as the delta itself."

She could make only tiny, protesting, futile noises.

I examined the gag. Heavy leather strips were bound tightly across her mouth, doubtless holding a heavy packing within, probably rep-cloth. Such a gag would not be pleasant to wear. It had been well done.

"At last," I commented, "someone has discovered a way to keep rence girls quiet."

There were tears in Telima's eyes. She squirmed in futility, in fear, in fury.

I patted her on the head condescendingly.

She looked at me in rage and exasperation.

I turned away from the girls, but stood before them.

I spoke loudly. "Now," I said, "let us release these wenches."

In that instant I heard, from down the passageway, a sharp whistle, and the sound of running feet, those of several men. I saw torches being carried.

"At him!" cried Lysias, helmeted, the helmet bearing the crest of sleen hair, marking it as that of a captain. Lysias himself, however, did not engage me.

Several men rushed forward, some of them with torches. Perhaps forty men rushed into the room.

I met them, moving swiftly, constantly shifting my position, drawing them after me, then pressing one or another of them back. I kept, as well as I could, near the girls, that the backs of the men would be, in turn, kept toward the entryway.

I could see, as they did not, a shadow moving swiftly behind them, it, too, rapidly shifting its position, moving about amidst the frantic shadows of men, torches and confusions, but always staying in the background, like an absence of substance but one which carried a blade of steel. Then the shadow had donned a helmet, and it was almost indistinguishable from the others. Those who fell before that shadow did so unnoticed, and without great cries, for the blade had crossed their throats as unexpectedly as a whisper in the darkness.

I myself dropped nine warriors.

Then we heard more shouting, and saw more torches.

Now the room was high with light and even the beams of the hall stood forth, heavy in their ceiling.

Now, discovered, Fish fought by my side, that we might, together, protect one another.

"Now, Slave," said I to Fish, "you should have stayed with the fleet."

"Be silent," said he, adding, "—Master."

I laughed.

I saw the boy, with a lightning thrust, flash four inches of steel through a body, returning to the on-guard position before the man realized he had been struck.

In fighting as we were, one did not use a deep thrust, that the blade might be more swiftly freed.

"You have learned your lessons well," said I, "Slave."

"Thank you, Master," said he.

He dropped another man.

I dropped two others, to my right.

I heard more men coming down the passageway.

Then, from one side, the door to the kitchens, a number of other men came forth, carrying torches and steel.

We are lost, I thought. Lost.

To my fury I saw that these men were led by Samos of Port Kar.

"So," I cried, "as I thought, you are in league with the enemies of Port Kar!"

But to my astonishment he engaged and dropped one of our attackers.

I saw that some of the men with him were my own, who had been left behind in the holding, to guard it. Others I did not know.

"Withdraw!" cried Lysias, wildly in the fighting.

His men backed away, fighting, and we, and those others who had come to help us, pressed them back even as they retreated through the great door to the high-roofed hall.

At the entryway we stopped and threw shut the doors, dropping the beams into place.

Samos and I, together, dropped the last beam into the heavy iron brackets.

He was sweating and the sleeve of his tunic was torn. There was a splash of blood across his face, staining the left side of his face, his short, white, cropped hair and the golden ring in his ear.

"The fleet?" he asked.

"Victory is ours," I told him.

"Good," he said. He sheathed his sword. "We are defending the keep near the delta wall," he said. "Follow me."

Near the bound girls he stopped.

"So here you are," said Samos. He turned to face me. "They snuck away to find you."

"They were successful," I said.

I slashed the binding fiber which, tying their wrists together, had passed through the slave ring, fastening them to it. They struggled to their feet. Their wrists, though no longer tethered to the slave ring, were still fastened behind their backs. They were still gagged. Vina ran to Fish, tears in her eyes, and thrust her head against his left shoulder. He took her in his arms.

Telima approached me timidly, head down, and then, looking up, smiling with her eyes, put her head against my right shoulder. I held her to me.

"So," Fish was saying to Vina, "you snuck away from the keep."

She looked at him, startled.

He took her by the shoulders, turned her about and started her stumbling down the kitchen passageway. Then, with a swift motion, he leaped behind her and, with the flat of his blade, dealt her a sharp, stinging blow. She sped down the passageway.

"You, too," I said to Telima, "apparently left the keep unbidden."

She backed warily away from me.

"Have you something to say to me, Rence Girl?" I asked.

"Umm-ummph," protested Telima, shaking her head.

I took a step toward her.

She shook her head. She had a don't-you-dare-you-beast-you look in her eyes.

I took another step toward her.

Telima, dignity to the winds, turned and fled down the passageway, but, before she had managed to make ten yards, she had been stung twice, and roundly, by the flat of my blade.

Twenty yards beyond, running, she stopped, and turned

to look upon me. She drew herself up in her full, angry dignity.

I took another step toward her and, wildly, she wheeled and, barefoot, fled stumbling down the passageway.

The dignity of the proud Telima, I gathered, could not endure another such blow.

I laughed.

"One must know how to treat women," said the boy, Fish, gravely.

"Yes," I said, gravely.

"One must teach them who is master," said the boy.

"Quite," I agreed.

The men about us laughed and, as comrades in arms, we made our way through the passageway, and then the kitchens, and the halls to the keep.

The next afternoon Samos and I stood together behind the parapet of the keep. Over our heads, high, between beams, was strung tarn wire. Heavy wooden mantelets, mounted on posts, were nearby, under which we might protect ourselves from crossbow fire from tarnsmen.

My large yellow bow of Ka-la-na, tipped with bosk horn and strung with hemp, whipped with silk, was at hand. It had helped to keep besiegers at their distance. There were few arrows left.

Our men were below. We were weary. We had caught what sleep we could.

Now, only Samos and I stood watch.

Before my return to the holding, Samos, with his men and mine, had withstood eleven assaults on the keep, both by tarnsmen and besieging infantry. Since I had returned yesterday evening, we had withstood another four. We now had left only thirty-five men, eighteen who had accompanied Samos to my holding, and seventeen of my own.

"Why have you come to defend my keep, and my holding?" I asked Samos.

"Do you not know?" he asked.

"No," I said.

"It does not matter," he said, "now."

"Had it not been for you and your men," I said, "my holding would long ago have fallen."

Samos shrugged.

We looked out over the parapet. The keep is near the

delta wall of the holding. We could, from the ramparts, look out over the marsh, stretching far beyond, that vast, beautiful delta of the great Vosk, through which I had come, so long ago.

Our men, exhausted, lay below, within the keep. The Ehn of sleep they could obtain were precious to them. They, like Samos and myself, were almost overcome with weariness. The waiting, and then the fighting, and the waiting again, had been so long, so long.

Also below were four girls, Vina and Telima, and Luma, the chief accountant of my house, who had not fled, and the dancer, Sandra, who had been afraid to leave the holding. Most others, whether men or women, slave or free, had fled. Even Thurnock and Thura, and Clitus and Ula, whom I had expected to stay, had fled. I did not reproach them, even in my heart. They were wise. It was madness to stay behind. In the end, I told myself, it was I, and not they, who was truly the fool. And yet I would not have chosen, at this time, to be any place other than where I stood, on height of my keep, in the holding I had made mine own in Port Kar.

And so Samos, and I, kept watch.

I looked at him. I did not understand the slaver. Why had he come to defend my holding? Was he so irrational, so mad, so contemptuous of the value of his life?

He did not belong here.

This holding was mine, mine!

"You are weary," said Samos. "Go below. I will watch."

I nodded. There was no longer any point, nor time, to distrust Samos. His sword had been much stained in my behalf. His own life, like mine, had stood stake on the parapet of my keep. If he served the Ubars, or Claudius, regent of Henrius Sevarius, or the Ubarates of Cos and Tyros, or the Others, or Priest-Kings, or himself, I no longer cared. I no longer cared about anything. I had come back. I was very tired.

I descended through the trap and climbed down the ladder to the first level beneath the keep's roof. There was food and water there, enough for another week of fighting. But I did not think we would need that much. Before nightfall doubtless more assaults would take place, and, in the first, or the second, or in another, we would surely fall.

I looked about the room. The men were sleeping. It was

dirty and littered. They were unshaven. Several of them, men of Samos, were unknown to me, but others, mine, I had cared for. Some were even slaves, who had fought with poles and hammers. Others were men who had been slaves, whom I had freed and trained with weapons. Others were seamen, and two others were mercenaries, who had refused to leave my service. I saw the boy, Fish, sleeping, Vina in his arms. He had done well, I thought.

"Master," I heard.

In one corner of the room I saw Sandra, the dancer. To my surprise, she had arrayed herself in pleasure silks and cosmetics. She was truly beautiful.

I went to her side. She was kneeling before a bronze mirror, touching an eyebrow with a brush.

She looked up at me, frightened. "When they come," she asked, "they will not kill Sandra, will they?"

"I do not think so," I said. "I think they will find her beautiful, and permit her to live."

She shook with relief, and returned to her mirror, anxiously studying her countenance.

I lifted her gently to her feet and looked into her eyes.

"Please do not disturb my cosmetics," she begged.

I smiled. "No," I said, "I will not. They will find you very beautiful."

I kissed her on the side of the neck, beneath the ear, and descended to another level.

She looked after me.

On this level, sitting against a wall, her knees drawn up, I found Luma.

I went to her, and stood before her.

She stood up, and touched my cheek with her hand. There were tears in her eyes.

"I would free you," I said, "but I think they might kill free women, if they found them."

I touched her collar.

"With this," I said, "I think you might be permitted to live."

She wept and put her head to my shoulders. I held her in my arms.

"My brave Luma," I said. "My fine, brave Luma."

I kissed her and, pressing her gently from me, descended another level.

There Telima had been caring for two men who had been wounded.

I went to one wall and, on a cloak that was lying there, sat down, my head in my hands.

The girl came to be beside me, where, in the fashion of the Gorean woman, she knelt, back on her heels.

"I expect," she said, after a time, "the fleet will return in a few hours, and we shall be saved."

Surely she knew the fleet, as well as I, had been driven pasangs south, and would not be able to reach the harbor of Port Kar for another two or three days, at the least.

"Yes," I said, "in a few hours the fleet will return and we shall be saved."

She put her hand on my head, and then her face was against mine.

"Do not weep," I told her.

I held her against me.

"I have hurt you so," she said.

"No," I said, "no."

"It is all so strange," she said.

"What is so strange?" I asked.

"That Samos should be here," said she.

"But why?" I asked.

She looked at me. "Because," said she, "years ago, he was my master."

I was startled.

"I was taken slave at the age of seven in a raid," she said, "and Samos, at a market, bought me. For years he treated me with great concern and care. I was treated well, and taught things that slaves are seldom taught. I can read, you know."

I recalled once, long ago, being puzzled that she, though a mere rence girl, had been literate.

"And I was taught many other things, too," said she, "when I could read, even to the second knowledge."

That was reserved, generally, for the high castes on Gor.

"I was raised in that house," she said, "with love, though I was only slave, and Samos was to me almost as a father might have been. I was permitted to speak to, and learn from, scribes and singers, and merchants and travelers. I had friends among other girls in the house, who were also much free, though not as free as I. We had the freedom of the city, though guards would accompany us to protect us."

"And then what happened?" I asked.

Her voice grew hard. "I had been told that on my seventeenth birthday a great change would occur in my life." She smiled. "I expected to be freed, and to be adopted as the daughter of Samos."

"What happened?" I asked.

"At dawn that morning," she said, "the Slave Master came for me. I was taken below to the pens. There, like a new girl taken from the rence islands, I was stripped. An iron was heated. I was marked. My head was placed across an anvil and, about my throat, was hammered a simple plate collar. Then my wrists were tied widely apart to wrist rings mounted in a stone wall, and I was whipped. After this, when I had been cut down, weeping, the Slave Master, and his men, much used me. After this I was fitted with slave chains and locked in a pen, with other girls. These other girls, some of them rence girls themselves, would often beat me, for they knew what freedom I had had in the house, and they knew, as was true, that I had regarded myself as far superior to such as they, only common girls, simple merchandise. I thought there was some great mistake. For days, though the other girls would beat me for it, I begged the Slave Master, the guards, to be taken before Samos. At last, kneeling, in a simple plate collar, beaten and shackled, stripped, I was thrown before him."

"What did he say?" I asked.

"He said," said she, "take this slave away."

I looked down, but held her.

"I was taught the duties of the slave girl in that house," she said, "and I learned them well. The girls among whom I had been first would no longer even condescend to speak to me. Guards who had formerly protected me would now, as they chose, take me in their arms, and I must well serve them or be beaten."

"Did Samos himself use you?" I asked.

"No," she said.

"The most miserable of tasks were often given to me," continued the girl. "Often I was not permitted clothing. Often I was beaten, and cruelly used. At night I was not even chained, but locked in a tiny slave cage, in which I could scarcely move." She looked at me, angrily. "In me," said she, "a great hatred grew, of Port Kar and of

Samos and of men, and of slaves, of whom I was one. I lived only for my hate and the dream that I might one day escape, and take vengeance on men."

"You did escape," I said.

"Yes," she said, "in cleaning the quarters of the slave master I found the key to my collar."

"You were then no longer wearing a plate collar," I said.

"Almost from the beginning, after my seventeenth birthday," said Telima, "I was trained as a pleasure slave. One year after my enslavement I was certified to the house by the slave mistress as having become accomplished in such duties. At that time the plate collar was opened by one of the metal workers and replaced with a seven-pin lock collar.

The common female slave collar on Gor has a seven-pin lock. There are, incidentally, seven letters in the most common Gorean expression for female slave, Kajira.

"It seems careless," I said, "that the slave master should leave, where a slave might find it, the key to her collar."

She shrugged.

"And, too," she said, "nearby there was a golden armlet." She looked at me. "I took it," she said. "I thought I might need gold, if only to bargain my way past guards." She looked down. "But," she said, "I had little difficulty in leaving the house. I told them I was on an errand, and they permitted me to leave. I had, of course, run errands in the city before. Outside the house I removed the collar, that I might move more freely, being unquestioned, in the city. I found some beams and rope, and a pole, bound together a simple raft and through one of the delta canals, which were not then barred, made my escape. As a child I had been of the marshes, and so I did not fear to return to them. I was found by the men of Ho-Hak and accepted into their community. He permitted me, even, to retain the golden armlet."

I looked at the opposite wall.

"Do you still hate Samos so?" I asked.

"I had thought I would," she said. "But now that he is here, and helping us, I do not hate him. It is all very strange."

I was tired, and I felt I must sleep. I was pleased that Telima had told me these parts of her story, which I had not heard before. I sensed that there was more here than I could clearly understand at the moment, and more than she understood, as well. But I was very tired.

"You know," I said, "the keep will be overrun and most of us, the men, at least, will be slain?"

"The fleet will come," she said.

"Yes," I said. "But if it does not."

"It will," she said.

"Where is the collar I took from your throat on the night of the victory feast?" I asked.

She looked at me, puzzled. "I brought it to the keep," she said. She smiled. "I did not know whether you wished me slave or free."

"The men will come with weapons," I said. "Where is the collar?"

She looked at me. "Must I wear it?" she asked.

"Yes," I said. I did not want her slain, if possible, when the men came. If they thought her a free woman, and mine, she might be swiftly killed, or tortured and impaled.

She found the collar.

"Put it on," I told her.

"Is there so little hope?" she asked.

"Put it on," I said to her. "Put it on."

"No," she said. "If you die, I am willing to die beside you, as your woman."

Port Kar does not recognize the Free Companionship, but there are free women in the city, who are known simply as the women of their men.

"Are you my woman?" I asked.

"Yes," she said.

"Then," I said, "obey me."

She smiled. "If I must be collared," she said, "let it be at the hand of my Ubar."

I placed the collar on her throat, and kissed her. In her tunic I saw, concealed, a small dagger.

"Would you fight with this?" I asked, taking it from her.

"I do not wish to live without you!" she cried.

I threw the dagger to one side. She wept in my arms. "No," I said, "life is what is important. It is life that is important. Life."

Collared, she wept in my arms.

Weary, I fell asleep.

"They're coming!" I heard cry.

I shook my head, and leaped to my feet.

"My Ubar!" cried Telima. "This I brought to the keep."

To my astonishment she handed me the sword that I had brought originally to Port Kar.

I looked at it.

I put aside the admiral's sword.

"Thank you," I said.

Our lips brushed as I thrust her aside, and ran to the ladder. I slipped the blade into the sheath and began to climb the rungs. I could hear shouts and the feet of men above me.

I climbed the ladder.

At my side I now wore the sword that I had brought originally to Port Kar, that which I had carried so many years before, even at the siege of Ar, and in Tharna, and in the Nest of Priest-Kings and on the plains of the Wagon Peoples, and in the streets of great Ar itself, when I had seemed to serve Cernus, Master of the House of Cernus, greatest of the slave houses of Ar. It did not have the jeweled hilt or the figured blade of my admiral's sword, but I found it sufficient. Telima had found it among my belongings, and had brought it to the keep, that it might be waiting for me there. Strangely she had apparently not expected me to do anything other than return to my holding. As I climbed the ladder I was glad that the old blade, the familiar steel, with its memories of another life and time, when I had been Tarl Cabot, was at my side.

If one must die, how could one better die than with such a blade in hand?

We fought on the height of the keep.

The last four arrows of the great yellow bow were fired, and four who threatened us fell from the delta wall beyond the keep, from which they were attempting to cover the climb of the besiegers.

Standing even on the mantelets under the tarn wire, with spears and swords, we thrust at the tarnsmen dropping to the wire, leaving go of the ropes to which they had clung.

We heard grappling irons with knotted ropes fly over the parapet, scrape across the stones, and wedge in the crenels. We heard the striking against the walls of the keep of siege poles, like ladders with a single upright, rungs tied transversely on the single axis. We heard the trumpets of the attack, the running feet, the climbing, the clashing of weapons, the shouting of men.

Then helmeted heads, eyes wild in the "Y"-like openings of the helmets, appeared at the crenels, and gauntleted hands and booted feet appeared, and men were swarming at the walls.

I leaped down from the mantelet on which I had stood and flung myself to the wall.

I heard the ringing of the steel of Samos, the cries of the men behind me.

I caught sight of the boy, Fish, running past, a spear held over his head in both hands, and heard a horrible cry, long and wailing, ending with the abrupt striking of a body far below on the stones.

"Keep more from coming!" I cried to my men.

They rushed to the walls.

Within the parapets we fought those who had scaled the walls.

I saw one invader climbing down the ladder to the lower levels.

Then he cried out and slipped to the level beneath, his hands off the rungs.

I saw Telima's head in the opening. In her teeth was the dagger I had seen. In her right hand, bloody, was the admiral's sword I had discarded.

"Go back!" I cried to her.

I saw Luma and Vina climbing up behind her. They picked up stones from the roof of the keep, and ran to the walls, to hurl them at point-blank range against the men climbing.

Telima, wildly, her two hands on the sword, struck a man from behind in the neck and he fell away from the blade. Then she had lost the blade, as an invader struck it from her hand. He raised his own to strike her but I had my steel beneath his left shoulder blade and had turned again before he could deliver his blow.

I saw a man on the parapet fall screaming backward, struck by a rock as large as his head, hurled from the small hands of Luma. Vina, with a shield, whose weight she could hardly bear, was trying to cover the boy, Fish, as he fought. I saw him drop his man, and turn, seeking another.

I threw a man whom I had struck, even before he

died, over the parapet, striking another, who, clinging
desperately to the siege pole, carried it back in a long
arc with him as he fell. I saw one of my former slaves,
with a spear shaft, beating another man from the wall.

Samos thrust his blade into the "Y"-shaped opening of
a helmet, parried a spear thrust from his body, and met
the steel of another man.

We heard the trumpet of retreat, and killed six as
they tried to escape back over the wall.

We, panting, bloody, looked about ourselves.

"The next attack," said Samos, indifferently, "will be
the last."

Samos survived, and I, and the boy, Fish, and the
three girls, and, beyond these, other than the dancer,
Sandra, who had remained below, only five men, three who
had come to my holding with Samos, and two of my own,
one a simple mercenary, one who had once been a slave.

I looked out over the delta.

We heard, behind walls, within the holding, the mar-
shalling of men, the click of arms. It would not, this
time, be a long wait.

I went to Samos. "I wish you well," I said to him.

The heavy, squarish face regarded me, still so much
the countenance of the predator. Then he looked away.
"I, too," said he, "wish you well, Warrior."

He seemed embarrassed to say what he had. I wondered why he had called me Warrior.

I took Telima in my arms. "When they come again,"
I said, "hide below. If you fight you will doubtless be
slain. When they come below, submit to them. They may
spare you." And then I looked to Vina and Luma. "You,
also," I said. "Do not mix in the matters of men."

Vina looked to the boy, Fish.

He nodded. "Yes," he said, "go below."

"I, for one," said Telima, "find it stuffy below."

"I, too," smiled Luma.

"Yes," said Vina, firmly. "It is very stuffy below."

"Very well," I said, "then it will be necessary, before
the next attack, to bind you to the foot of the ladder
below."

"I think," said Samos, looking over the parapet, "you
will not have time for that."

We heard the trumpets signaling a new attack. We
heard the rush of hundreds of feet on the stones below.

"Go below!" I cried to the girls.

They stood away, feet fixed apart, in the garments of slaves, obdurate, rebellious.

"We acknowledge ourselves your slave girls!" screamed Telima. "If we do not please you, beat us or slay us!"

A crossbow quarrel swept overhead.

"Go below!" screamed Fish to Vina.

"If I do not please you," she screamed, "beat me or kill me!"

He kissed her swiftly, and turned to defend a wall.

The girls took up stones and swords, and stood beside us.

"Good-bye, my Ubar," said Telima.

"Farewell," said I, "Ubara."

With a great cry the hundreds of men swarmed to the foot of the keep. Again we heard the striking against the walls of siege poles. Again irons, on their ropes, looped over the parapet wall. And across from the keep, on the delta wall, boldly, there stood crossbowmen, now without fear, for our arrows and bolts were gone, to cover the climbing men.

We heard the men nearing us, on the other side of the wall, the scraping of swords and spears on the vertical stones of the keep.

On the delta wall, opposite, I saw the leader of the crossbowmen, standing even on the parapet of the delta wall itself, directing his men.

I heard the climbers approaching even more closely.

Then, to my amazement, I saw something, like a streak of light, leap from the delta behind the wall, and the leader of the crossbowmen spun about as though struck with a war hammer and dropped, inert, from the wall.

"You're hurting me!" cried Telima.

My hand clutched her arm.

I leaped to my feet.

"Stay down!" cried Samos.

Suddenly more than a hundred irons with ropes struck the delta wall, wedging in the crenels, and I saw the irons tighten in the crenels and strain with the weight on them. One of the crossbowmen looked over the delta wall and flew backwards off the wall, his hands not reaching his head. Protruding from his forehead, its pile stopped by the metal helmet in the back, was the long shaft of an arrow, one that could be only from the peasant bow.

We saw crossbowmen fleeing from the wall.

We heard the men climbing closer on the siege poles.

Then, swarming over the delta wall, were hundreds of men.

"Rencers!" I cried.

But each of these men, over his back, carried a peasant bow. In perfect order they stood in line within the parapet on the delta wall. As one their arrows leaped to the string, as one the great bows bent, and I saw Ho-Hak on the height of the wall bring down his arm with a cry, and I saw, like sheets of oblique rain, the torrent of gull-feathered shafts leap toward the keep. And I saw, too, on the wall, with Ho-Hak, Thurnock, the Peasant, with his bow, and beside him, with net and trident, Clitus. There was a great screaming from the siege ladders, and I heard men crying out with death, and terror, and heard the scraping of the ladders and then their falling back, showering bodies on those crowded below, waiting to scale them. Again and again the great line blasted shafts of pile-tipped tem-wood into those packed at the foot of the keep. And then the invaders began to scatter and run, but each archer picked his target, and few there were who reached cover other than the side of the keep away from the archers. And now archers were running down the side walls, and leaping to other roofs, that every point at the foot of the keep might be within the assailing orbit of the string-flung missiles, and the girls, and the men, too, flung stones from the top of the keep down on the men trying to hide behind it, and then, again, the invaders scattered, running back toward the holding. For an instant, white-faced, wild, I saw below Lysias, with his helmet with its crest of sleen hair, and beside him, with the string of pearls of the Vosk sorp about his forehead, the rencer Henrak, who had, long ago, betrayed the rencers for the gold of Port Kar. And behind them, in a rich swirling cloak of the fur of the white, spotted sea sleen, sword in hand, looking wildly about, was another man, one I did not know.

"It is Claudius!" cried the boy, Fish, beside me. "Claudius!"

So that, I thought, was Claudius, who had been regent for Henrius Sevarius, and who, doubtless, had attempted to have him killed.

The boy's fists were clenched on the parapet.

Then the three men, with some others, fled into my holding.

On the wall Thurnock waved his great bow over his head.

"Captain!" he cried.

Clitus, too, raised his hand.

I, too, lifted my hand, acknowledging their salute.

And I lifted my hand, too, to Ho-Hak, the rencer. I saw how his men used their bows. I had little doubt that having been taught the might of the great bow in the marshes, when I had freed them from the slavers in the barges, they had traded for the weapons and now had made them their own, and proudly, as much as the peasants. I did not think the rencers would any longer be at the mercy of the men of Port Kar. Now, with weapons and courage, perhaps for the first time, they were truly free men, for they could now defend their freedoms, and those who cannot do this are not truly free; at best they are fortunate.

"Look!" cried Samos.

From the height of the keep, we could see over my holding, even to the canal and sea gate beyond the lake-like courtyard.

Men were fleeing from my holding but, even more important, approaching down the canal, oars flashing, mast down, came a tarn ship, and then another.

"It is the Venna!" I cried. "And the Tela!"

Standing at the prow of the Venna, shield on his arm, helmeted, spear in hand, was Tab.

He must have brought the Venna and the Tela into the wind, cutting away even the storm sails, and risked the destruction of the two ships in the high sea, not to be driven from Port Kar, and then, when the storm had lulled, they had put about and raced for the harbor. The rest of the fleet was still doubtless a hundred or more pasangs to the south.

"A seaman truly worthy of Port Kar," said Samos.

"Do you love the city so?" I asked.

Samos smiled. "It is the place of my Home Stone," he said.

I grinned.

We saw the two ships, the Venna and her sister ship, the Tela, knife into the courtyard and swing about, their bowmen firing on the men running on the promenade and trying to escape about the edges of the courtyard.

We saw men throwing down their weapons and kneeling. They would be roped together as slaves.

I seized Telima in my arms. She was laughing and crying.

I then seized one of the ropes attached to a grappling iron wedged in one of the crenels and began to descend the outer side of the keep wall. Fish and Samos were not far behind me.

With other ropes the men behind would lower the girls, and then follow themselves.

At the foot of the keep we met Thurnock, Clitus and Ho-Hak.

We embraced.

"You have learned the lesson of the great bow well," I said to Ho-Hak.

"You well taught it to us, Warrior," said Ho-Hak.

Thurnock and Clitus, with Thura and Ula, had gone for aid to the rencers, traditionally enemies of those of Port Kar. And the rencers, to my astonishment, had come to risk their lives for me.

I decided I did indeed know little of men.

"Thank you," said I to Ho-Hak.

"It is nothing," said he, "Warrior."

It is such nothings, I thought, that are our manhood and our meaning.

"Three are cornered within," said a seaman.

Samos and I, and Fish, and Thurnock, Clitus and Ho-Hak, and others, went within the holding.

In the great hall, surrounded by crossbowmen, stood three men, at bay. Lysias, Claudius and Henrak.

"Greetings, Tab," said I, saluting him as I entered the room.

"Greetings, Captain," said he.

By now the three girls, Telima, Vina and Luma, had been lowered from the height of the keep, and were close behind us.

Lysias, seeing me, flung himself at me. I met his attack. The exchange was sharp. Then he fell at my feet, his helmet rolling to the side, blood on the sleen-hair crest, that marking it as that of a captain.

"I am rich," said Claudius. "I can pay for my freedom."

"The Council of Captains of Port Kar," said Samos, "has business with you."

"My business is first," said a voice.

We turned to see the slave boy, Fish, his sword in hand.

"You!" cried Claudius. "You!"

Samos looked at the boy, curiously. Then he turned to Claudius. "You seem disturbed," said he, "at the sight of a mere slave boy."

I recalled that there was a price on the head of the young Ubar, Henrius Sevarius.

And he stood there, though branded, though collared, though in the miserable garment of a slave, as a young Ubar. He was no longer a boy. He had loved, and he had fought. He was a man.

Claudius, with a cry of rage, the cloak of white, spotted fur of sea sleen swirling behind him, leaped at the boy, sword high, raining blows upon him.

The boy smartly parried them, not striking his own blows.

"Yes," said the boy, "I am not an unskilled swordsman. Now let us fight."

Claudius threw aside his swirling cloak and, warily, approached the boy.

Claudius was an excellent swordsman, but, in moments, the boy, Fish, had stepped away from him, and wiped his blade on the flung-aside cloak. Claudius stood unsteadily in the center of the great hall, and then, he fell forward, sprawling on the tiles.

"Remarkable," said Samos. "Claudius is dead. And slain only by a slave."

The boy, Fish, smiled.

"This one," said Ho-Hak, indicating Henrak, "is a rencer, and he is mine."

Henrak regarded him, white-faced.

Ho-Hak regarded him. "Eechius was killed at the rence island," he said to Henrak. "Eechius was my son."

"Do not hurt me!" cried Henrak.

He turned to run, but there was no place to run.

Ho-Hak, solemn and large, removed his weapons, dropping them to the floor. About his neck there was still the heavy iron collar he had worn as a galley slave, with its links of heavy, dangling chain. His large ears laid themselves flat against his head.

"He has a knife!" cried Luma.

Ho-Hak, carefully, approached Henrak, who held a knife poised.

When Henrak struck, Ho-Hak caught his wrist. Slowly Ho-Hak's great hand, strengthened from years at the oar, closed on Henrak's wrist, and the knife, as the men sweated and strained, dropped clattering to the floor.

Then Ho-Hak picked up Henrak and, slowly, holding him over his head, carried him screaming and struggling from the room.

We went outside, and saw Ho-Hak slowly climb the long, narrow stairs beside the delta wall, until he stood behind the parapet, at its height. Then we saw him, outlined against the sky, climb to the parapet itself, hold Henrak over his head for a long moment and then fling him screaming from the wall out into the marsh beyond.

At the foot of the delta wall there would be tharlarion.

It was now late at night.

We had supped and drank, on provisions brought from the Venna and the Tela.

We were served by Telima and Vina, who wore the garments still of Kettle Slaves. The young man, Fish, sat with us, and was served. Serving us as well, though uncollared, were Midice, and Thura and Ula. When we had been served the girls sat with us, and we ate together.

Midice did not meet my eyes. She was very beautiful. She went and knelt near Tab.

"I never thought," Tab was saying, "that I would find a free woman of interest." He had one arm about Midice.

"On a peasant holding," said Thurnock, defensively, as though he must justify having freed Thura, "one can get much more work from a free woman!" He pounded the table. Thura wore talenders in her hair.

"For my part," said Clitus, chewing, "I am only a poor fisherman, and could scarce afford the costs of a slave."

Ula laughed and thrust her head against his shoulder, holding his arm.

"Well," said Samos, chewing on a vulo wing, "I am glad there are still some women slave in Port Kar."

Telima and Vina, in their collars, looked down, smiling.

"Where is the slave Sandra?" I asked Thurnock.

"We found her hiding in your treasure room in the keep," said Thurnock.

"That seems appropriate," said Telima, acidly.

"Let us not be unpleasant," I cautioned her.

"So what did you do?" I asked.

"We bolted the door from the outside," said Thurnock. "She screamed and pounded but is well contained within."

"Good," I said.

I would let her remain there for two days without food and water, in among the gold and the jewels.

"When you release her," said Telima, "why don't you sell her?"

Telima was Gorean.

"Would you like me to sell her?" I asked.

"Yes," said Telima.

"Why?" I asked.

"Beast," smiled Telima.

"In my arms," I said, "I have found her a true slave."

"In your arms," said Telima, looking down, "I am a truer slave than Sandra could ever be."

"Perhaps," I said, "I shall let you compete anxiously against one another."

"Good," said Telima. "I will compete. I will win."

I laughed, and Telima looked at me, puzzled. I reached across and seized her by the arms, and drew her to me. She was so utterly Gorean. Looking down into Telima's eyes I told her, "In two days, when I free Sandra from the treasure room, I am going to give her her freedom and gold, that she may go where she wishes and do what she pleases."

Telima looked at me, startled.

"It is Telima," I said, "whom I will not free."

Her eyes were wide. She squirmed in my arms.

"It is Telima," I told her, "whom I will keep as a slave."

She laughed, and lifted her lips eagerly to mine, and it was long that we kissed.

"My former mistress kisses well," I said.

"Your slave," said Telima, "rejoices that master finds her not displeasing."

"Is it not time for some of the slaves to be sent to the kitchens?" asked the young man, Fish.

"Yes," I said. I then addressed myself to Fish and Vina. "Go to the kitchens, Slaves," said I, "and do not permit me to see you until dawn."

Fish lifted Vina in his arms and left the table.

At the entryway to that passage leading to the kitchens he stopped, and then, as she laughed and kissed him, he swept her, once the Lady Vivina, who was to have been the Ubara of Cos, now only a young, collared slave girl, in a brief, miserable garment, through the portal and disappeared down the passageway. And I do not doubt that the Lady Vivina would have found the couch of the Ubar of Cos less joyful than did the slave girl Vina the blanket and the mat of the kitchen boy, Fish, in the house of Bosk, a captain of Port Kar.

"I see," said Ho-Hak to Telima, "that you still wear the golden armlet."

"Yes," said Telima.

"It was by that," said Ho-Hak, "that I was to recognize you, when years ago you were to have fled to the marshes."

Telima looked at him, puzzled.

Samos put down a cup of paga. "How do you suppose matters in the city will proceed?" he asked Tab.

Tab looked down at the table. "The Ubars Eteocles and Sullius Maximus," he said, "have already fled with their ships and men. The last holding of Henrius Sevarius has been abandoned. The council hall, though partly burnt, is not destroyed. The city, it seems to me, is safe. The fleet will doubtless return within four or five days."

"Then," said Samos, "it seems that the Home Stone of Port Kar is secure." He lifted his goblet.

We drank his toast.

"If my captain will permit," said Tab, "it is late, and I shall withdraw."

"Withdraw," I said.

He bowed his head and took his leave, and Midice slipped to her feet and accompanied him.

"I do not think it wise for Rencers," said Ho-Hak, "to be over long in Port Kar. Under the cover of darkness we shall depart."

"My thanks to you and your people," said I.

"The rence islands, now confederated," said Ho-Hak, "are yours."

"I thank you," I said, "Ho-Hak."

"We can never repay you," he said, "for having once saved many of us from those of Port Kar, and for having taught us the lesson of the great bow."

"I am already more than paid," I said.

"Then no longer," said Ho-Hak, "are we in one another's debt."

"No longer," said I.

"Then," said Ho-Hak, putting out his hand, "let us be friends."

We clasped hands.

"In the marshes," he said, "you have friends."

"Good," I said.

Ho-Hak turned and I saw the broad back of the ex-galley-slave move through the door. Outside I heard him summoning his men. They would return to their rence craft tied at the foot of the delta wall.

"With your permission, Captain," said Thurnock, with a look at Thura, "it is late."

I nodded, and lifted my hand, and Thurnock and Clitus, with Thura and Ula, left the table.

"Good-night," said I, "my friends."

"Good-night," said they.

Now only Telima, and I and Samos, remained at the table, alone in the great hall.

"It must be nearly morning," said Samos.

"Perhaps an Ahn till dawn," I said.

"Bring cloaks," said Samos, "and let us climb to the height of the keep."

We found cloaks, I that of the admiral, and we followed Samos from the room, across the tiled yard behind the great hall, and into the now-opened keep, and climbed behind him to its height.

From the height of the keep we could see the men of Tab, from the Venna and the Tela, here and there on guard. The great sea gate, leading out into the city, had been closed. The rencers, one by one, were climbing down ropes over the delta wall, returning to their small craft below.

We saw Ho-Hak, the last to climb over the wall, and we raised our hands to him. He waved, and then disappeared over the wall.

In the light of the three moons the marshes flickered.

Telima looked at Samos. "Then," she said, "I was permitted to escape from your house."

"Yes," said Samos, "and you were permitted to take the golden armlet, that Ho-Hak, with his men, would recognize you in the marshes."

"They found me within hours," she said.

"They were waiting for you," said Samos.

"I do not understand," said Telima.

"I bought you when you were a girl," said Samos, "with these things in mind."

"You raised me as your daughter," she said, "and then, when I became seventeen—"

"Yes," said Samos, "you were treated with great cruelty as a slave girl, and then, years later, permitted to escape."

"But why!" she demanded. "Why!"

"Samos," said I, "was it from you that the message came, months ago, which I received in the Council of Captains, seeking to speak with me?"

"Yes," said Samos.

"But you denied it," I said.

"The dungeon of the hall of captains scarcely seemed the place to discuss the business of Priest-Kings."

"Priest-Kings?" breathed Telima.

I smiled. "No," I said, "I suppose not." I looked at him. "But when the message was delivered," I said, "you were not even in the city."

"True," said Samos. "I hoped by that ruse to make it easier to deny any connection between myself and the message, should denial seem in order."

"You never again attempted to contact me," I said.

"You were not ready," said Samos. "And Port Kar needed you."

"You serve Priest-Kings," I said.

"Yes," said Samos.

"And it was for this reason, to protect me, one who once had served them as well, that you came to my holding?"

"Yes," said Samos, "but also because you had done much for my city, Port Kar. It was because of you that she now has a Home Stone."

"Does that mean so much to you?" I asked. Samos was the predator, the cruel, insensitive larl of a man, the hunter, the killer.

"Of course," he said.

We looked out. Disappearing now in the rence of the marshes, under the three moons, were the many small craft of the rencers.

Samos, on the height of the keep, regarded me. "Return to the service of Priest-Kings," he said.

I looked away. "I cannot," I said. "I am unworthy."

"All men," said Samos, "and all women, have within themselves despicable elements, cruel things and cowardly things, things vicious, and greedy and selfish, things ugly that we hide from others, and most of all from ourselves."

Telima and I regarded him.

Samos put, not without tenderness, a hand on the shoulder of Telima, and another on my own shoulder.

"The human being," he said, "is a chaos of cruelties and nobilities, of hatreds and of loves, of resentments and respects, of envies and admirations. He contains within himself, in his ferments, much that is base and much that is worthy. These are old truths, but few men truly understand them."

I looked out over the marshes. "It was no accident," I said, "that I was intercepted in the marshes."

"No," said Samos.

"Does Ho-Hak serve Priest-Kings?" I asked.

"Not to his knowledge," said Samos. "But long ago, when he was running from the galleys, and hunted, I concealed him in my house. I later helped him get to the marshes. From time to time he has aided me."

"What did you tell Ho-Hak?" I asked.

"That I knew of one from Port Kar who would soon be traversing the marshes."

"Nothing else?" I asked.

"Only," said he, looking at the girl, "that the girl Telima be used as the bait to snare you."

"The Rencers hate those of Port Kar," I said.

"Yes," said Samos.

"They might have killed me," I said.

"It was a risk I took," said Samos.

"You are free with the lives of others," I said.

"Worlds are at stake," said he, "Captain."

I nodded.

"Did Misk," I asked, "the Priest-King, know of any of this?"

"No," said Samos. "He would surely not have permitted it. But Priest-Kings, for all their wisdom, know little of men." He, too, looked out over the marshes. "There are men also who, coordinating with Priest-Kings, oppose the Others."

"Who are the Others?" asked Telima.

"Do not speak now, Collared Female," said Samos.

Telima stiffened.

"I will speak to you sometime," I said, "of these things."

Samos had spoken gently, but he was a slaver.

"We anticipated," said Samos, "that your humanity would assert itself, that faced with a meaningless, ignominious death in the marshes, you would grovel and whine for your life."

In my heart I wept. "I did," I said.

"You chose," said Samos, "as warriors have it, ignominious bondage over the freedom of honorable death."

There were tears in my eyes. "I dishonored my sword, my city. I betrayed my codes."

"You found your humanity," said Samos.

"I betrayed my codes!" I cried.

"It is only in such moments," said Samos, "that a man sometimes learns that all truth and all reality is not written in one's own codes."

I looked at him.

"We knew that, if you were not killed, you would be enslaved. Accordingly, we had, for years, nursing in her hatreds and frustrations, well prepared one who would be eager to teach you, a warrior, a man, one bound for Port Kar, the cruelties, the miseries and degradations of the most abject of slaveries."

Telima dropped her head. "You prepared me well, Samos," she said.

I shook my head. "No," I said, "Samos, I cannot again serve Priest-Kings. You did your work too well. As a man I have been destroyed. I have lost myself, all that I was."

Telima put her head to my shoulder. It was cold on the height of the keep.

"Do you think," asked Samos of Telima, "that this man has been destroyed? That he has lost himself?"

"No," said the girl, "my Ubar has not been destroyed. He has not lost himself."

I touched her, grateful that she should speak so.

"I have done cruel and despicable things," I told Samos.

"So have we, or would we, or might we all," smiled Samos.

"It is I," whispered Telima, "who lost myself, who was destroyed."

Samos looked on her, kindly. "You followed him even to Port Kar," said he.

"I love him," she said.

I held her about the shoulders.

"Neither of you," said Samos, "have been lost, or destroyed." He smiled. "Both of you are whole," he said, "and human."

"Very human," I said, "too human."

"In fighting the Others," said Samos, "one cannot be human enough."

I was puzzled that he should have said this.

"Both of you now know yourselves as you did not before, and in knowing yourselves you will be better able to know others, their strengths and their weaknesses."

"It is nearly dawn," said Telima.

"There was only one last obstacle," said Samos, "and neither of you, even now, fully understand it."

"What is that?" I asked.

"Your pride," he said, "that of both of you." He smiled. "When you lost your images of yourselves, and learned your humanity, in your diverse ways, and shame, you abandoned your myths, your songs, and would accept only the meat of animals, as though one so lofty as yourself must be either Priest-King or beast. Your pride demanded either the perfection of the myth or the perfection of its most villainous renunciation. If you were not the highest, you would demand to be the lowest; if you were not the best, you would be nothing less than the worst; if there was not the myth there was to be nothing." Samos now spoke softly. "There is something," he said, "between the fancies of poets and the biting, and the rooting and sniffing of beasts."

"What?" I asked.

"Man," he said.

I looked away again, this time away from the marshes, and over the city of Port Kar. I saw the Venna and the Tela in the lakelike courtyard of my holding, and the sea gate, and the canals, and the roofs of buildings.

It was nearly light now.

"Why was I brought to Port Kar?" I asked.

"To be prepared for a task," said Samos.

"What task?" I asked.

"Since you no longer serve Priest-Kings," said Samos, "there is no point in speaking of it."

"What task?" I asked.

"A ship must be built," said Samos. "A ship different from any other."

I looked at him.

"One that can sail beyond the world's end," he said.

This was an expression, in the first knowledge, for the sea some hundred pasangs west of Cos and Tyros, beyond which the ships of Goreans do not go, or if go, do not return.

Samos, of course, knew as well as I the limitations of the first knowledge. He knew, as well as I, that Gor was a spheroid. I did not know why men did not traverse the seas far west of Cos and Tyros. Telima, too, of course, having been educated through the second knowledge in the house of Samos, knew that "world's end" was, to the educated Gorean, a figurative expression. Yet, in a sense, the Gorean world did end there, as it also, in a sense, ended with the Voltai ranges to the east. They were the borders, on the east and west, of known Gor. To the far south and north, there was, as far as men knew, only the winds and the snows, driven back and forth, across the bleak ice.

"Who would build such a ship?" I asked.

"Tersites," said Samos.

"He is mad," I said.

"He is a genius," said Samos.

"I no longer serve Priest-Kings," I said.

"Very well," said Samos. He turned to leave. "I wish you well," said he, over his shoulder.

"I wish you well," I said.

Even though Telima wore her own cloak, I opened the great cloak of the admiral, and enfolded her within it, that we both might share its warmth. And then, on the height of the keep, looking out across the city, we watched the dawn, beyond the muddy Tamber gulf, softly touch the cold waters of gleaming Thassa.